MYSTERIES of PLANET ANDROID

MORE BY THE AUTHOR

Planet Android series:

Marooned on Planet Android

Standalone:

Goddess Found

MYSTERIES of PLANET ANDROID

Planet Android Book 2

CALANTHE COLT

CENTAURI PUBLISHING

Copyright © Calanthe Colt 2025
Calanthe Colt asserts the moral right to be identified as the author of this work.

Published by Centauri Publishing.

ISBN 978-1-0670666-0-4 (paperback)
ISBN 978-1-0670666-1-1 (kindle)
ISBN 978-1-0670666-2-8 (epub)

A catalogue record of this book is available from the National Library of New Zealand Te Puna Mātauranga o Aotearoa.

Cover design © Centauri Publishing Services — cover uses stock images purchased by the designer.

Typesetting © Centauri Publishing Services

To all who were misunderstood because the patterns of social interaction either didn't make sense to you or didn't work for you.

CONTENT WARNING

If you would like a warning about sensitive content, please read this section. If you don't need the warning and would prefer not to risk seeing spoilers, please skip forward to the illustrated map.

~

~

~

~

~

~

~

~

OK, here be warnings and spoilers.

Mysteries of Planet Android contains a murder that may be upsetting for people who are sensitive to such topics, though the murder itself takes place off page. There are a few instances of violence in the book, and mortal peril. Previous deaths are mentioned but not detailed.

This book discusses themes of memory loss and mind control, including mind controlled individuals being used to perpetrate violent acts. It also lightly details emotional and physical neglect of a child. These topics may also be upsetting for some, so please take care.

Drug use is mentioned, and the instance of voyeurism from the previous book is mentioned again.

The book extensively details a character's experience of ADHD and their anxiety about loss of access to medication.

The book also contains explicit sexual content, though always with full, enthusiastic consent between the parties involved.

If any of these topics are triggering for you, but you still want to read the book, please read with caution, and choose a time to read when you are well-rested and your resilience is high.

All the best
Calanthe

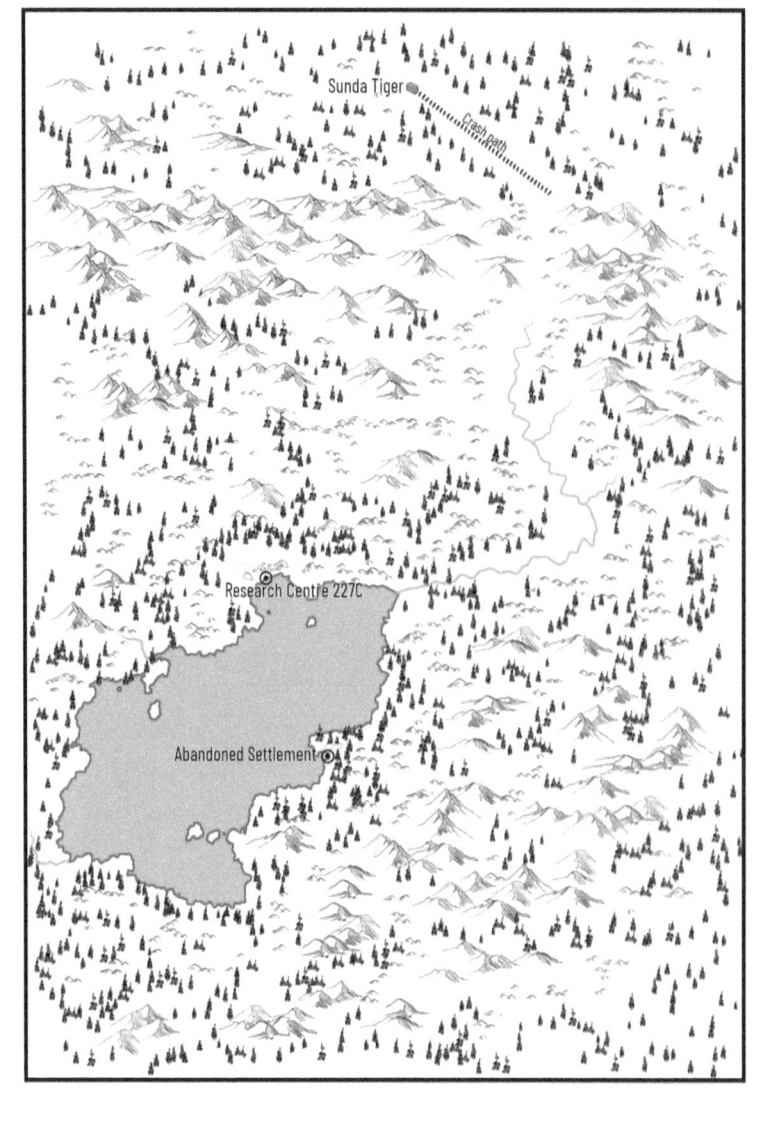

CHAPTER 1

F or 29 years, 8 months, and 11 days, the android repair lab had been Shaula's domain. Other androids
came and went as needed. Her colleagues in the building, Bellatrix and Tiaki, used the lab on occasion. But
despite this, the lab was Shaula's place, her home, and
had been every day since the beginning of her memory.

Sure, she had existed before what the androids called
the Event Horizon, the moment when their memories
began. But those earlier memories had been locked to
cover up a massacre. How she wanted those memories
back. How she feared their return.

"Did you get the notification that I detected another
memory discrepancy this morning?" asked Lieutenant
Marcie Martin-Palmer from where she sat hunched
over a spare android brain. Marcie was a small dark-
haired human woman in a blue dress, who Shaula had
only known for a few weeks.

Shaula was no longer alone in her lab. Marcie now worked here too. The human engineer had two tasks. One was to help the androids unlock their memories so the Orion Navy could uncover what had happened in the colony and who may have sabotaged their ship. The other was monitoring her android paramour Altair to see if she could catch any new alterations to the androids' memories. Since the humans arrived, they had learned someone had been altering the androids' memories for years without their awareness. Shaula disliked sharing her space with the Orion Navy officer. However, her dislike of the arrangement was not the fault of the efficient and knowledgeable engineer. It was Shaula herself who simply disliked people.

"I received the notification. Something was wiped from our memories last night. I have spent the last three hours rechecking the mobile engineering lab."

Shaula would soon leave the settlement for the first time since the Event Horizon, joining a salvage operation to the wreck of the *Sunda Tiger*, the Orion Navy ship that had crashed on 227C. They would salvage goods essential for the humans' wellbeing. Shaula was not fond of leaving her lab, let alone the android engineering centre. Leaving the settlement was far beyond her preferred parameters. Undertaking the mission with a mobile lab sabotaged by whoever was lurking about, controlling the android settlement against their will and endangering the human crew, would be a disaster.

Thankfully, some quick-thinking human had programmed the wreck to crash relatively close to the settlement. If it had crashed in the ocean or on another continent, or even more than a thousand kilometres away, they would not have had the range to mount a salvage at all.

"I can report that the mobile engineering lab is safe, as far as I can tell," she said to Marcie. "Tiaki checked the mobile medical lab. I reported to Mayor Sirius that we are still safe to leave tomorrow." She had almost hoped to discover otherwise. Almost.

Marcie sat upright and stretched her back, her small blue bird-shaped android familiar, Delichon, shuffling to keep its balance on her shoulder. "It must be odd for you to go and leave me here." Marcie would not be on the salvage team, as her work was critical and time sensitive. She would stay in the settlement, with Bellatrix, the android familiar engineer, remaining to offer support. But Shaula and Tiaki had been told to go with the salvage crew to make up numbers.

Despite her favourable opinion of Marcie, she still wished she did not need to leave the human engineer as the sole worker in her own lab. To make matters worse, Shaula would not even be in charge of the salvage mission. She was not used to taking orders. She barely tolerated being told what to do by Mayor Sirius. It was inefficient listening to others' opinions when her own were solid and reliable. But on the salvage mission, the officer in charge would be Lieutenant Commander Ife Kikelomo, and Lieutenant Sandeep Chaudhary would be second in command. The third most important person would be Dr Camryn McArthur, who would be in charge of salvaging as much essential medical equipment as possible. Some humans needed medicine for chronic conditions that could not be managed in the settlement, and the humans who were not coping with the gravity needed a special therapy that could be provided by equipment on the wreck of the *Sunda Tiger*. Shaula was only going to provide *engineering assistance*, and to fix any damaged androids on the salvage team.

"Yes. I dislike it. But I trust your work. I simply do not want to go."

Marcie grinned at her. "I understand. Needs must, though, right?"

"Not all of it is essential, surely," she said. "I have been ordered to attend a 'team-building dinner' at the Welcome Centre this evening. Why would that be necessary?"

Marcie pulled a face. "If it's any consolation, most humans dislike team-building exercises too. Most people are just there for the catered meal."

"I do not eat."

"I really don't know what to tell you, except 'sorry, friend'. Altair and I will be upstairs at the Welcome Centre if you need help."

Altair was Marcie's partner, a fact which scandalised many. Shaula would never be personable enough to have a relationship with a human, but she was not against other androids doing so. She simply did not know how to express encouragement, so Marcie was unaware that Shaula supported her.

The door swung open, and another android, Bellatrix, entered the lab. She wore a pink dress that accented her purple skin. She held her white cat familiar Bastet. Bellatrix was the android familiar engineer, in charge of assigning android familiars and repairing them when necessary. "I have assigned two pigeons to the salvage team," she announced. While the salvage team was away from the settlement, they would be in contact only via android familiars, since they still did not have a communications satellite aloft. Several of the team had their own bird-form familiars who would be asked to run messages along with the pigeons. Shaula's own familiar, a bronze scorpion she had called Charm because it always seemed to do the opposite with anyone who saw it, would not be useful in this circumstance. As an arachnid familiar, Charm could not go far. That was not often a problem, because Shaula was usually only sending messages as far as Tiaki at the android engineering centre front desk.

"What else must be completed before your departure?" Bellatrix continued.

"I will shortly complete my analysis of the inventory," said Shaula. "I still need to reorganise the routine servicing schedule, communicate the schedule changes to the androids in question, lodge requisition and restock requests with the Quartermaster, report to Commander Mori about the backup gravity acclimatisation plan... yes, that is all."

"Shaula, that's a *lot*," said Marcie. "You take on too much. How about you let me tell the androids whose servicing needs to be moved about the scheduling change? I have a winged familiar, after all." Marcie stroked one finger down Delichon's back.

"Tiaki can communicate with the Quartermaster," said Bellatrix. "You don't get along with them."

It was true. She ought to have delegated that work to Tiaki, but she was a poor delegator. Tiaki always took on the work that Shaula could not complete because she was on someone's bad side. She relied on him. She just did not know how to tell him in a way that would not sound like an abrupt demand for more of his time.

Shaula was glad Tiaki would be coming too. She would need him, not only because of her own lack of people skills, but because certain other members of the team had similar issues. It was an unavoidable consequence of the skills needed on the salvage team. Tyler Simons, who had once been head of the human engineering section before being stripped of his rank for how he had treated Marcie, needed to go for his engineering expertise. None of the human crew wanted to spend time with him, but they had no choice. Sublieutenant Doriane Gagnon also was required for the mission because she had been in charge of storage areas that they would need to access, though she was uncomfortable and even hostile in the presence of androids.

Then there was Naos, an android medical specialist who did not get along with the human Dr Camryn McArthur. And to top it all off, one of the security officers going was a human who baffled Shaula with his inability to stop talking. He was cheery and gregarious.

Shaula disliked cheery and gregarious.

All considered, the mix of personnel was ill-advised, but the best they could do with who they had available.

"Understood," she said. "But I will still attend to the backup gravity acclimatisation plan. It is my own project."

If they could not salvage the medicine for the therapy that would help those with gravity sickness, they would need a tech solution instead. Shaula was working on repurposing some of the android muscle fibril tech into a structural support for the afflicted human crew members. She would rather continue with that project, but it would have to wait until she returned. Commander Mori was keen for Shaula to complete the project, because her own spouse, who had been born on Mars and had never been in gravity stronger than 1/3rd Earth, was one of the afflicted crew.

"Mayor Sirius wanted an update on our progress," said Bellatrix. "Shall I take care of that?"

"Please do."

Bellatrix left to meet with Mayor Sirius, and Marcie returned to her own work. Shaula finished the inventory early and had free time before she would need to report to Commander Mori. Delegating work was perhaps efficient, but it led to unfortunate moments of idleness.

She went for a walk outside the lab. It was not something she did often. Tiaki, her closest colleague, and Dr McArthur, the chief medical officer of the human crew, were leaning on either side of the android repair centre front desk, engaged in a conversation. They were talking about the mobile med lab and its facilities, a dry topic one would have thought, but the doctor seemed to be enjoying the conversation. She was smiling up at Tiaki, who loomed over her, and she even laughed and brushed her blonde hair back from her face.

Some humans were taking better to interacting with androids than others. Dr McArthur seemed to have no problem talking with androids. This was not the first time she had seen her talking with Tiaki at the front desk.

Shaula did not want to bother them, so she stepped into the familiar storage area. She would be alone there, as Bellatrix would still be visiting Mayor Sirius.

Shaula looked around the quiet lab with all the unused familiars in cubbies. At the moment, they were focussed on fixing the unreliable android memories. This problem stemmed from a perpetrator in an unknown location, putatively Dr Rebecca Neale, the previous head of this research centre. However, the android familiars may also be compromised. They ought to investigate them too. If only Shaula had time.

Charm's weight on her head had always been a comfort, but sometimes she wondered about what it saw about her movements and who it told. Could she trust her small companion?

Also, could they trust the familiars that were going with them on the trip? It was possible that the pigeons assigned to them were compromised too. Bellatrix had checked them as well as she could, but what was being hidden from Bellatrix's perception with memory wipes? There were too many unknowns, too many variables. Shaula wished she could make a plan of how to solve these issues, but one led on from another, so she could only navigate one step at a time.

What if she organised for another familiar to be with the team, one that no android or familiar knew about so that there would be no opportunity for it to become compromised?

She walked down the line of cubbies. They were low on birds now. Insects would not be useful when they were so far away. She paused by one of the biggest cubbies, one with a large grey animal within.

"Do you have a task in mind here?" asked Charm from on top of her head. "Shall I fetch Bellatrix for you?"

"No, thank you, Charm. I am merely in here so as not to bother Tiaki and Dr McArthur's conversation."

"Understood." Charm settled back down into her curls.

She disliked she had just lied to Charm, but the deception was necessary. If any other android knew what she planned, they would have questions. It was logical to be wary of the humans they had only recently met. Humans were unpredictable. Selfish. But she was considering relying on a human, one she did not know well and who had even annoyed her in the past, purely because a human brain could not be hacked like an android's, and because she had no choice but to trust in the roles the humans had allocated themselves.

Should it not make more sense for her to trust in her fellow androids, and her own familiar in particular, more than a single chatty human? But the inescapable reality she faced was that she trusted no android on 227C to be fully in control of their own mind.

Not even herself.

CHAPTER 2

I t was a wonder to Faolán how often things his Mam had said to him as he was growing up turned out to be true. In this case, he was reminded of how she'd always said, *No matter how hard done by you think you are, there's always someone worse off.*

Faolán was worried about his wellbeing, now that they were stranded on 227C — he had a med implant that was going to run out, and the fallout wasn't going to be pretty. But at least he wasn't spending hours a day floating in a kiddie pool in a medical centre.

Damon Mori was not doing well. They looked grumpy, tired, and embarrassed. Their asymmetrical dark hair was plastered to their forehead, and they were breathing rapidly in the air that was uncomfortably thick and humid for them. Commander Mori, their wife, sat in the pool with them in a drenched outfit of shorts and t-shirt, holding their head up in her lap to do the hard work of keeping their head above the water.

Before the crash, Faolán never would have guessed the hard-arsed Laura Mori was heavily tattooed. No one had seen her out of uniform before. But now, Commander Mori was multi-tasking, doing as many of her duties as she could from her spouse's bedside, or rather poolside, and reporting to her while she sat in the pool was a common occurrence.

"I checked all the vehicles again today, commander. All looks perfect, near as I can tell. We'll keep an eye on things during the trip as well, of course."

"Understood. Thank you for your diligence," said the commander, sloshing in the pool as she changed position. "How about the personnel?"

Faolán exhaled through his nose and rocked on his feet. "I have my concerns, of course. We have some prickly personalities coming along. I wish we could get out of taking Simons." Faolán held a grudge against Simons for how the man had treated his friends Marcie and Altair before the crash of the *Sunda Tiger*.

"I understand, lieutenant, but his specialty will be needed."

"A few others concern me. That Shaula might be the worst of all. She has a rep for being disagreeable. Among the *androids*."

The commander raised her eyebrows. "She's brusque, sure, but does that mean she's the worst?" An assessment that could be expected from a similarly brusque woman.

"She wears a *scorpion* on her *head* like a *crown*."

"It's her familiar."

"It *hissed* at me."

"You called the head android engineer of 227C a 'cute wee elf'."

Faolán held his hands up in a gesture of resignation. "I'm sorry. My gob was off on a tangent, leaving my brain far behind." That was a problem of his, one he needed to get a hold of, especially around green women who wore lethal creatures as decoration.

Damon gave a huff of laughter. "I would have loved to see that," they said.

"I would have loved to have you there. Maybe you could have cut me off before I put my foot so far in my mouth."

Truth be told, Faolán was likely to be more chaotic soon if their salvage mission didn't go well. The ADHD meds in his implant would run out soon. It's not as if he was a different person without them. But then again, he hadn't been able to finish his culinary training when he'd been undiagnosed. In fact, he'd messed that up so badly he'd needed to fall to a backup plan (the not-so-rewarding security work he was doing now), so it wasn't nothing, either. Especially if he was going to make a habit of saying stupid shite around android women who didn't suffer fools, and who always had sharp tools (and scorpions) on their person.

In short, he needed this salvage trip to work. Not as much as Damon, but pretty well.

"On your best behaviour on the salvage trip, lieutenant," said the commander. "Keep an eye out for anything suspicious. If there is anyone else here on 227C, which we're thinking there must be, they might also want to salvage goods and equipment."

"Aye, commander."

"And... keep an eye on our hosts in particular. We still don't know if they're all telling the truth. Pay particular attention to the engineers. If anyone would know more than they're letting on, it would be them."

"Yes, commander."

"Good. Safe travels, lieutenant."

Faolán snapped to attention and gave a quick salute. "Yes, sir." Then he looked at Damon again. "Anything you need me to look for on the wreck that would make things easier for you? Something from your quarters, if they're in good shape?"

Damon gave a quick dispelling motion with their hand, though it looked like it felt like it weighed a ton to them. "I'm fine, Faolán. Don't worry about me." They smiled. "I'll be out of here in no time, anyway. I just want as much of my hydroponic equipment as I can get."

Faolán gave a smile and a nod, acting like he believed them. But Damon was just putting on a brave face. Gravity sickness was no joke.

Faolán saluted the commander and nodded at Damon. When he turned, there was an angry hiss at his feet, and he jumped back. On the ground in front of him was a scorpion. Not just any scorpion: the familiar of that engineer, Shaula.

"Your presence is required in the android engineering centre, Lieutenant O'Donoghue," hissed the creepy bronze bug, and then it scuttled away.

Faolán shivered and then looked at his commanding officer.

"Seems like you have another report to make, lieutenant," she said, shifting her arms into a different position around her spouse. "Don't let us keep you."

Faolán tried again to leave. He walked around a pink android in a white shift dress who was approaching Damon's pool — probably their nurse carer — and then out into the square in the middle of the 227C settlement.

The crew still spent most of their time in the tent camp on the landing field. Fair enough. They were thrown into living on the colony world without warning, and hadn't had a chance to prepare themselves mentally. Faolán hoped people would move further into the settlement with time. As a security officer, he had to stay where his people were, and he was getting right sick of sleeping on a camping cot in a tent with three other snoring fellows.

Maybe he could warm some people up to the idea at the team building party that evening?

But for now, most of the people he could see around the town were androids. They were clothed now, too. No more dingly dangly bits hanging out all over. Everyone was wearing basic clothes: t-shirts, plain trousers, shift dresses. It was all coming off one production line.

Faolán himself was wearing a similar outfit; a white t-shirt and grey trousers. Everyone had got off the *Sunda Tiger* with nothing but the uniform on their body, or in many cases their pyjamas, and they weren't sure yet if they could salvage replacement uniforms. So the captain had given them all leave for now to accept the basic clothes offered by the androids. It made sense, and also made laundry day easier to manage.

Faolán strode along the road to the android engineering centre. The first day he'd been a part of the away team to 227C, he'd felt like a specimen under a microscope as he walked these roads. All the androids stopped to stare. But he was not such an unusual sight round these parts anymore.

One android stopped him with a raised hand, though. Vega, a security android who held a similar role as Faolán, but who dealt with the role in a very different demeanour. He now wore a dark blue outfit that went with his purple skin. Vega was also a part of the salvage crew.

Faolán nodded to Vega. "Good afternoon," he said.

"Yes," said Vega. "It is sunny. I received a report that you rechecked the vehicles."

Faolán looked up, spotting Vega's large dark eagle familiar circling high above them. "Sure did. Wasn't my role to check the systems, of course, though they got checked too. But I checked all the cupboards and whatnot for gear or devices that aren't supposed to be there. Didn't find anything."

"Acknowledged. Will you be checking again before we depart?"

"Probably a few times, to be honest, up to and including inspecting the undercarriage right before we leave. I've got an itchy feeling between my shoulder blades, and I have done ever since we crashed here. I'm expecting something; I just don't know what."

Faolán would be a fool not to expect something, considering the manner of their marooning on the planet. Vega would be a fool not to expect something too. And Vega didn't seem like a fool.

"Acknowledged."

While they spoke, Bellatrix, another purple android, approached them. "Vega, may I have a moment to discuss the needs of your familiar on your trip? I'd like to add an extra navigational routine so that it may run messages back to the settlement." She carried a handheld unit with a cable, something he'd seen used to side load commands into familiars before.

"Of course," said Vega. "But I must report in to the security hub. Please accompany me."

Faolán watched the two purple androids walk down the road towards the square. Neither had acknowledged him as they left. Oh, well.

He put them out of his mind. He had an even less friendly android to go contend with.

When he stepped into the android repair centre, he found it uncharacteristically quiet. Shaula stood in a sunbeam from the window over the door, her arms crossed as she waited in the foyer. For him. He stopped and looked her over. If she didn't scare the bejeezus out of him, he'd find her beautiful. She was an emerald green colour, and her wavy hair, usually in an up-do, was a dark forest green. She wasn't a giant statue, either.

Most of the female-shaped androids were considerably taller than him and made him feel little. She was smaller, just about the same size as him. She was wearing basic grey clothing that draped nicely over her sculpted curves. She also, for some reason, had pointed ears like an elf. That was what had caused Faolán to make the fatal error of calling her a 'cute wee elf', something he wished he could take back. Because it was most probably the reason she was scowling at him with those bright golden eyes of hers.

"Did you see Bellatrix?" she asked him without preamble.

"Yeah, she was with Vega."

"Will they be back soon?"

"Don't think so. They were going the other way."

"Good. Tiaki is running an errand too." Shaula grabbed his arm. "Hurry. I need you." She began dragging him further into the building. She had a strong enough grip on his arm that he hadn't a hope of resisting her.

Needed? "Uh, what? What for?" he managed to utter.

"In here." She dragged him through a door he knew didn't lead to her lab. Instead, it was the android familiar facility.

The wall of sleeping animals was creepy. They just laid there in little cubbies, waiting to be needed. Each android had one, and also Marcie had been given one during their first mission here, before the ship had crashed. Faolán didn't think many of his crew mates would want a small animal android following all their movements.

Shaula let go of his arm and strode over to the wall. She opened one of the largest cubbies and bent over, then stood up, carrying a...

...that's a wolf. A full-sized *wolf.*

It was nearly as big as she was, and was a dead weight as it was asleep, but she carried it over to the workbench as if it weighed nothing. Faolán imagined her picking him up with ease, maybe giving him a squeeze to crack his back, that horrible tangle that kept knotting up in there that he had trouble getting out on his own. It was a silly mental picture, but he could almost imagine how good the click would be. A real satisfying crunch. Maybe if he asked nicely...

"Over here," she interrupted his inappropriate thought train.

He approached the workbench. "What's all this about?"

"This is preparation for the trip," she said as she fiddled with a handheld device. "We are uncertain whether the familiars are safe and unhacked. But they will be our communications."

"For sure. It's a security flaw, but one I don't know how to mitigate. I mean, we just don't have that much in the way of..."

"This is the mitigation," she interrupted him. "Your name has something to do with wolves?"

He blinked at the sudden non sequitur. "Yeah, why?"

"We match familiars to names where applicable."

He looked down at the sleeping wolf on the workbench. "Oh. No, I'm not sure..."

"Yes," she said, still hard at work. "I have decided to allocate an undocumented familiar to a member of our team."

Faolán was having trouble keeping up. "Why? You want to get in trouble with Bellatrix?"

"I get in trouble with others no matter what. I may as well put the tendency to good use." She looked at him, and his belly flopped. He was not at all prepared for being roped into hijinks.

"You think I'm the kind to go along with crazy plans?"

"I had already decided this wolf was a useful familiar. It is not a bird, but it will have the range to run messages between the wreck and the settlement. Then your name was the deciding factor. But as a bonus, you are a security officer, so you ought to understand what I am doing."

That was a surprising amount of faith she was putting in him. "You want to make sure that no one knows this familiar will be with us until we're on the way."

She looked back at the device. "No one but you. I will wipe my own memories so the knowledge cannot be hacked out of me. I will program the wolf to stay in the cubby overnight and then catch up with us tomorrow."

For the first time, Faolán noticed she didn't have her scary scorpion crown on. Shaula looked up and noted his line of sight. "Charm is charging. I logged this meeting as a discussion about the safety of the mobile engineering lab. We need to talk about that afterwards, so that when I wipe this event from my own memories, it makes sense to me why I invited you here."

Faolán wouldn't have described it as an invitation, but whatever. "Ok." He sighed. "You're going to be all confused and angry with me tomorrow, aren't you? I'm going to have a devil of a time convincing you that you organised this yourself and I'm not hoodwinking you."

Shaula paused and stood upright, staring at the wall. "Slip the word 'diadem' into the conversation. It will be a password of sorts."

"I don't even know what that means."

"It is another word for crown."

"Grand. That's just... grand." He gulped. She was sure asking a lot of him.

Shaula pushed a few more buttons, and the dark grey wolf sat up, its bright apple-green eyes glowing. Now he could get a good look at the creature, he could see the grey of its fur looked unnatural. It was far too monochrome, too blue-tinted, to look like a natural wolf's pelt.

Shaula pressed a button on the device. "Bonding protocol engaged. Please state your full name," she said, then looked at him expectantly.

"Faolán Michael O'Donoghue."

"Please state a designation for your familiar."

Faolán's eyes widened. He didn't like being put on the spot like this. He took in a deep breath, let it out. Tapped his fingers on his thigh. But then he remembered his granddad's old dog, the one he'd had when Faolán was a boy. "Madigan," he said.

"Bonding protocol finished. Calibration protocol engaged. Your familiar will now say a series of words. Please repeat each one. Your familiar will also look at you from several angles."

The wolf, now called Madigan, stood up on the bench and began pacing back and forth, staring all the while at him. It was so large it had to look down at him, and the hairs stood up on the back of Faolán's neck at being looked at like that by an apparent predator.

"Perturbed," said the wolf in a low growl of a voice.

He sure was. "Perturbed," Faolán parroted.

"Terrestrial."

"Terrestrial."

"Donut."

Faolán smirked. "Donut." Where had this word set come from?

"Cunnilingus."

"Excuse me?!" That was not a word he expected to hear growled at him by a wolf! Faolán looked at Shaula in shock, only to find her avoiding his gaze and jabbing at the device.

"Word skipped," said Madigan. "Obstacle."

Faolán felt a wash of relief. "Obstacle."

All up, he repeated a dozen words back to Madigan. Then the wolf jumped down from the work bench and stood by Faolán's hip.

"May I pet you?" asked Faolán, not sure what else to do with the wolf.

"Petting protocol engaged."

Faolán sat down on his haunches and stroked Madigan's thick neck ruff. The fur was as soft and pleasant as a real dog's. Er, wolf's. Madigan's tongue lolled out, so Faolán rubbed a bit more vigorously, giving the wolf a bit of a scratch, and got that sweet spot between the ears. Would an android animal enjoy this the way a real animal would? Or was this 'petting protocol' for Faolán's benefit alone?

Shaula had moved over to a terminal and was typing what looked like code.

"Those the instructions?" he asked her.

"Yes. I am coding Madigan in for the electrofilm window in the meeting room so he may leave the building without assistance, and directing him to chase down our expedition and find you. Once you have reminded me of all of this, I will assist you further in the bonding process during our journey to the wreck."

Goodness only knew what the others would think when a large grey wolf chased him down. But that was a problem for tomorrow. "I look forward to working with you, Madigan," said Faolán as if greeting a new co-worker.

"Likewise," said Madigan. "Please indicate to me what information you would like conveyed to you upon first meeting in a day."

"Uh, I'll let you know tomorrow when I've had time to think."

Shaula led Madigan back into its cubby, then walked across the hall to a meeting room. Faolán followed. It was time for him to pretend he'd just arrived. "What can I do for you?"

He then had a normal meeting with Shaula, all the while wondering how well their reunion with Madigan would go the next day. It would be a huge hassle, surely. Yep, beyond a doubt.

What an inauspicious start to the trip.

CHAPTER 3

"**Y**ou must enter," said Charm.

Shaula stood outside the Welcome Centre, looking at the front door. Inside was a social event that she was expected to attend.

"No one would miss me if I left," said Shaula.

She heard footsteps behind her, and then an arm wrapped around her waist. "You have to enter the building for it to count, Shaula," said Marcie. She tugged at Shaula, who chose not to be budged by the much lighter woman.

"I do not want to count."

"I understand. Really, I do. But when it's a work thing, you kind of can't wriggle out. If you can't handle it, come on up and hide in our living room for a bit."

Shaula begrudgingly allowed herself to be led inside. Marcie escorted her to the dining room. "Try not to kill anyone," she said, and then she left, taking the stairs up to her abode two at a time.

Several people noted her presence within the dining room, and so now she must either enter or be seen as weak. She drew back her shoulders and walked into the room, veering right and standing with her back to the wall, away from anyone else.

"Thank you for coming, Shaula," called the leader of the salvage team, Lieutenant Commander Ife Kikelomo, who stood at the head of the table with a glass in her hand. She was a dark-skinned human with her hair in many tidy braids against her scalp.

Shaula nodded at the woman and returned to her silent waiting. She wondered if she could stay where she was during this 'team-building exercise'.

The long table in the middle of the dining room bore bowls of fruit from the gardens and glasses of beverages, all for the humans, of course. Dotted around the room were most of the members of the salvage team, some in small conversation circles, and some standing alone.

With Kikelomo near the head of the table stood her fellow human engineer, Lieutenant Chaudhary, and Ensign Hernandez, a midship who was on the team to, as far as she could tell, carry things. Chaudhary was nearly as dark-skinned and dark-eyed as Kikelomo, but Hernandez was paler and green-eyed, though his hair was still dark. From a professional point of view, Shaula took a moment to admire how all three humans had skin that could be called brown and hair that could be called black, and yet they were all very different, with different undertones and hair textures. How did humans look so different when their colourings were so similar, and androids look so similar when their colourings were so different? She needed to study more about colour theory and hair texture to allow the androids of 227C to express their individuality.

Near the window stood Tiaki and Naos, the dark blue android doctor, with Dr Camryn McArthur, the human doctor. Tiaki would normally have greeted Shaula when she entered a room, but he seemed distracted with his current conversation. Naos's familiar, a teal seagull called Beaufort, sat on her shoulder, and Tiaki's red-feathered crane Zephyr sat on his shoulder. Tiaki and McArthur were standing beside one another facing Naos together. Though Naos's face was, of course, placid, there was a frown line on the tanned blonde human doctor's forehead and a tension in her body. Were they discussing or arguing? Tiaki looked over and caught Shaula's eye. She understood. He had looked at her that way many times when someone was being problematic at the front desk, but he was dealing with it. So, an argument of sorts, but she could trust Tiaki to attend to the matter.

Further along the electrofilm window wall stood Sub-lieutenant Doriane Gagnon, a pale-skinned, orange-haired woman, and the now rankless Tyler Simons, a large blonde man. It was interesting that anyone at all was talking to Simons. He was not popular, and for good reason. If it were up to Shaula, he would be in custody. She understood he would face a Court Martial once the humans were rescued and returned to Earth. He deserved it for what he did to Marcie. But for now, his engineering expertise was begrudgingly needed.

Near the door she had come through stood Diphda, a bright green security android. Diphda was an eyesore ever since the androids had allocated themselves clothes because of her tendency to wear bright colours such as yellow or orange. Shaula had toned down her own green skin with grey or brown clothes, but Diphda leaned into being far brighter than a human could ever be.

Further along the wall Shaula stood against was one person standing alone: Ensign Latu, a young curvy woman with light brown skin and a long dark braid. She was also a security officer. Shaula was not sure if she was standing alone because she was providing security for the event like Diphda, or if she was socially awkward like Shaula herself.

There were two people missing from the gathering, both of them security officers: Vega ought to be here, as should Lieutenant O'Donoghue. Vega was likely doing a perimeter sweep, but Shaula was surprised that O'Donoghue was not present. Was he not a gregarious person who enjoyed talking to other people? Was this not the sort of environment in which he thrived?

Vega strode in and approached Latu, having a quiet word with her while looking around the room. The interaction had the air of a professional consultation.

"It looks like we're all here now," said Kikelomo, drawing the attention of the room. "Could you all take a seat?"

Shaula frowned. They were still short one person. But then Lieutenant Chaudhary opened the door to the kitchens and beckoned to someone within. Lieutenant O'Donoghue entered the room, an apron over his white and grey clothes. He wiped his hands on a cloth, which he then slung over his shoulder. To her surprise, his eyes sought her out, and he gave her a nod. *Why me?* wondered Shaula. Sure, she had met with him not long ago to ask him further questions about mobile engineering lab security. But that was a routine meeting.

Shaula took a seat at the table at the end of one of the long sides. She chose that spot because it was far from the head of the meeting, and no one was sitting beside her yet, so she left deciding who would sit next to her up to someone else. The spot beside her did not fill quickly. Across from her sat Sublieutenant Gagnon, who gave her a cool look for a long moment before turning her attention to Kikelomo at the front of the room. Beside Gagnon sat Simons, who kept a smirk on his face as he looked around the room. Beside Simons sat Dr McArthur, though she turned in her seat, giving him the cold shoulder and angling her body towards Tiaki instead. Shaula looked through the electrofilm window visible between Gagnon and Simons, focussing on the trees swaying in the breeze outside.

The chair beside her moved back and O'Donoghue took a seat. Shaula looked at him in surprise. The brown-haired, green-eyed man pointed at his own eyes, and then at Simons, then crossed his arms and sat staring at the disgraced engineer. Of course. O'Donoghue was here on important security business.

"Thank you all for coming," said Kikelomo. "We've talked with each other over the last few weeks while planning this salvage mission, but we've not yet gathered together as one group. I thought we could all meet before we head out tomorrow, to go once more over the practicalities of our trip, and to get to know one another better. We're going to be spending a lot of time together over the next ten days. So, let's do a team-building exercise before we move on to more technical discussions."

The humans around the table groaned.

"'Tell us one interesting thing about yourself,' and all that?" asked O'Donoghue.

"No," said Kikelomo. "Let us not put such pressure on ourselves. How about 'Tell us one *boring* thing about yourself', because then there's no need for anyone to compete, or feel pressure to come up with something interesting on the spot?"

A few people around the table laughed.

"I'll go first," said Kikelomo. "I'm Ife; I'm from Nigeria; when I'm on leave, I live on the Moon; and I don't like fried eggs because they're too squeaky." She held out a hand to Chaudhary, who sat beside her.

Shaula paid little attention to the rest of the introductions. She did not need to know minutiae about the team. While they played their inane game, Shaula instead looked around the table and listed the group dynamics, trying her best to memorise the interpersonal relationships. She was not good at this sort of thing, and she feared making a *faux pas*. Kikelomo was the team leader, and Chaudhary was her second in command. They were Marcie's friends, and also friends with O'Donoghue. Both referred to them by their given names 'Ife' and 'Sandeep'. Most other people called each other by their surnames as they were work colleagues. Ensign Latu worked with O'Donoghue, but did not seem to be his friend. Dr McArthur was liked by everyone except Naos. Simons was hated by most. Sublieutenant Gagnon was also disliked, but Shaula did not know why the humans did not like her. The only thing she had noticed was a hostility towards androids, but how did that affect the humans? Shaula did not understand. Ensign Hernandez was well liked and seemed eager to please his superiors. Perhaps he was still new to his job.

All the others were androids and therefore not so inscrutable as the humans. Vega was as intent and professional as ever. She thought there would not be any interpersonal clashes, other than herself with everyone else. However, Naos was surprisingly not keen on her new colleague Dr McArthur, and Diphda was vying with Shaula for the title of least personable android. Thankfully, they would have Tiaki with them at the wreck. Since he excelled at mollifying Shaula, he could help with Naos and Diphda.

O'Donoghue nudged her with his knee. "Hey, you're up."

Shaula looked around at expectant faces. She did not want to participate, but now O'Donoghue had drawn attention to her... "I am Shaula. I... have a scorpion for a familiar."

"We can see," said O'Donoghue, and made a show of ducking his head away from Charm who, for some reason, played into the joke by hissing at the security officer from within her hair. Their double act garnered laughs from around the table, but Shaula felt like the butt of the joke.

She looked across the table at the orange-haired Gagnon, who looked straight at Kikelomo to answer. "I'm Doriane. I'm from Montreal, Canada, originally, but I've lived in Hellas Basin, Mars, since I was a child."

"That explains a few things," muttered O'Donoghue under his breath, low enough that the humans around the table probably did not hear him.

"I'm a weightlifter," finished Gagnon. Now that she mentioned it, the woman had sculpted shoulders more similar to the androids than many of the human women of the crew.

They all looked at Simons. He gave a disturbingly toothy grin. "Hi, I'm Tyler. I'm from Richmond, Virginia, and that's where I hang my hat on leave."

"That's in the USA," said O'Donoghue to Shaula in a low voice. "Americans often do that: forget to mention the country or planet."

Simons gave O'Donoghue a cool look, but continued, "My father's in politics and my younger sister is in holo-dramas."

Dr McArthur nearly cut Simons off by talking immediately after him, saying she was from Brisbane, but Shaula returned to not paying as much attention. This was the perfect time to ponder her engineering problems further...

Before long, the uncomfortable team-building exercise was over, and they spent the following 20 minutes discussing the logistics of their trip. Ten minutes in, O'Donoghue rose from his seat. Shaula looked up, surprised, expecting Kikelomo to tell him to stay. But O'Donoghue pointed at the kitchen, and Kikelomo nodded to him. He then went into the kitchen, the door closing behind him.

After their discussion concluded, Kikelomo rose to her feet. "Thank you all. Now, let us break bread together in the spirit of camaraderie. Have fun, but don't go too late. We have an early start."

Break bread? Shaula was not aware of what Kikelomo was referring to. But then the door at the far end opened, and O'Donoghue returned, this time carrying a tray of fresh-baked bread. There were also a few bowls on the tray: one seemed to contain an oil and the other a mixture of small particles. He placed the tray in the middle of the table, Latu leaning to the side to give him room to do so, and then stood up straight, wiping his hands on the cloth on his shoulder.

"Bread with dips to make it more palatable. I've salted the heck out of everything to mask the long-life taste. It's... not dukkha, sorry, but hopefully this mix will do. Enjoy!" He walked back towards the kitchen.

The humans all moved to partake of the meal, and they did in fact *break* the bread, since it seemed to be made to pull apart into bits. Those who could reach seated did so, and those at the end of the table rose and stepped closer.

Shaula looked around at her fellow androids to see what their reactions were. What were the androids supposed to do while the humans ate? Tiaki seemed fine in the company of humans, as per usual. He sat and talked with McArthur while she nibbled on bread dipped in oil. Both Vega and Diphda rose and stood with their backs to the wall, their role as security officers always giving them a task to attend to. Naos went to the electrofilm window and raised an arm for her familiar Beaufort to take flight through the window.

Shaula felt like a loose end. She was separated from the others, the seat beside hers empty. She raised a hand and brushed Charm with a finger, reminding herself she was never truly alone. Her familiar was not like the others, flying or running about the settlement. It was usually right with her, on her person. "Are you all right there?" she asked her familiar.

"Affirmative," replied Charm, and she felt it settle further into her hair.

Shaula needed something to do. She could not just sit there and observe everyone else have a purpose when she had none.

Tiaki must have noted her distress. He had much experience in her particular troubles. He wandered away from Dr McArthur and came to stand by her side.

"You are glaring. Please do not cause others anxiety."

Shaula smoothed her face over. "Better?"

"Yes." He gave her a closer look, his piercing blue eyes gleaming in his yellow face and making his eyelashes look green. "You are finding this difficult," he said.

"Yes."

"I understand."

"You are not finding this difficult." She tried not to sound accusing.

"There are challenges..." he said. But of course, his challenges were not the same as Shaula's. That was why they made a good team.

"I do not think I can socialise with all these people. I am bound to insult someone accidentally."

"Then do not try to socialise. You have made an appearance. You have participated. Now you may rest. Stay in the building in case you are needed, but go somewhere quieter. I will answer any engineering questions that come our way."

Tiaki left her side and returned to Dr McArthur. The doctor smiled up at him at his approach. Something in

Shaula felt... empty at the sight. She was simply bereft of the ability to use Tiaki as a shield. That was all.

But he made a good point while she had his attention. Somewhere quieter...

She wandered over to the kitchen door. She was curious about what O'Donoghue was doing. At first, she nudged the door open and peered through the gap. She had never been in the Welcome Centre kitchen. It was a big room, with equipment and storage around the edges and a large work surface in the middle, everything in black, steel, and white. She could only see O'Donoghue's elbow from where she stood. He was busy doing something. But there was hubbub behind her and only the whir of machinery ahead, so she stepped into the room, letting the door close behind her.

A sense of peace surrounded her. She never would have guessed that a kitchen would be so similar to her lab. But the ovens and other food preparation devices reminded her of the equipment she used to make and apply silicone skin, and the food preparation surfaces were like her own work benches.

The whir belonged to some sort of mixing machine with a hook that turned in a large bowl. O'Donoghue stood at the middle bench, piping something viscous onto small baked goods.

He looked up at her, and his eyes widened. "Uh, hi there. What can I do for you?"

"What are you doing?"

He grinned at her, baring his teeth. His grin was lopsided, one of his cheeks creasing more than the other. "Icing cupcakes."

Shaula moved further into the room and peered into the bowl of the mixing machine. Some sort of pale dough turned in there.

"Are you making all the food for this gathering?"

"Yup." He continued his work as he talked.

"Why? You are a security officer."

He ran the inside of one elbow over his face, keeping his hand well away. "Sure. But there's no one on the crew who's a designated cook, because we used a food prep machine on the *Tiger*. I can cook, so I volunteered."

Shaula tilted her head. "You have skills unrelated to your occupation."

He paused his work and looked at her. Some shadow passed over his features, but Shaula could not interpret its meaning. "Uh, yeah," he said, looking back at the cupcakes. "Humans often do. I bet you androids do too, though, right?"

The door opened again, and Gagnon stepped in. "I've been sent to fetch some..." She froze in place, staring at Shaula.

"Some?" prompted O'Donoghue.

"Drinks."

O'Donoghue pointed to a tray with three pitchers on it. "There. Options are limited, of course. But I've made two flavours of iced tea — made from packaged stuff, but it's not as if it goes off — and a handmade lemonade. Altair's been tending to a lemon tree, bless him."

Gagnon made no move to pick up the tray. Instead, she glared at Shaula and folded her arms.

"What's an android doing lurking in here?"

"What do you mean?" asked O'Donoghue, an edge to his voice.

"I am just standing here," said Shaula.

"Are you? Or are you looking for an opportunity to sabotage the meal?"

Shaula felt her forehead crease. No one ever thought the best of her. Only the worst.

"She's allowed to be curious," said O'Donoghue.

Gagnon took another step forward. "Don't be naïve. These androids need to be watched. Isn't that your job?"

Shaula outright frowned. Gagnon was questioning O'Donoghue's professionalism when he was in the middle of going above and beyond his duty?

When Gagnon stepped forward again, Shaula braced herself for an argument. This was her lot in existence: to butt heads with others, and she prepared herself for the confrontation in a mere moment.

But then there was a body between her and Gagnon.

"Oi, sublieutenant," said O'Donoghue. "Just pick up the drinks and go back to the party."

Shaula stared at the back of O'Donoghue's head. He was intervening?

Really?

She must be mistaken. Other than Tiaki, no one ever intervened.

CHAPTER 4

H e stared Gagnon down. This, right here, was what he'd been complaining about to his superiors. Some people were more trouble than they were worth for the salvage team. Surely.

Gagnon set her mouth mulishly and frowned at him. Thing was, he'd just understood that her issues with androids had more of a reason than just dickishness: anyone from Hellas Basin probably had their own reasons borne of personal experience. But then she had to go be annoying in a kitchen he was cooking in, that is to say, in *his* domain.

"Take the drinks to the dining room, sublieutenant," he said.

"Forgive *me* for being concerned about you being alone in here with one of them." There was precious little deference in her voice. Not that Faolán usually wanted to pull rank on anyone. But he did outrank her, and her behaviour was making her a security concern, so he was well within his lane.

"I don't need your concern." He realised with a start that he believed that fully. Shaula was prickly as hell, and he sure wasn't looking forward to their inevitable confrontation about Madigan tomorrow. But he wasn't worried about his safety around her. She was too direct to harbour hidden malice. Shaula was a 'stab a man in the chest, not the back' sort if ever he met one.

Faolán stepped forward. He'd been intending to pick up the tray and hand it to Gagnon, but he reckoned she misunderstood his intention, because she grabbed his arm and braced her feet. All of a sudden, he was going *nowhere*. He'd always thought she was quite slender; turned out that while she may have been, she was also as strong as an ox.

But Faolán had plenty of training in how not to look intimidated when outmatched in strength. He looked Gagnon straight in the eye. "Let go of my arm. That's an order."

Her eyes flickered over his face, and a laden moment later she let him go. Faolán pushed past her and picked up the tray of jugs and handed it to her. "On your way."

Gagnon turned towards the door, then paused for a moment, looking back over her shoulder at first him, then Shaula. "Watch yourself. The Hellas Basin Massacre androids were well known for seducing people to get information for their attack." She pushed through the door and let it swing closed behind her.

Faolán let out a sigh. He was tired of this, and they hadn't even left yet. He looked at Shaula, who was still standing where she had been throughout the confrontation. She raised an eyebrow at him, but made no comment.

"Sorry 'bout that. Gagnon seems to have her hang-ups."

"Her behaviour is not your responsibility. However, should I not be here?"

Faolán shrugged. "It's fine by me. Whenever I'm feeling socially awkward at a party, I end up in the kitchen too, so I'm not exactly in a position to call you out on it."

She tilted her head at him, and he'd be damned if he couldn't read surprise in it. "You feel social awkwardness?"

Faolán flushed and turned back to the cupcakes. "Sure, well, yeah. I probably hide it well with excess verbiage, but sometimes my brain gets real noisy, and I inevitably end up in a kitchen." It was ironic. Because he'd known that about himself, he'd been so sure that a culinary career would be right for him, would help with his noisy brain. But the fast-paced, stressful environment of a professional kitchen had been exactly wrong for him. He'd executive dysfunctioned himself right out of culinary school.

Casual cooking, though, was fine. And kitchen lurking, pilfering snacks and talking to people one at a time as they came into the kitchen, was best of all.

Too bad that wasn't a valid career path.

Faolán finished icing the last of the cupcakes and then turned to check on the pizza dough. He had to step around Shaula to get to it. She watched him as he turned off the dough mixer, tested the dough's consistency, and then switched an oven on to heat up. He was getting awkward about her presence, but like he said, he wasn't going to hold kitchen lurking against anyone.

It sure would be easier if he could offer her food, though. That's what he would have done for any human hanging around him while he cooked.

"Can I help you with anything?" he asked to fill the silence.

"No. I am merely interested in how the apparatus of cooking works."

He grinned as he dusted a board with flour. "You're such an engineer."

"Yes."

He divided the dough and started preparing pizza bases, putting each one on a tray. There weren't any pizza stones in this kitchen, alas, but the trays would do in a pinch. He was itching to ask Shaula more about why she assigned Madigan to him, but he couldn't until he had reminded her she'd done so. But the words were right there, on the tip of his tongue. He needed to distract himself...

"May I ask you a question?" he asked.

"You may."

He looked over his shoulder at her, trying to judge how she felt about him asking, but he couldn't read her. He turned away again and grabbed a bowl out of the fridge. Earlier he'd mixed up a tomato paste using powdered tomato he'd found in storage. It tasted like shit, but he was hoping everyone had been without pizza for long enough that even this processed version he was making would be welcome. "Do you think this Dr Neale is still around the settlement?"

She stayed quiet for a long moment while he started spreading the paste on the pizza bases, the only sounds the hum of the oven and the low hubbub from the party through the door. "I do not have enough verifiable information to give a probability of her presence."

"I know. I've been briefed about all the tampering of your memories. Just, do you think it's possible?"

"Yes, I do. Something is wrong here. I have been trying to investigate the issue for a long time, but have never reached the end of my investigation. I feel... tampered with. Hindered." She shifted position. "Why am I talking to you about this?"

He grinned. "I'm good at getting people to open up." He fetched a vacuum-sealed pack of processed parmesan he'd investigated earlier. It was the only cheese they had to hand. Like the tomato paste, it tasted terrible if compared with the fresh stuff, but perhaps people would let it slide because *pizza*.

He didn't like the thought of her struggling with what they were doing. Although she didn't remember it, she'd flattered him by trusting him with Madigan. For some reason, he now felt responsible for her experience of the salvage mission. He knew enough about her to know it was already not going well. Hence why she was lurking in the kitchen to avoid people when she didn't even eat.

"I get the feeling you don't really want to be on the salvage team."

"I do not."

He shrugged. "I'm not judging. But what would you prefer to be doing?" He took out the few fresh tomatoes and basil leaves Altair had provided from his garden for this dinner and placed them on the pizzas. He had to spread them out quite far to make them even.

"I would prefer to be investigating the missing memories of the androids, or searching for the abandoned settlement that Altair remembered."

Faolán nodded. "I can see that. But I just want to say thank you for coming on the mission to the *Tiger*. It's really important for us humans."

"Because you need the food supplies."

"Yeah, but as you can see, we can get by for a bit. But it's the medicines that we really need. And fast."

Shaula peered into the oven, looking at the elements heating inside. "The people with gravity sickness need help."

"Yeah." Faolán sighed. "I saw Damon Mori today. They aren't doing well."

Shaula turned to him. "That is another project I would like to be working on rather than the salvage."

"Oh? But the salvage is that project."

"I am working on a technical aid that may help. But finding time for the project is proving difficult."

"Let's try to get the salvage sorted as fast as we can, then."

Faolán heard a door bump open. He turned, expecting someone to have come through from the party, but instead Marcie peered in from the door to the hallway. "Hello~!" she said in a cheery voice. She caught sight of Shaula in the kitchen, and her eyebrows rose.

Faolán grinned. "You want a cupcake, don't you?"

"I want a cupcake."

"Go on; why don't you?" He waved her in and pointed to the cupcake tray, then let her take her pick while he put the pizzas in the oven. Shaula moved out of his way and towards Marcie. He turned to find Marcie already half-way through a cupcake, her mouth too full to speak. She gave Faolán a thumbs-up in thanks. Since she was also drowning in a long-sleeved shirt that looked like it was Altair's, with the sleeves rolled up, she looked fecking adorable. He'd always thought Marcie was cute, but she'd always been in relationships, so he'd never tried flirting with her. Now she was with Altair, and he couldn't blame her. Altair was both awfully nice *and* smoking hot. Truthfully, Faolán was a bit jealous of them, but he wasn't sure which of them he was more jealous of.

When she finished her mouthful, Marcie grinned at him. "Thanks. I can't tell if that was good, or if it's just been so long since I had a cupcake, but either way I enjoyed it." She grinned at Shaula. "You in here to talk to Faolán, or are you hiding from the party?"

"Can I not be doing both?"

"Oh!" said Marcie, clearly not expecting that answer.

"We were talking about all the things that need doing," he said.

Marcie sighed. "So many things! Ugh!" She rubbed her forehead. "Bring Shaula and Tiaki back quickly, please!"

"We'll do our best."

The door to the hallway opened again, and Altair stepped into the kitchen. "Have you seen... ah. Marcie. I found you."

Marcie smiled up at Altair as he approached. "You found me. I was sneaking snacks." She held up her half-eaten cupcake.

"Is O'Donoghue's baking up to par?"

In answer, Marcie took another large bite.

Faolán wiped his hands on the cloth and then he clapped Altair on the shoulder, having to reach up a way to do so. "Hey, Big Blue. What's the story?"

"What story?"

Faolán winced at his own folly. He *had* to learn to scrub his natural slang out of his speech. The androids hadn't been programmed with Irish slang, and he kept confusing them. "How's your day going?"

"Well, thank you. Are you prepared for your salvage operation?"

"As well as I can be. Though I have a task to complete first. Please excuse me."

He picked up the tray of cupcakes to take them to the party. Before he got far, Marcie's hand darted out to grab another one.

"Lieutenant Martin-Palmer!" Faolán fake-scolded, but really, he was pleased by that reaction to his baking.

As he left the kitchen, he heard Marcie, Altair, and Shaula start a conversation about their hopes for investigating the old abandoned settlement after the salvage trip.

When he delivered the cupcakes to the party, he was cheered. Actually cheered. Sandeep took one bite of a cupcake, made a joyous noise, and gave Faolán a side-hug. A man could get used to that sort of praise.

"Are you joining us now?" asked Ife.

"I've still got something else in the oven. I'll be back in a bit."

When he reentered the kitchen, he could smell that the pizzas were coming along nicely. He'd made them thin base since he hadn't had much time for cooking. The group in the kitchen had grown by one in his absence: Bellatrix, the android familiar engineer, was present. Faolán didn't know her well, but he knew she worked with Shaula. He'd thought when he first met her that she was a bit out of place with the rest of the androids. She didn't seem to match. But then he'd learned that 'Bellatrix' was also actually the name of a star, so she did match the naming convention after all. She was talking with Shaula and Marcie about pigeons. He assumed she was talking about the familiars for the salvage operation. If there was an update, he would hear it when the rest of the team did.

He walked past the group nattering in his kitchen, half-listening to talk of pre-programmed homing routines, and rotated the pizza positions in the oven so they would cook evenly.

The door from the dining room opened behind him again, and he turned, hoping that someone pleasant like Sandeep had followed him.

No such luck.

Simons stood in the kitchen doorway, surveying the group. There was a smirk playing around his mouth. Faolán wondered, not for the first time, if his smirk was real arrogance or a shield he was putting up to hide, say, shame over what he had done.

He ought to be ashamed.

The conversation nearby ground to a halt, and Faolán could feel the tension radiating off Marcie.

"I was wondering who I could hear chatting in here. Lovely to see you, Martin-Palmer."

That arsehole. "Hey, now; out of here," said Faolán. "You know you've been forbidden from talking to Marcie." It shouldn't be up to Marcie or Altair to deal with Simons.

"Hey, loosen up. I didn't know who was in here. It was an honest mistake." He stepped further into the room. "While you're here, though, I just want to say how sorry I—"

In a flash, Bellatrix stood eye to eye with Simons. She was close to his height and stared him down. "Leave my workmate alone," she said.

Simons reared back. "Get out of my face!"

"Don't speak to me like that."

Simons glared at her. "I don't even know who you are. Why are you so aggro?"

"I work with Shaula, and now Marcie. I know what you did to Altair too. I will never forgive you for that. Now, get out of this room."

Simons looked around. Faolán was considering pushing Simons out of the room when Shaula stepped up to stand shoulder-to-shoulder with Bellatrix. "Your conversation is not wanted in this room. No one here wants to talk to a sexual harasser with a penchant for torturing androids. The only reason you are not in a brig is because there is no brig available."

Simons held his hands up. "Fine, fine; I'll go." He gave a mocking salute and sauntered back through the door to the dining room.

"I don't need protecting, you know," said Marcie.

"We know," said Shaula. "I just wanted an excuse to make my opinion of him known."

"I feel so sorry for you both, needing to go on a salvage trip with that arsehole," said Marcie, looking from Shaula to Faolán.

41

"Hey, it'll give you a break from being in the same settlement as him, at least," said Faolán. "Enjoy it while it lasts."

"I too have concerns about how you will fare," said Bellatrix to Shaula. "This is not right. Use the pigeons to send a message if you need any assistance. I will check in with you regularly while you are away using one of the settlement's remaining pigeons. If there is anything I can do to assist remotely, please let me know. Should I try to get myself allocated to the team as well? I have asked before, but was denied."

"Your expertise is needed here," said Shaula.

"That's true. But please stay in contact as much as possible. I will help."

"That is appreciated," said Shaula.

"Yeah, thanks a million," said Faolán. He started cleaning up the area where he had topped the pizzas. When he turned to the oven again, he was surprised to see Bellatrix had wandered over there. She leaned over, peering in the glass door of the oven.

"Something caught your eye?" he asked, peering around her. The pizzas looked like they needed five more minutes, so he left them in there. "I didn't think you androids would be interested in food."

"I'm watching the oxidisation process. It is interesting," she said. He could have sworn she licked her lips, though. "Is security for the salvage in place?" she asked.

Faolán raised an eyebrow. She was no commanding officer of his. He figured she was a busy-body, though. "Sure."

"What measures of security will you have in place on the wreck?"

Faolán crossed his arms. "Those are details I discuss with my superiors only, thank you."

Bellatrix stood straighter. "Of course. I was merely interested. I wish for Shaula and Tiaki to return safely."

Faolán relaxed his posture. That made sense. "Of course. But I still can't discuss it, sorry."

"Understood. I shall let Lieutenant Commander Kikelomo know about the extra checks I am planning," said Bellatrix. "And perhaps glare at that man again." She stepped through into the dining room.

"It's nice you all have a good working relationship at the android engineering centre," he said to the others.

Marcie smiled. "Yup. Right, Shaula?"

Shaula tilted her head in confusion again.

"It's true, Shaula," said Marcie. "Stop selling yourself short. Now, we should stop crashing your party. If I don't see you before you leave, good luck on your mission."

"Thank you."

"Thanks."

Marcie took Altair's hand, and they headed for the hallway again. Faolán watch the pair from behind as they walked. They were so different from one another and yet they matched so well. Scandalous though they may be, he got it.

Faolán checked the oven, then started removing the pizzas. "I like how you gave Simons a piece of your mind," he said to Shaula, who was still present, standing still.

"It was... invigorating."

He laughed. "You going back to the party?"

"I am not well suited for parties."

"Well, OK. You can hide out here. I'm getting pretty hungry, though, so once I deliver the pizzas, I'm going to stay and partake. OK?"

Shaula shrugged.

Well. This was more like the Shaula he expected. Social battery at 0%.

"OK. If you do sneak off soon, which I expect you shall, then I'll see you in the morning?"

She gave a curt nod.

He took the first two pizzas through, to a chorus of cheers, then by the time he returned for the third, she was gone.

Hopefully, she would remember he had been nice to her when she discovered he'd bonded with Madigan to-morrow.

He'd need every bit of favour he could get.

CHAPTER 5

S haula sat in a passenger seat in the front of the mobile engineering lab and pondered. She felt like she
had forgotten something. For decades, until the humans
of the *Sunda Tiger* arrived, they had been unaware of the
constant alterations to their memories, thinking erro-
neously that they had only been wiped once. But now
Marcie was bringing their attention to the times when
their memories changed, Shaula was developing a sense
for when it had happened. She felt that now.

But she seemed to be the only one.

"Are you sure you do not feel like your memories
changed yesterday?" she asked Tiaki.

He was sitting in the middle seat, driving the lab vehicle up a riverbank away from the lake. "I felt nothing
yesterday. But I agree with Marcie that something happened to our memories the evening before."

If she and Tiaki were alone in the vehicle, she would
have talked more about her concerns. She trusted Tiaki

above anyone else, as she had worked closely with him for so long. But Kikelomo sat on Tiaki's other side.

Instead, Shaula looked at the vehicles ahead of them. The salvage team was taking six vehicles: three large multi-terrain vehicles with six large wheels apiece and with solar panels atop, and three small all-terrain vehicles that a rider rode on, each with a small trailer unit behind. Each of the technical vehicles, the engineering lab and the medical lab, had small living quarters in the rear with a sofa that converted to a stack of three bunk beds and an ensuite bathroom. The third large vehicle, the cruiser, had full facilities for the humans: two stacks of bunks, a kitchen, a dining table, a larger bathroom, and clothes washing facilities.

The large vehicles were driving in a row up the riverbank, trying to avoid crushing the lupins that were preparing the river valley for a more complex ecosystem to come later. The ecosystem of 227C was still ageing up after the terraformation process, so they could not afford to damage anything that would slow erosion and help fertile soil form. The hills to either side of the river still looked sparse, mostly covered in gorse. But gorse, too, was a good nursery ecosystem for sapling trees, which were already climbing their way up the slopes. To their right, the braided river ran in channels over rocks and around sandbanks, the greenish tinge indicating that the algal portion of the ecosystem was also ageing well.

Shaula had never seen this part of 227C. The hills around the settlement were forested, but some trees had been planted to speed the process. Further out, things were still changing, still developing, still becoming. But it was doing so on its own, with no maintenance. The life the terraformers left did not care whether it was being maintained. It just kept on doing what it did best: proliferate.

One of the ATVs that had been lagging behind caught up with them and passed ahead, staying to the hill side of the riverbank. The driver was O'Donoghue. Having O'Donoghue as one of the ATV drivers was not only a good idea from a security standpoint, but also must be a relief for those aboard the cruiser, his designated vehicle for the trip. The lieutenant talked too much. Words poured out of him, whether or not they were needed. Shaula could not fathom where they all came from. Even more disturbing, he somehow pulled excess words out of Shaula too, such as when she had been hiding in the kitchen last night. She did not like being manipulated by his presence into seeming more social than she was. No one should have that kind of power over her.

Ahead of them, the vehicles slowed down, and Tiaki followed suit.

"Sandeep must have found a good space to have lunch," said Kikelomo.

Sure enough, the vehicles all settled into an area where a bend had conspired with an instance of the braided river swerving away towards the other bank to create a wide stony area where they could park the three large vehicles along three sides of a square, and the three ATVs on the fourth.

Shaula, Tiaki, and Kikelomo exited their vehicle just as Naos, Dr McArthur, and the security officer Latu exited the mobile medical lab. Gagnon was supposed to be aboard that vehicle too, though she did not emerge.

O'Donoghue, Vega, and Diphda dismounted from the ATVs. That day, Diphda wore an orange t-shirt and trousers over her apple green skin.

The cruiser occupants, Chaudhary, Simons, and Hernandez, were still inside their vehicle, though clattering sounds emerged from within, indicating they started preparing lunch for their fellow humans. From on top of the cruiser, Boris, a spider-shaped android, watched the proceedings below. He was docked on the top of the vehicle because he was not a good shape to use the vehicle interior, and because he rather frightened the humans. They did not seem comfortable around a teal blue spider the size of a sheep. If Shaula were shaped like a spider, or perhaps a scorpion, would she also have been left out of the dinner the previous night?

The humans entered the cruiser to partake of their meal, while the androids moved to the rear portions of their vehicles to spend time on a charging dock. When Shaula stepped out of the vehicle to move back to the rear compartment, she found O'Donoghue staring at her. He started when they made eye contact and then began walking to the cruiser behind his fellows.

Tiaki had already taken the sole charging cupboard in the engineering lab, so Shaula stepped through the sliding door into the rear cabin. A pack of Kikelomo's personal effects lay beside the wood-look coffee table that could double as a bed support if the bottom bunk were pulled out into a double bed configuration. Shaula did not convert the sofa into either a double bed or a stack of bunks. She simply reclined along the grey upholstery, positioning the middle of her back over the charge port built into the furniture. She magnetised on and slipped into a light charge cycle, one that would leave her otherwise alert. Charm crawled out of her hair and sat on the armrest behind her head, also magnetising on and beginning to charge.

Shaula floated in the charge cycle, wondering why O'Donoghue had been looking at her like that. At first, she thought it was because she had bothered him in the kitchen the previous evening. But no, that did not feel right. She felt sure she ought to remember something. Something to do with him. But what? Had something to do with O'Donoghue been deleted from her memories in the last wipe? How could she remember if so? She could think of no way except asking the man, but that thought did not appeal. What would he think of the question?

Twenty minutes into her recharge, a croaky voice sounded outside. "Security alert! Security alert!"

She stopped charging and darted out of the engineering lab, grabbing Charm as she did so. She was not the only one whose first instinct was to run out of a vehicle. Vega was present, of course, as the voice was sounding from his own familiar, who now sat perched on his shoulder. Diphda, Latu, and O'Donoghue had all appeared to look as well, which was understandable for the security officers. And Kikelomo had emerged, her 2IC Chaudhary at her shoulder.

"There," said Diphda, pointing between the cruiser and the engineering lab to the tree line.

A large dark shape stood there. Animal, not human. Latu took a pistol from her belt and held it up towards the creature.

"No! It's all right!" cried O'Donoghue, pushing her hand down.

"Explain," said Vega.

"I was waiting for it to catch up," said O'Donoghue.

Shaula walked away from the group towards the creature. With a moment to observe, she recognised it as a familiar that had for many years been in storage in the android familiar centre. A large grey wolf. She had never seen it awake and upright, and so was surprised by its size.

The wolf trotted towards them. O'Donoghue pushed past her and strode towards the wolf as if its presence did not surprise him in the slightest. The wolf stopped in front of him and looked up at his face.

"Good afternoon, Faolán. The time is 12.43 pm. The high for today is 21°C." It then sat down on its haunches and wagged its tail.

O'Donoghue scratched the wolf on the head. "Thank you for catching up to us."

Shaula clenched her teeth. He'd taken a familiar? Without anyone's permission? Bellatrix kept a tight leash on the allocation of the familiars. She would have told her if there had been another familiar assigned to the team!

She stalked up to him and crossed her arms. "What is the meaning of this?"

O'Donoghue turned to her and grinned, rubbing the back of his neck. "I knew this would happen," he muttered.

"That is one of the android familiars," she said. "You have not been assigned a familiar. How did you bond with it?" Charm hissed at him from within her hair for good measure.

O'Donoghue rocked back on his heels, then forward onto his toes. He looked over at the others who were watching the exchange with a variety of expressions on the humans' faces, and watchful miens on the androids'. "It's all above board, honest," said O'Donoghue, "so don't get your *diadem* in a twist." He eyed the hissing Charm.

Shaula froze. That was a key word she had chosen for herself, one she had decided to pass on to a human to help verify the truth when she was not sure she would remember. If he knew to use it...

"Ah." She looked at the wolf again, a familiar that would have the range to run back to the settlement from the wreck, and up at the man before her whose given name had something to do with wolves in his own language. He was watching her with an eyebrow raised and a crooked smile playing at the corner of his lips. The sunlight caught in his eyes and made them look greener.

"Do you remember now?" His grin reappeared.

"No. But this is a decision I would have made."

"What's going on here?" asked Kikelomo as she stopped near them. The woman was frowning, and Chaudhary still stood at her shoulder, giving O'Donoghue a questioning look.

"In summary," said Shaula, "in my wisdom, I have at some point assigned a secret familiar to Lieutenant O'Donoghue, and then wiped the knowledge of it even from my own memories."

"Why would you do that?"

"Because I am still not sure how closely our memories are being monitored, or whether the familiars are safe or trustworthy."

O'Donoghue patted the wolf on its shoulder. "Madigan here is our communications backup plan. In case all the others are hacked."

Kikelomo looked back and forth between them all. Then she nodded. "Good work. Carry on."

When they got underway again, Latu drove the ATV that O'Donoghue had been driving before. He instead sat cross-legged on the floor in the cabin at the rear of the mobile engineering lab next to Madigan, who took up most of the rest of the floor space. Shaula sat across from them on the sofa.

"Please tell me what special programming you think we need to add to Madigan for the salvage operation. I will help you get him customised and teach you what you need to know about caring for a familiar."

That afternoon, as the mobile lab bumped along the riverbed, and the light through the window alternated from sunlit yellow to cloudy grey, Shaula taught O'Donoghue about how to make sure Madigan was well charged, how to take care of his fur, when to take him in for a service, how to send people messages via the wolf, and how to alter the information that Madigan gave him the first time they talked each day. Faolán listened and

repeated the information back to her fine, but he interrupted a lot, asking about unimportant things like
whether she remembered the list of words Madigan had
used in the calibration protocol (she did not). He also
had trouble staying still. Sometimes he was on the floor,
sometimes on the sofa beside her, sometimes staring
out the back window at the river behind them. At one
point, he even opened the sliding door and walked in
circles around the work station in the middle of the lab,
opening drawers and cupboards.

"You've got sheets of skin in here. That's so creepy."

"Someone may be damaged. I need to be able to fix
them."

"What are all these sharp things?"

"Careful! Those are hair re-rooting tools."

"This cupboard is empty."

"It is for the hydroponics equipment, if we can salvage it."

"I knew that."

"Then why did you mention it?" Shaula demanded.
Charm hissed, letting Shaula's annoyance be known to
him.

Faolán looked over his shoulder at her in surprise,
then sat down again by Madigan. He ran his hands
through the wolf's fur. For once, O'Donoghue was quiet,
withdrawn, though he seemed to draw comfort from his
familiar. That was good. He would be more likely to take
good care of the familiar if he saw it as a companion
rather than a tool. Shaula brought up the petting protocol
for Madigan on her tablet and made some adjustments to
the parameters, programming Madigan to provide extra
petting time and have more patience for it when
O'Donoghue looked stressed. She had not uploaded the
changes to the animal yet; without a working network,
Shaula would have to side-load the changes via cable,
which she would do all at once at the end of their session.

Shaula hoped this was all worth it. Adding a familiar to the team was a good idea, but it would only pan out if the team was free from tampering now they were away from the settlement. They still had no idea how the perpetrator, putatively Dr Rebecca Neale, was accessing them and tampering with their memories. The working theory was the recharge stations, but Shaula had found nothing yet to confirm that. There was also the possibility Dr Neale had some sort of cloaked broadcasting technology they had not located. If so, it was possible they would experience tampering even at the wreck of the *Sunda Tiger*.

If that was the case, Shaula was not sure how she would ever solve the technical problem she faced. She was an android too. She was as susceptible to hacking as anyone else.

Though thankfully the mystery hacking from yesterday had been herself, not anyone nefarious.

Shaula uploaded the modifications to Madigan soon before the vehicles found a place to stop for the evening.

She emerged from the lab ahead of the still subdued O'Donoghue into an inquisition.

Rather than setting up the evening camp, everyone was gathered and looking at them. Or rather, at Madigan.

"I require more data," said Vega. Diphda stood at his side.

"About what?" asked O'Donoghue.

"The familiar."

"There is nothing more to discuss," said Shaula. "As I already said, I allocated one more familiar to the team, one that will be free of any nefarious meddling that may have been implemented. That is all."

"Were you aware of this, Tiaki?" Vega asked.

Tiaki approached the group. "No, but I could not have been for this plan to work."

Tyler Simons stalked over, not towards Shaula but towards Kikelomo, who also stood nearby, having ridden in the engineering lab. "How could you just accept this?" He waved his hands around, gesticulating at Madigan. "It's probably here to take us out in our sleep. It's a wolf!"

"It is a familiar," said Shaula. "Not a wolf."

Simons waved her off without even looking at her. "You don't have what it takes to lead engineering," he said straight into Kikelomo's face, invading her personal space. "You can't make the hard decisions."

Kikelomo drew herself up to her full height and stared him down. Chaudhary stood at Kikelomo's shoulder and also stared at Simons, his hands on his hips.

Kikelomo opened her mouth to speak, but Simons cut her off. "And here's your lil' pet, ready to bark at whoever calls you on your bullshit. Hey, Sandeep, you think if you do her bidding often enough, she'll finally put out?"

Chaudhary's brown complexion did not hide the deep blush that arose in his cheeks.

Kikelomo sucked air in through her teeth.

As if the team's interactions were not bad enough, Sublieutenant Gagnon approached the group. "I don't care about engineering team dynamics," she said. "But I do care that we've got yet another android putting things in place to monitor us, or worse. Simons is right. What if that thing attacks us in our sleep? We can't trust it."

"Hey, now," said Faolán. "It's not like that. If you can't trust Shaula, then at least trust me."

Gagnon snorted. "You? Everyone knows you're friendly with Marcie and her fucktoy. I bet you're screwing an android too. I bet you're screwing that one."

Shaula was disturbed to see the woman was pointing at her. Was this because she had hidden in the kitchen while O'Donoghue cooked? Gagnon now thought Shaula was intimate with O'Donoghue? That's all the woman saw her as: a sum of her parts? She felt a surge of ill-will within her, and with it... the sense of the colour purple. What? What was purple?

The security officer at her side flushed as red as Chaudhary had. "Now, wait just a minute..."

"Let us not throw recriminations around," said Tiaki, holding up quelling hands. "Even if something like that were to occur—"

"IT HAS NOT," interrupted Shaula.

"—Even if it did," continued Tiaki, staring her down now, "what is the harm? We are all learning to work together, after all."

"Work together, not *sleep* together, yet certain people seem so keen to jump straight to that?" said Gagnon.

"Is this all because we supported our friend when she was harassed by Simons in public? Is that it?" demanded Kikelomo. "None of us who stood with her that day regret it for a moment. We were in the right, and he was so wrong." She took a moment to glare at Simons. "Regardless, it has nothing to do with what we are doing now, which is *getting camp ready for the night*."

"My apologies, sir," said Tiaki. "I am merely concerned by Sublieutenant Gagnon's fascination with that topic."

Shaula felt frustration as the argument flared up again. She could usually count on Tiaki to smooth interactions over for her, but he had miscalculated in this instance.

"Are you calling *me* a freak, freak?" demanded Gagnon. "See? We can't trust them. I bet they're trying to use whatever methods they can to hoodwink people for nefarious purposes."

"That is not how we operate on 227C, and I take exception to you implying as such," said Vega.

"That yellow one's been flirting with the good doctor, you know. Ask her!"

The group all looked at Dr McArthur, who had just arrived to stand beside Tiaki. She tossed her blonde hair behind her shoulder and held her chin high. "Oh? You trying to find someone else who is intimate with an android so Simons can take voyeuristic videos of them without their knowledge too?"

Naos, the medical android, followed Dr McArthur over to the group. "Are you not denying that you and Tiaki may have been flirting? As a fellow medical professional, I find your priorities to be questionable. We must focus on the salvage of medicines. You are the key person for that facet of the salvage."

"Excuse me?" said Dr McArthur. "You are jumping to some massive conclusions there!" But something about the way Tiaki and the doctor stood as a pair, shoulder to shoulder, made Shaula wonder if Gagnon was right.

Shaula wished she were anywhere else. People were so noisy. And chaotic. They had started off mad about Madigan, but they had forgotten the wolf. It now sat on its haunches, looking back and forth from group to group like a spectator at a game of tennis.

O'Donoghue stepped past both of them and held his hands up. "Everybody, just calm down. I think you're all letting your stress from the last few weeks get to you."

"Like I'm going to trust your judgement. You accepted an android animal without consulting anyone else!" said Gagnon.

O'Donoghue ran a hand through his thick brown hair. From behind him, Shaula could see tension in the muscles of his back as they pulled against his brown jacket.

"ENOUGH!" roared Kikelomo. "You're all out of line! Everyone split up and perform the tasks you need to do to set up camp for the evening. If I see anyone arguing anymore, I will split you up and send you to opposite corners like unruly children. Do I make myself clear?"

There was a smattering of assent from the group.

"Dismissed."

Everyone walked to their vehicles to get the camp ready for the night. Shaula could not face it, though. Too many people, too many words. Too much anger. This was why she stayed in her own quiet lab and interacted with others in controlled, scheduled appointments.

She walked away from the vehicles towards the river. She sat on a boulder and looked out over the sunset sparkling on the chattering water. Would it always be like this around other people? Was it impossible for her to enjoy interacting with another?

She looked back over her shoulder at the camp. Kikelomo and Chaudhary stood close together having a whispered conversation. Tiaki was staring in Shaula's direction with a forlorn sort of look about him. Zephyr was sitting on his shoulder and combing his hair with its beak. Perhaps Shaula should have stayed to make sure Tiaki was all right. He rarely got embroiled in arguments. He would feel out of his comfort zone too. But as she watched, Dr McArthur approached him and ran a hand down his arm. He would be fine.

Shaula's eyes drifted. She made eye contact with O'Donoghue, who also looked in her direction. Madigan sat at his side, also watching her.

She looked away, out over the river once more.

CHAPTER 6

It took three more days to reach the wreck of the *Sunda Tiger*. On the second day of travel, they travelled the rest of the way up the river until it was a narrow stream, too small for them to use as a road for the larger vehicles. The following day, they cut through some gorse to a pass between the hills. It was slow-going, and they only just made it to the other side of the small range by nightfall. The third day was much easier: all they had to do was follow the trail of destruction the ship had carved through the new growth forest as it crashed.

It was all exactly as the familiars who had done recon had described.

Faolán spent a lot of time on the ATV, Madigan loping along at his side. Even when they were caught in a downpour one afternoon in the hills, somehow it was more pleasant for him that way. Faolán liked people, liked being around people, but not when they were acting the way everyone had when they stopped that first night to make camp. A lot of angry words had been said, and few apologies offered afterwards. All the goodwill from the dinner party the night before had gone up in smoke.

He understood why. They'd been through a lot since the *Sunda Tiger* had arrived at 227C. Tensions were high, resources were scarce, and everyone was worried about a threat they couldn't locate. Not everyone had made it off the *Sunda Tiger* alive, so some people had even lost coworkers. Friends.

It was a recipe for disaster. All in all, they were lucky all they'd had was a flaming row, and not a punch-up brawl.

Even knowing all this, Faolán still wanted to avoid his fellows as much as possible until tempers had cooled. Not rock the boat. And he was not the only one.

He had something that no one else had, though: a new familiar to get used to. Travelling through a wild landscape was an adventure. Travelling through it with a wolf at his side was like something out of a fairytale. And being able to talk with said wolf about the land-scape was a total acid trip.

He could say, "Look at those spiky trees!" and Madigan would say, "*Cordyline australis*, known as the cabbage tree. Endemic to Aotearoa on Earth. Selected by most terraforming companies as a good nursery species to precede forest establishment. Permission to use the germplasm and mātauranga granted by the Kīngitanga."

Or he could say, "Look at that pretty stripy rock!" and Madigan would say, "Gneiss; a metamorphic rock formed in the tectonic action that raised this range of hills."

No matter how technical the information the wolf offered, it was delivered in a deep growl of a voice.

During the last day of their travel, while the going was easier, it was also more grim. The ground was scraped bare of scrub and early forest, forming something like a wide dirt road, leading them straight to their destination. But it was the damaged hull of their crashing ship that had formed that road. Low-scudding grey clouds added to the mood. Even if they hadn't all been grumpy from the argument, they would have been subdued.

They reached the wreck late in the afternoon. The *Sunda Tiger* lay on its back, so all the rooms inside would be upside down, which would complicate the salvage. It was mostly intact, other than a lot of damaged or missing hull plating, and of course, the engine section was entirely missing. It was a good thing, too, or the whole thing would have gone up in a matter / anti-matter explosion before it crashed.

Faolán had been living mostly aboard the *Sunda Tiger* for nearly five years. While the remains weren't small, hulking like a toppled skyscraper in a semicircle of dirt caused by its own movement while crashing, they somehow didn't look big enough to encompass all he'd experienced aboard the ship, either. All the people he had served with, all the missions they had been on. In death, the *Sunda Tiger* was reduced to nothing more than a crumbling building with a shattered façade.

They set up camp far enough away from the wreck that nothing would fall on them, away from the bottom of the vast ditch in case rains came and turned the bottom into a stream, and also not so close to the edge that the trees around the scar rent through the young forest would topple in on them. They kept their vehicles to the square formation they had been using on the riverbank. It's not as if there were large predators on 227C, but keeping together seemed safer nonetheless.

Or at least, Faolán thought so. But as he lingered in the square formed by the vehicles, he saw the remnants of the argument all around. People stayed scattered, forming pairs or small groups, or even staying alone like the antisocial Shaula.

Faolán had protected his own mind long enough. He had gathered energy for an attempt at mending the atmosphere.

First, he put Madigan on to charge in the engineering lab. The wolf was big enough that he had to use a bunk bed. Ife was the only human using the beds in the engineering lab, so he'd been getting Madigan to charge there each evening and then getting him out of the way before Ife went to bed. Afterwards, he gathered wood from the toppled trees and carried it to the square. He also found stones that had been churned up and constructed a campfire. Everyone liked gathering around a campfire and telling stories, right? How could anyone stay mad while looking into the mesmerising flames?

It had been a long time since he'd learnt how to make a fire on a school camp, but he found he still knew how. It helped that he could grab a light and some accelerant from the kitchen, of course. There was no need for rubbing sticks together. Within 20 minutes, he had a merry fire crackling away. He sat back and held his hands out to the warmth, waiting for people to drift closer like moths.

It worked a charm.

Ife and Sandeep were the first to arrive. They brought a blanket and their bowls of dinner. Sandeep handed Faolán a bowl of the mystery stew as well. He nodded his thanks, though he was not so sure he was all that thankful. It was made of previously dehydrated mystery foods. Hence why it was so important for them to salvage as much of the food stocks and hydroponics equipment as they could. Faolán had some ideas of how to jazz up their supplies, but he wouldn't be on dinner rotation for a few nights yet.

"This is a good idea," said Ife, nodding at the fire as she settled on the blanket. "A campfire always cheers people up."

"I thought so too."

Sandeep sat down beside Ife and took a mouthful of his stew. He made a face. "People need cheering up," he added.

Soon after, Hernandez sat down with his own meal. He gave Faolán a nod, then tucked into his stew. Faolán was glad to see him approach. Hernandez was likely feeling lonely out here as he'd only just started a romance with Ensign Bailey, who was not on this mission. Or maybe they'd only just let on that they were a couple. Either way, Hernandez likely wanted to be back at the settlement with his boyfriend.

Latu drifted towards the fire soon after. She brought not only her own stew, but also a tray of rolls. They'd been made from that long-life bread mix the androids had in storage. It made rolls that came straight out of the oven tasting as stale as 4-day-old bread, but whatever; beggars can't be choosers. Faolán took a roll.

Vega approached them and stood looking at the group. "This is not wise," he said. "Eating out of doors is not as safe as indoors."

"We need this," said Ife. "At least us humans do."

Faolán understood where Vega was coming from. He lifted a hand to draw the android's attention. "Latu and I will keep an eye on everyone. And Boris is still up there, with a great line of sight of the entire area. Don't worry. You can safely go charge now, so you're ready for the night shift."

Vega gave him an inscrutable look. Then he gave a terse nod and headed for the cruiser, his own designated vehicle.

By the time Faolán was half-way through his meal, Dr McArthur had joined them.

"You looking forward to getting into it?" he asked her.

The doctor sighed. "The ship being upside down will make it harder," she said in her broad Australian accent. "But, yeah, I'm eager to get stuck in."

Tiaki, the yellow engineering android, approached them. "Are there any engineering solutions we could provide that would make your salvage in the upside down rooms easier?"

"Hm, I don't know. The biggest problem is how the cabinets will have been thrown about. But also getting some of the heavy units out over the tops of the doorways, which will be quite a barrier in some rooms..."

The pair began talking about the minutiae of how to extract items from the wreck. As a security officer, the minutiae were not Faolán's business, so his attention wandered. He stared into the crackling flames, feeling satisfaction about being the one who brought the fire into existence, and thereby helping to bring everyone back together.

Well, maybe not everyone. Beyond the fire, Shaula paced in the fading twilight. She glanced at the group by the fire, but did not join them, instead standing by the corner of the med lab and looking out over the wreck of the *Sunda Tiger*, all alone.

A gusty sigh snagged his attention. Tyler Simons, creep at large, sat down beside Faolán. He held out a mug to Faolán. "You drink tea, right?"

Faolán eyed the cup warily. "I do," he said.

Simons held the mug out further. "Take it. It's not poisoned." He laughed as if he'd told a grand joke.

Faolán took it, though he wasn't thinking for a single moment that Simons had prepared him a cuppa out of any sort of altruism. He wanted something.

Also, the tea was freeze-dried crap, so like the stew, not exactly a grand prize.

He took a cautious sip. It was hot at least.

While he waited for Simons to make whatever case, or cause whatever trouble, he was intending, Faolán had a look round the circle. Ife and Sandeep at least were listening. He knew they'd both had trouble with Simons when he was their superior officer. They wouldn't trust the man as far as they could throw him, either.

"So," said Simons. "You think that android is monitoring you with that familiar? Is that what they're going to do to all of us?"

Tiaki seemed to be listening now too, though he was still paying most of his attention to Dr McArthur.

"No," said Faolán. "I don't think Shaula cares enough about what I do to have bothered with that sort of thing. Madigan's just a backup plan in case whoever has been hacking the androids has hacked the familiars too and our communications fall through. No more, no less. Don't worry about it." He took another swig of the tea.

"Are we even in contact with the settlement?" said Simons. "I'm used to something more concrete than this."

"Aren't we all," said Ife. "But one of the pigeons returned today with a message from the captain saying all was well. It's all we can go on for now."

"And you're OK with this?" Simons asked in a recriminating tone of voice.

"Uh, *no*," said Sandeep. "That's why we're here. To start salvaging what we can of the *Sunda Tiger*, so we have better options available." Now that Simons was no longer Sandeep's commanding officer, the latter was no longer hiding the scorn in his voice. Go Sandeep. Faolán had used to see the engineering specialist as too mild-mannered for the Orion Navy, but he had real bite when one of his friends was being challenged.

"So we'll be getting better comms tech in this salvage, right?" asked Simons.

"Probably not," said Ife. "We'll get that next time. Food and medicine are priorities one and two. They trump everything else."

"You think that's a safe option?" Simons said out the side of his mouth, probably hoping that only Faolán would hear, but of course, his voice travelled.

"People first," said Faolán.

"I'm glad to hear you're of that persuasion after all." Simons gave Tiaki a cool glare, then took a large gulp of his coffee.

Faolán rolled his eyes. Is this what this was all about? "I didn't mean it that way. The androids are people too. I just mean, let's look after the crew before we worry about comms. We got a distress call out before the ship went down. What's the hurry to send more comms? We need to wait anyway."

"But who knows what threats could be out there? It's not only the Orion Navy we might need to contact." Simons lowered his voice even further. "We need long range comms up much faster than any of these idiots seem to think. As a security officer, you must appreciate that. If you see any opportunities to get comms up, let me know and I'll sort it. I can get it working again so long as I have the units to fix." Simons tapped his nose and then stood, taking his mug with him to the cruiser.

Faolán looked at Sandeep, who was watching him. Faolán rolled his eyes again, and Sandeep shrugged.

"While I have most of you here," said Ife in a loud voice, the snap of command in her words, "I just wanted to thank you all for getting us here. The engineering team is a few members down for a few more weeks, and so this is a tough task we've been given. We have a mandate to focus on food and meds, but we're also going to be the first team in the wreck since it crashed. We have a solemn task ahead of us. We also potentially have an upsetting task. Not all our fellow crew made it down to the surface. We think that most of the missing crew members were lost to space when portions of the ship depressurised. But it is possible that people were trapped in rooms along those corridors, unable to get to an escape pod. If we find those people, we may need to perform burials. Dr McArthur and Naos are with us to take point on such things, but be prepared for some heartache." Ife nodded at McArthur and at Naos, who lurked beyond the firelight, almost impossible to see in the twilight because of her navy blue skin and grey clothes.

"Otherwise, I think we all know our tasks. Tomorrow we'll split into two teams, one to do a sweep of the ship and see what we're working with. Engineering staff will take point on that. The other team will prepare a cargo bay or some other convenient place to collect salvaged goods. I'll let you know your assignments in the morning. Spoiler: it's going to depend on who has been playing nice with whom lately. Now, get some sleep. We're going to have a big day tomorrow."

As Faolán stood to head back to the cruiser with his empty bowl, his eyes caught the glowing gold gaze of Shaula in the gloom. She still stood near the corner of the med lab, away from anyone else, her scorpion draped in her hair. He wished he'd had a chance to talk to her around the fire too. By assigning Madigan to him, she'd given everyone else the impression that they were on good terms. He felt like he now ought to get on good terms with her for real, just in case it all came back to bite him on the arse. Well, he'd have to do that later, because she didn't look his way for long. She broke eye contact and strode over to the engineering lab. He didn't even have the excuse of going to get Madigan to go talk to her, because mere moments later, his familiar was turned out and sheepishly slunk over to Faolán's side.

"How may I assist you this evening?" Madigan asked.

"I'm going to get some sleep now," said Faolán. "Vega and Diphda will be taking the night watch. Perhaps you could help them by keeping an eye out?"

"Keep an eye out for what?"

"Anything suspicious."

"Define 'suspicious'?"

Hm, it seemed Madigan would need more specialised programming if Faolán wanted to use him as a security familiar. "How about this? You keep note of everyone who's up and about out of their vehicles overnight. Not everyone will be causing trouble. Like I said, Vega and Diphda at least will be up for work. But tell me who you saw in the morning, and I'll tell Ife if anyone sounds suss. OK?"

"Understood. Good night, Faolán."

Being bade goodnight by a wolf. Who would have thought?

Faolán napped for a bit, but then he tossed and turned on the top bunk. He was in the bunk stack in the main room of the cruiser, near the dining table and the kitchen. Someone sat at the table nearby, making noise. Giving up for now, he sat up and climbed out, dropping to the floor as quietly as he could. He shouldn't have bothered. The two bunks below him were assigned to Simons and Vega (so that two security officers could keep an eye on Simons). Vega was out on patrol, and Simons was the one sitting at the table. According to the schedule, Diphda would be in the charging cupboard across the way. Faolán peeked into the room at the back and saw both Hernandez and Sandeep fast asleep. He hadn't awoken them.

"Can't sleep either?" asked Simons. The man was turning a mug around on the tabletop.

"Nah. You might have better luck if you didn't drink coffee so late, though."

"I don't get affected by caffeine like that."

"Sure." Faolán didn't care if Simons tortured himself with caffeine. He pulled his trousers on and grabbed a drink of water from the kitchen. "Just going for fresh air," he said, and stepped outside.

It was a starry night, the sparse local star field providing next to no illumination. 227C didn't have one large moon like Earth, rather a few small ones like Mars, so the night was always dark no matter what. Madigan was a large darker shape in the night nearby. Faolán squatted down beside him to have a quiet word. "Simons is still awake in there. Please tell him to stay in the cruiser if he tries to go for a walk."

"Simons has already been for a walk."

Faolán exhaled through his nose. He had only told Madigan to note who was up and about, not to stop anyone from wandering.

"Who has been wandering around so far?"

"Many people have been walking around the camp. From this vehicle, Tyler Simons and Diphda have both left and returned, and Vega has left and not returned. From the medical lab, both Naos and Doriane Gagnon have left and returned, and Camryn McArthur has left and not returned. From the engineering lab, Tiaki has left and not returned. All have walked beyond my line of sight into the dark at some point. I could not follow and remain here at my station."

It really was an unsettled night. Why were so many people walking out into the night? Actually, he knew the answer. Tensions were high, and no one had privacy in the vehicles. Everyone who went for a walk just needed a bit of alone time.

"Will you be walking beyond my line of sight?" asked Madigan.

"Not sure," said Faolán. "I never had a chance to check in with Shaula after we arrived. I just want to have a quick word with her." He was still feeling miffed about her stubborn refusal to talk to him after lumping him with an admittedly cool source of group contention.

He tiptoed into the engineering lab. If Madigan was right, though Tiaki wasn't there, both Shaula and Ife would be inside. Faolán didn't want to wake Ife up if he could avoid it.

He checked the charging cupboard first, but it was empty. Then he entered the rear cabin. Shaula slept on the middle bunk, or rather recharged, and Ife was up the top, fast asleep. It seemed they'd left the bottom for Madigan. Or maybe neither Shaula nor Tiaki used the cupboard.

Faolán tapped Shaula's shoulder. Her eyes snapped open, and her scorpion hissed at him, alerting him to its presence on a small shelf behind Shaula's head.

"What did I do this time?" she asked.

"Uh, what? You were just asleep. I came to ask you if I could have a word," he whispered.

Shaula's eyes flickered. "It is 11:07pm."

"Sorry. You're still charging, aren't you? I'll come back later."

"No," said Shaula. "Now is efficient." She detached from the bunk with a click and swung her legs over the edge. The scorpion scuttled up her arm and onto her head.

She led him out of the vehicle. Faolán looked over at Madigan, aware that he'd be yet another human stressing the wolf by walking beyond his line of sight. Also, he should have grabbed his jacket. "I'm sure we could talk in the lab without waking Ife if we slid the door shut," he said.

"If you are going to have harsh words for me, I would rather no one overhears," she said, and led him out of the square of vehicles and up the slope towards the tree line.

"What makes you think I have harsh words for you?"

"I caused trouble for you. And now you keep staring at me. I assume you bear me ill will."

"And so you're walking off into the dark with me?" He tripped over a rock but caught his balance before he face-planted.

She paused and looked at him. "You could not harm me if you tried."

He remembered that time she'd carried Madigan with no trouble. She was no doubt right.

She led him up a groove in the slope that made the walk easier. There were already footprints before them. It was the path of least resistance, after all.

They reached the top of the ridge and began making their way between thin tree trunks. "Speak," said Shaula.

"I just wanted to check in with you. The group dynamics have been rough over the last few days."

She kept walking ahead of him. She was a dark blob in the shadow under the trees. "That is no concern of mine."

"Some terrible things were said the other day, some of it thrown in your direction. I was just wondering if you were OK. You've been avoiding everyone ever since." He clipped a tree with his shoulder and winced. "If I'd known we'd be going for a walk in the forest, I would have brought a torch."

A soft gold glow lit up the trees ahead of them, just enough for him to see. The glow came from her eyes. "Your concern is misplaced. I would be keeping to myself regardless."

"Tiaki sat with us at the fire this evening."

Shaula slowed a moment, then resumed her normal walking speed. "Tiaki has always been better at interpersonal interactions than I am. If you need to discuss anything related to engineering with us, please direct your questions to him. That has always been our dynamic."

Faolán sighed. He felt like he was wasting his time. Here he'd been worried about her, but if anything, everyone being vaguely discombobulated with her was exactly what she wanted, or at least what she expected.

"Is there anything you do need? Any concerns you have?"

She looked back over her shoulder at him. "Did you really wake me up for this? My apologies; you were right. We could have had this pointless discussion at the camp. It would not have mattered to me if others heard you fretting over nothing."

"It's not nothing, you know. And you should try being nicer from time to time, rather than relying on Tiaki to do it for you. You catch more flies with honey than vinegar, you know."

"I do not wish to catch flies. What would I do with them?"

"It's a turn of phrase."

Suddenly, Shaula stopped and held an arm out, barring his way. "I see something."

"What?" Faolán's heart thumped. He didn't for a moment think that Shaula would startle over nothing.

She stalked forward and squatted, looking at something on the ground. He joined her. It the dark, he saw a bedraggled... something.

"It is Zephyr. Tiaki's familiar."

Now she had identified it, he recognised the red crane. "Is it hurt?"

"It is destroyed."

The gold glow grew brighter, and Shaula stood, stepping over Zephyr and towards what Faolán thought was a log in the dark.

"Faolán, please. Come here," said Shaula. She never sounded like that before. Never even said his name. He hurried over.

In the gold glow from her eyes, he saw them. A yellow and red prone form on the leaf litter: Tiaki. No light shone in his eyes. And beyond him, lying at his side, was Dr Camryn McArthur.

There was no light in her eyes, either. But there was blood dripping down her neck.

CHAPTER 7

T iaki had been laid out on her worktable many times before. But never like this.

It was early morning, and Shaula was performing an autopsy. Lieutenant Chaudhary and Ensign Latu were both watching her. Under the circumstances, no one wished to let an android do this investigation unsupervised.

She had already investigated Zephyr, because that was the easier task. Its memory banks had been crushed and nothing was salvageable. Now she had to check Tiaki, who was laid out wearing the red clothes he had worn the previous day. But Shaula was hesitant to begin. Either Tiaki would be fixable, or he would not. Until she plugged the cable in, he was like Schrödinger's cat, both alive and dead.

But that was a false perception. His fate was already determined. She just had to perceive it.

She attached the cable to his datapoint. Nothing registered on her tablet. She clicked her tongue and tried again, hoping she had not inserted the cable properly. As if she would have ever made a mistake like that.

Nothing.

Then she took out a multimeter, looking for any activity hiding within. It was not a check she would usually resort to, having no subtlety or nuance. But there must be something present, surely. Even if his datapoint had been damaged. Surely there was some process running, locked within his brain, out of reach. Some part of his personality remaining.

Nothing.

She stood still for a few long minutes. She did not know what to do. It was Tiaki who got her moving in moments like these, who gave her the push she needed.

"Anything?" Chaudhary asked in a quiet voice.

Shaula looked up at him and shook her head.

"I'm so sorry for your loss." His voice was gentle. She did not thrive on gentle words, but she appreciated it nonetheless. Appreciated being perceived as a person who had lost someone.

Kikelomo entered the lab, followed by O'Donoghue and Vega. Kikelomo had one of the messenger pigeons perched on her forearm.

"I need whatever details you can tell me now to add to my report to Captain Rodriguez," said Kikelomo.

"Tiaki and Zephyr are dead," said Shaula. "As dead as the doctor is. They cannot be fixed."

"Can you access any of their memories? Any indication of what happened?"

"Zephyr was crushed. Nothing will be recoverable. I may be able to access some of Tiaki's memories, given time. But given the trajectory of the murder weapon and the fact that I am not detecting any activity, I will most likely have to remove his brain and mend connections before I can access anything."

Kikelomo sighed. "Understood. Can you tell what the murder weapon was?"

"I have not yet identified the weapon. It was something thin and sharp. I can tell you that if the same murder weapon was used for both Tiaki and McArthur, then Tiaki was murdered first. There is no residue of her blood in the wound in the back of Tiaki's head. Also, he would have been attacked from behind in an upward motion, with the weapon stabbing from the top of his neck up into his head."

"OK, I'm going to go make the report."

"I expect Sirius will receive a copy of the report too," said Vega.

"Of course," said Kikelomo. "That's how Captain Rodriguez and Sirius are doing things." She stepped outside and could be heard recording her message for the pigeon to take.

"I want you to find conclusive evidence of who did this," Vega said to her. She did not appreciate how he sounded like he thought he was in charge.

"I will do my due diligence," said Shaula. "Tiaki was my fellow engineer. I wish to know." Though, since there had been a memory alteration the previous night, one she had been aware of as soon as she had awoken to O'Donoghue's touch, she herself may be the culprit, and she would not know.

O'Donoghue had already reported what Madigan had told him about the movements of people during the evening. But if a memory alteration had happened all the way out at the wreck of the *Sunda Tiger*, then even Madigan's account must be treated as suspect. He could have missed another person moving around under those circumstances.

Kikelomo returned, now without the pigeon.

"I expect full compliance from your people," Vega said to her.

Kikelomo's eyes hardened and she stood straighter. "No, I expect full compliance in this matter from *your* people," said Kikelomo. "Your unreliable memories mean androids are under more suspicion than humans."

"In instances of murder, security staff should investigate. Therefore, I should be in charge."

"We have security staff too." She nodded at O'Donoghue and Latu. "And it will be Captain Rodriguez and Sirius who designate who will be in charge of the murder investigation." She rolled her shoulders and let out a weary sigh. "Sandeep, you're with me. We're going into the *Sunda Tiger* to see if we can turn the morgue pod on. We need to get Camryn on ice as soon as Naos has finished examining her. Ensign Latu, could you go watch Naos? She's not to start a full autopsy yet, not unless we get permission. Just an examination. Can you do it? Faolán already found her body, so I don't want to send him. Diphda is there for security too."

"I can do it, sir," said the young strong-framed woman with the dark braid.

"Thank you. Faolán and Vega, provide security here. Vega, if you could look around the camp occasionally too, that would be good."

"Yes sir," said O'Donoghue.

"That is acceptable," said Vega.

Soon it was just the three of them, and Tiaki, and Shaula could not delay any further. She handed a pair of gloves to each man. "Could you help me undress him?" she asked. "I ought to examine the rest of him."

"Sure," said O'Donoghue, taking the gloves and pulling them on.

Between the three of them, they removed Tiaki's clothes. While they had him tipped on one side, Shaula took a closer look at the wound. She already knew the

75

murder weapon must have been slim and sharp, but on closer examination it must have been yanked around once it was in there. Which explained why such a thin weapon had such a terrible impact on Tiaki.

"Excuse me," said Vega. "I am just going to take a turn around the camp." He clipped his shoulder on the door-frame as he left, slamming the door behind him.

"He seems shaken," said O'Donoghue.

"This has never happened before. It is unfamiliar territory for 227C."

Shaula laid Tiaki on his back and began examining his front. She spotted something sticky on Tiaki's penis. "There is a residue here. I should take a swab for analysis. Surely Naos will need such samples."

"Sure, but I can tell you straight away what that is."

"Oh?"

"Lady cum."

"I beg your pardon?"

"Sorry; vaginal secretions. You can swab for DNA if you like, but I bet it'll come up as Camryn's." He sounded unfazed by the crude turn of the conversation.

Shaula thought about all the time Tiaki and the doctor had been spending together over the last few weeks; O'Donoghue was most likely right. She took a swab anyway. "During the argument the other night, there were certain people who seemed against the time Tiaki and Dr McArthur were spending together. They seemed against the idea of any android and human pair."

"Yep, there sure were. Someone should look closer at those people, I think."

"So the argument may have been the motive behind this murder?"

"Could be. Someone caught them having some hanky-panky in the forest, lashed out in anger? I mean, stabbing an intimate couple in the head sure does sound like a crime of passion." He sighed, and added, "poor Camryn," under his breath.

Shaula inspected what she could of Tiaki's epidermis, but soon there were no more investigations to be done other than to remove Tiaki's brain so she could begin working on it. She readied a storage receptacle and all the tools she would need. Then she stood at the head of the worktable and looked down at the form before her.

"I am the android engineer who fixes and reskins most of the settlement," she said, somewhat to O'Donoghue, but mostly to herself. "But when I need fixing or servicing, Tiaki is the one who does it."

"That makes sense. Are you wondering who will help you now?"

"No. One day a few years ago, I needed an epidermis repair. I had recently started using a new colour, this green. I used to wear a bronze epidermis. I paid little attention while Tiaki worked. Then when he was finished, I looked in the mirror and found that he had installed these pointed ears." She touched the tip of one ear. "I think he did it as a joke of sorts, and expected that I would ask him to make me rounded ears again. But I liked them and I have kept them ever since."

She looked up and found that O'Donoghue was watching her closely.

"Hey, you are shaken, aren't you? You just don't show it all too well. Is there anything I can do? What comforts you?"

Shaula shook her head. "I do not know. I have never needed comfort before." She set her shoulders and took up the tools she would use to peel away Tiaki's scalp.

It took her little time to remove all the mechanics that had encompassed Tiaki and put it in the brain container. She replaced Tiaki's cranium and scalp, attaching everything so that he looked as normal as possible.

Then she took his brain over to a workstation along the wall, flicked on an overhead light, and took a toolset out of a drawer.

"What are you going to do next?"

Shaula looked up. "The damage to Tiaki's brain is preventing me from accessing what is left of his memories. I am going to mend the connections."

"Does that mean you can fix him? That he'd come back to life?"

"No. Too much of his personality matrix was damaged. I can swap in new parts and repair his body. But he would be a fresh android. I suppose you could call it a factory reset. It would look like Tiaki, but it would be someone new. It is not my decision to make. I would only do that if Sirius ordered me to."

"Wow, yeah. I can see that would be rough. It would be like he had amnesia?"

"I suppose. But even more so. Tiaki became Tiaki during a long period of individuation. The same happens when humans grow up. When a human has amnesia, all that individuation exists even if they cannot remember the experiences that led to them becoming who they are. But Tiaki's individuation, his ability to be the gentle path of least resistance, it is all gone."

Thankfully, O'Donoghue quietened down as she worked. She was vaguely aware of him making himself a cup of tea in the tea nook, and visiting the human waste facilities. Shaula kept her head down, carefully mending the connections between the information port and Tiaki's memory banks.

Vega looked in on them occasionally, though he only glanced at her work before leaving in a hurry again.

Madigan came in to tell O'Donoghue about the locations and activities of all the people in the camp. It seemed the security officer was already learning how to do on-the-move programming to turn Madigan into a useful aid in his job.

Otherwise, Shaula worked, and O'Donoghue lurked, never sitting still for long, but keeping his movements to the kind that would not disturb Shaula.

Eventually, she gained access to a portion of Tiaki's memories, but only the short-term banks covering his last few days. They were fragmented and incomplete, and longer term memories were as yet unreachable. Shaula scrolled through the transcript on her tablet.

O'Donoghue came over to stand behind her chair and leaned one hand on the back. "You find anything?" he asked.

Shaula shook her head. "This is Tiaki's last memory. As you can see, he was in the middle of a sentence, talking with Dr McArthur about her home country of Australia, asking her about what it is like. Then nothing. Tiaki saw nothing suspicious before he was attacked. If he had, there would be a tag here in the transcript. He was attacked from behind, and unawares, before the doctor, as we already suspected."

"Can you see what he saw before he was attacked? In case he missed something."

"No. Android memories do not record video accessible outside of our own minds, for privacy reasons. We are not cameras."

The door opened and Kikelomo and Chaudhary stepped through. The latter was carrying a bowl that he held out to O'Donoghue. "Here, you must be starving," he said.

It was only then that Shaula noticed it was well beyond the time that humans ate their midday meal.

"You are a blessing, Sandeep," said O'Donoghue as he took the bowl and stepped through into the rear cabin to eat over the coffee table, leaving the door open.

"We got the morgue pod up and running," said Kikelomo. "We'll move Camryn there soon. The messenger pigeon has already returned. It's fast, for sure. But first, have you made any progress here?"

Shaula put her tools aside. "Tiaki's memories are fragmented and scrambled, but I found his last memory. He did not see his assailant. He was attacked from behind while in the middle of a conversation with Dr McArthur."

"Also, we think they'd been having sex shortly beforehand," added O'Donoghue between mouthfuls.

"Well, that complicates things," said Chaudhary.

"Or provides a motive," said Kikelomo. "Good work, you two. And I'm glad you're working well together, because Captain Rodriguez and Sirius have designated the two of you to lead a murder investigation. They want you to figure out who killed Dr McArthur and Tiaki before we finish the salvage run."

Shaula froze a moment, then disconnected her tablet from Tiaki's brain. "I beg your pardon?" She put the receptacle cap on to keep the brain safe.

"You will be helping Faolán with the murder investigation. Sirius says your android engineering expertise may be key, and the recording included Bellatrix recommending you for the job too."

Bellatrix's belief in Shaula was appreciated, if surprising, but even so. Shaula stood and placed Tiaki's brain in the most secure cupboard in the lab, locking it with a password and identity-triggered lock. She turned to the humans. "There has been some mistake. Murder investigations involve talking to people, empathising with people. I cannot do that."

"It'll be fine. I'll do that part. You'll be the tech person," said O'Donoghue.

Shaula shook her head. This was not playing to her strengths. If she were the one who had been murdered,

Tiaki would have been perfect to investigate who killed her. But the other way around, how could she possibly do him justice?

"There's more news," said Kikelomo. "Another wipe of android memories was detected in the settlement just as we were leaving. And then another last night."

"I think our memories were altered here too," said Shaula, "though we are not monitoring as closely here as Marcie is monitoring back at the settlement, so I cannot be sure."

"See; this is why we need you. You were already working on the memory problem. Your expertise will be needed to verify what you androids actually remember."

Shaula paced from one end of the lab to the other. "And what if I did it, but I do not even remember that I did?"

"Madigan didn't see you leave the engineering lab until you left with me," said O'Donoghue in a soft voice. "You're in the clear."

"Only if Madigan's memories may be trusted."

"Isn't that what you gave him to me for?"

She looked O'Donoghue in the eyes. "What if I was in error with my supposition? I am sorry, but I do not think I can do this."

He stared at her as she turned and headed for the door, bursting her way out of it as Vega had done before her.

CHAPTER 8

Faolán couldn't help but see Shaula's exit as a rejection. It was silly; he knew that despite Shaula's icy exterior, she was suffering from grief. Her storming out of the lab was 100% about her own feelings and 0% about not wanting to work with him. But he was self-aware enough to know that he had a sensitivity about being perceived as dumb by smart people. It was a side effect of having fucked up his life's A plan.

Knowing what the problem was and avoiding feeling like a failure were two different things, though.

"Sorry about lumping you with her, Faolán," said Ife. "I know that no one wants to work with Shaula, but her expertise will be needed, as I said."

Faolán frowned. "What do you mean?" He ought to get in the habit of tacking a 'sir' on the end there, now that Ife had been promoted, but he hadn't remembered very often so far.

"I just mean, everyone knows that she's difficult to work with, and you've even had your own troubles with her in the past."

Faolán cleared his throat. "I think those troubles were all my fault. I insulted her accidentally early on."

"She just stormed off, though. I hear it from both humans and androids; she's tough to get along with. Please let me know if you need any help smoothing anything over with her."

"I'm going to give her a pass for that one. She's grieving."

"You think so?" asked Sandeep. "Were they that close?"

"As far as I can tell, Tiaki was the closest Shaula had to a friend. She's not coping well with this. Let me talk to her. See if I can get through to her."

"OK. Get her on board," said Ife. "We're going to need this murder solved quickly, before tensions boil over. I can't do it, because I'm still in charge of the salvage, which has to go on regardless. We need that food production and those meds. We can't take too much time."

"Understood. Sir."

He went in search of the errant engineer, Madigan falling in at his side as he left the boundary of the vehicles. He found her sitting on a boulder and staring at the wreck of the *Tiger*, afternoon sunlight glinting on her green hair and on her familiar's carapace, half hidden amongst her curls. The delicate points of her ears stood out from behind.

"May I join you?" he asked.

She looked over her shoulder at him, and Faolán drew in a breath as the light played on the finely sculpted lines of her face, her upturned nose, her bright eyes. She really did look like a cute wee elf. Or rather, a beautiful leannán sídhe there to tempt him. Or drive him mad.

"Suit yourself," she said, and returned to her contemplation of the wreck.

Good thing she didn't act like it.

He stood beside her rock and looked at the wreck for a minute.

"I know this is hard on you," he said. "But you're not the only one, you know. We lost Camryn McArthur last night. She was a workmate, she had friends. She was a key part of our crew, one whose loss we're going to have trouble compensating for. She was key to some major parts of this salvage mission. We were relying on her knowledge of where things are in the med bay and what we need to bring back. We have a list, of course. But it's not the same as hands-on experience. They were both important people."

"You are labelling me as troublesome," said Shaula. She had turned to look at him.

"Well, kind of, I suppose. I'm not trying to tell you not to feel your feelings, though. It's OK to grieve Tiaki. But remember, other people are grieving too. And... this is something practical you can do that would help Tiaki."

"I cannot help Tiaki. He is gone."

Faolán winced. OK, sure, his wording had been poor.

"My job is to support this salvage," said Shaula. "I did not consent to investigating a murder. And I am not grieving. I am... inconvenienced by Tiaki's loss."

She almost sounded like she believed that.

"None of us ever expected to be investigating a murder. We're not homicide detectives. But someone's got to do it, and we're the ones who've been shoulder-tapped."

"Do you do everything you are told to do?"

He gave her a wry smile. "Well, I'm an officer in the Orion Navy, so, kind of, yeah. Within reason. Some joker I've angered tells me to jump out an airlock, I won't do it."

She just gazed at him, unfazed by the joke.

"Anyway, you always this stubborn? I bet you give Sirius headaches."

"Androids do not get headaches."

"Yeah, I'm sure you don't. Anyway, what if this investigation helps you figure out that memory problem you're working on with Marcie?"

"How?"

"I don't know. It might be good incentive, at least."

Shaula shook her head and looked back at the wreck. Well. Maybe his idea was foolish, but there was no need for her to rub it in.

Faolán looked around for inspiration, but instead spotted an incoming problem. Simons was striding their way, his face in a frown and looking like a man on a mission.

"Heads up, approaching annoyance," said Faolán.

Shaula's familiar hissed.

"What are you two conspiring about over here?" demanded Simons when he was nearby.

"Not conspiring," said Faolán. "Discussing a task we've been assigned. Don't be weird."

Simons stood between them and the wreck, his arms crossed. "Do you two really not realise how shady you look? First the wolf, then you 'find' the bodies in the forest, then you examine the destroyed android. Now you're having a shady conversation outside camp?" He made the 'I'm keeping an eye on you' gesture.

"Please," said Faolán. "You think we're, what? Partners in crime? You know as well as anyone that we raised the alarm about Camryn and Tiaki straight away, and that the whole camp came right over, and Camryn's blood was already cooling. Whatever happened, it happened before we got there. That's probably part of the reason we're the murder investigators."

"You two?" Simons laughed. "You make sense, I suppose, O'Donoghue. You're a security officer. But that android there? What input would it have? It probably led you right to the bodies to make it look more innocent."

Faolán unclenched his teeth. What was up with this guy? Why was he always causing trouble? "I woke Shaula from a charge cycle myself last night."

"Convenient. What for?"

"A quick word."

"I bet. Maybe it does have its hooks in you. I thought it might sabotage this salvage somehow. After all, if we have our own tech back, it's not important anymore."

Shaula's familiar hissed again, and she stood from her rock, approaching Simons. "Enough," she said. Her voice wasn't loud, but there was no mistaking the firmness in it.

"Fuck off, arsehole," said Faolán. "How dare you? Shaula lost a friend last night, and you're accusing her of murdering him so she can keep some nebulous 'status'? That sounds like projection to me."

Simons stepped into Faolán's personal space and stared down at him. The American had over half a foot on Faolán, but Madigan stepped up to Faolán's side and let out a low growl. Simons flinched and took half a step back. "What did you say?" he demanded.

"I'm just pointing out that what you were doing to Altair on the ship was very similar to what you're accusing Shaula of."

"That's ridiculous. And you should be more polite to me. I outrank you."

"No, you bloody well don't. The captain stripped you of your rank. And for good reason, too."

"We should start by investigating this man, Lieutenant O'Donoghue," said Shaula, standing shoulder-to-shoulder with him. "He seems very suspicious."

"Doesn't he just. We should reconstruct his movements. Can you pull data from all the familiars in the camp who may have observed him?"

"Yes, indeed, I can pull that data, using my skill set, which is absolutely relevant to a murder investigation. I could do that very easily."

"Why, thank you, my dear investigation partner. Let's put Simons at the top of our list for now, huh? After all, intimidating the investigators is absolutely something a guilty person would do."

"Attempting to intimidate."

"Hm?"

She looked at him. "I was not intimidated. Were you?"

"I guess not. Attempting to intimidate it is." He clapped Shaula on the shoulder. "Let's get to it, partner." He turned and headed back towards the camp, whistling a random tune. "So I take it you're in?" he asked her when they'd left Simons behind.

"I am." There was a finality to her delivery.

Faolán grinned. He may have failed to get Shaula to accept the responsibility of the investigation. But where he had failed, it seemed Simons had accidentally succeeded.

She was competitive, this Shaula. Duly noted.

CHAPTER 9

They started at the murder site. The scene had been taped off the previous evening, and all members of the salvage team forbidden from entering.

But now Shaula, O'Donoghue, and Madigan were within the cordon, their feet covered in bags, gloves on their hands (at least, those who had them), and their hair in nets. Charm perched on Shaula's shoulder instead, observing. Shaula did not know exactly what she would be doing, other than the logical attempt to avoid contaminating the crime scene and the need to find whatever evidence they could.

The area looked different during the day. The forest, which was dominated by pine at this point in its development, was light and airy, the canopy sparse. Pine needles decreased the undergrowth, but did not suppress it entirely. The scrub species that had grown in the area first were still present. It would be a pleasant spot, if not for the dark stain under a tree and the scuffs all around.

They only had so much light, so this would merely be their first pass through the site. They were looking for the most obvious evidence, particularly the murder weapon.

O'Donoghue stood up and stretched his back out with a groan. "We all should have been more careful when we recovered their bodies," he said. "There's footprints all over."

"Agreed." Shaula was taking pictures of all the footprints she could find so they could be measured and perhaps matched to their owners. If they were lucky, a pattern may emerge.

"I can't see anything but footprints and blood to show that anything happened here. No weapon. I can't even see any fibres. Madigan?"

The wolf sat on his haunches. "I have nothing of note to report."

O'Donoghue sighed. "We're losing the light too. We need to finish this tomorrow."

"Were you not intending to interview everyone tomorrow before they started the salvage?"

"Yeah, that too. We'll have a busy day, for sure."

"Understood." Shaula finished taking the last few pictures of the footprints. "Let us return to camp."

While they walked back, Shaula brought up a topic that she felt she could not avoid discussing even though she worried about how many of her own private concerns she let on by speaking. "Lieutenant O'Donoghue, I have come to a conclusion."

He smiled at her. "You can call me Faolán, you know. You're not an officer. And you've called me it before, anyway."

"If you insist. I believe we have to take the alteration to android memories seriously during this investigation."

He nodded. "Sure. What do you suggest?"

"I suggest a similar approach to what Marcie and Altair have been using."

Faolán's eyebrows rose. "Uh..."

"Not like that. I am referring to how Marcie has been monitoring Altair's experiences via conversation and noting any discrepancies. It may be wise for each android in the salvage crew to be allocated a human who will monitor them in the same way. The android and human pairs would stay close together throughout the investigation. Any memory wipes that occur may delete important information. We require the backup of your human memories to ensure we gather all the clues."

"I see what you mean. Some people are going to be less thrilled about it than others, though."

"That is inevitable."

"If this murder has something to do with Dr Neale, looking out for memory alterations might be even more important. You know, if someone has been hacked."

Shaula stopped walking. "You think that might be the case?"

Faolán stopped and looked at her, his eyes wide. "I don't know. I mean, out here, far from the settlement... I *think* it's just us here. And as we said, it looked like a crime of passion. So the murderer is probably one of the salvage team. But we can't rule anything out." He put his hands in his pockets and hunched his shoulders.

He was right, loathe as Shaula was to think about it. Because if this was all tied to Dr Neale, that made this murder investigation all the more daunting.

They found Kikelomo when they returned to the camp, and she concurred with Shaula's assessment. While they conferred on pairings, Faolán built another campfire as he had done the evening before.

The group soon gathered, the humans bringing their evening meal. The humans told stories about Dr McArthur. Hernandez told them about how he could not work the food printer on his first day on the ship, and Dr McArthur had shown him how. Gagnon told a story about how Dr McArthur had set her broken leg when a loose unit had fallen on her in a space battle. Dr McArthur had told her off-colour jokes throughout the procedure to keep her mind off her woes. Their stories moved them to smile, to laugh. It seemed to be some human grieving ritual.

"Shaula, can you tell us a story about Tiaki?" asked Faolán in a lull in the conversation.

She had been intending to lurk on the edge of the group as she usually did. But between Faolán's chastisement that afternoon and his conversational hook now, it seemed she had no choice but to socialise.

She was intensely aware of the eyes on her as she walked over and sat on the blanket beside Faolán. "What kind of story?" she asked, looking only at him.

"Something that would tell us about the kind of person he was. If you're not sure what's right to tell, I think that story you told me earlier about," he tapped his ear, "would be just about right."

Shaula was not sure if she wanted to tell that story. It was personal, and it had been a risk enough for her to let that much of herself be perceived by one person alone. But it was also a story about Tiaki. Perhaps she could alter the perspective.

"I usually change the epidermides of the androids when they need a refresh. But Tiaki has always changed mine. One day, he played a trick on me. As far as I was aware, the procedure passed as normal. Later, when I looked in the mirror, I discovered that I had pointed ears."

Kikelomo chortled. "Did he say why he did it?"

"Not as such. He mentioned he had been reading about an old Earth story, and he had thought of me, and the pointed ears had come from that. But when I searched the database, I found multiple relevant references. I do not know which one he intended, and therefore which pointed comment he was making about my nature is still a mystery to me."

There was a titter of laughter around the campfire. She looked at Faolán. Only he knew the most private part of the story: that she liked the ears and kept them on purpose.

Kikelomo let them finish their meals before getting to business. "All right, people. I've some updates for you. As many of you are aware, Lieutenant O'Donoghue and Shaula have been designated by the captain and Sirius as the investigators of the murders. They're going to be focussing on finding out what happened while the rest of us focus on the salvage. They have a few announcements to make about the investigation, so listen up. Faolán?"

Faolán sat up straighter. "Thank you. First of all, tomorrow morning I'm going to be talking to each one of you about anything you may have seen last night, or even earlier, that may have been out of place. I want to talk to you all, one at a time, before you start the salvage. So we'll be starting bright and early, to get it over and done with as soon as we can. All right?"

There were murmurs of assent and nods around the fire. Only a fool would think that was unreasonable.

"Also, Shaula has made a very good point, which we've already discussed with LC Kikelomo. Shaula?"

There he went, pushing her to socialise again. She looked into the fire, finding it easier to talk without making eye contact with anyone. "I do not trust the memories of us androids." Vega made a move to protest, but Shaula held up a hand to him. "The problem of alterations to android memories has been lingering for a while. I consider it to be an extreme risk to our endeavours here. Therefore, I propose that each android be paired with a human who will stay close to them and monitor their memories and perceptions, so that we can catch any further alterations to our memories as soon as we can."

"What would that look like in practice?" asked Diphda. "I do not need my hand held."

"For the last few weeks, Marcie has been asking Altair about what he did and what he saw that day. If he seems to forget anything or perceive it differently, she alerts Sirius and Captain Rodriguez. I propose we do the same here, and alert Kikelomo if we find any discrepancies."

Simons was frowning, of course, as was Gagnon. But Kikelomo did not intend to assign them androids because of their own personal tendencies. Everyone else was either nodding at the sense of her words, or remaining quiet.

"I think this idea of Shaula's is a good one," said Kikelomo. "We don't know what we're dealing with here, and it's a sensible backup."

"We can't watch them round the clock, though," said Hernandez. "We need to sleep."

"Sure, but they need to charge too. And there's a way to send a ping to our tablets when an android finishes a charge cycle. Right?"

"That is correct," said Shaula. "It is based on ancient locational technology since we cannot be networked for security reasons. But it will work."

"I've picked out the pairings myself," said Kikelomo. "We're going to reshuffle berths to make sure that we can keep pairs together. Sorry for the inconvenience, people, but pairing up people who were already in the same vehicle didn't always make sense from a work team perspective. For practicality's sake, the pairings are based on who is going to be working where, and vehicle allocations are to do with mixing people up between teams so that we keep our lines of communication as open as possible. I don't have the patience to keep things gender segregated as well. Just behave yourselves. We have no privacy here, and the two who sought it found trouble." Kikelomo stood. "Ok, first of all, Ensign Latu, please pair with Vega and move into the cruiser. You're both on the med bay team and you're both security officers, so it makes sense. OK?"

"Yes, sir," said Latu. Vega did not respond, though he did give Latu a long look.

"Next in the cruiser, Hernandez, please keep an eye on Boris."

"Uh, the spider... sir?"

"Yes. He's also an android, and you're both on portage duty. Just ask him every now and then what he's seen, that's all. Are you scared of spiders?"

"Uh, no, but... yes, sir." Hernandez gulped.

"Simons, stay on the cruiser. No android pairing for you. Gagnon, move to the cruiser as well, please. No android pairing for you, either. I know you have... opinions that might interfere with the task."

Gagnon looked relieved. "Yes, sir."

"Sandeep and Diphda, you're both on hydroponics salvage duty, so please move to the med lab and pair up."

"Why the med lab?" asked Diphda.

"Because I want a security officer on the med lab, and two on the cruiser, so you're in the med lab."

"Why am I paired with him?"

Chaudhary sighed and raised an eyebrow at Kikelomo. She shrugged. "Because you're both on hydroponics. There's no other reason, Diphda."

"I do not wish to be paired with a human at all."

"You must be," said Shaula. "This is my professional opinion. Please honour it."

"I will try my best to inconvenience you as little as possible," said Chaudhary.

"Moving on," said Kikelomo. "Since I'm on med lab duty, I'll pair with Naos myself and move to the med lab."

"As I expected," said Naos. "Is this because I disagreed with you when you said I could not do a full autopsy of Dr McArthur, because a human should do it?"

"Those were our orders from the settlement. You know that."

"That leaves just O'Donoghue and Shaula in the engineering lab," said Simons. "You sure we can trust them with all the important equipment in there? All the evidence?"

"It makes sense for the investigators to have the evidence and a lab in which to process it."

"But what about keeping an eye on them?"

"I'll be keeping an eye on Shaula," said Faolán, his forehead creasing with annoyance. "You do remember that I'm not an android, right?"

There were a few snorts of mirth around the fire. Shaula, too, was amused. Faolán was the least android-like of the humans present.

Kikelomo sighed. "You want to move in there too?" she said to Simons. "Keep them company? I'm sure Shaula could put you to work. Or maybe you could groom the wolf. I bet its fur picks up all sorts of burrs."

Simons shuddered.

Shaula expected that no one else would volunteer to move into the engineering lab with her. She had that sort of reputation. Pricklier than Diphda even.

Kikelomo clapped her hands together. "All right, you have your assignments. Get settled in for the night, sort out a system with your buddy to monitor their memories, and get some sleep. We have a big day tomorrow."

The grumblings did not start in earnest until Kikelomo had gone to the engineering lab to fetch her things for the move. Shaula did not wish to listen, so she went to her lab too. She nodded at Kikelomo as she left, and then began sorting her tools, tidying up her work bench for the evening. She draped a sheet over Tiaki for now. Someone could help her move his form into the charging cabinet the next day so she would not need to keep looking at him.

The door opened, and both Faolán and Madigan entered. It was good that the familiar had come too. If the murder motive was anger over humans and androids becoming close, then Faolán himself might be in danger. It was well known that he had supported Altair and Marcie's romance. Also, Gagnon had been putting foolish ideas in people's heads, ones that she hoped had not taken root, but it was hard to tell.

Faolán gave her a stiff salute. "Permission to come aboard?"

Shaula frowned at him. "You have been aboard this vehicle before."

"Yeah, but," he hefted a bag. "Not in a moving in sort of way. Sorry for the intrusion."

"These are our orders, and you do what you are told, right?"

He gave an odd huff of a laugh. "Right. Right." He shut the door behind him. "I'll just, uh." He pointed towards the rear cabin. "I'll get myself sorted." He moved into the cabin, Madigan on his heels, and shut the door behind them. Shaula turned back to her work bench. But then the door opened again and he stuck his head through. "Uh, where will you be? Cupboard or bunk? I mean, I don't want to inconvenience you at all. I wouldn't like the cupboard personally. But then if I were you, I also wouldn't want to share a bedroom with me either. So just do whatever is comfortable for you. I'll work around you. OK? Am I making sense?"

"Precious little, and yet nonetheless I parsed something from your rambling."

He flushed and rubbed the back of his neck. "Yeah, sorry. I'll just get to sleep. Which bunk should I use?"

"Top bunk."

"Roger that." He disappeared into the cabin and shut the door again. Why was he so awkward all of a sudden?

CHAPTER 10

If Faolán was in need of one thing at all, it was a better organisational structure on his tablet. The amount of information he would need to keep track of was daunting, and it was not his strong suit. He would need to record all the information about the investigation and everything anyone said to him about it, either in an official interview or in off-the-cuff remarks. On top of that, he would need to track Shaula's experiences, looking for memory gaps.

He'd have his work cut out for him. And that was while his implant was still working. Heaven help him if he ran out of ADHD meds before he concluded the investigation.

When he'd first woken that morning, he'd laid in his bunk, peering over the edge at Shaula lying on the bunk below. She had looked up at him, her eyes hard gems in the early morning light filtering through the dimmed window. "What?"

"Sorry. Just, run through for me what we did yester-day, would you?"

"Ah. A memory check."

He had laid on his bunk and made notes on his tablet of all she said. He couldn't see anything out of the ordinary. Then they'd both risen and made ready for the day. It was now barely 7 am, and Faolán was sitting in the cabin at the rear of the engineering lab, now converted back into a sitting room. He'd put a folded blanket on the coffee table to turn it into an additional seat so that the people who he interviewed could sit across from him. He was now poking at his tablet, trying to figure out how best to organise his information. He wanted something he could use immediately, because he knew if he ever put off writing something down, he'd likely forget it entirely.

"Do you have a good system for organising inter-views and whatnot? Like, lots of information and notes?"

Shaula looked at him through the open double doors between the cabin and the lab. She was organising her tablet and cable, readying herself to download all perti-nent information from each familiar in the camp. "I do not know what will work best for you. However, why not ask Madigan to take a transcript of all the interviews? Then you would have a backup in case your own notes prove lacking."

"He can do that?"

"Of course. He cannot record video. He does not have that upgrade, and Sirius controls which familiars have it. But he can take a transcript or an audio record-ing that can be offloaded via cable at a later time, similar to what I will be extracting from the familiars today."

"Hm." Faolán looked at the wolf, who reclined in the corner by the ensuite door, his tongue lolling out in a calculatedly good-dog manner. "Can you help me by recording the interviews I do this morning?"

"Affirmative. I will record audio and transcript files."

Faolán nodded. "That's fantastic. Thank you."

Then he jumped up and went to find his first victim.

Not everyone was as happy with being grilled for information as others, of course. He caught Diphda first, as she was doing a morning patrol of the camp. He asked her to come in, and leave her familiar with Shaula to extract all it knew about people's whereabouts the night of the murder.

"I saw Tiaki and the doctor leaving the camp," Diphda said to Faolán when he began questioning her.

"Why were you up and about? Vega was on duty that evening."

"I do not like to settle in for a long charge until I have done a perimeter sweep at the very least. That is when I saw them leave the camp."

"And you didn't call them back?"

"I knew what they were intending to do, and I did not want to know the details. Under these circumstances, anyone seeking alone time is likely to leave the camp to do so. I did not designate their behaviour as a security concern."

"Did you see anything else out of place?"

"No."

The next person he waylaid was Hernandez, who said he slept through, though he remembered seeing Vega leave the cruiser.

He found Naos next. The android doctor was reluctant to hand her seagull familiar over to Shaula before taking a seat in the cabin, but did so when Shaula glared at her long enough. "I have already reported all of what I could discover by examining Camryn McArthur, which was precious little, as I could not extract her brain as Shaula has extracted Tiaki's."

"Run me through it. I didn't get the full report."

"McArthur had leaf litter and dirt smears on the epidermis under her clothes, indicating that she had been unclothed prior to her murder. She was killed with one wound dealt by a thin, sharp implement, yet to be determined. The wound begins underneath her chin and travels up into her brain."

Faolán shuddered. At least it would have been quick, but it was such an execution-style death. "Thank you. Did you leave the med lab that night?" He already knew she had, but would she admit to it?

"Yes. I saw Dr McArthur leave. I thought it was unwise, considering her importance to the mission, so I went to tell her to go back inside."

"And how did that conversation go?"

"I did not find her. By the location of the bodies, I now know I guessed the wrong direction when looking for her. I walked towards the wreck."

"What did you do when you couldn't find her?"

"I went back inside. I decided to berate her when she returned. But I never had the opportunity."

Berate. What a word to be used about a grown woman who could make her own choices. Even if those choices had led her to being murdered.

Faolán made a note to look more into Naos's whereabouts, just in case. She really didn't seem to like that Camryn and Tiaki had stated seeing each other.

"Ok, moving on. Did you see anything suspicious that evening?"

"Yes."

Faolán waited a moment. "Uh, what did you see?"

"I saw Gagnon lurking around the charging cupboard and the bunk charging connection in the medical lab. She seemed to be inspecting their operation."

"OK. Anything else?"

"No."

That seemed like a nice lead, so he went and dragged Gagnon into his lair next. She came unwillingly, a rock-hard bread roll still in her hand from breakfast. She was dipping it in a mug of coffee to make it edible.

"Does she need to be here while we talk?" Gagnon said, nodding her head in Shaula's direction. "I'd feel more comfortable without an android listening in."

"I'm monitoring her experiences too, so yes. She stays. Now, what did you see the night of the murders?"

"Nothing."

"And everyone from your vehicle stayed put?"

She shrugged.

"I've heard that you were snooping around the charging facilities. What's that about?"

Gagnon huffed. "I mean, can we really trust that the androids are 'asleep' when they're charging? What if they're listening to us the whole time? Half of them aren't even using those cupboards. Those at least give us some measure of security. But the beds? Just open in the room? I was just trying to figure out how it all works, is all."

"OK. And what of the others in the med lab that night? Are you sure you can't say if you saw them?"

"I saw nothing, OK. I was tired."

"Did you leave the vehicle that night?"

"No."

"You sure? Because we already have one eye witness account of you being up and about." No need to let on that it was Madigan who saw her.

"OK, fine. Come to think of it, I did step out for a moment."

"What for?"

"Just... it's no big deal."

He crossed his arms. "People were murdered, you know. We need to know everything."

Gagnon sighed. "Fine! Whatever! I had a gassy belly. I went out to let out some stinky farts into the night. You satisfied? Or are you going to ask me any more invasive, personal questions?"

Faolán dismissed Gagnon. She had her hackles up, so he wouldn't get any further with her. But just as with Naos, he wasn't satisfied he had the full truth from her. Was she up to something? Or was she just still having trouble with the presence of androids?

Next he ran down Vega, who seemed reluctant to come in for a chat, dragging his feet up the steps into the engineering lab.

"I'm keen to get your take on things, Vega," he said after the android had handed his eagle familiar to Shaula and taken a seat.

"Why?"

"Because you were on night watch, of course. What did you see?"

"Nothing."

Faolán blinked. "How can you have seen nothing? I've already had confirmation that multiple people were up and about that night."

"Correction: I saw a few people walking around the camp. But I did not see anyone leave the camp."

"Not even Camryn and Tiaki?"

He paused. "No," he said in a quieter voice.

Faolán crossed his arms. "Does it seem likely to you that you would have missed them?"

"It does not."

Faolán looked over at Shaula, then back at Vega. "Do you think it's possible something was wiped from your memories during that memory glitch?"

"It is possible."

Shaula stirred from her own work. "Where were you in the camp when the memory glitch occurred?"

"I am not sure," said Vega. "I have not pinpointed the moment in my own memory."

"Could you have been on the side of the camp closest to the murder site?"

"I do not believe I had cycled around that side before you roused the alarm. I remember having to walk through the vehicles to head in that direction."

"Hm, thank you."

After Vega left, Faolán and Shaula looked at each other. "How could he not have patrolled one whole side of the camp after several hours?" asked Faolán.

"He did patrol there. His memory has been wiped."

"Does that mean he saw something, or participated in something?"

"Possibly. Or it may be a coincidence caused by an android-wide memory wipe occurring at a time that is inconvenient for us. We need more evidence to tell."

"Did his familiar see anything?"

Shaula shook her head. "I cannot tell. Every familiar I have checked so far saw nothing of note for a suspiciously consistent gap of time lasting about half an hour. I cannot yet identify the exact boundaries of the memory alteration."

"I sure wish we knew if that was a coincidence."

Faolán rose to go fetch the next person, but Shaula grabbed his forearm for a moment as he passed.

"Did you see any indication that I had been up and about before you woke me for our conversation?"

"No. Why?"

"Like Vega, I would not know what had been removed from my memory. I do not believe I left the vehicle between when I settled for the night and when you arrived, but I cannot be sure."

Faolán crossed his arms. He couldn't imagine how worrying it must be for the androids to have their own memories proved unreliable.

"You didn't smell like the night at all, I don't think. I don't remember there being any leaf litter or dross on you. And Madigan didn't see you walking around. So I think you're good."

"That is all we have at the moment, though. Suppositions."

"Yeah. From what I understand, murder investigations usually feel like this at the beginning."

He tracked down Simons next. The man looked tired and kept yawning. He claimed not to have seen anyone acting suspicious. "Here's an idea," he followed up with. "What if that Tiaki killed the good doctor first, and then someone took him out because he was dangerous? I mean, have you thought of that possibility? It makes perfect sense to me."

The evidence that Shaula had extracted from Tiaki's memory banks didn't support that theory, but Faolán didn't want to let on to Simons what they did know in case he was the murderer. "Thanks for your input," he said instead, committing to nothing. "Now, what were you doing the night of the murders?"

Simons scoffed. "You yourself saw me drinking a coffee in the cruiser."

"And before that?"

"Nothing."

"Really? Because we have an eye witness account of you leaving the cruiser for a bit."

Simons laughed and crossed his arms. "Do you now? And who said that? I'd be interested to hear. Because it seems someone is trying to pull wool over your eyes."

As if Madigan would be doing that. Shaula's idea of bringing in an untampered familiar was the gift that kept on giving. Faolán shrugged, giving Simons nothing.

"Actually, I think I stepped out for a bit of fresh air, and to check the camp fire had been put out properly. But I didn't go far."

"Did you see anyone else while you were up?"

"Nope." Something about how quickly he said it made Faolán suspicious he was lying.

"You sure?"

"Yes, of course."

He wouldn't get anything else out of Simons, that was for sure, so he dismissed him.

He pulled Latu off duty for a few minutes to interview her. "I'm sorry, sir. I don't think I have any relevant information," she said. "I was tired that night and slept deeply."

"That's OK. Who did you see in the med lab before you went to sleep?"

"I know Naos went to charge in that cupboard thing. Gagnon was still up and about. She spent time that evening reading on her tab and was still using the bathroom when I went to sleep. I don't know when she went to bed."

"How about Camryn?"

"She was in her bunk when I went to sleep, I think. But I don't think she was asleep. I think she was reading too. I don't know when she left the vehicle." Latu hung her head. "I'm sorry, sir, for failing at my duty."

"In what way do you think you failed?" he asked in a gentler voice.

"Someone I was supposed to be providing security for got murdered. Of course I failed."

"No, ensign. You're not responsible for Camryn leaving the vehicle for a tryst. She was a smart woman who knew what she was doing, and chose to take that risk."

Latu nodded. "Thank you, sir."

After she left, Shaula turned from her current work, downloading data from one of the messenger pigeons. "You seem convinced it is not her."

"Call it intuition. Hey, run through who I've talked to so far?" He opened his notes of Shaula's memories.

"That is a good idea." Shaula recited for him everyone he had spoken to so far, and the main points. He jotted it all down. It all matched up with what he'd done, and made a handy summary besides.

"All good," he said. "No memory weirdness detected."

He finally got a hold of Sandeep and Ife, who had been busy getting everything ready for the salvage to begin. He spoke to Sandeep first.

"I slept through, sorry, Faolán. But I sleep light, so I think that if Hernandez had gotten up, I would have noticed."

Faolán had seen both Sandeep and Hernandez asleep himself, so he believed that.

Ife too said she was asleep and had nothing to add. Again, he'd seen her asleep himself when he went to get Shaula.

But his intuition pinged. They were both very quick to assure him they were asleep. What was up with that?

There was one final android who he had to speak to, the one who he had been dreading somewhat.

They eased Boris into the engineering lab, making sure he didn't clip any of the equipment. Madigan sat beside Faolán on the sofa to give Boris room to take up most of the floor. His front four legs, which ended in pointed tips, were up on the coffee table. Faolán wasn't sure which of his eight eyes to look into when speaking.

"OK, uh, thank you for coming. Can you tell me what you saw the night of the murder?"

"Many people moved around the camp, but few left its bounds," said Boris in a voice like tumbling gravel, like a much deeper version of Charm's metallic hiss. "I did not... I believe I would have looked at everyone, but I assume my memories have been tampered with. I saw some movement in the forest, but what that movement was has not been recorded. I do not know if I could not identify the movement, or if I did, but then the knowledge was removed."

"Where did you see it?"

"In the general direction of the murder site. Something on the tree line, I believe. In my memories, it is a mere flicker on several of my sensors, including visible spectrum and infrared."

"Uh, thanks." Faolán wasn't sure about all the different ways Boris could perceive the world; he was a very specialised android left over from mining activity. Perhaps Shaula could enlighten him later. "Did you see anyone else make any notable movements before your memory was tampered with?"

"I observed Dr McArthur and Tiaki leave the camp. They were holding hands. I observed each of Naos, Simons, and Sublieutenant Gagnon walk towards the *Sunda Tiger* away from the camp. Naos was only gone for a few minutes. Simons was gone longer, but also returned. Gagnon... I believe she must have returned during the memory alteration, because I did not see her return, but I saw her leave the mobile med lab when you called everyone to the murder site. I also observed yourself and Shaula leave camp. You were walking close to one another."

That's because it was dark, and he'd been using the light from her eyes to make sure he hadn't tripped over!

How lucky they were to have Boris; he'd confirmed a lot. He definitely wanted to figure out more about where both Simons and Gagnon had gone. Walking off to the wreck didn't align with either of their testimonies. But for now, Boris was freaking him out a bit and he wanted the spider to go now, thanks. "Thank you for your time, Boris. We'll let you know if you have any further questions."

Faolán sighed and stretched his aching back out once Boris had left. He leaned his elbows on the bench beside

Shaula's workstation. Now that she'd finished dealing with the familiars, she was comparing two sets of photos on her tablet: pictures of the footprints at the crime scene, and pictures of people's feet, all taken just inside the door to the lab. He turned and spied the small camera set up inside a glass-front cabinet near the door.

"Sneaky woman. I like it. You're figuring out who was standing where at the crime scene?"

"Yes. I will try to determine if anyone's footprints are in places we did not see them after we found the bodies. I am not yet sure if I will find anything important. There are several pairs of people with similar-sized feet in our group, so being exact in identification will be challenging."

"Good work. What did you think of the interviews?"

"Better you than me," she said, still not even looking up from the tablet.

"Off the top of my head, Gagnon, Simons, and Naos were all up and out of the camp when they shouldn't have been. No one knows how long Diphda was up and about, no one knows exactly where Vega was patrolling, Simons is sketchy as fuck, Gagnon's hiding something, but it may just be her own opinions. Ife and Sandeep are hiding something, but I don't think it's the murder. I think they're just withholding something for another reason."

"They have already been on the wreck. They may know something about the status of the items we are to salvage that would damage morale."

Faolán imagined the medicine manufacturing unit in pieces and unfixable. That would be a huge inconvenience. "It's possible," he said. "It worries me, but it's possible." He sighed. "I don't have a good read on Boris and what he can and can't perceive. Could the wounds on the bodies have been caused by his legs? They're pointy."

Shaula stared at the wall ahead of her for a moment. "No. They are not pointy enough."

"OK. Then, how does he see? Is it likely that he wouldn't have been able to identify movement in the forest?"

"No, it is not. Boris is equipped with eight eyes, two for stereoscopic vision, and six for alternative viewing actions. He has two night vision eyes, a telescopic eye, two different infrared eyes covering different ranges, and an ultraviolet eye."

"So what you're saying is that his memories must surely have been tampered with, because if there was something to see, he would have seen it."

"Yes."

Faolán leaned back against the bench and crossed his arms. How the heck was he supposed to untangle all this and figure out who killed Tiaki and the doctor?

CHAPTER 11

Shaula wondered if Faolán knew that by lurking near her workstation, he was interrupting her work. Probably not. He seemed like the gregarious sort whose thought processes were aided by the presence of others.

"We should go report to Ife," he said. "She wants to get the salvage underway ASAP, and we don't need to keep people from doing their jobs any longer."

Shaula did not need a further interruption to her work, but she complied. It was not as if he were interrupting her work for frivolous reasons. He was still focussed on his assigned task. "Let us not delay."

They found Kikelomo talking with Chaudhary and Naos near the med lab.

"Hey boss," said Faolán. "Can we give you an update when you're free?"

"I'll make time for you right now," she said, and led them away from the vehicles so the three of them could have a private conversation.

"Have you finished with the interviews?"

"Yup. We've got some things to look into, so it wasn't a waste of time either. And we've got some stuff to get on with this afternoon that we don't need anyone else for, so if you want to start the salvage, please go ahead."

Kikelomo breathed a sigh of relief. "Good. That's good news. Not 'we've found the killer' good, but something. What will you be doing?"

Faolán looked at Shaula. It seemed it was her time to talk. "Footprint analysis, and a re-examination of the murder scene using the updated data."

"Good. You'd want to get that done before it rains."

That was a good point. Without access to satellites, accurate meteorological data were not available to the 227C colony, so the next rain could come upon them unawares.

"There's something else you should know," continued Kikelomo. "We've had another message from the settlement. News of the murders has flared up some tensions. There have been a few altercations, a few arguments. The captain and Sirius have their hands full smoothing things over. Also, some people suffering from gravity sickness have taken a bit of a turn for the worse over the past few days and are starting to look frail. We need to get the salvage completed as fast as possible, and figure out who the murderer is too."

"That sounds rough," said Faolán. "I forgot to think about how the news would be received by the others."

"Yeah. Plus, we have to face the idea that one of our own has done something so awful."

The three of them looked back to the camp at all of their work colleagues going about their business. Indeed, one of those people was a murderer. It was a troubling thought.

They left the rest of the team preparing to enter the wreck, including Madigan, who would guard the camp after the others left, and took Shaula's list of footprint comparisons with them to the crime scene. She held the tablet out between them. "I have labelled the footprints on this map with who I think they belong to." Charm was the one who had recorded a schematic of the murder site she could map the footprints onto.

"Nice," said Faolán. He swayed closer to her as he studied the diagram, his shoulder bumping hers. Shaula noted how they were very close to the same height. Somehow it made it much easier to talk to him than her fellow androids, who were taller than her. "You've tagged Ife over there, which is just how I remember it. She stood there."

"The prints over here also align with my memories." She pointed to some prints labelled 'Hernandez' near where the bodies had been. Hernandez had indeed helped lift the bodies onto a hoverbed.

"But over here, you have prints labelled just 'android-male' and here are some called 'android-female.'"

"Yes. Unfortunately, our foot sizes are standardised. It is impossible to tell between Tiaki and Vega's prints, just as it is impossible to tell between Naos, Diphda, and my prints, with the exception that my prints may be shallower as I am shorter and therefore lighter than Naos and Diphda."

Faolán wandered away from Shaula to look at the scene from a different angle. "So we can't tell if this trail here is Tiaki arriving in the clearing after a round of hide the pickle with Camryn, or Vega approaching from a different direction than we saw him walk from on the evening."

"Hide the pickle?" Shaula asked in bemusement.

"Sorry. That's a euphemism for sex." His cheeks were flushed.

"Ah." She wandered in that direction, being careful about where she put her feet. "We are lucky we had rain shortly before we arrived. The ground would have been too hard to preserve prints otherwise."

She inspected the prints near where the bodies were found. "I presume these are Dr McArthur's prints. I wish I had measured her feet before she was put in the morgue pod."

"Ah, don't worry yourself about it. Neither of us are trained homicide detectives." He gave her a crooked smile. "We can only do the best we can."

It was a pleasant sentiment. Shaula had always aimed for perfection and frustrated herself when she did not achieve it. But Faolán's expectations of her were far more achievable.

Shaula measured Dr McArthur's presumed footprint. "I shall seek to reconstruct her movements."

"OK. Let me have another look at that map and I'll see if I can spot anyone else's prints in places they shouldn't be."

They searched in companionable silence for a few minutes. But Faolán was not known for keeping quiet for long.

"Hey, so, tell me more about the memory problem you've been working on."

She looked at where he sat crouched, a sunbeam piercing the canopy picking out red tones in his brown hair. "Tiaki's memories, or the alterations to all our memories?"

"The alterations."

"It is a complex issue that would take much time to explain. Is there a particular facet you would like to know about?"

"How about the bits relevant to this investigation? Oh, and keep it simple. I'm not such a technical person."

"We do not know how our memories are being altered. We also do not know how to access what has been hidden. That is what Marcie is researching, as Altair's experiences indicate that hidden memories can be re-covered. If so, and if I can figure out how to do it at will, I may be able to recover hidden memories from the memory wipe that happened at the time of the murder."

"Right. So those conspicuously absent memories from Vega and Boris."

"Yes."

"This sounds pretty high priority, actually. Think you'll have time to work on this too?"

"I will fit it in."

"How did Altair unlock his memories?"

"Some of it was accidental while Simons was hacking him. That is Marcie's primary means of investigation. Unfortunately, Simons did not pay enough attention to exactly what he did, and the effect has not been repli-cated. They discovered another way, but it is not my place to say."

"Am I not on a need-to-know?"

"That is not the problem. It would be an invasion of privacy. I wish I did not know as many details as I do." Supporting their romance was one thing. Knowing what sex acts they had partaken of to unlock memories was too much.

Faolán pulled a face. "Never mind. I get the gist. I'll leave it at that."

Shaula had not expected her words to elucidate the matter. She was often caught unawares by the humans' ability to intuit beyond what an android would. And what of that face he pulled? Did he find the idea of inti-mate relations with an android to be distasteful?

"It is not that bad, surely," she said.

"What?"

"What they have been doing. It is not that bad. You made a face."

He waved his hands about in a chaotic fashion. "What? What face?"

"A disgusted face."

"Oh, that." He laughed and rubbed the back of his neck. "No, I'd make that face about any two of my friends getting it on. I don't want to think about my friends naked. I get intrusive thoughts sometimes that I have trouble controlling, and I don't want that sort of mental picture to be one of them."

Shaula huffed. It sounded plausible, and she hoped it was the case. The thought of Faolán also secretly harbouring anti-android sentiments irritated her.

"Uh, you're not weirded out talking about a topic like that?" His voice sounded strained and awkward.

"So long as I do not know the details."

He busied himself, looking in another direction. "Huh."

"What do you mean, 'huh'?"

"Don't take this the wrong way, but I thought you'd be more prudish. Sorry."

He thought she would not support Marcie and Altair, or would be like Naos and be against intimate relations. But that was not the case. She was no prude. Also, her eagerness to learn more about how android bodies worked was stronger than her desire to be alone. If she thought anyone would be interested in her sexually, then she would jump at the chance to try it out for herself. For interest's sake and to see if she could unlock memories, not for romance. But she was not a friendly android like Altair or Tiaki. Who would want to be intimate with her?

She put that thought aside for now. She had work to do.

"I believe I have found a trail of Dr McArthur's footprints over here by the android-male footprints. It looks as if she was walking normally here, but then about five metres further out she walked backwards for several paces. Further out here," she said, following the trail, "she was walking normally. The trail leads from further in the forest." She stopped and put her hands on her hips. "Why would she have been walking backwards? Did she see something?"

"Or was she having a flirty bantering conversation with Tiaki, and she turned around to look at his face while she delivered a particularly pointed remark? I've seen people do that before. It's a flirty sort of thing to do."

"Walk backwards? It makes no sense."

"It's an eye contact thing." Faolán followed her over. "I can't see anything out of place over there. Does this prove those footprints are Tiaki's after all?"

"It seems so. I am going to take a wider pass around the site to see if we missed anything further out."

"Good. I'll do the same, going the other way."

Shaula walked in a semi-circle around the site. The ground made a complex substrate to search: there were fallen leaves and needles strewn about, but also many stones and rocks thrown by the ship as it ground to a halt nearby. Then there were many footprints layered over the top. The ecosystem was advanced enough in this area that she even saw insects moving about over the site. A large grasshopper of some kind paused in a footprint and then bounded away. She ignored the footprints for now, as they were satisfactorily documented. She spotted a few broken low branches on trees and took pictures. None of them seemed to have any fibres attached to them.

When she reached the other side of her arc, she found Faolán crouched down. "Look at this," he said. There were footprints in front of him, in a place that would have been out of sight from the clearing, behind a bush. "Was anyone standing over here?"

"Not that I recall."

"What do you make of the prints?"

"These prints have an Orion Navy standard tread. They are a similar size to both Dr McArthur's and Gagnon's feet."

"Human or android?"

"This soil is similar to that over there. I believe these are human footprints or they would be deeper. In fact, I believe they belong to a very light person."

"So Gagnon or Camryn again?"

Shaula crouched and gently poked at the soil, away from the prints but in soil that looked similar. It was soft and giving. "Lighter. Very light indeed."

"I think you're right." He looked at the surrounding forest. "I have a bad feeling about this. They might be from someone in our team coming back for a nosey. But also, this might be evidence that someone else is here."

Shaula also looked out into the forest. "Maybe our memories were not altered at distance after all. Maybe Dr Rebecca Neale is somewhere nearby, monitoring us."

"If so, is she just an observer, one who came for a snoop to see what happened, or the murderer?"

They both stood and looked each other in the eye for a long moment. "We have another suspect to add to our list, one we do not even know how to locate."

CHAPTER 12

As if things weren't already complicated, he had to worry about Dr Rebecca Neale lurking around too?

It had always seemed far-fetched that the infamous android researcher was lurking about on 227C somewhere unseen. He was sure he wasn't the only one who thought so. They hadn't seen anyone else moving around: no other habitations, no vehicles, nothing. But Altair had remembered that she was responsible for the Event Horizon. And, as only a few knew, an intruder had been detected on the *Sunda Tiger* shortly before it was sabotaged, and a DNA sample had been taken. If they could salvage the DNA database, the first person they were going to run the sample by was Dr Neale.

As crazy as it seemed, it might just be true. Who else would have made this strange android research centre far away from other colony worlds other than an infamous android researcher who had gone missing from Mars under mysterious circumstances a few years before this colony was formed, presumed dead in an android-performed massacre? It was the stuff of comic book villains, and truth-is-stranger-than-fiction news holos that keep people on the edge of their seats for weeks.

Faolán had heard a lot about Dr Neale over the years, more than other people had. His oldest sister, Aoife, had been obsessed with the story when she was younger. The whole sordid affair had scared the bejeezus out of her, but in a way that she couldn't help but read about. He'd heard all about the conspiracy theories that it was a coverup of a political assassination. All about the theories that Dr Neale'd gone mad after her only child died some years before. All about the theories that the massacre was a coverup of an assassination of Dr Neale herself (which he now knew wasn't true).

There was nothing he could do about her now, other than keep an eye out for evidence. He didn't have the resources to mount a wide search of the forest. Though, of course, he'd let Ife know of their suspicions as soon as he had a chance to tell her in person.

"Do you think an elderly woman could have been the murderer?" he asked Shaula as they made their way back to camp.

"No. It would take a lot of force to inflict such damage to Tiaki. It would be beyond the strength of most human women, even in the prime of their lives."

"But a man could do it? Or perhaps a woman who was a bodybuilder?"

"I believe most men could, yes, though not all. And yes, I suppose a female bodybuilder could."

"That puts Ife and Ana in the clear. But they're the only ones we've ruled out. And if Dr Neale was here, she couldn't be the murderer either."

Shaula was quiet for a long moment as she picked her way around a thicket of bushes. "Not unless she used an android as the murder weapon."

A chill settled into Faolán's stomach. "I know the idea has been bothering you, but is that really possible? Memory wipes are one thing, but if you were all under her control, surely it would be more obvious? You can't all be faking your individuation."

She looked at him solemnly. "I hope you are right. But I cannot verify that until I solve the problem of the memory alterations."

"It's a far more important problem that I thought." He sighed. He wished he could help with that, but it was ridiculously far outside his area of expertise. "If someone in our camp was the murderer, who do you think may have had motive?" he asked.

"I do not trust either Simons or Gagnon. They both seem to be causing trouble for their own reasons, and I do not know why."

"I agree. I wish either of them would just come clean about whatever bug is in their bonnet."

"Naos seemed angry at Tiaki and Dr McArthur because of their relationship."

It was interesting she'd described her fellow android as 'angry'. In his experience, the androids tried to avoid labelling their experiences as 'emotions' and instead explained them away as mere logic. Shaula didn't seem to do that to the same extent.

"Anyone else?" he asked, stepping around a bush in his way.

"What do you think about Diphda?"

"She also seems to be sketchy to me. She seems to be annoyed about us humans being here. Do you know what that's about?"

"I do not. Though many of the androids of the colony have their own individual trauma responses to the Event Horizon."

"I'd still like to keep her on the list. Her whereabouts were unaccounted for on the night of the murder."

"And Vega. I cannot see a motive. But his where-abouts were also unaccounted for."

"Vega seems to me to play things close to his chest. I'm not sure if we'd know if he had a motive yet."

"That is true."

They reached the tree line. Faolán stopped, looking at the foliage along the edge. "New growth is coming up here now after the crash," he said, squatting down. "Look."

"Are those weeds important to the investigation?"

He grinned up at her. "Nope. But they might be important for dinner. These are all young dandelion plants. The young leaves can be eaten as a salad."

She watched him as he picked some leaves. "You would trust these weeds?"

"A weed to one is a treasure to another. These are good, and super easy to identify. I did a unit on foraged foods when studying... well." He cleared his throat. "Dandelions have got nutrients and whatnot. They'll be good for people." He stood and held out the leaves. "We may end up out here at the wreck longer than we intended. If I can stretch the rations, it'd be a good idea."

They started down the slope towards the camp.

"Hey, uh. I'm sorry if I made you upset before." It had been nagging at him, the way he'd fumbled over his words when they'd been talking about Marcie and Altair, the way she'd grumped at him.

"When?" she asked.

"When we were talking about Marcie and Altair. I'm not sure what about it made you upset, but I'm sorry."

"I was merely mistaken," she said. "I thought for a moment that you harboured anti-android sentiments too. But you explained yourself adequately."

He flushed. "Ah. Sorry for making you think that. No, I support Marcie and Altair. They have the right to choose to be together."

"I think so too. All I am concerned about is that they are probably taking advantage of me being away to be together in my lab."

He gaped at her. "Why would you even think that? Neither of them seem like kinksters who'd be into that!"

"Perhaps. But doing 'that' while Altair is hooked up to the specialised diagnostic equipment in the lab might be elucidating for Marcie's research."

"Eugh!" he said. "You've gone and put a mental picture in my brain after all! Flush, flush!" He pushed an imaginary toilet flush button on his head. Then he pointed at the cruiser. "I'm going to go make a salad and try to forget this conversation."

"I will have another session of fixing Tiaki's connections."

They both nodded at Madigan as they went into the separate vehicles.

"Androids and their inability to grasp what is a polite topic of conversation!" he muttered to himself as he rinsed the dandelion. "Why'd she go and talk about that! She's been all 'sex, sex, sex' today. It's enough to give a man ideas." Did she not realise how little control over his libido a human could have when talking to a beautiful person like her about topics like that? Actually, she probably had no idea. So he shouldn't say anything about it. His reactions were his own, and nothing she was responsible for.

And really, she was talking about memories, not sex. It was just his depraved brain that kept focussing on that aspect. He could understand why she kept worrying about the memory thing. It was a huge handicap, one that she must angst about a lot. He could relate. Didn't he keep worrying about whether he was about to be hit by an ADHD bomb?

The only difference here was that she had been open about the struggle she was facing, and how it may hamper the investigation. He pulled a face. He really should tell her about his own struggles, so she'd be aware of what was going on if he suddenly had trouble with his executive function and couldn't keep track of the investigation or her memories.

Speaking of which, he should check in on her soon. He quickly chopped the leaves, and rummaged through the condiments looking for something to jazz them up. He had to settle for a slug of cooking oil, salt, and desiccated garlic flakes that were goodness knew how old. He shook the basic salad together in a lidded bowl, popped it in the fridge, and stepped outside.

"Seen anything?" he asked Madigan on the way.

"No, Faolán."

"OK, thanks. Please let me know when the rest of the team's on their way back."

He bustled into the engineering lab. "Hey, Shaula, I just wanted to check up on..."

He forgot how to speak.

Right across from the door, by the far bench, was Shaula's arse. Her *bare* arse. What was worse, she was bent over looking at something closely, so he could see *everything*. He'd seen her naked before because he'd met her before the androids had got the clothing production online. But not like this. And last time he'd been a good boy and kept his eyes up. Not today. He gulped. Her arse was beautiful. Pure perfection.

There was an insistent part of his brain telling him he should look away because he was acting like a creep. But what with his thoughts from before, and being caught unawares, he just wasn't prepared. He couldn't.

"What do you want to check up on?" she asked, not looking away from her work.

"Why are you *naked*?" His voice sounded breathless. He untucked his shirt, hoping to hide that he was, er, *responding* to the view she'd just inadvertently given him.

She stood upright and looked down at herself. "Oh. I took the opportunity while you were in another vehicle to take a break from the clothes. They still feel uncomfortable to me, especially under my arms and between my thighs." She put down the tools she'd been holding and turned around. "If I am distressing you, I can redress."

He now couldn't take his eyes off her front, which was just as bare. Beautiful, rounded breasts, made with just the right amount of weight and hang to make her look mature and real. A toned stomach with a feminine curve. Thighs that looked like they could crush a man. And between, a green thatch of hair. She could have gone with anything, but she'd gone with the natural look on purpose.

She leaned back against the bench for a moment, crossing her arms, then turned around and began tidying up her work area, putting the lid back on Tiaki's brain and then locking the container back in the cupboard. He watched her every move in a daze. She wasn't telling him to look away after all.

"You done already?" he managed to ask with his last two operational brain cells.

"No. But I thought I might seize the opportunity, so to speak, and switch to another task."

"Oh?"

"You advised I should prioritise figuring out the memory problem too, and even offered assistance."

"Yeah."

"Well."

"Well what?"

"This is an opportunity, is it not? Would you assist me? Such an inquiry may prove useful."

He blinked. "What?"

"I have been thinking about it since our conversation earlier. Maybe I would understand better if I tried it for myself, to see if I can access any memories via that method."

"I don't understand."

She pointed at his crotch. "You are aroused."

He looked down. Sure enough, his t-shirt was not hiding his *reaction* as well as he'd thought it would. "Jesus fucking Christ, I'm so sorry." He tried adjusting his trousers to make it less obvious, but it was a losing battle. Her drawing attention to it was only making the problem worse.

"Do not apologise for it: make use of it."

He gaped at her. "I'm sorry; are you suggesting we have *sex*?"

"Yes."

"As in, 'Drop your trousers; it's for science!'"

"It *is* for science."

"You don't even *like* me!"

"I do not like anyone. Please do not take it personally. Can you help me? It would perhaps further our investigation."

"Is this something you want to do? Or something you feel obliged to do for your investigation? Because I don't like the thought of the latter. It sounds morally questionable to me."

"I do want to." He must have looked sceptical, because she followed up with, "I do. I honestly want to know what it is like, and whether I recover memories too."

He believed her. He knew the androids well enough now to know they were people perfectly capable of knowing their own minds. But he still didn't understand why she was asking it of him. "Why me?" He wasn't under the mistaken impression that he was some paragon of human beauty. He was just some average guy.

"You are respectful of others. I feel safe with you."

He flushed, and couldn't help but look away. That was just about the nicest thing anyone had ever said about him. He'd had no idea she thought of him that way.

She must have read his silence as hesitance. "If you do not want to, I would not take it personally if you took care of your situation by yourself in the bathroom."

Somehow, it was her talking about him having a wank that tipped him over the edge. His cock throbbed. "Fuck it, I'm in. This job's ridiculously stressful; I could do with blowing off some steam."

They went into the rear cabin. Faolán closed the blinds and started taking his clothes off while Shaula folded the sofa out into a narrow double bed and draped a sheet over it. "We will have to be quick in case the team comes back."

He snorted. "Today, I think I have no option but quick. I've got a lot of pent-up frustration."

She sat on the edge of the bed, and he stood before her.

"So, how do you want it?" he asked.

"I am programmed to provide pleasure, and to simulate an orgasm whenever you like." She ran a finger down his stomach, then along his shaft. She dabbed at his pre-cum, and pinched it between her fingers, as if analysing the texture.

"That doesn't sound like fun for you. That sounds like it's for my benefit. If we're going to shake your memories free, we need to do what's good for you. So, what do you want?"

"I do not know," she said in a quieter voice than he'd ever heard her use. She ran her fingers over the hairs on his left thigh, and he shuddered, caught somewhere between tickled and pleasured.

"OK, how about this: this is an exploratory trial. We have a quick go, see if we can figure out what you like.

Anything else is a bonus, given the time constraints. OK?"

"That seems reasonable."

"So, what would you like to try?"

"The basics. Whatever you would consider 'basic sex'."

He gave her a crooked smile. "I know what you mean." He gently pushed her shoulder. "Lie down." He lay beside her and propped himself up with an elbow. He then stroked her face, marvelling at how normal her green skin was starting to look to him. "Sex usually begins with a kiss." He leaned down and pressed his lips to hers.

Soft didn't seem to be what she wanted. She opened her mouth to him and pulled him down with a hand on the back of his head. *Rough it is*, he thought, tangling his tongue with hers. He grabbed a handful of her hair, held it tight. Thank fuck the scorpion was not in there. He'd forgotten about it until then. He felt the tip of her ear press against his wrist, reminding him again that she was not human.

With his free hand, he stroked one of her breasts. She didn't seem to want gentle there, either, thrusting her breast up into his hand. He grabbed, pinched, rolled her nipple. She moaned into his mouth. Yeah, it was pretty clear now that what she wanted was something quick and hard. He could do that.

He reached down between her legs and slipped his fingers between her labia. To his surprise, she was wet. "Hey, what's this made of? Do you have vaginal secretions like a human?"

"Similar. It is made of the same substances that lube for human interactions is made of. I triggered it to release from a receptacle into my vagina when you consented."

She made it sound very non-sexy. But it felt good, so whatever. He slid the fluids up from her opening to the nub of her clit with his thumb. He didn't know if her clit was functional or just for show, but he'd give it a go anyway. He circled her nub with his thumb and slid two of his fingers into her, hooking them slightly and massaging her depths. It felt like fingering a human's vagina.

She clamped her thighs around his wrist and arched her back. Something seemed to be working, at least. He couldn't tell if it was a well-programmed routine or genuine pleasure. He figured he'd rather know later, or maybe not at all. Because the way she reacted to his ministrations, he so badly wanted it to be him.

He added another finger and ramped up his speed. She gasped and threw her head back. Then she took him in hand and stroked him.

"Careful; you do that and I won't last long."

"I do not think I need you to." Her words sounded as flat as always, but her body was telling him another story. And she was right, too. Her auto-lubing or whatever had made her wet enough that they didn't really need foreplay, and by the way her thighs opened and then closed again, gripping for something that wasn't there, he could dive right in.

He knelt between her legs and held onto one of her thighs with one hand and himself with the other. "You want me to put it in?"

"Yes, please."

Again, not the sexiest of word choices, but the sentiment was the right one. He eased just the tip in. He huffed with laughter; she *was* a leannán sídhe, leading him into the passage in her green mound. He certainly felt inspired.

"Something funny about this, O'Donoghue?"

He gulped. Her eyes were hard. "Just filled with a wild energy, Shaula," he said as eased out and back in again, still keeping it shallow. "Pay it no mind."

She gripped him with her legs, digging her heels in and pulling him until he bottomed out. "Less laughing, more fucking."

He'd never heard a word like that from her, and the incongruity did things to him. "Yes, ma'am."

He pounded into her, and she kept up the pace with him, gripping him, pulling him, fighting him. He was on top, but she didn't relinquish a single bit of power to him. It was rough and wild, and they were surely making the whole vehicle shake. The bunk at least was screaming in protest.

He was grunting and moaning, and probably as red as a tomato, but he didn't care what she thought about it.

She wasn't as loud as him, but she did let out small squeaks, rising in pitch. Her eyes screwed tight, and she bucked harder and harder as if chasing a really good orgasm. "Ah, Faolán!"

That did him in. He groaned so loud it probably echoed around the camp as he reached his peak. As predicted, he was fast. He reached between them for her clit. He still wasn't sure if it would do anything for her, but there was no harm in trying. He looked into her eyes and found her staring at him intently. She thrust her pelvis up into his hand, and then tipped over the edge. She moaned and bucked, and gasped, then fell still. He untangled himself from her and rolled to lie beside her, gasping for breath.

"Was that satisfactory for you?" she asked.

"Woman, you fucking wrecked me. My arse muscles are going to ache tomorrow." He turned his head to look at her. She lay on her back, her hands crossed on her stomach. "That orgasm at the end was simulated though, right?"

"Yes. I figured there was no point in dragging it out once you had finished."

Faolán tried to suppress the uncomfortable pinch he felt in his stomach to hear his suspicions confirmed. This was an experiment, not lovemaking. "OK. Did you experience any memories?"

She was quiet for a moment. "No."

"Oh. I guess this was a bust, then."

"Perhaps. But did you release some of that pent-up frustration?"

He *was* feeling loose and boneless. "Yeah. It was a good orgasm for me, if nothing else. I'm just sorry you got nothing out of it."

She turned her head to look at him in turn. "I did enjoy it. My favourite part was watching your face as you finished. You lost all control of your expression. I could not tell if it was pleasure or pain. I found that fascinating, and gratifying."

He grinned at her. He could understand that and identify with that sense of power. "Well, that's something, then." He chortled. "I've never been with anyone who was so blunt and factual about sex."

"My apologies. Should I have run a flirt routine first?"

"Nah. It was kind of refreshing, actually. You cut through all the anxiety-inducing parts and got us right to the good bit. Now, let's jump in the shower real quick. We're both sticky."

While she stood, he gave the hand he'd had in her a quick sniff. Then he licked it. "Wait a goddamned moment! Your pussy juice tastes of *passionfruit*?!"

"Yes. Is that a problem?"

He knelt on the bed. "Is it a problem? Is it a *problem*? You should've said! I would have eaten you out like a dog at an unattended buffet!"

"We did not have time for that. Come on, into the shower."

They got in together and washed each other, quickly rather than in a sexy way. Faolán, rather than being filled with warring senses of affection and anxiety like he usually was after a hook up, was instead filled with a comfortable sense of camaraderie. Like they'd been doing a team-building exercise that had gone well, instead of getting hot and heavy in a bed.

"I have changed my mind; this is my favourite part," Shaula said as he knelt in front of her and soaped up her legs.

"This? Really?"

"Do you remember when you asked me what comforts me, and I did not know?"

"Yep."

"It is comforting being looked after."

He grinned up at her. "It is, isn't it?" He stood and put more soap on his hands, and began soaping her back and buttocks. "Run through for me what we saw at the crime scene earlier."

"We verified whether the footprints I had tagged on my tablet matched up with our memories of where people stood after we found the bodies."

"And?"

"Everything looked fine. We identified from which direction Tiaki and Dr McArthur entered the clearing."

"And then?"

"We did a circular sweep around the camp, looking for anything else unusual."

"And?"

"And... you picked dandelion?"

He paused in his washing. "What did we find on our circular sweep?"

"Nothing." She turned to look at him. "Something is different. Correct?"

"Yeah. It is. We need to take another look."

Ten minutes later, they were dressed and standing by the bush near the clearing again. The footprints they had seen were gone. The ground was disturbed, as if it had been brushed by something and leaves carefully placed back over.

"And they were here?"

"Yes," he told her. "You even took pictures."

Shaula flicked through the photo stream on her tablet. "There's nothing here."

They looked at each other. "Whoever is here with us clearly doesn't want us having evidence of their presence. For one reason or another."

CHAPTER 13

A s the wreck was upside down, they had to step over the top of every doorway they passed. And in a ship designed to minimise atmospheric loss when the hull was damaged, there were a lot of doorways. They also had to step around the light panels that were underfoot, lit with a pale orange low-power emergency lighting running off the battery banks the team had got running while they were investigating the crime scene (and each other) the day before.

It was Shaula's first time aboard the *Sunda Tiger*. How unfortunate she was not seeing it in its best light.

They were aboard the wreck to talk to the rest of the team as they worked, Madigan following along in their wake. The investigation could not wait, but neither could the salvage. The previous evening, they had reported to Ife about the mysterious disappearing footprints and the mysterious missing memories. Faolán had sketched out the footprint as he remembered it, because that was now the only record they had.

They had also received communications from the settlement. Kikelomo had received the normal report and request for updates, carried by a returning pigeon familiar. But Shaula too had received a message borne by a smaller dark purple bird of a type unknown to her. It had contained a recording from Bellatrix. She had sat in the cabin of her lab beside Faolán as she listened to the message, with the bird perched on her finger. Bellatrix asked if there was anything she could do to assist the murder investigation, and what she had uncovered so far.

Bellatrix was not usually this attentive to Shaula's work. She wondered what was keeping the other android's thoughts on her, even when she was not present in the settlement. Was Bellatrix privy to some information that Shaula was not? She could not ask for more detail until she returned. Whatever the origin of Bellatrix's extra scrutiny, Shaula had appreciated the offer of help, but there was nothing anyone at the settlement could do. And as for her request for information, Shaula and Faolán had looked at one another, and she knew their thoughts were unanimous: no matter how well intentioned Bellatrix was, they could not risk transmitting what they had uncovered. Not while they were unaware of what they were dealing with. It was a security risk. Shaula had recorded a brief message of thanks and sent the bird on its way.

Now their investigation was continuing aboard the wreck, around the salvage operation, and she should keep her mind on the task at hand. She looked at the man at her side. They had not talked about what else they had done the day before. Rather, they were both carrying on as normal. He had not tried to join her in

135

bed or in the shower again. He had simply said 'Good night' the previous evening and then gone to sleep.

Shaula was relieved. She was still unsure if she had made the right decision. This was why she usually kept to herself. She could compartmentalise, but could he? And had it hurt his feelings that they had not uncovered what they hoped to with the act?

Why was she even worried about his feelings? Perhaps she was just tailoring her responses to his in the interests of collegiality. Yes, that was surely it. True connection was beyond her. It had been an experiment. Nothing more.

Nevertheless, she had found the experience to be interesting. She did not know if she would do it with him again, but he had performed adequately. Anything lacking in their intimacy was a lack within herself.

"This way," he said, pointing along a side corridor. "No, wait: the other way. The fact everything's upside down keeps doing my head in."

He stepped ahead of her. She looked at his broad shoulders. She now knew he had a tattoo of a tree on the back of his left shoulder and a compass and star field on his right arm. None of the androids had tattoos. Why not? It would be easy to print designs into any android's epidermis while she was manufacturing it. She could even make embossed designs. She could change them whenever the epidermis was changed. Perhaps she could find an artist amongst the crew of the *Sunda Tiger*. Maybe they could make some designs for her to offer as a service.

But first, the murder investigation, salvage, memory problem, gravity sickness problem, Dr Neale problem...

She ought to table that idea for a while, as intriguing as it was.

"If we have time, I'll take you to the engineering labs for a quick look-see. They're in the body of the ship, so didn't break off with the engine. But for now, here's the med bay."

He led her into a large room that would have been a warm and calming light green if lit properly, but was instead dingy and cavernous in the dimmer orange glow. The static parts of the room, such as storage units and some larger computer banks, hung from the ceiling, which used to be the floor. The mobile items in the room, such as beds, equipment, and assorted sundry items, were on the floor, or rather the ceiling. Vega and Latu were tidying the jumbled piles of items into sorted stacks and collections. They were about a third of the way across the room. Naos was sorting through a pile of small boxes, presumably medicine or medical equipment, and placing them into three different storage crates. There was already a pile of four crates by the door, each labelled 'Salvage' and with a list of technical terms listed underneath. The last person at work in the room was Kikelomo, who was performing a task that was much more within Shaula's realm of knowledge: running a diagnostic on a boxy piece of medical equipment, checking whether it was still in good working order.

"Permission to enter the work area?" asked Faolán.

"Permission granted," said Kikelomo.

"We're here to ask a few more questions related to the investigation. Can we talk to each of you one-by-one?"

"Sure. Take Ensign Latu first."

"Stay here," said Faolán to Madigan, who sat on his haunches.

Shaula tailed Faolán and Latu into an office off the side of the main med lab. There was a built-in desk hanging from above, but they righted some chairs and pushed a smashed cabinet out of the way to make an area they could interview in. There was a window looking out over the med bay. Shaula wished she were out

137

there. These interviews were Faolán's work. She was only following him so he could keep monitoring her memories. If not for her assigned task, she would be doing something useful for the salvage right now.

"We've just got some follow-up questions because we're on to the next stage of the investigation," said Faolán. "We won't keep you long."

"OK, sir. How can I help you?"

"Could I ask you to run through who you saw where at the crime scene after we alerted everyone to the bodies?"

"Sure." Latu confirmed where she had seen people that evening, which all lined up with the reconstruction Shaula had made.

"OK, thanks," said Faolán. "Have you seen anything of note with Vega? Is he missing any memories?"

"Not that I've seen. I've been checking in regularly, just as you said." She nodded in Shaula's direction. "He does sometimes seem hesitant to make a move, though."

"What do you mean?"

"Like, if I say 'We should get going. Our shift is going to start,' or whatever, he'll stay still a moment, or delay, before he gets up. Just kind of stares at the wall or into the distance for a bit."

Faolán turned to her. "Is that normal for Vega?"

"If he is thinking of many things, then perhaps. Compared with you humans, us androids stay still when our thoughts are turned inward. Is that what you have seen?"

"Perhaps," said the ensign. "I just thought it was a little weird."

"OK. Thanks for telling us," said Faolán. "And have you seen anything weird here on the wreck since you started coming aboard?"

"Now you mention it, the doors are strange. They sometimes open when they shouldn't. If we had more crew, maybe someone would be free to check the sensors. We don't have enough people for this now."

Faolán sighed and nodded. "Thank you. Anything else of note? Have you remembered anything new about the night of the murder?"

"No."

"Sure. Do you have any more questions for her, Shaula?"

"No."

"OK, could you please send Vega in next, ensign?"

While they waited for Vega to come in, Faolán turned to her. "What do you think?"

"She is right about there not being enough staff for the salvage now. I wish I could help."

He patted her on the knee. "I know. It must be frustrating the hell out of you. You want to be doing things, right?"

"Yes."

"We'll get there. We just need to push through."

Vega entered the office and lowered himself into a seat, staring at Shaula as he did so. He said nothing in greeting, as would be expected of Vega. His familiar was not present.

"Thanks for coming," said Faolán. "Can you run through for me who you saw at the crime scene after we alerted everyone to what had happened and where they were standing?"

"Affirmative." Vega too gave a summary that aligned with what they had reconstructed.

"What direction did you arrive from when alerted?"

"I followed everyone else up the slope and straight to the clearing."

"Has your familiar seen anything odd in the forest? Anything he's brought to your attention?"

"No."

"Latu said you sometimes seem hesitant to get moving. Do you have any concerns that are bothering you?"

"I am concerned about whether it is wise for us to continue the salvage under these circumstances."

"So you have reservations."

"Yes. But I am not in charge."

There was a sting in his words. She remembered he had initially wanted to be in charge of this investigation.

But Faolán moved on. "And have you seen anything odd on the wreck?"

"Do you suspect sabotage of the salvage?"

Faolán shrugged. "I'm trying to keep an open mind. Have you seen anything?"

"No. Though Latu mentioned that the way the doors are behaving is not usual."

"Thank you. Any more questions, Shaula?"

"Yes. Would you please deliver any security recordings Romulus has taken of the forest while we have been here?"

"You accessed Romulus's transcript the other day."

"I took its transcript of the evening of the murders. But I would like everything since we arrived until the present time, including recorded footage."

Vega paused. This was an unusual request, and Vega may deny her, citing security concerns. But after a moment of thought, Vega relented. "Affirmative. Though please note: recordings Romulus have captured include compromising footage of the two of you."

That seemed unlikely, though possible. "Please clarify."

"Footage shows that the two of you often walk or stand too close together. You brush arms and bump shoulders."

"That is not compromising. We often discuss the investigation in low voices. Of course, we must stand closer together. Please deliver the recordings. And send Naos in next."

After he left, Faolán let out a sigh. "Whew. For a moment there I thought his familiar had peeked in the curtains or something."

"I did for a moment as well." She did not want others to know that she had been intimate with Faolán. Although she did not regret her choice, it had the potential to complicate group dynamics further. Also, was she forming an attachment to him that would compromise her logic? The thought worried her. She also worried that her curiosity about the memories would make her do it again.

"Wait, his bird can record video?" he asked her, his thoughts already off on another tangent. "I thought familiars couldn't do that."

"Not unless they have received permission to be upgraded, which Romulus did. Diphda's familiar can do the same, as she is also security staff."

"Come to think of it, I'm not sure I've seen Diphda's familiar. Is it a bird?"

"No. It is a bronze frog. It is very good at pretending to be a rock, so you have likely been in its presence and not noticed it. I have seen it sitting around the campfire in the middle of camp, listening. I have not asked, but I suspect that she has been wearing bright clothes to draw humans' attention so you do not notice her familiar nearby spying on you."

"Wow."

Naos entered the office. She was wearing a white doctor's coat over grey clothes, and her teal seagull familiar Beaufort perched on her shoulder. "I trust this will not take long. I am busy," she said.

"We just need a few minutes of your time," said Faolán.

They asked her the same question about who stood where at the murder site and again shook nothing new loose. "And how about the forest itself? Did you or your familiar see anything odd?"

"No."

"How about here on the ship?" asked Shaula.

"I am not familiar with the ship. There are, of course, many things out of place because of the crash. Though there are fewer of some supplies than Dr McArthur had indicated."

"Stuff's missing?" asked Faolán. "What kind of stuff?"

"I do not know if it is missing, or if McArthur was too *distracted* by her affair and gave me incorrect inventories. But I believe that there ought to be more bandages and antiseptics than are in stock, more basic analgesics of the kind humans take for minor complaints, and more sanitary supplies for the human menstrual cycle. These are top priority in the salvage, but there is little to take back with us."

"That is odd," said Faolán. "That's all the kind of stuff that the Orion Navy keeps a good supply of. We shouldn't have been short. Have you remembered anything else from the night of the murder you would like to tell us about?"

"No."

"OK." He cleared his throat. "What did you think of Camryn and Tiaki being romantic?"

"It was unprofessional," said Naos.

"Why?" asked Shaula.

"You should not need to ask that question," said Naos. "The potential for conflicts of interest is far too high. They may have been murdered because of it. They should have not behaved so."

Shaula felt sure that Naos would be just as scandalised about herself and Faolán. She looked at him out of the corner of her eye. Colour dusted his cheeks. He was thinking the same.

"Thank you," he said. "Please send Ife in."

Naos stood and left without a word.

"I'm seeing a pattern here," said Faolán.

"Distrust of human / android interactions?"

"Well, that too. But I meant, this is all reminding me of something odd that happened shortly before the *Sunda Tiger* was sabotaged. You heard about the doors and the DNA sample?"

"No."

"It seems there was a stowaway on the runabout when we returned to the ship after our first visit. Someone we couldn't see on our cameras. Doors were opening randomly, and a DNA sample was found. If we can salvage the DNA database, we're going to check it."

"To check if it is Dr Neale's?"

"Correct. We already suspect that someone is lurking around, and she's the most likely candidate. This would have been a good place for her to have come for supplies. Seems someone's raiding the med bay, at least. Maybe she was here for supplies and was surprised by our arrival? And so she has nothing to do with the murder; it's just a coincidence?" He crossed his arms. "Though it still doesn't sound quite right. Dr Neale would be in her 70s by now. She shouldn't need menstrual stuff."

Kikelomo entered the office, cutting off their conversation. "What can I do for you?"

Faolán checked in with her as well about who was where at the murder site (no further information) and whether she had seen anything unusual in the forest (yet again, no).

"How about Naos? Have you seen anything odd about her?"

143

Kikelomo's eyebrows lowered. "Naos is in the 'doesn't like humans and androids spending too much time together' bucket. She's weird about it. But I don't know if she actually harbours anyone ill will. She just seems to think that mixing socially is a bad idea." She shook her head. "That sort of thinking makes me uneasy."

Faolán nodded. "Have you seen anything weird here on the wreck?"

Kikelomo looked through the window to see if the others were watching them, but everyone seemed busy. "OK, there is something weird. Something Sandeep and I have sent a message back to the settlement about, but we weren't sure if we should bring up here yet. You remember how we suspected there would be bodies trapped in rooms along the corridors that depressurised?"

"Yeah."

"There aren't. Even though there were a few rooms with blood smears. The bodies weren't there. Also, we think that the emergency lighting and door mechanisms had already been turned on for a while at some point, then turned off again."

"Someone has already been here. Naos told us medical supplies were missing that she had expected to see. The kind of thing someone would hoard to look after themselves on an ongoing basis, like painkillers and whatnot."

"That's right. I think we should suspect the putative 'observer', perhaps Dr Neale, has already been here, and may have moved the bodies of the deceased."

Faolán exhaled heavily. "OK. Anything else?"

"That's all I have for now. Though I have a favour to ask of you. Faolán, is your wolf free? At the moment, just Vega's familiar is watching the pile of salvaged goods. They're in cargo bay 4. Do you think you could get your wolf to watch them too?"

Faolán looked at Shaula. "Madigan will be adequately programmed for such a task," she said.

"Then, sure," he said to Ife. "I'll just go ask him." Faolán left the office, leaving Shaula and Kikelomo alone.

"While I have you a moment, may I ask: would it be possible for me to at least look at one of the hyper-core units that were used to hack Altair? I know we are unlikely to be able to transport one, but if I could at least take a look..."

"I get it. You're keen to do your research. But please look into the murder first. We can think about the hyper-cores afterwards if we have time."

"What if it could help solve the murder?"

"It'd be a long shot, and likely would take more time than just finding the murderer the old-fashioned way. Please, just ignore it for now." The human woman sighed, rolled her shoulders, and rubbed her temples.

Fine, she would not speak of the topic more. For now. "You look like you are experiencing stress," said Shaula.

"You think so?" said Kikelomo. "Who wouldn't under these circumstances? Urgent salvage, murder, disappearing corpses, lurking evil scientists... and that's all just today's problems. Who knows what we'll face tomorrow?"

"I suggest finding time to do something that will decrease your stress."

Kikelomo snorted. "Forgive me. You just didn't strike me as the type to espouse self-care."

"Do as I say, not as I do. We will be adrift without your leadership, so please protect your ability to provide it."

"Noted. I'll schedule that in... sometime." She sighed and stood. "There is no rest for the wicked."

Shaula followed her out. Faolán was waiting by the door for her, a light in his eyes as he watched her walk towards him. She almost smiled when she saw him there. Her. Shaula the Not Very Personable Android.

"Let's go check in on the hydroponics crew." He gestured for her to go ahead of him. She was touched by his unfailing insistence on treating her as a person he respected. Charm did not even hiss at him from within her hair as she passed. What had she unleashed yesterday?

CHAPTER 14

It had been weird to see the med bay upside down. It was even stranger to see the mess hall upside down.

All the tables were fixed, so they were hanging from above. Someone had stacked the fallen chairs at the side of the hall. But the real problem was the devastation all around. On three sides, electrofilm windows had bordered the mess hall, and on the other side of those windows were the hydroponics racks. But the electrofilm generators had gone offline in the crash, and the hydroponics racks had spilled everywhere.

Foetid water and rotting plants were strewn all about the facility, and the hydroponics racks themselves were twisted and crumpled.

When they arrived, Sandeep and Simons were working on the food printer, the unit that had 3D printed personalised nutrient meals for each of the crew. They had somehow removed the machine from where it had been bolted down and lowered it to the new floor. Diphda was loading boxes of the raw materials for the printer out of a cupboard adjoining the mess hall onto a hoverbed, and Gagnon was in the hydroponics area, sorting packets of something that had spilled out of a cabinet.

Shaula stood beside him, looking around at the space. So far that day, she'd been acting as if nothing untoward had happened between them the day before, and to avoid the anxiety-inducing prospect of talking about it, Faolán was following her lead.

That didn't stop him from stewing internally, however.

The previous day, he'd been carried on a wave of adrenaline, endorphins, tiredness, and a whole lot of horniness. But after a sleep, reason had kicked back in, and now he was wondering what the heck he'd been thinking. Sleeping with his investigation partner was *bad*. It was *so bad*. What the hell kind of impulsiveness was that? All sorts of thoughts were competing for prominence. What would other people think if they knew? What did Shaula think? He was just an ordinary guy, after all. Maybe he'd given her a lacklustre view of humans. And he'd failed to help her, which was the real kicker! They'd done it for a specific purpose, and that had been a bust. He could barely look her in the eye, sure she must be thinking of him as a failure.

A dishonest failure, at that. He hadn't come clean with her about his struggles with ADHD before he'd been intimate with her, as he ought to have done. For both their professional relationship and their personal one. She was so perfect. She ought to know about the ways in which he was flawed.

All he could do was promise himself that he'd bring it up as soon as he could.

He was brought out of his Thought Spiral of Doom by Shaula brushing his arm with a finger. "This is where you partook of meals?" she asked.

He blinked, remembering with a start where they were. "Uh, yeah. It was much nicer when the electro-films were in place and the hydroponics were all bursting with healthy vegetables." He looked around. "Where should we set up to ask people questions?"

Sandeep must have overheard him, because he stood up and walked over. "Do you need a place to hold meetings?"

"Yeah. What do you suggest?"

"Damon's office is tidy. They didn't have much junk in there to get thrown around in the crash."

"Damon has an office?"

"It's at the far end of the hydroponics. Sort of a glorified closet with a terminal in it."

"How about you show us, and then come in for a quick word first?"

Sandeep led them through the wreckage of the hydroponics. Along the way, Faolán looked around. "It's such a shame it took us a few weeks to get out here," he said. "Some of these plants may have survived if we'd been able to get them watered and in sunlight quick enough."

"Yes. But Damon had a large store of seed. That's what Gagnon's trying to sort at the moment. If we can salvage some of the equipment, the nutrient packs, and the seeds, then we can get things growing again soon."

"To be sure." Faolán stopped. "Hey, some of these herb plants here might be useful as is. They've kind of dried themselves naturally. They could be crumbled up to flavour things."

Sandeep gave a nervous laugh. "I don't think anyone wants to trust plants that have been mouldering away in here."

Faolán squatted down and peered at the plants in the dim emergency lighting. "This isn't mouldering. It's just desiccated. It'll be edible. Probably."

"Faolán; can we focus on the investigation?" Shaula stood looking down at him. Behind her, Sandeep had his eyebrows raised.

"Sorry. Got a bit distracted there." He worried at his lip. Was he just distracted by the plants because of curiosity? Or was this it: the end of his ADHD meds? His stomach roiled. He really did have to come clean with Shaula about his troubles, and that very day, if he could. He wasn't looking forward to it. She was just so perfect, in almost every way. Really, she was just a bit abrupt and grumpy. Otherwise, she was a pinnacle of achievement.

The office was very tidy. They didn't have to shove any filing cabinets or papers out of the way. There was a print of a Martian landscape and a Pride flag on the wall, both well affixed so they'd stayed in place. Otherwise, there were just a few chairs lying around, which had made dents in the wall during the crash.

"They are a tidy sort, huh?"

"You surprised?" asked Sandeep.

"Guess not. Those Martians really lean into keeping only what's necessary, huh?"

Faolán and Sandeep took the chairs, and Shaula stood with arms crossed by the door.

"We've just got some follow-up questions for everyone because we're at the next stage of the investigation. Can you tell us where everyone was at the crime scene after we alerted the camp to the bodies?"

"I think everyone was there. The security androids were a bit slow to arrive, though?" He ran through where he saw everyone, which again aligned with the footprints.

Ever since Shaula said that the different android footprints couldn't be told apart other than by gender, some instinct had told him that there was something there to uncover. Shaula probably thought he was flogging a dead horse. But he wanted to make sure he had asked everyone.

Upon further questioning, Sandeep said that he hadn't seen anything odd in the forest. But the ship was another matter.

"Things are weird here. If you've already talked to Ife, you may know some of this. But I haven't had a chance to talk to her yet this morning, so she may not know all of it. We've got signs that someone has been here in the mess hall, maybe often."

"What kinds of signs?"

"There were a whole heap of tomato plants that I'm sure should have had tomatoes on. I remember looking at that rack through the electrofilm the night of the crash, and there were heaps of tomatoes. But the plants had all been picked over. I didn't notice it at first, because everything was so jumbled. But then I realised that there should have been smashed smears of tomatoes everywhere, and there weren't. I think lettuces have been harvested too, but I'm not sure."

He looked at Shaula, who nodded. "Stuff is missing from the med bay too. Pain killers, bandages, antiseptics. Tampons."

Sandeep sighed. "I hadn't heard that yet. I knew the bodies were missing. That's what I thought Ife would have told you."

"You think someone has been here, stocked up, and then, what, buried the bodies?"

"Crazy as it sounds, yes, I do. Ife and I aren't talking about it in such terms yet, not until we have more evidence. But we're telling people to keep a look out and be on their toes. Certain people are interpreting that as us warning them about androids being untrustworthy. But that's on them. Whatever keeps them alert and taking their own safety seriously."

"You're a lot more calculating than you look, Sandeep."

He shrugged. "We all have no choice but to be under the circumstances."

"True. OK, how about Diphda? Have you seen anything odd with her?"

"She is odd, but I think that's just who she is. She's been on task, and I haven't seen any memory discrepancies."

"Thanks. Anything else, or can I ask you to send Diphda in?"

"I'll get Diphda."

"What do you think?" he asked Shaula while it was just them in the office.

"It is more evidence to support what we are already suspecting."

Faolán sighed. "Yep. This all makes me very uncomfortable, though. I don't like the feeling of being watched."

"I dislike it too."

Diphda entered the office without knocking. She was wearing a bright yellow t-shirt over orange trousers which, together with her apple-green skin, was excessively bright.

"Thanks for coming," he said.

"I am busy. Will this take long?"

"No." He ran through the same questions, with little difference in the answers of the first two.

"And have you seen anything strange on the ship during the salvage?"

"I do not trust Lieutenant Chaudhary. He is hiding something."

Faolán shared a look with Shaula. Sandeep was probably the least suspicious person in the group. But Diphda hadn't bonded with Sandeep in any way yet.

"What do you think that might be?"

"I do not know. But he and Lieutenant Commander Kikelomo are often whispering to one another."

"But it's just Sandeep you don't trust. Ife's fine? Why's that?"

"She seems well in control of the group. I just wondered if he were whispering incorrect information in her ear."

"Is there anything in particular that makes you think that?"

"I believe he knows things he is not letting on."

Faolán gave a sage nod, as if taking in Diphda's information. But he was pretty sure that what Diphda had picked up on was the information Sandeep had about someone lurking around the wreck. "Thank you for your information," he said instead.

And he would keep it in mind. No one was truly above suspicion except himself. Shaula didn't even fully trust herself, he knew. It was just very unlikely to be Sandeep who was the killer.

"Could you send in Gagnon next, please?"

While they were alone again, Shaula ran a hand along Faolán's shoulder, a risky move for her. "You're carrying a lot of tension here," she said. "Are you worried your friend might be untrustworthy after all? Are you suspecting him?"

"No," he said. "I mean, I'm keeping an open mind. But the group dynamics are so tense. We need to sort this out before there's another bust-up argument."

Shaula dug her thumbs into the muscles at the base of his neck, getting straight to the worst of the tension, and he let out an embarrassing little whine at the relief. Before she'd worked the knots out, though, they heard footsteps outside. Shaula stepped away from him to look at the print of Mars on the wall, and Faolán cleared his throat, trying to get his face under control.

There was a quick rap on the door, and then Gagnon entered. "Morning," she said, and took a seat.

Faolán got straight to questioning her. She, like the others, had little to say about the crime scene and more about the ship. "I know the ship crashed and all, and it's upside down. But there are some things that just aren't where they're supposed to be," she said. Her eyes flicked to Shaula. "Are we sure the androids haven't already been here? What if the murder was a cover-up for something?"

"We are sure no androids have been here before our team arrived," said Shaula. "No androids were unaccounted for before we left."

"Since when?"

"We have not had an incident of a missing android for 16 years, so long before the *Sunda Tiger* arrived in orbit."

"What happened 16 years ago?" asked Faolán.

"An android went missing for over a year. She was found lying in the forest later. It was an unfortunate accident; her battery meter was faulty and so she had stayed away from a recharge station for too long. I fixed the damage to her epidermis, recharged her, and she has been fine since."

"Odd. But not related to the current mystery." He turned his attention back to Gagnon. "Have anything else?"

"Aren't you concerned about things being moved around by someone unknown?" she asked, incredulously.

"Well, yes. But we need to get all the information we can and put it all together. So, anything else? Say, for example, are you ready to tell us where you went on the evening of the murder?"

"I already told you, and I don't want to repeat myself!"

Faolán flicked his eyes towards Shaula, but she was standing still as a statue. "So, you went to the wreck to... relieve your gas?"

Gagnon scoffed. "I may have been drawn towards the ship to take another look. I love this ship, you know? It's hard to get my head around seeing it like this. Anyway, if you're worried about people walking too far from the camp, look into what Vega's been up to. I saw him walking around the camp while I was up."

"Like... a perimeter sweep? You know, what security does while on guard?"

"Where exactly did you see Vega?" asked Shaula.

With a start, Faolán remembered that Vega's movements were unaccounted for during part of that evening.

For once, Gagnon didn't sneer at needing to talk to an android. "Circling around the camp from the side farthest from the murder site, up past the wreck, and I think back towards the camp? Maybe? It was dark." Faolán wasn't sure what his face looked like, but Gagnon must have read something. Disbelief? Annoyance? Because she hastened to add, "Something just isn't right with that android, and I can't put my finger on it."

"Is this something you feel just about Vega?" asked Faolán.

"Well... no. That Naos is aggravating for a supposed medical practitioner."

"Uh, huh."

"And Diphda is truly strange. Literally no one thinks ill of Lieutenant Chaudhary, and yet she does?"

"I see."

"And that Shau—" she cut herself off.

"Do go on," said Shaula.

"...Whatever."

"Yeah, I catch your drift," said Faolán. "I don't agree, but at least you're being honest about your opinions. Have anything else to tell us?"

"...No."

"OK, please send in Simons."

"You do know that she distracted you from asking many questions about her activities that night?" said Shaula after she had left.

"Shit. She did too." Faolán crossed his arms. He would have to figure her out later. Gagnon was up to something. And with how little she liked androids, and how she was strong enough to have been able to hurt Tiaki? Yeah, he'd have to keep an eye on her. "Do you think her concerns about Vega are valid?"

"What she described sounds like a perimeter sweep."

"It does, doesn't it? And it doesn't sound like she saw him anywhere near the murder site."

Faolán was looking forward to Simons' interview least of all. The man entered, took a seat, and gave them both a smarmy grin. "What can I do for you?"

This arsehole. "Tell us who the murderer is? Or failing that, tell us who you saw where around the murder site the night we found the bodies."

Simons shrugged. "I don't remember. I do remember that you two found the bodies because you were going for a starlit stroll in the forest."

"That's a fanciful way of describing a private conversation about work matters."

"Oh, is *that* what we're calling it these days?"

It annoyed Faolán that Simons was right about what they'd been up to, just wrong about the timing. "Think what you like," he said. "Seen anything out of place in the forest? Other than in the crime scene, of course."

"Nope, can't say that I have."

"And here on the ship?"

"I don't trust any of the androids as far as I could throw them. Present company included."

Faolán frowned at the man. He'd say that right in front of Shaula?

"But also," continued Simons, "I think Sandeep and Ife are being sketchy. You know, I think there's an engineering section conspiracy. They colluded to get me taken off the team."

"You took voyeuristic footage inside someone's private cabin, then showed it to the crew without *anyone's* consent. That's on you. How could it possibly be on anyone else? Did they twist your arm?"

"We needed to know what we were up against."

"What? Great sex? Allegedly."

"*Allegedly*," said Simons with a smirk.

Fuck. "Don't involve us in your sordid imaginings," Faolán sighed.

"Indeed," said Shaula. "We are getting off topic. Do you have any more information for us?"

Simons shrugged. "Beats me."

"I have run out of patience with this man," Shaula said to Faolán. "His information is worthless. Let us move on with the day."

"Yes; let's."

They only had Hernandez and Boris to check in on now. That pair were porting the boxes of salvaged goods to the cargo bay, so Faolán figured they'd catch them on the way out.

They left the office, Simons pushing past them and heading back to the food printer.

On the way, Faolán stopped by Gagnon to look at what she was sorting: hundreds, perhaps thousands, of packets of seeds that had spilled out of boxes in the crash and got all muddled up.

"Hey, what have you got here? Anything good?"

"Tomato seeds coming out my ears. Lettuce. Spinach. Some herbs. Mostly stuff that's good in the hydroponics. But there's weird stuff too. There's chia seed. I don't even think Specialist Mori was growing that in the hydroponics. Shouldn't it be in the food stores?"

"Prioritise that one, please!" said Faolán. "It's chia for growing, not eating. We can sow it and harvest more. Chia helps with desserts, extra nutrition in smoothies, some interesting baked goods. Actually, I think I could turn the long-life bread mix into something edible if I had chia. Hm..." he stood there imagining it. The chia could hold moisture in the bread mix, stop it from going so dry...

"Faolán, can you think of that later?" asked Shaula.

Faolán felt a stab of shame. He was distracted again. He had to come clean with Shaula.

"As fascinating as this all is, we've got a problem," said Simons as he walked over.

Faolán sighed. Oddly, Diphda was walking with Simons, creating one of the more unlikely pairs he'd seen in a while.

"What's the problem?"

"Sandeep took the opportunity while we were all distracted to sneak off. I told you there was something up with that guy."

"I mentioned it too," said Diphda.

"Maybe he's just checking in with Ife."

"We've already salvaged the backup walkie-talkies for comms. He didn't need to go," said Simons.

"Whenever he has reported to Kikelomo in person, he has either taken me with him, or told me where he would be, because of how he is supposed to be paired with me," said Diphda. "This time he did not. It is out of pattern. But I have sent Hops to follow him and report back on his location."

"We need to go find Lieutenant Chaudhary, Faolán," said Shaula. "This is an odd time for him to have left without telling anyone."

Faolán sighed. They were right. He hadn't wanted to suspect that Sandeep would be up to something sketchy. But he couldn't look past anyone. Not even his friend.

When Hops, who was Diphda's frog familiar, returned, it said in a croaky voice, "I have located Lieutenant Chaudhary." Faolán now understood how he'd never seen the familiar. Sure, it stood out here on the ship. But it looked so much like a rock that he was sure he could have easily missed it outside.

They followed the frog down a hallway and up to another floor. It wasn't easy going up what had been the stairwells because the stairs were above them. But at least the ceilings of the stairwells had been sloped, so there was a ramp to scramble up. The frog hopped along another corridor.

"What is along here?" asked Diphda.

"Offices and meeting rooms, mostly," answered Gagnon. "Though there are also some storage rooms."

"Storing what?" asked Shaula.

"Extra uniforms, bedding. Electronics like tablets. All kinds of personal items like that."

Hops stopped in front of a door. "Lieutenant Chaudhary went in here," it said.

As they approached the door, Faolán heard a rhythmic thumping. He felt a squirm of recognition in his belly. "Uh, I think we should leave him to it..." he said, but the others weren't listening to him. Diphda and Gagnon both pushed past him and threw open the door. "No, don't!" he said, as a voice within sounded in a moan that rose to a frightened shriek.

The room beyond was one of the bedding storage rooms that Gagnon had mentioned. Two entangled forms within were making use of a bedspread on the floor. *I did not know Sandeep was so ripped!* He averted his eyes before any more stray thoughts could cross his mind.

"Close the door, ladies," he said to Diphda and Gagnon. But they seemed frozen in shock as the people within scrambled to cover themselves.

"Why are you all here and not at your posts?" demanded Ife. Faolán peeked and found she was now in a blanket burrito, only her tidy braids and her *very* annoyed eyes showing. Sandeep knelt beside her, his clothes clutched in front of his crotch, burning so much with embarrassment that it was showing through his dark complexion.

It was ironic, really, considering that Ife had been the one to tell people to behave. 'Do as I say, not as I do,' apparently. But he wouldn't hold it against them. He'd just do his best to pretend he didn't see what he just saw.

"Sorry," said Faolán. "Diphda said Sandeep had snuck off, and Shaula and I are obliged to look into any questionable behaviour now. But, mystery solved. Come on, people. Let's go." He tried to wave everyone back towards the mess hall.

"Did you all leave Simons unwatched?" asked Ife, her voice crackling with annoyance.

Faolán looked around, but only saw Shaula behind him, her arms crossed and eyes averted. No Simons. "Fuck. We got played."

Shaula looked up at him in shock, and then they both took off running.

Shaula was faster and pulled ahead. By the time he got to the stairwell slope and started sliding down, she was already disappearing around the corner.

He jumped over the sill at the bottom of the door into the mess hall and skidded to a stop, bumping into Shaula from behind. She barely budged. Simons sat at the food printer, working diligently.

"What's the hurry?" he asked. But the big, smarmy grin on Simons' face said that they'd missed something, and now they had no evidence of what. It looked like Simons had been there the whole time. But had he?

CHAPTER 15

She followed Faolán to an office labelled 'Deck 3 Security'. Luckily, there was little in the room to have moved around in the crash. They needed only to right a few chairs to make the space useful. Worryingly, there was a large buckle and rent in the far wall, indicating that structural integrity in this area was compromised. But there were no creaks or groans of imminent structural failure.

"How credible is Simons as a suspect?" asked Faolán. "He's always suspicious, so I'm not sure what to think of his latest behaviour."

Shaula crossed her arms. "I do not like him. I am concerned that he has just fooled us about something, and I believe we must investigate. But I also have serious concerns about Gagnon, and about Naos, and of course whoever is present who should not be."

Faolán rubbed his face. "Yeah. We still don't even know who's around. Is it Dr Neale? That's what Altair remembered. But how could an elderly woman be out here, and how could she have moved and buried bodies? That's no easy task!"

That line of inquiry greatly concerned Shaula. It was hard enough to believe that one human had been present on 227C for 30 years without being detected. But what if an entire community was here, hidden from view? How could Shaula ever trust her senses again if that was the case?

"We should investigate one person at a time. Shall we start with Simons?"

"Yeah, that sounds like a great idea. But, how?"

"Are there any security cameras active within the ship?"

Faolán sighed. "No. That whole system was taken out in the crash."

Shaula plucked Charm from her head. "Charm, please shadow Simons as secretly as you can. Please see where he goes and report to me at the end of the day."

"Affirmative," said Charm.

Shaula placed it on the ground and opened the door for it to exit. She watched her familiar scurry away. Charm's bronze carapace camouflaged well with the dim orangish emergency lighting. Its speed, as usual, was slow; possibly the slowest in all of 227C. Charm had always suited her needs before; it was not as if she wanted to be in regular contact with others. As such, Charm's speed was usually sufficient. It was not Charm's fault her needs were currently different because of the circumstances. Though, why had she been approved for a familiar that kept her isolated in the first place? Why had no one else noticed that it was too easy for her to remain difficult to contact? She did not mind. But she knew others did.

When she closed the door and turned to Faolán, one eyebrow raised, he just nodded at her.

"Nice work," he said. "What should we do while Charm does recon?"

"We have not yet spoken to Hernandez or Boris."

"Oh. Right." He cleared his throat. "Let's go"

They found Hernandez and Boris in cargo bay 4. It was a large room, but presumably one of the smaller cargo bays in the ship. The team chose it as the place to gather the salvaged goods because there was a hole rent in the outer hull that opened out onto relatively level ground, making it easier to remove the salvaged goods from the ship later.

For now, crates, boxes, and machinery were gathered in a collection in the middle of the cargo bay. Around the edges of the room, dirt, dust, leaves, and even a few insects had gathered. Shaula would have chosen a more enclosed and clean area, even at the expense of ease of access.

Madigan also sat at the edge of the room, surveying the space with keen eyes, and Vega's familiar perched on a high railing too.

When Shaula and Faolán approached, Hernandez was moving crates off a hover bed that Boris was holding steady. "Can I ask you a few questions?" asked Faolán.

They stopped their work. Hernandez gave a relieved smile. "You're here!" He peered around, looking towards the doorway, then gestured them closer.

Faolán and Shaula looked at one another, then complied.

"I'm so glad you're here," said Hernandez. "I have something important to tell you, but I wasn't sure where you were."

"Go on," said Foalàn.

Hernandez peered around again, then lowered his voice further. "It's about Sublieutenant Gagnon."

"Gagnon?" asked Shaula. Too bad it was not about Simons, but they needed to investigate Gagnon too.

"Yeah. She's been sneaking around. We followed her to figure out what she was up to. Didn't we, Boris?"

"Affirmative," said Boris.

"Anyway, I'm not sure what she's doing. But I have the location, if you want to investigate and see if it has anything to do with the murder."

Faolán touched her arm and raised an eyebrow, as if asking her a question. She could not intuit his meaning, so continued to look at him.

"Switch?" he asked in a low voice.

Ah. Of course. They had just decided to investigate Simons first. But this was too good an opportunity to ignore. He was asking if they could switch targets.

"Please show us," she said to Hernandez.

They followed the man and the spider out of the cargo bay, up several floors, and along a corridor that ran the length of the ship. Faolán lagged behind. Shaula dropped back to walk with him.

"What do you think?" he breathed into her ear.

"About this new information, or the investigation as a whole?"

He shrugged. "Either."

She tilted her head. "We must follow this line of inquiry now, in case Gagnon hears of Hernandez's discovery and hides something important. As for the investigation, it turns out that it may have been inadvisable to leave both Simons and Gagnon free of androids to monitor. They have been left with much more time to cause trouble and evade prying eyes."

"I reckon you're right, though I'm not about to tell Ife that. You can if you want to, but please leave me out of it."

"Did you know that Kikelomo and Chaudhary are in a relationship?" she asked him as they walked.

"No! Either that's new, or they kept it real quiet. I've never even heard a whisper of a rumour about them."

"It may explain why they were both so quick to say they had been asleep the evening of the murder. Perhaps they had a rendezvous earlier and were back in time to be asleep in their bunks later on."

"Sounds plausible."

Ahead of them, Hernandez waved to get their attention, and then pointed towards a door. He waited for them to catch up before making a move. "I saw her coming out of here," he said. "I had a look, and it's just a normal storage room. There's not much in there, at least not that I could see. But she seemed... furtive, I guess?" The young man wore a puzzled look on his face, and he was biting his lip.

Faolán clapped him on the shoulder. "You did good work, Hernandez. Thank you."

Hernandez beamed at the praise. Shaula had not considered the respective ages of the humans until that moment, but it was clear Hernandez was a lot younger than Faolán, and looked up to him. She wondered about how old Faolán was. Perhaps in his mid-thirties? If that was the case, they might be about the same age.

Faolán opened the door, and they all looked in. As described, the interior was a storage cupboard of some kind. Someone must have tidied up since the crash, because the boxes inside were on the shelves, which were shaped in such a way that it did not matter which way up the ship was: they were still functional.

"I couldn't find anything suspicious, but maybe you could double check?" said Hernandez.

Shaula stepped into the room. She looked into a nearby box and found folded white fabric with black piping. The next box had folded white fabric with green piping.

"Spare uniforms," said Faolán. "These aren't on the list of urgent salvage goods, since you androids have been so kind as to provide us with clothes."

He moved past her and started checking more boxes, as did Hernandez. Boris, in consideration of his bulk, stayed outside in the hallway. "Could you check the walls?" Faolán asked her.

"What for?"

"Anything."

A frustratingly vague request. But he was distracted with his task, so she would allow it. Perhaps he meant that there may be a false wall. She left the humans looking through the boxes and instead began inspecting the room itself. She tapped at the walls, listening for discrepancies in the structure.

The walls to either side, the floor, and the ceiling all seemed normal and as solid as she was expecting. But when she tapped on the back wall, she stilled. She tapped again. "Faolán? This wall does not sound right."

He was at her side in a moment, tapping at the wall himself. "You're right."

Shaula worked her fingers around the left side of the back wall, and Faolán the right.

"What do you think we're looking for?" he asked.

"I do not know. A hidden button? A catch?" But the wall was a single, featureless panel.

Shaula began sliding her fingers over the entire surface of the wall, searching for discrepancies. For a long moment she found nothing. But then a patch on the wall caught her attention. It was tackier than the rest of the surface, as if there was a sticky residue on it. Or perhaps a buildup of faint traces, deposited over time.

"Here," she said. "I believe someone puts their hand here often." She pushed on the spot, and the wall clicked. It slid away from her and then rotated about its axis. It then slid over to one side, forming a doorway.

Inside was a dark cupboard roiling with humidity. Shaula increased the glow of her eyes to light the space.

It contained three growth units of some kind, and grow-ing in the cabinets were mushrooms.

"Well, I'll be damned," said Faolán.

"Is this a food source?"

"Uh. Some of it is, yeah. But that back cabinet? I'm pretty sure that contains psilocybins."

"Which are?"

Faolán looked at her with wide eyes. "Uh, drugs. Hal-lucinogens."

"So, contraband?"

"*Oh*, yeah. Big time."

CHAPTER 16

Of all the things Faolán expected to be doing that day, standing hunched over staring at mushrooms growing inside electrofilm-fronted cubbies would have been at the bottom of the list. Who would have thought that the person with the relevant technical expertise of the day would be him? But he'd done a unit on culinary mushroom identification and cultivation back at school, which he had never guessed would actually come in handy.

"What's the verdict?" Ife stood nearby watching his investigation.

"These ones are definitely just button mushrooms. We could eat these. And these ones here are saffron milk caps. These are also for eating. They're delicious. Too bad it looks like the pine root section got bashed up in the crash." The cabinet used sections of pine tree roots hooked up to fake xylem and phloem to trick mycorrhizal mycelia into thinking they were growing on full-sized trees. This was top-of-the-line fungi production tech, usually only available in the richest settlements on the Moon and Mars.

From what they could tell, since they had arrived at the crash site, Gagnon had righted the mushroom growing cabinets and started cleaning up and fixing the growth media, focussing on the more 'exotic' mushrooms in the rear cabinet.

"Any expensive mushrooms like truffles?" asked Hernandez from where he lurked by the door.

"It looks like there were some over there, but they didn't survive the crash. Frankly, I'm impressed she managed to keep the saffron milk caps going. These cabinets are notoriously difficult to grow mycorrhizal fungi in."

"This is all well and good, Faolán, but what about the contraband mushrooms over there?" Ife asked, her voice dripping with impatience.

Faolán winced. He looked up at Shaula, who stood nearby watching him. What would she think of all of this? He walked over to the cabinet in question. "My knowledge is in culinary mushrooms, but I learned a bit about poisonous mushrooms and, ah, *recreational* mushrooms, so I know what to avoid serving people. I can't identify all of these, but the ones I can identify, I certainly wouldn't serve to anyone." Privately, though, he might have eaten extracts of some of them himself at one time in his life. For fun.

"So, definitely contraband?" asked Ife.

"I have no doubt about it."

More people arrived in the storage cupboard: Gagnon, who was being led by Diphda. Gagnon was white as a sheet.

"Care to explain?" asked Ife.

Gagnon drew her shoulders back. "What is all this?"

"This isn't your secret hobby?" asked Faolán.

"No." But she was a terrible liar: it was clear she knew about the mushrooms and knew she was in trouble.

Diphda stepped behind her and held her biceps as if she expected Gagnon to run.

"This is a technologically interesting find," said Shaula. "I would like to take it apart to see how it works."

"No!" said Gagnon. "We're going to need this."

There she went. "Oh? So you *do* know something about this setup?" asked Faolán, propping his hands on his hips.

Gagnon ran her hands through her hair. "Look, OK. Fine. I know this looks bad. But please hear me out: these mushrooms could be really, really important. Please, please, please, let's make use of them."

Faolán pointed at one of the edible mushroom cabinets. "You mean to boost our food supply? I don't think there's enough here to make much difference. Though we could eat some for dinner tonight, I guess."

"I suppose, but that's not what I meant," she said, pointing towards the rear cabinet. "I meant those."

Ife snorted. "The magic mushrooms? Really? You want us all to pass our time until rescue tripping off our gourds?"

Gagnon sighed. "Do none of you know about the medical applications of psilocybin?"

Faolán had heard a bit. Psilocybin treatment was legal under certain conditions, though of course it was difficult to find a doctor who could prescribe it. "You think we're all going to get depressed and need microdoses of 'shrooms to get through?"

"No. Well, maybe. But I mean the people with gravity sickness. There's some compelling research about how the neuroplasticity effect of psilocybins can support gravity acclimatisation. It's going to be a long road for them, and every little bit will help."

For once, Gagnon seemed truly in earnest.

Ife sighed, then looked at Hernandez. "Ensign, please fetch Naos. We need a consult."

While they waited, Faolán looked closer at the mushroom cabinets. They were very well designed and utilised. "How did you get these cabinets in here in the first place?" he asked.

"I didn't," said Gagnon. "I inherited them, I suppose. Someone installed them in the last ship outfit. When I got assigned to the *Sunda Tiger*, I ended up volunteering, then I took over when the other person was reassigned."

"Who used these before you?" asked Ife.

Gagnon shook her head. "I'm not ratting anyone else out." She made a gesture as if zipping her mouth shut.

Faolán peered again at the saffron milk caps. "This is no idle activity. You're doing this at a specialist level."

He looked up to see a proud smile at the corner of Gagnon's mouth. "What, you think normal people can't be good at something? You think it's just engineers and androids who have impressive skills?" She nodded towards Ife and Shaula.

"No, I never said that," said Faolán. "But you must have learned these skills somewhere."

"My mother's a mycologist. I didn't have the patience to study science at university and become a scientist myself. Too much report writing; ugh. But I've picked up the hands-on skills along the way."

"And you used the skills your mother taught you to become, what, a drug manufacturer and dealer?" asked Ife. "Is she proud?"

Gagnon's face closed down again, and she looked away, her jaw set mulishly.

But Ife had a point: these cabinets weren't just a hobby; she was selling these.

"I get how she could have turned a profit off the psilocybins," he said, "but the button mushrooms? Were they worth the effort?"

"With how repetitive the food can get on long missions? Anything different sells. You should have been more industrious, O'Donoghue. I bet if you made some of those pizzas, you could have sold them."

He frowned. "How would I have cooked them? There's no working kitchen here, just a food printer and salad prep."

"Where there's a will, there's a way." Gagnon squatted down and opened a box on a low shelf. Instead of uniforms, it contained a small integrated cooking unit like the type used for camping. "See?"

Faolán clicked his tongue. She was going to all the trouble of growing these mushrooms aboard ship, and yet she was massacring them on a camping stove? "I'll do you a favour: assuming I get the go-ahead, I'll cook them properly for dinner. The *culinary* mushrooms, not the *magic* mushrooms, I hasten to add." He shook his head again.

Their conversation was interrupted by Hernandez showing Naos to the door. "What emergency has taken me away from my assigned task?" she said.

Ife raised one eyebrow. "First, since it turned out that I wasn't stepping away from the med bay for only a moment after all, you should be here with me. But more importantly, do you know anything about psilocybin mushrooms and whether they can be useful for gravity sickness?"

Naos looked around at the growth area for a long moment, taking in everything. "Psilocybin mushrooms?" she asked eventually.

Shaula worked her way through the tight knot of people and waved Naos into the room as she left, giving up her space. Faolán wanted to follow her, but as the one with mushroom knowledge, he ought to stay. Shaula didn't go far, though. She just stood in the hallway with her back to the wall.

"We've found an illicit growth area," said Faolán to Naos. "It isn't sanctioned. Some of these are culinary, but some are... well, they're drugs." He glanced at Gagnon. "But Gagnon says we should put that aside for now as psilocybin microdoses might help those with gravity sickness."

"What do you think?" added Ife. "They're your patients now that Camryn is gone."

Naos huffed. "This is highly unusual."

"What isn't these days?" said Faolán.

Naos stepped closer to the psilocybin cabinet. "I would like to consult further with the settlement database, as I have stored only general knowledge of psilocybin in my personal database. But if I can positively identify species and ascertain correct dosages, then potentially, yes, these could help."

Ife rubbed her temples. "Here's what we're going to do people: On the last day of the salvage, Gagnon and Naos, please sample these mushrooms in whichever way will make potential medicines, OK? I'm assuming what you harvest will be small enough to be stowed in a bag. We'll have space for that."

Gagnon breathed a sigh of relief.

"Do not be hasty," said Ife. "You still have the hounds of hell breathing down your neck. We'll be reporting this to Captain Rodriguez. Tonight."

Gagnon gulped, but then nodded.

"This is all highly irregular," said Naos. "The behaviour of your human crew leaves much to be desired. I warned Dr McArthur about her own behaviour, but it was not just her. It was all of you."

Faolán frowned and went to retort, but Shaula beat him to it. "We are not in a position to comment," she called in from the hallway. "Our entire settlement, and indeed our existence, is most likely unsanctioned and in breach of many rules and guidelines."

Naos looked at Shaula. "You are more like Tiaki than I ever expected."

Faolán usually couldn't read Shaula, but at that moment he saw her jolt in shock. "Thank you," she said.

"I did not mean it as a compliment."

Faolán shook his head. None of this was helping. "Hey, boss," he said to Ife. "Is it all right if we ask Gagnon a few questions related to the murder investigation?"

"Sure."

He led Gagnon out of the cupboard and down the hallway out of earshot. Shaula followed. "So," he said when they stopped. "When did you first come onto the wreck to check on your mushrooms?"

Gagnon folded her arms and leaned against the wall. "The first night we arrived."

"So the 'going out for a fart'? Really? That was the first excuse you thought of?"

"Well, I didn't expect to be seen! I hadn't come up with a better story."

"Did you see anything else while you were sneaking onto the wreck?"

"Not really. I saw Simons up and about, but only close to the camp. Oh, actually, I did see something. I thought I was the first person on to the wreck, but I was wrong. When I first entered through the open cargo bay, I saw footprints in the dirt on the floor. So someone was there before me. That dirt wasn't there before we crashed." She glanced at Shaula. "Are we sure the androids weren't here before us?"

Shaula just stared at Gagnon.

"We're sure," said Faolán. "Thanks for your time. Go back to LC Kikelomo, please."

Once she had gone back to the cupboard, Faolán sighed. "Well, that was all very weird and unexpected. But I think we've ruled Gagnon out."

"You do not believe that Gagnon could have attended to her hobby and committed the murders? She still seems to dislike androids and those who are close to us."

"Sure. But the amount of work she's put into those cabinets since we arrived? I don't think she would've had time."

"Indeed. We have at least decreased our list of suspects. That is something."

He grinned at her. "It is indeed."

CHAPTER 17

Shaula watched as Faolán leaned against a wall in a corridor and rubbed his temples. "Why do we keep running into more problems?" he lamented. "I just want to solve the murder, not every problem among the work crew." He rolled his shoulders as if his back were giving him trouble.

Shaula was growing worried about him. Stress was tightening his shoulders and etching lines on his forehead.

"Shall we take a break?" she asked. "While we are aboard, would you like to salvage anything from your quarters?"

He stood upright. "That's a good idea. Yeah, I would."

He led her along a corridor and up several floors. They passed a long row of doors that were all closer together than many others on the ship. Then he typed in a code on a panel beside a door, which swooshed open onto a small, dark room. He said a word that sounded to her like 'Fahl-cheh' as he waved her into the room with a wide gesture. Shaula had not been programmed with Faolán's native language, but the gesture indicated he was welcoming her in.

There was no emergency light in the cabin, but it did not need one as a porthole let in natural sunlight, casting a beam on the jumbled mess. Shaula picked her way in. A mattress and blankets lay tangled in a heap on what had once been the ceiling; clothes and other sundry items had fallen out of drawers that had opened in the crash; and items that must have usually been on the desk were strewn about. Faolán closed the door and then stood, arms crossed and one shoulder leaning on the wall, watching her survey his belongings.

"I take it the room was tidier before the crash?"

"Uh, marginally." He squatted and started digging through the mess. "Actually, that's something I ought to talk to you about. You may have noticed that I'm not always the tidiest." He did not look up at her as he talked.

"I had noticed," she replied.

He was silent for a minute, shaking dross out of a backpack and then shoving in items such as clothes and a tablet. "You deserve to know something about me," he said, "because it might affect the investigation." He flipped the mattress over so the padded side was up, then sat on it, patting the spot beside him. Shaula took a seat and waited for him to continue. He ran a hand through his hair, and his knee jiggled. "I... have a condition called ADHD. Have you heard of it? I usually tame it somewhat with the help of medicine that's on slow release from an implant I have. But I think it's running out. Anyway, without the meds, I mean, I'm still me; my personality doesn't change or anything. But I lose track of time, get distracted. Have trouble getting started on tasks I know I have to do, I *want* to do. I just can't start. It's called executive dysfunction. Oh, and my medicine tends to keep my emotions on an even keel. When I don't have access to them, I'm not quite as stable."

Shaula nodded. It explained a lot about Faolán. His distractions, his talkativeness. How his self-confidence was waning. "Understood. You think this condition will be difficult to manage with the investigation?"

"Yeah. I'm sorry."

She frowned at him. "It is nothing to apologise for."

"But I'm faulty. That must frustrate you."

"You are not faulty. Did you think I would not understand?"

He looked up at her. "But you're perfect."

He thought that? Of her, Shaula, the least personable android? "I am not, no matter how much I would like to be. Of all the androids, I am the one who understands best that none of us androids are, that perfection is impossible. I am the one who knows what ailments the androids of 227C have. I am the one who builds and programs the work-arounds and modifications needed to get everyone working in their allotted places well enough. I, more than anyone, know that we all do the best we can with what resources we have."

He stared at her for a long moment. He looked like he was having a revelation. "Thank you."

"What helps you?"

He snorted. "Well, the meds. I hope we can salvage a production unit from the med bay in good enough working order."

"Sure, but if that does not work out, how can we mitigate? What else helps?"

Faolán rubbed the back of his neck. "I know this sounds weird, but being squeezed or squished can help. Like, light touches do nothing, or even distract me more. But heavy pressure sort of fixes my brain chemistry a bit? It's to do with the—ah, what's it called? Part of the nervous system. Uh... para... I'm after forgetting. But anyway, pressure helps. For me, at least. Not everyone who has ADHD has the same experience, but that's mine."

Shaula nodded. She did not know the details, but she could search in the database later for more information. "That sounds like something we could program Madigan to help you with."

His eyes lit up. "Really?"

"Yes. I could program Madigan to, for example, sit beside you and lean against you when you look stressed. Even perhaps sit on your lap? He is heavy, but perhaps that is the kind of weight you need?"

"Fully on me might be too much. But against? Especially as he's fluffy and pettable? That sounds great."

"Let us do that, then. And of course, *I* could always lie on you if needed."

His green eyes twinkled, catching the sunlight from the port hole. "Oh? You could lie on me, could you?"

"I assure you, I would squish you thoroughly."

"Mmm. Sounds delightful." He grinned.

Shaula frowned. She failed to see how being squished could be delightful.

Faolán noticed her confusion and gave a huffing laugh. "You *on top* of me. Sounds nice." He waggled his eyebrows.

She finally caught on. He was making an amorous comment. "Ah. I see."

Faolán smirked and began rummaging through his stuff again.

Shaula idly began organising the mess, moving things into piles that seemed to have similar functions: gadgets in one pile, clothing in another, personal hygiene products like shampoo and toothbrush in another. She picked up a folder with a plain blue cover. "What is this? Where should I put it?" She began to open the folder.

Faolán glanced over, then did a double take. He went bright red and grabbed for the folder. "I'll take that!"

But Shaula had already opened it. Inside, she found a printed animated loop of a red-haired woman in a forest, naked and touching herself.

"Who is this?" she asked. She felt an unpleasant roil within her. Did Faolán already have someone in his life?

"No one!" he exclaimed, grabbing for the folder. But she turned the page. There was another animated loop on the next page, this one of three people in bed together, one man and two women, all doing things to each other. The red-haired woman was not one of them, and the man was not Faolán.

"Ah. Is this your pornography stash?"

"Shaula!"

"There is no need to be ashamed. You are a single person on a long-range space mission. It would have been stranger for you to not have material like this to keep you company." She turned the page. The next animated loop showed a naked, muscled man. "You like men too."

"Don't look." She looked up in surprise. Faolán looked ashamed, perhaps upset.

She closed the folder and put it down. She had miscalculated, and looking at the folder was more of a violation to him than she had thought it was. She should not have opened it. "My apologies. Has there been a regression in human society while we have been isolated? Has there been a resurgence of homophobia or biphobia?"

"It's not that," he said, his head hanging. "I don't care if people know I'm into guys too. It's just..." he sighed, looked up at her. "That guy is way hotter than me! I don't want you to see how hot human guys can be and see that I'm really not all that." He looked distressed by the idea.

"Did we not just have this discussion?"

"Huh?"

"You are worried about not being perfect again. I understand. I am often in that space too. But that image in your book is of a man who would not look like that in life himself. How can your own image in a poorly lit bathroom mirror, the only time you are ever likely to look at yourself, ever compare to a touched-up professional recording?"

Faolán nodded. "True. You know, you're surprisingly good at confidence-boosting pep talks."

"You are the only one who has ever said so."

"Maybe I'm the only one you've tried building up, because I'm the only one who has come undone in front of you like an unspooling ribbon of worries and self-flagellation?"

"Or maybe it is because you are the only one who has come undone *in* me, and so I'm putting in extra effort."

He chortled. "I did do that, didn't I?" He bumped her shoulder with his own. "That implies that I'm winning you over with my charm, you know." He snorted. "Or at least, with my cock."

Shaula stilled. He was right. It did. How had that happened? Maybe she was wrong about simply altering her responses in the interests of collegiality. Maybe she was being truly drawn to him? This had never happened to her before. Why was it happening now? And was it in Faolán's interests to spend social time with her?

His confidence had taken a beating lately. It seemed it must have been his worries about his condition. But perhaps being surrounded by implausibly sculpted android forms had not helped. Her words seemed to have helped, but this new closeness she felt with him made her want to lock in the ego boost. Would doing what they did the previous afternoon help?

No, because despite getting his own pleasure, perhaps the fact that her own orgasm had been simulated had been another contributing factor to his low self-esteem today.

He needed to feel achievement. She thought about how pleasant it had been, how gratifying, to see what she had done to him. That feeling was the one she wanted to share with him.

"I want you to make me orgasm," she said.

Faolán dropped the bag he was holding. "I beg your pardon?"

"I am feeling selfish. Make me orgasm."

His face turned red. "We're not sure that's something that works for you."

"You will have to work for it." She stood up and took her clothes off, folding them and putting them aside.

"Fuck," said Faolán. He dithered a moment, then went to lock the door.

Shaula lay on the mattress and put her arms behind her head. She let her knees fall open, exposing herself to him. Faolán whipped his t-shirt off and knelt between her legs. Shaula lifted a foot and put it on his chest, wriggling her toes in the patch of chest hair he had in the middle.

"That's a new one," he said, bracing himself against the mild pressure she applied. He grabbed a pillow and put it near her backside. "Lift your hips." She did so, and he slipped the pillow underneath. "All right, I'm going in. Feel free to release as much of that passionfruit stuff as you like." He kissed the inside of her knee.

"It is not passionfruit today. I had to put a fresh pod in." She let a little of the new pod release, enough that he'd be able to smell it.

"You change your flavour? Just like that? You're like one of those fancy coffee machines." He leaned forward and put his nose to her nether regions, inhaling deeply. "Hmm, that's..." he gave a quick lap with his tongue. "Fuck me, that's sticky date pudding!"

"Is that OK?"

In answer, he ran his tongue all the way up her slit. He moved away from that area of her for a bit, instead moving up and taking one of her nipples in his mouth, and fondling the other with his hand. It felt... nice. Maybe not quite in the way he was aiming for. It felt comforting rather than erotic. He let the nipple go from his mouth with a pop. "How does that feel?"

"Nice, but mild. Try your teeth."

He raised an eyebrow at her, but bent his head back down to comply. This time, he took the other nipple in his mouth and rolled it between his teeth.

"Harder."

He bit down, still with care, but it was more like she needed. Her leg curled around him against her will, bringing him closer to her core. She could feel his smug, lop-sided grin against her breast. He nibbled again, and she bucked. The sensors in her breast sent urgent signals, asking for more, more. But he pulled away, trailing kisses down her stomach.

He settled between her legs again, kissing her there the way he had kissed her mouth. "More," she gasped. "I want more."

"Mhmm, you're selfish today," he muttered against her.

"Yes. So selfish." She thrust up at his face.

She could feel the confidence returning to him, making him more decisive, more forceful. He sucked her into his mouth and slipped two fingers into her, curling and pumping them.

"Does this do much for you?" he asked, then sucked her clitoris again, letting her know which body part he was talking about.

"There are a lot of sensors there. I can feel the exact temperature of your mouth, measure how much pressure you are applying."

"But is it good?"

The sensors there were sounding off constantly, a repeated message of *Just right, just right.* "Yes. Good."

He paid more attention to her, making sounds that ought to be obscene and revolting, and yet they made her proud of herself, proud for trying something new. Her life had been the same for year upon year, never forging anything new, never being other than what she was programmed to be, the role assigned to her at the Event Horizon. But now she lay back, a human man between her legs, her knees in the air, not a care in the world for propriety, not a care in the world for the endless list of tasks everyone kept heaping upon her, so sure that she would efficiently get through it all and never buckle. He was not asking her to do anything but lie there and feel.

She felt the texture and wetness of his tongue. The rough strength of his fingers. The brush of his hair on her low abdomen. Her skin sensors were always accurate and well tuned, but now she felt more keenly than she ever had, her focus on such a small area of her body.

Something sparked in her code. Something new. Something old. Something forgotten. A program that had laid dormant for too long. Had it ever been active? She did not know. Her thighs wanted to close around his head, but she was afraid she would hurt him. She had enough power in her hip joints to crush his skull. So she held her legs open with her hands, straining against herself to stay open and safe for him.

He must have sensed some change in her she was not aware of herself, because he switched to placing his tongue against her and providing pressure in a constant rhythm, and pumping her with his fingers again in the same rhythm. As he kept up the pace, she struggled to control her limbs. Her feet planted on the mattress, and her hips rose off the cushion, chasing his mouth, chasing the feeling coursing through her.

"Ngh!" she cried, and then bucked. It was like the programmed orgasm from the day before, but she did not choose it. Faolán merely brought it out in her. She did not know if it felt similar to a human orgasm, but it was good. All the data flooding into her brain from her sensors should have overwhelmed her. But she just felt alive.

She stilled, and the tension dropped out of her limbs. Faolán looked up at her. The whole lower part of his face was wet. He grinned. "How did I do? Did I work hard enough?"

"Yes. You did well. That felt..."

"Sufficient?"

"I have not finished processing, so I have not chosen an appropriate adjective. But it was beyond my control."

He grinned, sitting up and wiping his face on his arm. "Did you have any memories?"

She frowned. She had forgotten about that. "No."

"Oh." He sat back on his heels. The bulge in his trousers reminded Shaula that Faolán had been so focussed on her pleasure he had not sought his own yet.

"Can I watch you?" she asked.

"Watch me what?"

"If you want to put it inside me again, that would be fine. But I want to watch you orgasm. If I may."

He looked frozen in shock for a moment. "Uh, yeah. I can do that." He stood and removed the last of his clothes.

"Sit on my stomach," she said. "I want a good view." She was interested to see what it looked like. Last time it had happened inside her, so she felt it all, but saw nothing.

He straddled her, keeping his weight on his own thighs. "Like this?"

"You can sit on me. You will not hurt me."

He settled more weight on her. "Like this?" His erect penis stood up beneath her breasts, his scrotum resting on her belly. His thighs, which were well sculpted despite what he seemed to think of himself, flexed to either side of her. And above his rounded belly and his pale chest with the brown hair, his flushed face looked down at her with blatant lust. "Like this?"

"Yes."

"You want me to pleasure myself like this?"

"Yes."

"I'll cum on your breasts and neck if I do it here."

"Please do."

He reached behind him and slipped his fingers into her again, scooping out some of her fluids, which he then used to lube himself up. Then he began stroking himself. "Like this?"

"Just like that."

She watched as he stroked himself: the way his hand moved; the way the muscles in his arm worked; the heaving of his breath. He thought he could not compare to others, but there was beauty in the flush on his chest, strength in the breadth of his shoulders, and comfort in the body fat under his real human skin that may have hidden some of the detail of his musculature, but also made him more pleasant to touch, to cling to.

He looked at her with heavy-lidded eyes as his arm moved faster, his gaze trailing over her breasts, meeting her own. His eyes looked dark, his green irises mere slivers around blown-wide pupils. He arched forward as if inexorably drawn towards her.

Then, with a grunt and a gasp, he reached his peak. She watched in fascination as the pearlescent semen squirted out of him and splattered on her breasts and neck, just as he said it would. He moaned, and more came out, some even reaching her face. Then he fell forward, holding himself up with one hand on the mattress beside her head, drooping over her and looking at the mess he'd made of her. He lazily gave himself a few last, soft pumps.

"Oh, wow," he gasped, and the look on his face...

...*watching a woman with curly steel-grey hair at work wrist-deep in a pink android's abdomen...*

What?

Faolán slumped onto the mattress beside her. Shaula, not sure what to think of what she had just seen, wiped at the sticky stuff on her face.

"I'm sorry I made such a mess," he gasped.

"I am not." She slid the stuff between her fingers, contemplating its nature. "This is what would make a human woman pregnant?"

"If deposited at the right time."

"It is full of gametes, but it just looks like slime."

"Gee, thanks."

"I am marvelling, not complaining. Evolution has created much more elaborate structures than technology has invented yet. No matter how much effort she put in, she could never fully recreate life. It was an asymptote. A white whale."

He propped himself up on an elbow and looked down at her. "You had a memory." It was not a question. "When you came?"

"No, when you did."

"Me? Why? I thought it was supposed to be orgasming that did it."

"That is what happened with Altair. But for me, it was the warm feeling I experienced knowing that I had a part in your pleasure. The satisfaction, I suppose you could say. I felt mighty, and then I remembered."

"What's the difference between you and Altair?"

"He has a special upgrade to his systems. Many of the androids of 227C have upgrades to different systems."

"Do you?"

"If I do, I have not yet figured out which system."

He grinned down at her. "Well, I think we just found out a big clue. And made some progress on your investigation, right?"

"Yes. I did."

Now, if nothing else, she knew what Dr Neale had looked like before the Event Horizon. But the memory brought more questions: if that really was Dr Neale, how could she be a threat? She must be an elderly, frail woman by now. Shaula had not previously understood what that would mean. The woman in her memories did not look strong enough to harm Tiaki. Add another 30 years to her age, and the idea became preposterous. Dr Neale was not the killer.

Faolán rose and found a towel and a bottle of water for them to clean themselves. There was theoretically a sink in the room, but it was hanging upside down, and the water system had likely been damaged in the crash anyway.

They were mostly dressed when there was a bang on the door. They quickly got themselves decent, and Faolán opened the door to see who was there. Madigan stood in the doorway. "Faolán. Your presence is needed. A fight has broken out near cargo bay 4."

They followed Madigan to the location of the fight. Simons, Vega, and Diphda were all yelling (or talking loudly, in the case of the androids), over the top of one another outside the cargo bay where the salvaged goods were being stored ready for transport. Latu stood nearby, trying to get a word in edge-wise. Vega's familiar Romulus sat on his shoulder.

"I have the recording my familiar took!" boomed Vega. "You have been stealing items from the ship. What for?"

"Why would I be stealing stuff? This is my ship; I'm part of the crew. We're literally here to salvage stuff!" shouted Simons in return.

"Then why were you moving things to an alternative location?" demanded Diphda.

"This is all a set up!" said Simons.

Naos walked out of cargo bay 4. "I have verified that the medical equipment, at least, is still present."

"Why would I have stolen medical equipment?" shouted Simons as he threw up his arms.

Shaula strode forward, Faolán at her side. "What is going on here?"

"Simons is behaving in a questionable manner," said Vega.

"So, what else is new?" said Faolán. "But what's he done now? You mentioned stealing?"

"I'm just protecting some sensitive stuff is all! Not stealing. I'm an engineer. I know what we need to be extra careful of."

Vega and Diphda both opened their mouths to retort, but there was a sudden bang. The floor lurched, and a compression wave knocked Faolán off his feet and blew him into her. She twisted and covered Faolán, shielding him from shrapnel. Smoke and dust billowed over the group.

It came from cargo bay 4.

CHAPTER 18

Faolán picked through the charred wreckage. They were working on the assumption that the explosion was linked to the murder. Therefore, Shaula and Faolán were the ones with their shoes and hair covered, examining the new crime scene, while everyone else lingered on the other side of the doorway behind a cordon, watching in a mixture of curiosity and interest.

Curiosity and interest. As if they hadn't just lost irreplaceable items. The medicine production unit, of all things. How could they have lost one of the most important things for the salvage? There was one more unit still in the med bay under repair, and thankfully it was the more important one that might help make medicines for the people with serious conditions. But there was now no hope of replacing Faolán's meds. None at all. That was it. His days as a productive member of this crew were numbered. All because they lost the unit. No, not lost. Someone had purposefully destroyed it. When he found out who...

He took some deep, calming breaths before he entirely lost his shit in front of everyone. All he could do was his job. That was the only action he could take. They were combing over the site of the explosion, examining every square centimetre of the large grey boxy room. It was slow going, because it was an utter mess. Not only because of the explosion, but also because of the large hole in the outer wall.

"What do you think of this?" asked Shaula.

He jolted at the sound of her quiet voice and moved over to her sector. "What have you got?"

"Paw prints. Are these Madigan's?"

Faolán squatted to look. The paw prints were in thick dirt and dust that had piled up against the side of the cargo bay. But the explosion had blurred the outline. "It's hard to tell. But they're about the right size. And Madigan was guarding the cargo bay until he came to tell us about the argument. Besides, there are no larger mammals on 227C, and no one else has a familiar with large paws, so whose else could they be?"

"I hope you are right," she said in a low voice. "The alternatives are all concerning."

He looked at the doorway to check that they were out of earshot of their observers, then turned away from them so no one could lipread his words. "Any evidence pointing to Naos?"

"None," she said.

As Naos was the last person in the cargo bay before the explosion, their suspicions had yet again turned away from Simons, this time to the android with the poor bedside manner. Naos seemed to have a problem with Tiaki and Camryn's relationship, after all. And perhaps she had some reason to sabotage the salvage, such as wanting to keep her place as the head doctor of the settlement.

Why was there no end to the list of suspects?

Faolán left Shaula taking pictures of the prints and turned back to his own area. He paused, catching sight again of the destruction. It wasn't just the important equipment they had lost. Everything they had gathered so far was damaged beyond repair, if not destroyed. Boxes of nutrients for the food printer. Extra blankets and bedding. First aid supplies that were newer than the expired stuff the androids had to hand.

The medicine production unit itself lay in a twisted heap of metal fragments and shattered component tubes. His stomach twisted at the sight, as it had been doing every five minutes or so.

This was all his fault. He should have been more on top of things. Maybe then it wouldn't have happened. If they'd finished the murder investigation already, Faolán could have been guarding the cargo bay. Maybe he could have stopped the sabotage.

Or maybe he would have just become another victim.

He plodded back to the area he had been examining. The curious faces of Hernandez and Gagnon were still in the doorway, and Ife and Sandeep were beyond, but the rest of the group was starting to disperse.

Faolán checked along a twisted piece of metal that had once been part of a hoverbed. He hadn't yet found evidence of an explosive device. Whatever had caused the explosion seemed to have vaporised itself. Whatever it had been must have packed a punch, though. The metal of the hoverbed was twisted like tinfoil.

He paid closer attention to a jagged corner that stuck out one side. Something glistened there, with a small tuft of brown fibres caught in it.

"Hey, I think I have something." He took a swab tube out of a bag slung over his shoulder and swabbed the sticky stuff as gently as he could. It came away on the swab dull red.

"Hey, Ife," he called. "Did anyone hurt themselves in here? Maybe while we were all having a quick health check after the explosion?"

"It should be just the two of you who have been in there. Why?"

"Because it looks like someone caught their shin on here and cut themselves after the explosion." Shaula came over and took out a sample tube of her own to collect the fibres.

"Is anyone in the group wearing brown trousers?" she asked, also loud enough to be heard from the doorway.

"No," said Ife.

Faolán took both tubes over to the doorway and handed them to Ife. "If you have that DNA database ready, think you could run an analysis on this blood?"

"On it. Naos, you're with me."

Faolán looked along the corridor. Most of the group was still there, actually. They had been out of his line of sight and quiet, but they were still nearby. Waiting.

After Naos turned around, Faolán made a 'keep eyes on' gesture towards her, catching Ife's eye. She nodded and turned to walk away.

He walked back over to Shaula. "Do you androids have anything in you that looks like human blood?"

"No, we do not."

"So, someone came in after the explosion, probably from outside, and hurt themselves. Were they just having a nosey? Checking their handiwork?"

"I do not know. Does this rule out Naos?"

Faolán crossed his arms. "Not fully. But it does make it less likely. Something else is going on."

They kept searching while Ife and Naos were gone, but it seemed they had found all the evidence. While he ineffectively searched, Faolán wondered about the argument that had been going on while the explosion happened. It had been an effective distraction. From what he had learned, the argument had started between Vega and Simons first, and spread to the others from there. Had either Simons or Vega started the argument as a distraction on purpose, or had someone else simply taken advantage of the argument for their own ends?

Neither man owned up to causing a distraction, of course, and they both blamed the other for causing trouble.

Faolán's stomach was rumbling for dinner by the time Ife returned and waved them over to have a word. "Anything more?" she asked.

"No. I think we're going to call it, right?"

"I have taken pictures of all parts of the cargo bay," added Shaula. "We have found no more evidence."

"We got the DNA database plugged into a unit in the mobile med lab, and Naos identified the blood as Dr Rebecca Neale's."

Faolán took in a deep breath, digesting that information.

"Also," continued Ife, "we've new orders from the settlement. They're concerned about our safety and want us back as soon as possible. So wind up what you can, and if you can't figure it out now, we'll have to rely on a full autopsy of Camryn back at the settlement. OK?"

"But there's a lot more going on than just the murder. We can't investigate if we don't stay."

"Sure. But at this rate, someone else could be lost. I don't want that, and neither do you."

Faolán shook his head. "Of course not. But we're still missing something important. How could an elderly woman be causing us this much trouble? Can we double-check the DNA on a different unit? One from the ship?"

"I'm sorry, Faolán. We just don't have the room to bring that equipment back with us."

"Even though we've lost so much?"

"We're taking the opportunity to bring more hydroponics back. The DNA analysis is solid. I double-checked it myself. We've got two days at most to make the best of this salvage as we can. I can't give you more time. Finish up here and then get some sleep. We all have a long day tomorrow. I want a report of your findings tomorrow, and then we'll all need to pull our weight for the salvage. We need to do the best we can to make up for what we lost."

Faolán nodded. "Sure thing. Understood, sir."

Beside him, Shaula frowned, but gave a curt nod.

They were left alone in the cargo bay. Madigan waited for them in the doorway, but everyone else had cleared out of the hallway while they talked with Ife.

Faolán turned to Shaula. "How are you with rule-breaking?"

"I am in favour of it whenever the person setting down the rules is being foolish. Ask Sirius sometime about his opinion of me. What do you have in mind?"

"Maybe it's foolishness, maybe its intuition. But I think the DNA evidence should be looked at more closely. Something doesn't feel right."

"Does the *Sunda Tiger* have small analysis units? Portable ones?"

"They're slow, but I think we have stuff in storage for away missions and the like that could get the job done."

"And this DNA database?"

"It'll be in the med lab computer."

Shaula took out another swab tube and took a second sample of the blood. "Let us get a unit."

Madigan kept watch for them while they broke into one of the storage cupboards near the hangar bay. Faolán was usually tasked with keeping people out of where they weren't supposed to be. It was frightening how easy it was to flip the script and get someone in instead. Maybe he was being foolhardy, but the roiling feeling in his stomach, the one caused by the loss of his access to his meds, was making him feel like he wanted to *do* something about it, no matter the cost. Someone had to pay.

They found the portable biological assay unit easily enough. But they had to wait for the others to leave the ship before they could sneak into the med lab, hook the unit up to the med lab terminal, and download the full DNA database. The unit only just had enough storage for the database, and Shaula had to hack the system to get it. Her fingers flew over the keys. The remarkable thing was that she was doing this the hard way out of an abundance of caution and a distrust of being networked to strange machines.

Faolán wondered what the androids would be capable of if they did network. For now, at least she could get the DNA database with relative ease. What they'd done would be obvious to Ife in the morning, but oh well. Maybe they wouldn't get in that much trouble if his hunch was right.

"We have the database and the sample. Let us attempt to smuggle this unit onto the engineering lab."

It folded up into a small suitcase shape. In the end, they doubled back to Faolán's cabin and dumped out most of the belongings he'd collected in his bag and put the assay unit in. It just fit with some clothes packed around it. Then they went back to the camp as casually as they could. Once they were in the engineering lab, they unstrapped the mobile unit and got it set up on a bench.

Shaula prepared the sample and then loaded it into the small intake tube. "What should I test for?" she asked. "You are the one with the intuition."

Faolán shrugged. "I don't know. The works?"

"You mean all the tests available?"

"Yeah. Everything you can."

"That will take many hours on a unit like this. It was made with portability in mind, not speed."

"Then we'd best start right away."

Shaula selected all the options on the display screen, then pressed 'Run'. "Estimated run time: 17 hours. This will take a while."

"Ah, fuck. That's even longer than I thought."

"It will have to do."

There was a scrabble at the door, and Shaula rose to let Charm in. She held her hand low and let the scorpion climb up to her head. "Report," she said.

"I observed no unusual behaviour by Tyler Simons," said the scorpion familiar.

Faolán walked closer. "Not even whatever shifty behaviour had Vega in a tizzy?"

"Negative."

"Thank you, Charm," said Shaula. "Maybe whatever footage Romulus captured of Simons happened while we were distracted by Kikelomo and Chaudhary."

"Yeah, you're probably right. He took the opportunity to move stuff around to his private stockpile, wherever that is. I damn well forgot about it, what with the explosion. We'll need to check that at some point. Uh. Tomorrow, I guess? After the blood sample finishes? It's getting too dark and unsafe to go back and check now."

"I concur. Now, I believe you require sustenance. Go have a meal with your fellow crew members. Be seen, and ease people's minds. We are going to need people on our side if our covert investigation bears fruit, and it is not something I can do."

"Are you sure? I don't want to leave you here all alone."

"I am used to being alone, Faolán. I am fine."

"Thank you for trusting in me," he said. "It must be hard for you to trust human instincts."

"Go."

Faolán went, but looked back at Shaula as he left. She was already getting Tiaki's brain out of the cupboard again for another attempt at accessing his full memories.

She looked so small by herself at the bench. Just because she was used to being alone didn't mean it was good for her.

CHAPTER 19

Shaula got back to work as soon as she had finished charging in the early hours of the morning. She left Faolán snoring gently in his bed. He needed his sleep, particularly after the shock of the day before. He had tried to hide how affected he'd been by the explosion, but she had noticed how often his eyes had slid to the twisted remains of the medicine production unit. She did not know exactly what he was feeling, but he must be suffering. The only way she could help him was by making sure they finished as much of the investigation as soon as they could.

She first analysed and mapped out all the data they had collected from the cargo bay. No matter how hard she looked, she could not find evidence of an incendiary device, unless some streaks of soot near the blast site were the only residue. Shaula was not familiar with the engineering of explosives. She did not know how easy it was to make a device that self-destructed beyond the ability to recover shrapnel.

The two sources of evidence she could find in the images were the two they already had: the DNA and fibres from the hoverbed, and the paw prints which may or may not have been Madigan's. She approached the wolf, who was recharging on the bottom bunk, and measured Madigan's paw to compare it with the images. She still could not be sure if they matched.

Shaula took a brief diversion to program in the special assistive routine for Madigan that she had discussed with Faolán the day before. Then she returned to the task of Tiaki's brain. At some point, Faolán rose, showered, and then left for breakfast. He returned shortly thereafter with several freshly baked rolls, each cut open and spread with something oily.

"Morning. Do you want to try one?" He held half a roll out to her.

She blinked up at him. "I am an android."

"Yeah, but you said you don't know if you have an enhanced body system. Have you tried eating?"

She looked at the roll. "I would know if that was it. The androids who can process food have specialised internal structures to do so, and must be topped up with acid. I do not have such structures."

His face fell. "Oh."

"It was a very thoughtful gesture, Faolán. Thank you for thinking of me."

He smiled. Shaula stared at the smile. It struck her for the first time that she had said something nice to someone, and they had felt happiness because of it. It was not the first time she had done so, but it was the first time she took a moment to reflect on it. Until a few days ago, she would not have thought she was capable of making people happy. But here she was...

...children laughing and squealing, splashing in puddles...

"Are you OK?"

She met his eyes again, this time in shock. "I think I just had another memory."

"Really? Something important for the investigation?"

"No. Just human children. But it was a memory from before. I am sure of it."

Faolán put the plate down and leaned one hip against the bench, crossing his arms. "What set it off?"

"I think realising that I had made you pleased with my words. But that makes no sense. What body system is that? How does it relate?"

"I don't know. Let's put a pin in that for later. It may become obvious in time." Faolán quickly scoffed his breakfast down. "We should get to the wreck as soon as we can. Ife has already hurried me along again this morning. We need to interview everyone again, and I think we need to search as much of the wreck as we can. We still don't know what Simons is up to. Plus, my instincts tell me someone else is here. "

"The evidence says someone else is here."

"Well, yeah, but I think they're *still* here."

"Sure. But should you not check my memories?"

Faolán stilled, then went red. "Yeah, you're right."

He fetched his tablet, then they ran through everything that happened the day before. He blushed as she gave a detailed account of their activities in his cabin, but dutifully wrote her words down. She hoped no one was checking his notes. Then soon after, they were aboard the wreck. Shaula wanted to return early in the afternoon to check the DNA results, but until then, they would keep investigating.

They were the first aboard the wreck, so they started with their hunt. They did not have time to search every room in the wreck, especially as the upper decks, which were ploughed into the ground, were not structurally safe. The command deck had apparently been nearly abraded away in the crash. But they paced the habitation corridors, opening all doors that were unlocked, and then checked the corridors near the mess hall, and several floors of offices.

They finally had luck in an exercise area. Some weights machines hung from the ceiling, while others lay in cluttered heaps, the bolts not having held up in the crash. A full wall of mirrors was cracked, though thankfully a shatterproof coating had kept the pieces contained. But it was a storage room that was of particular interest. Drag marks in the dust led from the storage room to the corner of an open exercise area. They investigated the storage room and found it full of crash mats and floor pads.

"Faolán, does it look to you like someone dragged a mat out and put it in the corner for a while, then put it back again?"

"Yep. Think someone was sleeping here for a while?" They checked and found a mat, the thickest one, had scratch marks under it consistent with the architrave of the storage room doorway. There was nothing else out of place in the storage area. Shaula wished they had a finger print kit. All she could do was swab the handles of the crash pad, though it likely bore many people's skin remnants, having been used by the crew of the *Sunda Tiger* for who knew how long.

"I can't see any sign that anyone is still camping here, though," said Faolán. "No belongings stashed in the cupboard or anything."

"But they were perhaps here from when the ship crashed until we arrived?"

"That'd be my guess."

They looked at one another. Somehow, Shaula read Faolán's thoughts in his eyes: they already suspected that someone was sneaking around on board the ship, and that person may have illicit cloaking tech. But they would not say that out loud, just in case they were being observed at this moment by someone unseen.

They should not let on all the information they had.

"We will need to make note of this," said Shaula, and she pulled out her tablet and took pictures of the space.

They headed back to the work areas, intending to interview everyone again, this time about the explosion. Shaula felt her wiring chafing at the delay. These interviews were Faolán's forte. She respected his ability to talk to everyone, to keep everyone at ease. But there was no need for her to be there too.

The most annoying thing about it was that it was Shaula's own recommendation that they pair up that had tethered her to Faolán's side. Which had turned out to be a more informative and enjoyable place to be than she would have guessed. But nevertheless, her skills could be of use elsewhere.

After he had interviewed Diphda, discovering nothing further about the explosion or the interloper than they already knew, Shaula put her hand on Faolán's shoulder. "I am no help here," she said. "Look the other way while I go investigate that hypercore unit Simons used to hack Altair. I believe it would be a better use of my time."

"We're supposed to stay together," he said.

"I understand. But feel free to interrogate me any way you want to later to be assured I did what I said I did. Clothing optional. Oh, and there are restraints in the fourth drawer under the aft end of the examination table that could hold me. If that is something that may help."

He blushed vermillion. "Excuse me, are you hinting that I should do a wee bit of BDSM roleplaying with you next time I verify your memories?"

Shaula shrugged. "I still do not know for sure what works for me. A bit of experimentation would not hurt."

He grinned that lopsided grin of his, the one that made her aware of just how human he was. "Safe word is diadem, right?"

"Correct."

She left the hydroponics area and walked through the mess hall into the corridor. She put a false scowl on her face as she walked. Her reputation did her justice. The other members of the team who looked up at her all winced or looked away. As expected, they thought she was in a foul mood, that perhaps she was annoyed at Faolán and storming off. No one stopped her. She hoped no one would volunteer to go track her down, cautious of her apparent ire.

Being known as one of the grumpy ones had its benefits, especially if you did not much like talking to people.

Once she was on her own, she followed Faolán's rambling directions to the engineering labs, the places on the ship where she would have worked if she were a crew member.

The *Sunda Tiger* had an impressive range of equipment. A further 30 years of progress had improved the technology noticeably. However, Shaula suspected 227C had been set up with state-of-the-art equipment that was black market, or secretive. They had much more in their settlement than the *Sunda Tiger* had, and some of what they had was more advanced.

Except for the hypercores. They did not have those. Shaula was not even sure if she could use these units. They were far beyond the quantum computers she worked with regularly. Rather, they used a deft reapplication of Weft-Skip technology to harness M-space to extend their computing power. Shaula had never worked with other universes.

The thought was terrifying.

But over the last 30 years, this technology had become first accepted, and now routine. Weft-Skip, after

all, had been around for a century, and no universe frac-
tures had occurred. At least, not that she was aware of.

Alas, the engineering labs had suffered damage in the
crash. They were in the rear of the ship, which had been
at the front during the last career of the ship across the
surface, with no engines to protect the space. Most of
the labs had torn open at the front end, and the rooms
filled up with debris, crushing the equipment within.
The first door Shaula opened loosened a pile of rock
and twisted metal to collapse into the hallway. The next
door did the same. She decided that whole side of the
hallway was a loss. So she tried the other side of the hall.
She was greeted first with two storage rooms in a row.
But the third door opened into the kind of room she
was looking for.

A grey and metal lab filled with jumbled equipment
showed itself to her in the low emergency lighting. She
increased the glow of her own eyes and then placed
Charm on the floor.

"Please look for a Witten 3.2 Hypercore computer in
this lab," she asked her familiar.

"Understood," hissed Charm, and then scuttled into
the piled heaps of equipment.

Shaula began organising and straightening the lab,
making it accessible for a being of her size. By the time
she had righted several units and tidied away the contents of a tool cabinet that had spilled everywhere,
Charm had done its assigned task.

"Shaula, the Witten 3.2 Hypercore is in one piece,
tipped on its side under the work table."

Shaula followed her familiar's instructions and soon
had the hypercore upright and connected to its power
source. While it booted up, Shaula tried her best to ignore the strange feeling in her wiring and distract herself by examining the ports and cabling on the unit. She
hoped she was just being wary about the unit, and that

the sensation was not actually the universe bending and warping as multiple dimensions were pinched together inside the unit. And if it was, would that be normal, or indicative of the unit malfunctioning?

She was so focussed on the unit and surmising about its operational parameters that she did not register the footsteps in the hallway until the door swooshed open.

"What do you think you're doing?" Kikelomo stood in the doorway, her eyebrows lowered and tension in all the lines of her body.

Out in the hallway, Shaula heard Faolán's voice calling from a distance, "Wait, Ife! I can explain!"

Shaula looked at the commanding officer, who was striding across the lab towards her. "I am doing something more productive than watching Faolán do work that I cannot do."

"Which is?"

"I am investigating a unit like the one Simons unlocked Altair's memories with. You know I wanted to do this, and how it could be beneficial."

"We do not have time or resources this trip. I gave you a direct order and you disobeyed it." Kikelomo reached out and aborted the hypercore's startup procedure.

"I am not one of your officers," said Shaula. "I am not beholden to you."

"If you don't play as part of the team, I have no choice but to remove you from the team."

Shaula's eyes narrowed.

Just then, Faolán reached the doorway. He hung onto the frame for a moment, panting, then stepped over the top of the doorway into the room. "She's not doing anything suspicious!" he said to Kikelomo. "She needs this."

"What she needs to be is off my ship. Now. I can't afford to trust anyone who is skulking around. Faolán, you too. You've got the rest of the day and tomorrow to write up a report and do whatever investigating you can at the murder scene and with Tiaki. But you're off the ship, understood? I'll investigate the explosion myself. But right now, go. Get that report done."

"But the hypercore—" said Shaula.

Kikelomo pointed at the door. "Now, Shaula. If you go now, this'll be between the three of us. If you stay and argue, I'll report it to Sirius."

Shaula did not care what Sirius thought. But she looked up at Faolán and saw how distressed he looked. She was causing trouble for him, and surprisingly, she did care about that. A lot.

"I am on my way," she said, and left the lab, scooping up Charm with one hand and Faolán's sleeve with the other.

CHAPTER 20

Faolán couldn't help but pace back and forth in the engineering lab.

"Like I get it, I really do," he said. "I know it probably looked suspicious to her that you'd wandered off. But it's so frustrating! We only have so much time left before we have to go back to the settlement." He leaned against the door frame between the cabin and the work area. Then, not finding that comfortable enough, he stepped into the lab proper and leaned against the recharge station. Then he remembered Tiaki's body was in there and, creeped out, he moved closer to Shaula, who sat at the bench dedicated to her work. The bioassay machine still whirred away on the bench nearby, running the sample from the explosion site.

"Tell me what you learned from the interviews," said Shaula, not looking up from her work.

He spaced out for a moment, looking at the beautiful line of her neck rising from her grey t-shirt to her updo of messy wavy hair. The point of her ear didn't even look weird to him anymore. She just looked like… Shaula. The way she wasn't looking at him as she spoke no longer made him think she was grumpy with him. She was just efficiently using her time.

"Not much. Everyone was seen by someone else, and they all had an alibi. Even Naos, if you can believe it. Everyone in that hallway said Naos had been called against her will to check the contents of the cargo bay, that she'd only been in there a few moments, and that she hadn't been carrying anything with her."

"It was not her, then. So we must suspect someone else. For just the explosion, or the murder too?"

"Who knows? I want to go look for Simons' stash and check what he's up to, but we'll need special permission from Ife for that now. I wish we could get one of our familiars to tail him, but Madigan would be too conspicuous, and it's too far for Charm to walk back and forth." He started pacing again. He walked over to the bioassay machine, but it still had a countdown of 2 hours and 37 minutes.

If only they'd been able to smuggle something bigger than this tiny field unit off the wreck. This was taking ages!

Shaula looked up at him then. "Looking at it will not speed it up."

"I know."

"You should start on the report. Please tell me if I can help. But I do not know what one of these reports is supposed to look like."

He sighed and flopped down on the sofa in the cabin, grabbing his tablet from the coffee table. He pulled up a report template and tried to get to work, but he just couldn't force himself to start writing. Instead, he looked up at Shaula, at the delicate lines of her back pushing against her top, at the flare of her hips. They'd fooled around a few times, and his thoughts kept returning to those encounters. But she was just trying to unlock her memories with him. They weren't having a romance.

If only he could get her off his mind.

He stood up again. Made a cup of tea at the tea nook. Went to take a piss even though his bladder wasn't full. He was wasting time, and he knew it.

"Did you know," he said to Shaula as he left he en-suite, wiping the remnants of the water he'd washed his hands with on his trouser leg, "that dandelion is a diuretic? Eat too much of it, and a man'd be peeing all day."

She gave him one of those long stares that made most people think she was scrutinising them like a bug under a microscope, but which was just her thinking hard. Then she got up and opened the door to the rest of the camp. "Madigan!" she called.

The wolf entered the engineering lab. "How may I be of service?" he asked.

"Parasympathetic activation protocol for Faolán, please." Then she pointed at the sofa. "Both of you. Over there."

Faolán smirked. "Yes, ma'am," he said, a little shiver that he steadfastly ignored running down his spine. He took a seat and picked up his tablet again. Madigan jumped up onto the sofa beside him and then leaned against his side. Faolán smiled, remembering his conversation with Shaula. But when had she had time to code this?

To his surprise, Shaula put Tiaki's brain away and then grabbed her own tablet, coming to sit on Faolán's other side. She turned her back to him and leaned against his shoulder. Without a word, she started sorting through explosion site photographs.

It... kinda worked, actually. He found it much easier to concentrate with the weight of the two androids leaning against him. His attention still wandered. Sometimes he started talking to Shaula about random crap. She would say, "That is interesting. Look at this picture. What do you think?" And somehow his brain would turn back to what he was supposed to be doing. A few times he nearly jumped up, but Madigan put a massive paw on his thigh and held him down.

It was still like pulling teeth, getting the words on the page. Each sentence had to be dragged from his psyche, kicking and screaming. But he never abandoned the task.

Plus, it was just so cosy, working together on the sofa like that. So... homey.

He wished he could do something for Shaula to show his appreciation. His automatic fallback was to feed people to show how much he cared. But he couldn't feed her. Not to say thank you. Not to flirt. Nothing. All he had were his words. So, he'd better use them.

"Hey, Shaula," he said in a soft voice. "Thank you."

"For what?"

"For understanding. For supporting me. For not judging me for needing support."

She turned around so she could look him in the eye. "Of course. It is what I do. I know I have a reputation for being unfriendly. But my mission is to fix what can be fixed, and compensate when appropriate, while knowing no one can reach the potential they wish they could, because we do not have the resources. Many people find me harsh for pointing that out. But is there not freedom in recognising that the limitations you face are not your fault?"

He gave her a crooked smile. "The same could be said of your memories, you know."

She looked away from him. He let her process her thoughts.

"I know," she said in the end. "As frustrating as it is, as dangerous as it may prove to be, I know. And I know that any solution I find will be flawed at best. There will be no miracles here."

"No miracles. Just people trying their best with the hand they've been dealt."

She met his gaze. "Yes. You put it well."

They were startled by a sudden beeping sound. "The results," said Faolán.

They both went over to the machine, and Shaula downloaded the results to her tablet. They leaned close together over the bench, scrolling through the lengthy output.

"DNA conclusively matches Dr Rebecca Neale, last known location: Hellas Basin, Mars," said Shaula. She scrolled down through the list. "Genetic predisposition for cancers of the digestive system, some types of Alzheimer's. There is a long list of epigenetic markers that have been methylated: deprivation, inconsistent access to food, multiple stress markers."

"What does that mean?" asked Faolán.

"I believe it is the genes that are turned on by environmental factors. So they are a record of the stresses that a person has experienced. She, or perhaps a parent or grandparent if hardship concurred with foetal gestation, has had a hard life." She scrolled faster. "There is a list of gene types here that have little relevance."

Faolán gasped. "Wait, what?"

Shaula stopped at the same point that had caught Faolán's eye. "That is impossible," she said.

"Telomeres. That's all to do with age, right? Why is the telomere length in the upper range?"

Shaula scrolled further.

Estimated age of subject: 12–16 years old.

"Excuse me, but what the actual fuck? Dr Neale's, like, in her 70s or something, right? Did she find the fountain of youth?" But then a sudden thought occurred to him. "Wait. What if we're dealing with a young clone?"

Shaula frowned. "A clone. I did not even consider that possibility. Why did I not?" She shook her head. "So Dr Neale cloned herself? Although, I suppose stranger things have happened."

She was right. Stranger things had happened.

CHAPTER 21

A clone. Shaula knew very little about cloning technology. It was hard to keep her thoughts on the possibility, so lacking in scope was it in her mind. Though
specific knowledge of cloning may have been withheld
in 227C for a reason. Time and again, they found the
important information that may have led to them having a breakthrough had been deleted at some point.

"Twelve to sixteen years," said Faolán. "So we might
be dealing with a little girl? What do we even do if a literal child is the murderer? It's a horrifying thought."

"Could an adolescent be strong enough to damage
Tiaki?"

"I don't know. She'd have to be a very strong teen to
pull that off." Faolán started pacing. "Twelve to sixteen
years... why do I feel like that should remind me of
something?" He slapped the bench top near him. "I can't
think while my hands are idle. I'm going to make a quick
lunch while I think. OK?"

"Go ahead," said Shaula.

While he was gone, Shaula got Tiaki's brain out again. A few last adjustments, and she would be able to access the fragmented files of Tiaki's whole memory back to the Event Horizon. She was closer to completing the task than she had estimated, and she made quick work of it. She looked at the brain for a moment, cable in hand.

"Sorry, old friend," she said, even though she knew he could no longer hear her. "Under any other circumstances, I would not invade your privacy like this."

She began compiling the transcript of Tiaki's memories and copying it to her tablet for later perusal. It would not be a quick transfer, as at least three decades of memories were stored in the brain. But it would not take anywhere near as long as the DNA analysis.

Faolán returned to the lab carrying a plate of food and with his other arm held behind his back. He put his plate on the coffee table, then disappeared towards the kitchenette. He reappeared with a glass of water. "I thought we could brighten the place up a bit. Just in this room. Don't want to contaminate your lab." He put a bunch of wildflowers into the glass of water and placed the display on the coffee table. There were small blue-purple flowers, larger white ones, and some longish leaves.

"You made a bouquet?"

He flushed and rubbed the back of his neck. "It's just a posy of wildflowers, Shaula. Nothing to get all that excited about."

She turned on her stool to face him, thinking of the ritual of gifting flowers. He wasn't meeting her gaze, but she read intentions in him anyway. He was growing fond of her. Somehow, despite all odds. Maybe it was just that they had shared orgasms. That was more plausible than her having won him over with her frosty personality. However it had happened, she had been given a place in his heart.

"Uh, so how are you going?" he asked her, perhaps uncomfortable under her scrutiny.

"I accessed Tiaki's memories. I am now compiling a transcript that will be easier to sort through."

Faolán let out a loud whooping noise, making Shaula startle. "Nice work!" He strode forward and took her face between his hands, stroking her cheeks with his thumbs. There was a smile on his face, so broad that the corners of his eyes crinkled. "You're amazing. You know that, right?"

... *"Test the subject's pain thresholds. I want to know if the upgrade to his nerve centres has had unintended consequences."*

There was nothing but compliance. No need for words. No need for questioning. Just her bronze hands reaching out for a sharp object and shoving it into the yellow hand strapped to the examination table in front of her...

"Hey. Shaula. Shaula!"

She looked up into Faolán's concerned face.

"Are you OK? Did you have another memory?"

"Yes. I did." What kind of memory, though? What was that? Whose voice was that? Why had she been following its directions without question, going so far as to cause pain?

That was Tiaki's hand. She had caused Tiaki pain.

"What triggered it, do you think?"

"Oh." Shaula had not thought of that yet. It seemed the least important part of the event. "I think seeing your smile, hearing your words of praise."

"Was the memory of use to the investigation?"

Shaula paused. She should say yes. But she was afraid of what the memory meant. So afraid.

Is it me? Am I compromised?

"No, it was not important to the investigation."

Faolán took Shaula at her word without question. He had not read the lie on her face at all.

CHAPTER 22

Faolán spent the afternoon living in that particular hell of second-guessing your social interactions and wishing you'd said or done something else.

He hadn't thought about it. He'd been affectionate towards Shaula. But in his defence, it was hard for him to not feel at least some affection for someone who had let him cum on their tits. It's the oxytocin. Gets you every time.

But she had withdrawn into herself since he had praised her while holding her face. It had been too much. He should have known there would be no affection from her. This was all an experiment. They'd known that going in. He had no business getting miffed over her reticence.

So he tried his best to act normal that afternoon while they pored over the explosion scene photographs while waiting for Tiaki's memories to compile. Unfortunately for Shaula, 'normal' for Faolán meant blathering about this, that, and the other thing. That afternoon, in an attempt to ignore the awkwardness, he told her all about Gráinne Mhaol, because he thought she'd like the story, being one who gives no fucks about rules herself; about the best chocolate mud cake recipe he knew, because he was hungry, and probably he needed the dopamine boost such a cake would give him; and about the time his sister Norah got drunk and woke up in a solar farm in a paddock outside town, for fuck knows what reason.

Each time, Shaula indulged him for a bit, then said, "Thank you for sharing, Faolán. Do you see anything of note in this picture?"

Unsurprisingly, it was the Gráinne Mhaol story that she stuck with the longest. The 'drunk sister in a paddock' story the shortest.

When Tiaki's transcript finished compiling, Shaula switched to reading it. It hit him in the feels to hear her whisper, "Sorry about this," before diving in. He kept forgetting how close Shaula must have been to Tiaki. Just because she didn't show it, didn't make it untrue. He looked over her shoulder, but she was reading much faster than he could. Trying to keep up made him dizzy.

"Just heading out for a bit of fresh air," he said.

Outside, Faolán stood with his back against the side of the engineering lab, his arms crossed. He gave Madigan, who was on guard in the middle of camp, a nod. The wolf trotted over and rested against his lower leg, settling down on the ground in a resting pose.

"Have you seen anything that might tell us who killed Tiaki and Camryn?" he asked Madigan.

"Negative, Faolán. I have seen movements in the forest, but when I look closer, there is nothing to observe. Such movements may indicate another presence nearby, but I have no solid proof to offer."

"Thanks. Keep an eye out and keep me posted." He sighed. "We've uncovered a lot. A clone sneaking about, probably camping on the wreck. Pressures and tensions within the crew. Several people who are acting shady. But why won't it come together as a full picture? Am I supposed to believe that a literal child killed two members of our crew and blew up a cargo bay? And now we can't even find her? Am I supposed to look at her presence as a red herring and see that one of the sketchy members of the team did it all? We haven't even found the murder weapon. I don't think I can do this. It's too hard."

"If you need any assistance, please ask."

Faolán looked down at the wolf leaning against him. He rubbed Madigan on the neck. "Thank you. I really appreciate it."

Movement caught his eye, and he saw Sandeep walking into the camp.

"Hey, is the salvage finished for the day?" he called out.

Sandeep walked over to stand beside Faolán. He wasn't wearing clothes borrowed from the androids anymore: he was in uniform, some backup set he'd salvaged with the correct orange engineering piping. Faolán felt underdressed in his casual clothes.

"The others are still going for a bit more. I just wanted to have a word before the others got here. Do you have a minute?"

"Yeah. Shaula's reading Tiaki's memory transcript at the moment, but she reads faster than I can, so I'm at a loose end."

"Ok." Sandeep shifted on his feet. He looked down in interest at Madigan, but said nothing about him.

Faolán felt a jolt of nervousness, realising what this might be about. "Hey, man, is this about what we walked in on yesterday? Because if so, I'm so sorry. That must've been so embarrassing."

"Oh. Oh! No, I wasn't really... but, um, thanks. That was rather awkward."

"If it helps any, you looked super hot railing her like that."

Sandeep flushed a deep maroon colour. "It doesn't really help all that much, but, uh, thanks?"

"Just a letting off steam thing, or something that's been going on a while? Wait, it's none of my business. You don't have to answer that."

Sandeep cleared his throat. "No, uh, yes, uh. It's not new. We've been keeping it on the lowdown."

"Sure. Yep, super lowdown. I hadn't even heard rumours. But congrats."

"Thanks."

They stood awkwardly side by side, Faolán watching the scudding low clouds. "Uh, if that wasn't what you were here to talk about... what did you want to say?"

Sandeep looked at him out of the corner of his eye. "Well, I noticed that you gave Shaula a lot of leeway today. Let her go off on her own?"

Faolán rubbed the back of his neck. "Guess I did."

"Are you OK?"

"What do you mean?"

"Well, Shaula has a reputation for being difficult to get along with, for getting on people's bad sides. And you've had your own run-ins with her before. She's not pressuring you, is she? It occurred to me we've left you with her pretty much 24/7 since the murder. You work with her, you share a cabin with her..."

Faolán felt his face going red, despite his efforts. Sandeep's eyes widened as he noticed.

"Oh. OH." He looked away. "Wait, really? But she doesn't seem affectionate or caring towards you, nothing like Altair is with Marcie, so the point stands: are you OK?"

"I'm fine, you great big mother hen, you." He sighed. "Look, at the risk of being TMI, I find being told what to do by women is comforting, like. Homey, even. So, no, I'm not upset when Shaula is terse with me. I'm just, like, 'Please, step on me more.'"

He looked over at Sandeep and saw a scandalised look on the other man's face.

"She's really thoughtful, actually."

"Are you sure?"

"She took the time to add some special programming to Madigan to make him more accessible for me."

"Uh, huh?"

"And she helped me with some stuff she didn't have to."

"Sure. But that's just normal."

Normal for Sandeep, maybe. But he was kinder than most.

"Everything is under control, Sandeep. Honest."

Sandeep sighed and stood upright. "I hope so. But let me know if you need help with anything. I won't tell anyone anything about... anything."

"Thanks. This wasn't a secret I was intending to let slip so soon."

"Yeah. I can sympathise."

They both winced.

Sandeep shook his head. "First Marcie, now you. Don't get me wrong: I see the androids as people. Even so, you've both kind of jumped right in without worrying about the consequences. I worry about you foolhardy types, I really do."

"You didn't jump right in with Ife?"

"No. We thought about it for a while. Workplace romances are risky. So we stayed friends for a long time. Thought about it. Visited each other at home on shore leave a few times. We only went with it when we were sure we wanted it enough to risk the consequences."

"I don't have enough forward planning capacity for that." He slapped Sandeep on the shoulder. "Come on. If the others will be back soon, we could at least get dinner started, right?" He was looking forward to the movement, the controlled chaos of the kitchen.

As ever since arriving on 227C, it wasn't the most enjoyable cooking experience. There weren't many ingredients to work with. But he had a few mushrooms to sauté, courtesy of Gagnon, and he managed to make something a bit more interesting with the long-life bread mix by mixing in dried garlic, rolling it into balls, drenching it in oil, and baking the bread balls in an oven dish. He hoped he'd end up with a pull-apart bread that would be perfect for dipping in the mystery freeze-dried stew of the day.

But was he ever looking forward to getting better food production online. Tasty food was so important to him. It was the hardest part of being in the Orion Navy: the lacklustre food. He'd learned to lean into the tastiness of a well-grown cherry tomato. But whenever he was on shore leave, he made himself all his favourite foods to boost up his brain chemistry for the next deployment.

Eventually, the others returned to camp. He got them set up around a campfire, eating their meal and marvelling at how the bread 'just tastes better like this; how did you do it?' Which was right flattering. Then he went into the engineering lab. "Shaula, I know you don't like to socialise of an evening, but could you come out so we can report our findings to Ife?"

"That sounds reasonable."

She put her tablet away and followed him to the fire.

"Hey boss," said Faolán. "We have some progress to report. You want to hear it here or in private?"

Ife glanced up at him, then tried to pass her bowl off to Sandeep, but he pushed it back into her hands. "You can take a few minutes to finish your meal, my dear. You too, Faolán. You cooked, but you haven't eaten yet."

Damn. He was right. Faolán had somehow forgotten to feed himself. "Fine, fine." He went into the cruiser and took a few of the bread bites, dipping them straight in the pot and eating them over the counter as quick as he could. Not bad. No wonder people were complimenting him. Not that he deserved it. It didn't take a genius to figure out you could make things taste better with garlic, salt, and fat.

When he went back out to the fire, Ife stood and motioned for him and Shaula to follow her to the engineering lab.

"May we have Naos's involvement too?" asked Shaula.

Ife paused a moment, considering, then asked Naos to join them. The medical android followed, her arms crossed.

"What have you got for me?" asked Ife when the door was closed behind them.

"We've got two things," he said. "Three, really. The scene examination of the explosion site is a bust, other than the DNA sample. That's number one. There's no hint of an incendiary device. I mean, obviously there must have been one, but we found no shrapnel. It self-immolated."

"I came to the same conclusion myself today," said Ife. "What's number two?"

"Shaula has got a clean transcript off Tiaki's brain."

They all looked at Shaula. "Anything?" asked Ife.

"Not yet, but the transcript is immense. I have read over his last week and found nothing yet. But I will read further for clues. The entire transcript from the moment the *Sunda Tiger* arrived will be of interest."

"OK. Keep on it. And number three?"

Faolán shifted on his feet and met Shaula's eyes. She, too, was looking at him, waiting for his initiative. She did that a lot, surprisingly. Faolán was beginning to understand what she had relied on Tiaki for, all the smoothing of social interactions. He felt an upwelling of pride that he was in a place to take over those functions for her in this time of need.

"We have a confession to make, boss," he started.

Ife frowned. "OK. Tell me about it."

Faolán crossed his arms and leaned back against the cupboard behind him. "I had a niggling feeling, like. I just thought something seemed off, that Dr Rebecca Neale couldn't be skulking about. She's in her 70s, for Chrissake."

"So, what's your confession?"

"We took a bioassay unit from the landing party storage cupboards and ran the sample ourselves, looking for wider data."

Naos stirred. "There is no need to do such a thing. The unit I ran the sample on is a state-of-the-art unit, with far more capabilities than any small field bioassay unit."

"I acknowledge that, Naos," said Shaula. "However, we wanted to run a wider analysis than simple DNA identification."

"DNA identification is the gold standard and has been for hundreds of years."

"About that..." said Faolán.

Ife was pinching the bridge of her nose. "I gave you both an order not to take extraneous equipment. I'm pissed that you disobeyed me. You'd better have found something worthwhile."

Faolán looked at Shaula. This was her wheelhouse. He wasn't good enough at technical stuff for this.

"While the DNA result matched Dr Rebecca Neale—"

"—Naturally," interjected Naos. "I did say so."

"—Further analysis," continued Shaula, glaring at Naos, "indicated that the individual who bled in the cargo bay had long telomeres on her chromosomes."

"In layperson's language?" prompted Ife.

"Telomeres begin long in infancy, and shorten over the course of an individual's life, because of copy errors and degradation. The bioassay estimates the individual's age range as being between 12 and 16 years."

"Impossible," scoffed Naos. "The DNA was that of—"

"I did not say it was not Rebecca Neale. I said it was a *young* Rebecca Neale. Our working hypothesis is that we are dealing with a young clone of the doctor."

"This is a preposterous idea. How could there have been a human child living on 227C who we were unaware of?"

Faolán cleared his throat, afraid that he would get his head bit off, but Shaula needed backup against the equally grumpy Naos. "You didn't know that your memories were being tampered with. Wouldn't it be easy, given the circumstances, for any evidence you saw to be wiped from your mind?"

"But why would there even be a clone? It makes no sense."

"Only because we do not know Dr Neale's motivations," said Shaula.

Faolán looked at Ife to see how she was taking the information. She looked thoughtful and disturbed. "If a child is behind this—"

The door opened and Madigan trotted inside. "Faolán, I am unable to locate Simons in the camp," he said, interrupting Ife.

"What? Since when?" asked Faolán.

Before the wolf could answer, the door to the engineering lab bumped open and Vega lurched inside.

"Pardon the intrusion," he said. "But this information is important."

Ife stepped forward. "Is this about Simons? Do you know where he is?"

"Yes. My familiar just reported to me that Simons has snuck away from the camp and to the wreck of the *Sunda Tiger.*"

Faolán squatted by Madigan and thought back, realising that Simons hadn't been there for dinner. How had he not noticed? "Fuck."

Ife ignored his expletive. "What's he doing? Did your familiar see?"

"Yes. It appears he is repairing some communications equipment and attempting to send a signal to an unknown person."

"Fuck," said Ife, apparently not above uttering expletives of her own. "We need to stop him, people. He might be in contact with Dr Neale. This might all be his doing."

CHAPTER 23

Shaula followed the others around the wreck to the far side. They had to scramble up the churned slope of the moraine formed by the crash, over the lip of dirt, to the edge of the forest beyond. The light was fading fast, and the forest was a dim collection of shifting shapes. Shaula turned on the glow of her eyes, as did Naos and Vega.

"Over there," said Vega, keeping his voice low. He was pointing to a round object with several protrusions adhered to the hull. A machine of some kind. The shape looked familiar. After a moment, she placed the object as one the androids had manufactured for the humans.

"That's the comms array," said Sandeep, who Ife had rounded up to join their little group as they left the camp. "The one Marcie nearly got herself killed installing."

"I remember," said Faolán, shuddering.

Shaula had heard the unpleasant tale from Marcie.

Simons was standing on a crate balanced on a pile of dirt, bringing himself in reach of the comms array, which dangled over the churned ground.

"Would the array even be usable at the moment?" asked Shaula. "I was asked early on if I could make a replica. But it is not the array that is the key at this time: it is the power source. We have nothing in the settlement that could substitute for the matter/antimatter Weft Skip drive." The comms array took a lot of power to communicate through the Weft, and that power had come from the now-destroyed engines.

"He can't power it. I'm sure," said Ife.

They walked in a line in the shadow of the wreck towards Simons. Was this the explanation for all the strangeness over the past week? For the murder of her long-time colleague?

No, thought Shaula. This was a distraction. She knew it. But they had to figure out what Simons was doing before they could continue, just in case.

Simons had his back to them. He was trying to attach something large and bulky to the comms array by cable, and failing if his stream of expletives was any indication.

"What is that?" asked Shaula in a low voice.

"It looks like a runabout engine," said Chaudhary. "Nice try, I suppose, but I doubt it'll give the array the boost it needs to get a signal to the Weft beacon."

"What if he is not trying to signal that far?" asked Vega. "What if he is contacting an unknown entity on the surface?"

Vega was right. The chances were slim, but they needed to consider the possibility that Simons was trying to contact Dr Neale.

Kikelomo stopped walking. "Stop what you're doing, Simons," she called out.

Simons startled and yelped, dropping the tool and cable he was holding. He tried to whip around on the box, but overbalanced. He cried out as he tumbled off the box behind-first into the dirt.

"Jesus Fucking Christ, why would you startle someone balanced on a box?" He winced as he rolled to one side and rubbed his tailbone.

"Sorry," said Kikelomo, but she smiled as she said it, negating her apology. "Did you break your arse?"

Simons glared at Kikelomo. "Fuck you."

Faolán walked ahead of them to Simons, who looked up at him warily. It was that wary look that made Shaula see Faolán in a light that she had not yet. Because he was so ebullient, it had never occurred to her to equate his role amongst the *Sunda Tiger* crew as similar to Vega's, but he was indeed security, and it now showed.

"Do you need medical attention?" asked Faolán. "We've got Naos here if you do."

"No. Nothing broken except my dignity."

"Good." Faolán then took hold of the man's arm and hefted him to his feet. "Now, what are you up to?"

Simons put his hands on his hips. "What everyone else should be doing, if they had their priorities straight!"

"Uh, huh. Who were you trying to contact?"

Simons tried to brush past Faolán, who, with a flash of speed, twisted the larger man's arm up behind his back and then pinned him against the curved hull of the ship. Madigan stalked forward and growled, and Simons whimpered at the sound.

"I asked who you were trying to contact," said Faolán.

"Ow, fuck off!"

Shaula was impressed. She'd had no idea Faolán had such capabilities.

Kikelomo leaned against the hull within Simons' curtailed view. "Answer the question, Simons. Because at the moment, you look suspicious as all hell, and if you don't, you might just get two murders and an explosion pinned on you."

"You wouldn't dare!"

"As suspicious as you are, you're at the top of the list," said Faolán. "Gotta say."

The blonde man's face twisted. "All right! All right! Just let go of my arm!"

Faolán let him go and stepped away.

Simons took a moment to shake out his shoulder while eyeing Madigan warily. Then he perched on the box he'd been standing on, the light set up for his work shining on his face. "I need comms up, OK? I've got to try, even if it's a long shot."

"Why?" asked Kikelomo. "Why you in particular?"

Simons flinched and looked down at his feet. He still held onto his wrist with the other hand. "Because someone is waiting to hear from me about something, and if they don't get word, they're going to do something bad."

"Lots of somethings there. What are you on about?"

Simons glared up at Kikelomo. "It's my dad, OK? They have him. He cut a deal; it went sour. I was supposed to feed them some information to buy him out. If I don't check in, they're going to assume I backed out, and my dad won't be safe."

Shaula did not like this development. She stepped up to Faolán's side. "The information these people want: is it about the colony?"

Simons started when she asked a question. "Y-yeah. I was supposed to tell them what kind of research colony 227C is, because it wasn't on the books. They want to know what tech's here."

"Of all the fecking..." said Faolán, running a hand over his face. "It's space pirates. You were trying to contact space pirates to tell them what's here to steal."

"Anything else?" asked Kikelomo.

"What do you mean?"

"There's more. You told us too easily, so there must be more."

Simons glanced around. Vega, too, walked closer and loomed over the man, who flinched away from him. Altair had once scared this man a great deal. Perhaps Vega's resemblance to Altair was working in their favour.

Simons sighed and put his face in his hands. "OK, so don't lose your cool. But my last communication from them made it clear my dad was being more of an asshole than usual, and so they asked for something else too."

"What?"

"...Porn. The guy my dad had dealings with has a side hustle in voyeuristic porn, apparently."

Kikelomo's hands curled into fists, and then she uncurled them again, with effort. "The recording of Marcie." Chaudhary came up and put his hand on her shoulder.

"I thought that since Marcie had been dumped, you and her might hook up, and that might sell well," he said to Kikelomo. "Girls in uniform are popular at the moment. Uh, apparently. I didn't know you and Sandeep were already banging."

As horrified by his disregard of his work colleagues' privacy as Shaula was, she had other concerns she had to pursue. "Did Tiaki discover you trying to send this communication?" she asked.

Simons gaped at her. "What? No! I had nothing to do with that, I swear! I'm not stupid enough to kill our head doctor when we're marooned out here! I hadn't even started on the comms yet when they were killed. All I'd done was scoped out the best route between the camp and the wreck. So what would they have uncovered?"

"Head human doctor," added Naos unhelpfully.

"When did you start?" asked Faolán, his voice sounding very casual, as if it were an idle question.

"After we started the salvage. I've tried a few things. Why are you asking? You'd know all this already. You've had your wolf stalking me."

Shaula frowned.

"What are you talking about?" asked Faolán.

"Your wolf android thing. It's been following me around."

Faolán looked at Shaula, and he too had a frown on his face. "Madigan hasn't been following you," said Faolán. "He's been with me or watching the camp or the cargo bay during the day, and charging at night."

"I installed no protocols that would have Madigan following you," added Shaula. Charm, yes, but Madigan, no.

"I've seen the footprints, and heard growls in the ship at night," said Simons. "You can't fool me."

Shaula glared at the man. What were these spurious claims? "No. That is incorrect."

"You've heard growls?" asked Faolán.

"Yeah. That's your wolf, right?" Simons looked around at the group. "If it's not the wolf, what else could it be?"

"You heard these growls on the ship?" asked Shaula.

"Yeah."

Shaula pulled on Faolán's sleeve and dragged him away from the group towards the tree line. "The paw prints in the cargo bay," she whispered to him in the dark under the trees.

"We were wrong. Those weren't Madigan's prints." He bit his lip and scanned the darkness as if looking for whatever had been watching Simons.

"I do not know of any other animal familiar with paws that size," said Shaula. "And large mammals were not a part of the terraformation of 227C."

Faolán gave her a long look. She thought she could read his thoughts: this was an important clue.

Kikelomo approached them. "Do you have any more questions for Simons about anything to do with the murder investigation?" she asked them.

"Nah," said Faolán. "We got what we needed out of that."

"You think he's the murderer?"

"I do not," said Shaula. "Though he is not definitively ruled out. He seems too self-centred to have been thinking of anything but his own narrow goal. Instead, I believe that this has all been a distraction from the murder investigation for us." Though it was a distraction that had given them another clue.

"OK. I'll ask Vega to escort Simons back to the cruiser and watch him there."

Shaula and Faolán stood side by side and watched as Vega led a protesting Simons away with Madigan following watchfully behind, and Kikelomo and Chaudhary started packing up the engineering supplies that Simons had set up by the comms array. Naos looked in their direction and gave them a long perusal, her silver eyes shining in the gloom, and her familiar Beaufort settled on her shoulder.

CHAPTER 24

When Faolán exited the ensuite in his pyjamas that evening, he found Shaula had folded the bottom bunk out into a double bed configuration. She had flipped the top most bunk out too, on which Madigan lay charging. Shaula herself was already in the bed under a blanket. She patted the bed next to her, inviting him in.

He stood and looked blankly for a long moment. She wanted to sleep beside him? Shaula did? He never would have guessed that she'd make an overture like this. Then, in a tired daze, he got into bed beside her. Her scorpion was charging on the arm at the foot of the bunk. It looked at him, but did not hiss.

He turned towards Shaula, who was lying on her back. "You all right?" he asked her.

"Yes. It has been an eventful day."

"Sure has. I think we made progress. Even if we did get yelled at."

She huffed. "We are still missing something of vital importance."

"Yeah. We'll get there, though." He debated whether he should ask her about her choice of sleeping arrangements. He decided he couldn't stand the wondering. "So..."

"Yes?"

"You wanted to sleep in the same bed?"

"I did." There was no hesitation in her answer.

"Why?"

"It is easier to speak with you."

He grinned. "Right. Speaking of which: run through for me what we did today."

They spent a half hour reminiscing about the day, supposedly for the memory check, but also to go over the clues they had so far.

"I think this clone of Rebecca Neale that we assume is around has a familiar," said Shaula. "It is the most plausible explanation I can offer."

Faolán propped himself up on his elbow and looked down at her. She looked beautiful in the dim evening light, her forest green hair splayed on the pillow. "A large, dangerous familiar might be a good idea for a teenager who is being hidden away by an evil scientist."

"No one has seen this girl, though."

"We've suspected for a while that the person who sabotaged the *Tiger* had cloaking tech."

Shaula frowned. "If so, I need to figure out how to negate it. How can we investigate if this girl is the murderer if we cannot find her?"

Faolán yawned. "Sorry. But perhaps we can leave that problem for tomorrow?"

"Of course. My apologies. Is it all right if I charge here next to you? Or would you prefer that I return the beds to the original stacked configuration? What would help you sleep best?"

Faolán thought for a moment. He wasn't sure what it would be like when Shaula finished charging. Would she move? She was very strong; she could do him some damage. But on the other hand, he liked the idea of snuggling up to her. "Here is fine," he said. "But could you wake me when you finish charging, if you're going to stay in the bed? I know you won't move while charging, but you might after you finish. I just want to know when you're mobile again."

"Understood."

It often took Faolán a long time to quieten his brain down enough to sleep, especially when he was having trouble, but that night, he was so tired that he fell asleep within minutes. Some time later, in the wee small hours of the morning, he was roused by a hand gently shaking his shoulder. He rolled towards her and looked up at her looming over him, propped up on one elbow. The gentle golden light of her eyes lit the cabin. He ought to find eyes like that disconcerting, but he was already so used to the androids that he merely appreciated the light.

"Done?" he asked, vaguely aware of how sleep muffled his voice.

"Yes. Do you want me to go?"

In answer, he slung an arm over her waist. She lay down on her side, and he pressed his forehead to hers, and tangled their feet. His eyes started sliding shut again, but her movements as she tucked in closer to him kept him at the edge of awareness. She put an arm around him too, and it was so heavy he was instantly comforted.

Without thinking about it, he sleepily kissed her. She soon reciprocated, and they kissed over and over in the dark, Faolán hovering on the edge of sleep. They tangled their legs more fully, and he reached down and grabbed a handful of her arse, tugging her towards him.

"You are aroused," she said.

"Hmmm."

"You are also half asleep. Do you consent to this?"

"I love sleepy sex," he muttered.

She took charge of things, easing his clothes out of the way, slinging her leg over his hip, guiding him into her. They rocked together, still on their sides. Shaula nibbled on his ear, and he moaned into her neck. For a long, hazy time, that was enough, but as they grew closer and needed more, Shaula rolled onto him, pushing him onto his back. She sat astride him and took off the shirt she was wearing as nightwear. He ran his hands up her stomach and over her breasts as she rode him, her hips rolling just right to drive him higher. The bunk creaked, and he couldn't help but moan and gasp.

From there, it didn't take long. He came with a deep grunt, and she also stiffened and moaned. He was too sleepy to tell if it was one of her real ones or a programmed orgasm. When she climbed off him, his eyes drifted shut again. But soon she returned with a cloth for him to clean himself up.

Then she was back in the bed, and they snuggled under the blanket, curled together once more.

"This also comforts me," she breathed into his ear.

"Cuddles?"

"Company in the night."

He held her hand and drifted off to sleep again.

Sometime later, sunlight peeked around the edge of the curtain and shone in his eyes. He winced and rolled over. He was alone in the bed. Naked.

Faolán rubbed the sleep out of his eyes and sat up. His clothes were strewn on the floor. The door to the lab was open a gap, and he could see Shaula, already dressed for the day in a grey shirt and slacks, at the bench hard at work. He checked his tablet: he hadn't slept in. She was just working early.

With dawning discomfort, Faolán realised that the sex they'd had during the night, while most enjoyable, may have been heard by people in the other vehicles. He'd been so sleepy that he'd forgotten to keep it down. His moans and the creaking bunk had probably been loud. He covered his eyes with his hand for a moment and chided his own idiocy. But what was done was done. He could only hope that anyone who had heard would be too polite, or too uncomfortable, to say anything about it. After all, most people were unlikely to say, "Hey, was that you I heard fucking?"

He was just going to put it down to another memory glitch. All in all, his ADHD was manifesting differently than it had when he was younger. He was having more 'brain farts', so to speak, but his sleep schedule and his temper were a lot better than they were before he was first medicated. Was the change because he was older? Because the meds hadn't worn out after all and he was just stressed? Because back then he'd been putting things down to his ADHD that were actually just him being an immature idiot? He didn't know. He couldn't know.

Whatever the truth, he had to stop dwelling on it, because if he did he'd just get incandescently angry about the loss of the med unit again and then he really would lose control of his temper.

He was nice and cosy where he was, and under any other circumstances he might have stayed there, pushing his get up time to the limit. But the thought of anyone else in the salvage team catching him naked and rumpled in bed motivated him to get moving. He padded to the ensuite, still naked, to have a quick shower. Shaula was still at the work bench when he emerged, groomed and dressed. She looked up at him. "Good morning."

It occurred to him that even a few days ago, she wouldn't have looked up from her work as he approached. She was changing right before his eyes.

He couldn't help but grin at her. "Top of the morning to you." Of all the cheesy... what was he, a walking stereotype? But it just kind of felt like that sort of morning.

She quirked an eyebrow at him. "I was the top of the morning, yes."

He guffawed. For a moment, he thought she might not have understood why he laughed, and she might be offended. But a small smile played at the corner of her mouth. She understood. She'd cracked that joke intentionally.

He pointed at the tablet she had before her. "Any progress?"

"Little today. I have a lot of data to comb through."

"You want to go for a brisk morning walk? That always helps my brain get into the right shape for thinking. And we could talk on the way."

"Sure. Let us do that."

Madigan followed them out into the golden morning light. The air was chilly. Dew had collected on the grasses and weeds. Vega stood at the far edge of camp. He acknowledged them with a nod, but otherwise ignored them and continued standing on watch.

They walked together up the slope towards the forest, further away from the wreck than the murder site. Once they were beyond the tree line, Faolán asked, "Anything about the investigation you need to talk through?"

"The investigation of Tiaki's memories will take time. But I am most concerned about locating our visitor. I believe an engineering solution may be needed. Who do you think I should talk to about this problem?"

Faolán smiled. It was nice to be asked for his opinion, even if he wasn't helpful on a technical level. Most people didn't think to ask security officers their opinion.

"Sandeep," he said. "He's just as technically competent as Ife, but he doesn't have the leadership responsibility on his shoulders at the moment."

"Thank you. I will do so as soon as I can arrange it." She stopped walking and put her hands on her hips.

"Something else is up," he said, stopping beside her. "What is it?"

She looked into his eyes. "I accessed another hidden memory last night."

"During...?"

"No. After, when you went back to sleep in my arms. I remembered talking about engineering in my lab with an android I do not know. A female-shaped android with an orange epidermis who I called Enif."

"And you've never known an Enif?"

"Not that I recall."

"Or that you were allowed to remember."

She was quiet a moment, peering through the trees towards the wreck. "There are very few android engineers in the settlement. Too few. Have some been decommissioned over the years for some reason? Did I used to have more colleagues?"

Although he couldn't directly see the fear and horror on her face, he knew she must be experiencing them. He tugged her into a hug. She leaned her face into the crook of his neck.

"I know the murder investigation is important," she said. "But the memory issue is also very important. Why am I having memories now at random moments? Why did Altair have them after a much more specific trigger? Why can I not solve this problem?"

"Hey, it's OK." He rubbed her back. "You're at an extreme disadvantage solving this, because of all the meddling. It's no failure that you've had trouble." He kept rubbing her back in circles for a minute. "There must be a trigger for you," he mused. "What's it been so far? Me

241

falling asleep in your arms? Complimenting you? Me, uh, jizzing on your tits? Anything else?"

"I think perhaps... although I did not recognise it at the time, I had a vague memory of something purple when Gagnon made me angry."

"Purple?"

"Like I said, it was a vague memory."

Faolán frowned. "What if it's emotions?"

She lifted her head. "What?"

"Your enhancement. What if you have more emotions than the other androids? Stronger emotions? More detailed emotions? Something like that. It'd be super hard to detect, because you won't find, like, a stomach full of acid or whatever. And how would you go about measuring your experiences against the other androids if you're not networked?"

Shaula froze in that particular way the androids had when they were thinking real hard about something. He waited her out.

"But I am known as a less personable android than others," she said.

He gave a wry grin. "If you don't have a good grasp of your emotions, they can often start expressing as anger and antisocial behaviour, a desire to be alone. Maybe disrespect for authority. Believe me. I went through a lot of that when I was young and didn't yet have my ADHD diagnosis. I had to see a therapist for a while to get back on top of things. You being known as 'grumpy', but not being grumpy with me lately, is a pretty big clue that you've got some emotional baggage to deal with."

"I have been grumpy with you. Surely."

"Oh, early on. But that was my fault for calling you a 'cute wee elf.' But lately? Not so much."

"We have been working through any tensions in another manner."

He nuzzled his nose against hers, enjoying how he didn't have to lean down to do it. "Have we ever."

"Make me feel something," she said.

It was his turn to freeze. How could he do that? He was just Faolán, the jokester, the one who keeps people entertained, but who gets left behind when those entertained people move on. But that was not what he was to Shaula. She wasn't seeing what other people did. He wasn't sure yet what she *was* seeing, but it was surely not the same.

He gently held her cheeks and rubbed his thumbs over them. "I've always been uncomfortable around smart people, because they make me feel unintelligent when I'm near them. But as crazy smart as you are, you've never done that to me. You treat me like a colleague who just happens to have a different skill set than you. I appreciate the way you treat me so very, very much."

Her wide eyes blazed golden, and she looked at him, still as a statue, for a long moment. "Oh. Oh!" She grabbed his face in turn and planted a firm kiss on his lips. "You did it!" She let go of him and started hurrying back the way they'd come.

He followed. "You've remembered something?" he called out.

"Yes!" she called back over her shoulder. "And it is important! It might be the most important clue we have found so far!"

243

CHAPTER 25

Tiaki was on her work table again. He was laid out naked on his back. Shaula was glad she had closed his eyelids before putting him in the recharge cupboard several days earlier. The lack of light in his eyes would have been distressing.

The salvage crew was already aboard the wreck for the final day of the salvage, and Faolán had gone over to the cruiser to have a quick morning meal. Only Madigan was with her in the engineering lab. The great grey wolf sat in a resting pose in the cabin, watching her through the open doorway.

Shaula rested her elbows on the bench near Tiaki's head and leaned down near his ear. His yellow skin was near blinding under the bright examination light. "You would never believe it, old friend, but I have ended up with a similar inclination as you did." She knew he could not hear her, but it eased her mind to say the words to the one who she would have shared them with, if she had been given the time. "Yes, me: antisocial Shaula. There is a certain human who I am getting along with much better than I ever would have guessed. If you experienced anything like I have over the last few days with your Dr McArthur, then I am glad your final days were happy ones."

She stood straight and walked further down the table. She pulled her magnifying glass down over her eye, picked up several tools from a tray, and let Charm scamper up her arm into her hair, where it could assist her. "Pardon the intrusion, my friend."

She worked carefully, peeling Tiaki's silicone skin away at the seam in his groin. She worked around a join across his abdomen until she could peel back a swathe and expose the workings within.

Tiaki's enhancement had never been on record. Or rather, she had not been aware of it being on record. It seemed the entire engineering team's enhancements had been wiped from her memory at some point, because she had not been aware of her own, and neither was she aware of Bellatrix's. Which was preposterous, because she was the one who fixed them. Was the knowledge wiped every time she had them on her table? Though, come to think of it, had she ever needed to fix Bellatrix? And she did not fix herself, of course.

From what she had remembered earlier, she had once been aware of Tiaki's enhancement. Because what she remembered had been herself and the missing orange android Enif taking Tiaki, and each other, to bed, and Tiaki visibly enjoying the experience in a way that was similar to Altair's description of his own experiences. Shaula had not remembered she and Tiaki had ever experimented in such a way. She had only known him as her friend, not as a former lover.

So much had been taken from them over the years, unbeknownst to them.

It did not take long for her to confirm that Tiaki had the same enhancement that Altair did. Which meant that the murder motive was now clear. Tiaki had remembered something in Camryn McArthur's embrace, and told that thing to his paramour, and then they had both been murdered to cover it up.

The murder was not about the argument, or tempers flaring, or the salvage. It was about the mysteries of 227C. About Dr Rebecca Neale.

She made Tiaki whole again, or as whole as she could. Then she returned to the transcript of his memories. She needed to read the rest of the transcript, starting from the beginning, not just the most recent weeks.

Faolán returned as she was examining the earliest records in Tiaki's database. "How are you going?" he asked.

"I have some good news and some bad news," she said. "The good news is that I have verified Tiaki had the same enhancement that Altair has, which shows the murder motive was to cover up a memory he retrieved."

He grinned at her and gripped her shoulder. "That's great! I knew you could do it!"

"The bad news is that the memory he retrieved does not appear to be from before the Event Horizon. There is nothing in his memories from before that same moment we all awoke."

"Meaning?"

"I will still have to trawl through nearly 30 years of memories to find whatever he remembered. It will take a while before we learn what he was killed to hide."

"Feck." Faolán sighed and crossed his arms. "What did you remember that led to this breakthrough?"

"...I am not sure if you would want to know."

"Try me."

Shaula looked again at Tiaki's form. "I remembered having sex with Tiaki. I remembered how it was for him." She looked closely for Faolán's reaction.

He gave a slow nod. "I figured it was something like that."

"Does it bother you?"

"What, that you've been with other people before me? Of course not. I wasn't an untouched virgin until you had me, either. We all have a history."

"Indeed. But I had not been aware of my own history."

"You had no idea?"

"None."

Faolán leaned against the bench. "Maybe he'd uncovered memories before, and you all got wiped. This time it escalated to murder because Camryn's memories couldn't be wiped." Then his eyes went wide. "Oh no, just a moment." He ran out of the engineering lab. Shaula watched him run into the medical lab and then emerge a moment later, one of the messenger pigeons on his arm. He was speaking rapidly to it, and then he gave a nod. The pigeon took off from his arm and sped away into the cloudy sky.

He returned to the engineering lab, his face flushed. "Sorry about that," he said, his voice breathless. "I just sent a message to the settlement warning them that Marcie and Altair may be in danger."

Of course. He was right. She had not seen it, but the murder motive that was emerging suggested they too might be in danger.

"There have been no attempts on their life yet," she said. "Other than Simons' attempts, of course."

"Because there was too much scrutiny on them, maybe? And because Altair's memories all seem to have been before you all woke up, and maybe the most important bit is where Neale is now, not what she did then? But I'd still feel better if I warned them to take care."

"Of course. Why did you use a pigeon, and not Madigan?"

"Because if there is another big, unfriendly familiar around, we'll need Madigan here for protection."

Shaula nodded. Though she was as strong as Madigan. Faolán was just as protected in her presence as he was in the wolf's.

"We ought to tell Kikelomo about our discovery," she said.

"Too right." He walked over to Madigan. "Would you please find Lieutenant Commander Kikelomo and ask her to come here? Tell her we've had a breakthrough we need to report."

"Understood," said Madigan as he stood and trotted to the door of the lab.

Shaula went to stand by Tiaki's side again. Now that she had a better idea of what had happened to Tiaki, his loss felt more real. With her uncovered memories, she knew that his loss to her had been greater than she had known. She had lost someone who had been her friend for many years, but also her lover.

And also at some point, someone she had been made to torture. How was it all linked? What had happened to them in the past?

She would uncover what had happened. But Tiaki would never know.

A tight feeling gripped her throat tubes, the ones that let her replicate human speech better than microphone-based voices in earlier generations of androids. She felt as if her neck were squeezing, and she could not relax. Her eyes prickled. She rubbed at them, but found no tears. Just the sensation of where they should be. The feeling of... the feeling of...

...running a test on the operational enhancement of a pink-skinned android. Dr Neale is hovering nearby. She is more attentive of this enhancement than any other. The distended belly. The rapid throb of a heartbeat. The synth-blood canister

that must be changed on the correct schedule to keep the placenta oxygenated.

Dr Neale hands a device to her with shaking hands. She is frail. Her time is short.

"Wipe your memories," she says.

Shaula takes the device. Finds her own name on the list. She runs the preprogrammed routine and walks out of the building...

...Out of...

...

...Why am I in the forest behind the android repair centre? Of course, I went for a walk...

"Shaula! Are you OK?"

She was kneeling on the ground beside the workbench, her face in her hands. Faolán knelt beside her, a hand on her shoulder. His face was worried, his eyes scanning her face for any sign of what she was feeling.

"I remembered something terrible," she said.

"Do you want to talk about it?" he asked in a gentle voice.

"I remember being made to do an engineering check on one of our community whose enhancement is an artificial uterus, like the ones used to raise foetuses outside a human womb. She was pregnant, a surrogate carrier."

"How is that terrible?"

"That android was Capella, the one who we thought ran out of power and got lost in the forest for more than a year about 16 years ago."

Dawning comprehension lit Faolán's face. "So you've remembered where the clone came from. Isn't that great? It's a major clue!"

"It is, but..."

"But?"

"Faolán, Dr Neale was sick. Frail. She made me wipe my own memories. My own memories, Faolán! She ordered me to press a button on a device, and I did it. I was fully, 100% under her control."

Various thoughts chased themselves across his face. "That's awful." He hugged her. "But also... A device... Does that mean, if we find it, you'll be able to unlock everyone's memories? Or at least stop the memory wipes?"

Shaula sat back on her heels. She thought of what she had seen of the device in her memory. Could it be? The answer to how they kept being reprogrammed... was a device they could find? A tablet? Could it really be that easy? "It could be," she said.

Faolán stood and cheered, and did a little dance. "We're getting there, Shaula! We'll have this all sorted out soon."

Shaula looked up at Faolán. She wanted to join him in his display of joy. She really did. But there was a buzzing, a sharp feeing right between her eyes. Her vision blurred, and she could not see him clearly any more.

Not again, she thought. *Not now. Not while he's here. I need to hold on! I need to—*

CHAPTER 26

He knew she'd make a breakthrough! She was always so on top of things.

"We can do this, Shaula. We can solve the murder and the memory problem." He held her face in his hands and stroked her cheeks with his thumbs. Her face...

She was frozen again. It wasn't the look of her thinking hard. Was she having another memory already?

"Shaula?"

Her hand shot out and grabbed him by the throat. He choked, grabbed her arm.

She stood, and he had no choice but to go with her.

Faolán was certain that, in a split-second, Shaula had become not-Shaula. This wasn't her who had him by the throat. This was pure over-ridden programming in an android body.

She could kill me in moments.

It was the self-defence training that saved his life. Instead of fighting as she pushed him towards a cabinet, he went floppy and boneless. Not expecting the change, not-Shaula's grip wasn't balanced right to hold him as he tilted his chin and slithered out of her hand. He dropped into a backwards roll and, still in motion, toppled sideways and around the corner of the work-table.

He reached blindly for the tray of tools she'd had on the edge beside Tiaki's form. He grabbed it on the third try, green flashing in his peripheral vision. Tools scattered everywhere as he brought it up just in time. The scalpel she tried to stab into his neck clanged against the tray, the blade snapping and pinging off. He had a moment to marvel at the dent she'd made in the steel tray, and then he flung it at her face.

Fourth drawer down, fourth drawer down... the mantra sang through his honed thoughts. She'd told him where the restraints were under different conditions. Had she suspected he'd need to know?

He checked the fourth drawer beside him, but he had the wrong one. It was full of bottles of silicone dye. He started crawling to the drawers at the other end. But then a hand grabbed his ankle. She had him again.

He kicked once, twice. "Wake up, Shaula! Please!"

No one was here but them. Not even Madigan. He pulled, but couldn't move away at all.

She was so strong. So heavy. He was like a rag doll in her hands.

Not-Shaula picked up another scalpel with her free hand. That was it. He was done for.

Then the door opened and Ife stepped in, Madigan on her heels. She took a mere moment to assess the situation, then grabbed a tool off her belt.

Ife flung herself on top of not-Shaula and plunged a screwdriver into her neck. Shaula stopped moving and collapsed to her stomach. There was still a glow in her eyes, unlike Tiaki. But otherwise, it was if she was dead.

Faolán panted as he watched Ife sit up and brush herself off. "Did you kill her?" he asked. His voice was wobbling. "Please tell me you didn't kill her."

"Faolán, she was trying to kill *you*."

He shook his head. "It wasn't her. She was taken over. She would never—"

"Faolán, get a grip. It must have been her. I can't believe we put the murderer in charge of the murder investigation. Did you uncover something that implicated her?" Ife started prising Shaula's fingers off Faolán's ankle, but he just sat there, unable to help.

"No, no, that wasn't it. We have evidence, but nothing that implicates Shaula. Dr Neale or her clone, one of them will have a device that can control the androids and wipe their memories. It wasn't Shaula! It was just her body! Now please tell me, *is she dead?!*"

Ife freed his ankle, then gave him a long look. "No. I just incapacitated her. Interrupted her synth-synapses. It's the same thing that Marcie said Simons did to Altair. But if she's dangerous, we should turn her off for good."

"I can't listen to this." Faolán crawled towards the drawers he'd been aiming for earlier and found some steel clip ties. He then went back to Shaula and put one tie around her ankles. He hefted her onto her side and brought her wrists together in front of her so he could clip her wrists too.

"What are you doing?" asked Ife. She was on her feet, tidying the chaos in the lab with shaking hands.

"Restraining her as a backup."

"Why? We're not turning her back on."

"Yes, we are. I'm 95% sure she'd be back to normal when she wakes up. These ties are just in case she isn't."

"It's too much of a risk, Faolán."

"No, it isn't."

Ife stopped and put her hand on his shoulder. "Listen. I know you've got your feelings all caught up in this.

Sandeep let slip about what's going on. And I'm so sorry you're going through this. But she *tried to kill you.*"

He glared at her. "No. *Rebecca Neale* tried to kill me. And frame Shaula."

Madigan walked back into the lab. Until that moment, Faolán hadn't even noticed the wolf had left. Naos followed him in. She also assessed the situation within moments. "Do you require medical attention?" she asked him.

"No. I'm perfectly fine." That wasn't quite true: he bet he had bruises forming. But he didn't care.

"It seems you have found the culprit. I am not surprised. I imagine she felt jealousy over Tiaki's relationship with Dr McArthur. This is why hurrying into relationships is unwise."

"It *wasn't her!*"

Naos looked at him in silence for a moment. "Evidence suggests otherwise."

"Just let us explain ourselves!"

"I will listen to your story, Faolán, honest," said Ife. "But Shaula stays off, for all of our safety."

They weren't listening. They'd made up their minds, and they wouldn't see any other scenario. He had to take matters into his own hands. He didn't think, he just moved.

"Faolán, no!" cried Ife as he reached down and yanked the screwdriver out of Shaula's neck.

CHAPTER 27

have to stop.

I have to regain control.

I have to...

ANDROID 26548 DELETED MEMORY 8907

Her bronze hands cup a synthetic stomach and lift it out of the chest cavity of an android that lay on her workbench. There is acid damage inside the android. Swathes of bright green skin lie to one side.

The stomach failed. Dr Neale designed a new version, but her hands are too unsteady to install it.

The bronze-skinned android does as she was bid and replaces damaged parts before installing the new stomach...

ANDROID 26548 DELETED MEMORY 10943

She has been told to turn off Izar. The device is in her hands. She watches until Izar is out of the line of sight of other androids, then presses the button. Dr Neale's preprogrammed routine triggers, and Izar stills.

The bronze android carries the pale grey Izar to her lab and disassembles her. Reusable parts get sorted back into the cupboards. The skin gets shredded for processing.

The brain goes to the incinerator.

The bronze android pauses a moment. She should feel...

...buzzing in her mind...

...the bronze android presses the button on the device and hands it to the white cat familiar that waits patiently. She turns away as all goes dim...

ANDROID 26548 DELETED MEMORY 11977

Pink-skinned Capella lies on the examination table. They are not in the normal lab. They are in a windowless lab with pale green walls. Dr Neale is observing from her wheelchair as she verifies Capella's artificial womb is operational.

Then dark blue Naos, her face as blank as the bronze android feels, inserts the embryo into Capella...

ANDROID 26548 DELETED MEMORY 12035

Feeding swathes of orange skin into the shredder.

Oh, my beautiful Enif. My dear...

...buzzing in her mind.

Feeding swathes of orange skin into the shredder.

ANDROID 26548 DELETED MEMORY 12061

Two examination tables. On one, the frail body of Dr Neale. She smells of human faecal matter and blood. The adult diaper she wears to catch what her cancer-ridden intestines can no longer control needs changing.

On the other table, a beautiful brand new purple body with tumbling waves of hair. All enhancements that have been well tested and verified have been added to the body.

This is the first major test of the research centre's ultimate aim.

The bronze-skinned android checks and rechecks the brain. The carefully mapped neural pathways have been faithfully recreated by Dr Neale. This is her life's work, and it shows. This brain is the pinnacle of android research to date.

"Ready for final transfer, Dr Neale."

"Do it," gasps the elderly woman. "For my children," she mutters under her breath.

The bronze android takes the final reading and inputs the last changes.

"Turn her on," says Dr Neale.

The bronze android activates the purple one with the device in her hands. The other android wakes up. She sits up on the table, runs her hands over her face, touches her hair, feels her own breasts, her waist. She laughs and looks over at Dr Neale on the other table. "I didn't realise I looked so old and frail."

"Of course I do," says Dr Neale. "Why do you think we're doing this ahead of schedule? Now, tell me, what did Aunty Helen give you for your seventh birthday?"

"She forgot to get me a present that year because cousin Matthew was in the hospital with a broken leg..."

ANDROID 26548 DELETED MEMORY 13098

The bronze android checks on the recovery of Capella's artificial womb. The nanofibrils are retracting on schedule, and the distension of her abdomen will be imperceptible in a week's time.

On the other side of the room, Dr Neale sits in an armchair feeding the tiny baby milk formula from a bottle. She coos at the tiny human cradled in her purple arms...

ANDROID 26548 DELETED MEMORY 14673

The green-skinned android attaches the new device to the large golden lion familiar before her and switches it on. The lion seems to disappear, but is still perceptible to touch. She uses the control device to turn the cloaking device off, and the lion reappears.

This cloaking device will keep young Bex safe.

Wait. Who is Bex?

...

Wait.

WHO IS BEX?

Bex.

I'm looking for her right now.

She's so young, even now.

...

Now.

When is now?

What did I—

Faolán.

Her eyes switched back on. She was lying on her side, and kneeling legs were in her field of view. Voices overlapped around her. "What did you do?" "She's not safe!" "Security!" "Cover her."

And above all Faolán's voice, "Just calm down! Everybody, calm down!"

"Diadem! Diadem!" Shaula gasped. *Spare me, please.* She tried to sit up, but her hands and feet were restrained. "What did I do? Faolán?"

He leaned down. He was the one kneeling by her. "Hey, hey, I'm here."

"Stay back, Faolán! She might try to hurt you again!" said Kikelomo.

But he ignored her and helped Shaula sit upright. She looked up into his face. She'd never noticed how the light caught in his eyelashes and made his green eyes sparkle, how there was a thin line of yellow around his pupils. How charming that lopsided smile of his could be.

"Are you OK?" he asked.

There was a large bruise blooming on his neck. A bruise that looked like the shape of her hand. "Oh. Oh,

Faolán," she said. She reached her bound hands up to touch the bruised area. "I thought I killed you."

Then, surprising everyone, most of all herself, she burst into tears.

She wailed uncontrollably and sobbed.

"There, there; you're OK. Let it out." He gathered her into a hug.

She slung her wrists over his head so she could gather him closer. "I thought I killed you. I thought I killed you," she said over and over through the sobs. He wrapped his arms around her and rocked her from side to side.

She was dimly aware that several other people were in the lab watching them, some with weapons trained on her, but she did not care.

Eventually, her sobs abated and she pulled back. He touched her face, wiped her cheek. "Hey, look at that. You even have tears."

"E-even androids ge-get dust in our eyes. Water helps." Her breath continued to catch.

"Are you OK now?"

"Let me run a diagnostic." She turned her attention inward and triggered all the diagnostics she could. All returned notifications to her that her operational parameters were within normal tolerances. The only thing of note was one of those 'blank' feelings that happened when there was a memory wipe. "I think I am fine now. I feel the evidence of memory tampering, but it has ended."

She looked up. The others in the lab were Kikelomo, Naos, Vega, and Latu. The security officers both held weapons.

Shaula did not know what to say to them to wipe the mistrustful looks from their faces. Should she even try to stop them from mistrusting her? It seemed right and good that they would.

"How did you all get here so quickly?" she asked. It must have been quick. How else could they have saved Faolán's life?

"It seems we've been under closer observation than we knew, ever since we got kicked off the wreck," said Faolán. "Makes sense, I guess. And I'm glad of it." He looked up at the others. "I told you she'd be back to normal, didn't I?" said Faolán.

"Is she?" asked Kikelomo.

Shaula removed her arms from around Faolán's neck. She stayed seated for now. She did not want to scare anyone further. "I understand your trepidation, lieutenant commander. But we have more important things to consider."

"Oh?"

"I retrieved a large parcel of memories while I was under control. I have remembered some very important details. We need to warn the settlement right away."

"Of what?"

"That Dr Rebecca Neale is with them and must be taken into custody. We were looking for a human, but that was in error. The doctor transferred her consciousness into an android body when she was dying of a terminal illness. We know her as the android Bellatrix."

All those years she'd worked side-by-side with Bellatrix, and never once had she suspected that the other woman was not a normal android like all the rest in the settlement. If someone had told her, she would not have believed it. But she had seen it in her own memories.

At her announcement, Vega strode to the door. "Romulus!" he called. They all waited. Nothing. "Romulus?"

"Why would it not respond?" asked Latu.

Somehow, everyone seemed to know.

Vega walked out of the engineering lab. The others followed. Faolán stayed behind with her and helped her undo the restraints.

By the time they too exited the lab, the others stood in a huddle around some bright shapes on the ground. Dark Romulus, teal blue Beaufort, and a light pink messenger pigeon. All the bird familiars capable of running a quick message back to the settlement. They were not damaged externally. But they were not operational, either. Hopefully the familiars could be revived with their memories intact.

Faolán nudged her with his arm. "Would you look at that? Your planning saved the day."

She looked to where he pointed. Madigan sat on his haunches, awake and ready for a task, with his tongue lolling out.

"Good job, Shaula," said Faolán. "Good job."

CHAPTER 28

adigan was already on his way to the settlement, both to warn them about Bellatrix and to ask them to look out for Marcie and Altair: they weren't sure the pigeon he'd sent earlier had escaped the great Bird Switchoff. But Madigan wasn't as fast as the birds. He would be gone a whole day, and so they would have to wait to learn if their warning had gone out in time.

Ife had paused the salvage for now and called everyone back to camp. Faolán had then herded everyone into the cruiser. They sat around the table and along the bunks and listened while Shaula told them about the things she had remembered. They were all still visibly worried around Shaula. Vega and Latu still had their weapons to hand, and Shaula had her chair pulled away from the table so no one had to sit directly beside her. But they were listening, which was the main thing.

Faolán wondered if there was something wrong with him that he *wasn't* flinching whenever he looked at her, despite the bruises of her hand aching on his neck. He ought to be worried, right? He ought to be afraid now, right? But she'd burst into tears with relief when she realised he was still alive. To see someone like Shaula in that state had more of an impact on him than the fear. And what fear he felt, he wanted to hide from her. If she saw him fear her for a single moment, it would hurt her too much. That might be it for them. So he leaned into the memory of her tears, her concern for him, and dispelled the rest.

Faolán couldn't sit still like the others, especially not at the more harrowing points. What she'd unknowingly been through all these years, the invasion of her mind, the abuse of her very self, made him want to scream, or punch a wall. Instead, he stood at the kitchen counter with a pot of soup on the stove, a basic American-style pie in the oven, and bread dough in a bowl that he was kneading and punching down with more force than necessary.

This, right here, was the situation in which his ADHD was a benefit. His fractious energy could be put to use at times like these.

"So these other androids: she made you disassemble them?" asked Ife.

"She made me murder them. Even androids that I think... may have been important to me."

"Why?"

"I have no memories of ever being given reasons. I was switched into a receptive state where my personality was suppressed, and given orders that I carried out without a hint of free will. I knew that our memories had been tampered with, but I had not suspected that we had been overridden entirely."

"Could they have uncovered things?" asked Sandeep. "Like Altair did. Maybe they remembered things that couldn't be patched over so easily?"

"But why not just wipe their memories?" asked Ife. "She can clearly do that too."

"Longer memories, rather than single instances? Or maybe more like thought trains, realisations, that sort of thing? That's more nebulous and hard to pin down."

"And you had no memory of doing these things until today?" asked Ife.

Shaula looked down at the tabletop in front of her for a moment. Faolán left the bread dough for a moment and gripped her shoulder. She reached up and touched his hand. "I have started having a few memories over the last few days. None were as indicative of the full extent of what happened. But I'd had a few memories that were clues of these events. I remembered an android called Enif. She is no longer here. And... I remembered being made to experiment with someone's pain receptors, but it was such a brief memory fragment, I was not sure of the context."

That one was news to him, but he didn't begrudge her the secret. It sounded like the kind of thing she would have needed to process first.

He went back to the kitchen and stirred the soup, then dumped the bread dough into a pan to rise.

"Were you made to do these things all along?" asked Ife.

"I do not think so." Shaula tapped on the table. "From what I have remembered, Dr Neale, in her original body, was always at least frail, if not in a wheelchair, while I was being made to carry out these callous experiments and acts. I postulate that she originally did these things herself, but started using me when she became too hindered by her terminal illness. After she became Bellatrix, she made less use of me again."

"Why you?" asked Vega.

"Because of my engineering expertise. My guess is that Tiaki at least may have been used in the same way, though I do not have evidence of that."

"And was it just the engineering androids?"

"No." She paused. Faolán looked over his shoulder and saw her staring intently at Naos. "I remember seeing Naos being used in such a way as well."

"What? I would never—" said Naos indignantly.

"I would never, either," said Shaula. "If I had any autonomy at the time, I would never have done the things she made me do. Never."

Naos hung her head. "What do you remember me doing?"

"Implanting an embryo."

"Excuse me?" said Naos.

"An embryo?" asked Ife.

"About sixteen years ago," said Shaula. "Naos and I were used to implant an embryo into Capella. She has an artificial uterus, like the ones used in fertility centres for infertile humans."

"Excuse me, a what?" asked Simons. "Is that even possible?" He sounded disbelieving.

"Yes. That embryo became a clone of Dr Neale, one she has raised as her daughter. The girl is called Bex, and I believe she is nearby."

"Oh, come on now!" said Gagnon. "This is all getting more ridiculous by the minute."

Faolán turned to glare at her. "Just because it sounds crazy doesn't mean it isn't true. We already had evidence of a young clone of Dr Neale."

While Shaula and Ife explained the telomere evidence and their postulations to the others, Faolán took the pie out of the oven and put the bread in. He'd decided to go dessert-first for people because, he reckoned, bad or worrying news always justified switching the order. Who wanted to eat the healthy stuff first when their knee couldn't stop jiggling with nerves? Better to get that dopamine boost from the tastiest food in as early as possible. At least, that's how he preferred it.

The pie was some basic experimental recipe-free thing he'd made, filled with a mixture of powdered egg, long-life flour, sugar, and a heap of cooking fat. It would be sweet and gooey, but otherwise probably a bit of a boring disaster. He let it cool for a few minutes while he seasoned the soup, then cut the pie into slices and started handing them around. Shaula tapped his arm as he passed her. "Give one to Diphda," she said in a low voice.

"What?"

"A portion of that food. Give it to Diphda. She has a stomach."

Faolán shrugged and took a plate to Diphda. The bright frog-green android looked up at him for a long moment, and did not take the plate.

"Shaula says you can eat this," he said.

Diphda cautiously took the plate and sniffed at the pie. She frowned. Then she tentatively licked the pie. Her eyes went wide, and then she took a nibble. After she swallowed, she looked past Faolán to Shaula.

"It is an intense feeling, testing out your special enhancement. Take it slow," said Shaula.

"This is pretty good," said Hernandez from where he sat next to Vega on one of the bunks. "How did you do this with the basic supplies we have?"

Faolán grinned. That's the sort of feedback he wanted to get! "Pretty simple, to be honest. Even old biscuits, egg powder, and long-life flour can be delicious if you put enough fat and sugar in them, and get a nice tasty tasty caramelisation going."

The room was quiet for a few minutes as everyone who could eat fed their faces. Faolán took a slice for himself and scoffed it down while he continued monitoring the soup. It wasn't great. The true edge this pie had was that no one had eaten any pies at all for months.

"Thanks, Faolán," said Ife after she'd finished. "Much appreciated. Now, we can't control what happens back at the settlement, but we can control what happens here. So about the clone: we've discussed that she's here, that she probably has a large familiar. We've all seen odd things on the wreck, so she may be sheltering in there somewhere, hiding from us. What should we do about the situation, people?"

"Do we think she is the murderer?" asked Latu.

"It is possible," said Shaula. "However, I think it is unlikely she struck the killing blows. She will not have the requisite body strength. She may have used the control device to activate a killer program in any android already here, similar to the program that was activated in me this afternoon. Whichever android did it... I can assure you, it was not you. You were a tool that was used, not a murderer."

"What if it was you?" asked Naos.

"It could have been."

"I still don't think so," said Faolán. "Like I've said before, I saw you charging quietly that night."

Shaula looked over her shoulder at him. "Let us not discount any android. Not even me. But also, let us not blame any android. We are victims of Dr Neale every time we do something she forces us to do."

He left the soup and gripped her shoulder, looked her in the eye. "Of course you are. That goes without saying." He gave her one last squeeze and went back to the kitchen.

Ife cleared her throat. "So, are we agreed that we have to find this clone?"

There was a smattering of 'yes's and 'aye's around the room.

"Not only to find her, but also to take possession of the control device," said Shaula. "I believe that once we have that device, we can delete any dangerous routines that have been uploaded into any of the androids of 227C so they cannot be triggered. We should also then be able to tell how the murder of Dr McArthur, Tiaki, and Zephyr was enacted."

"Good. That sounds like it would solve several problems at once."

"Just one moment," said Gagnon. "I agree we need to find the clone, but can't us humans take care of that? If you androids are so dangerous until we get that device, then shouldn't we just turn you all off until we have it in hand? We're risking our safety with every minute that we leave you all active."

There were more sounds of assent around the room. And Faolán had to admit she did have a point. But...

"Dr Neale is an *android*," he said. "And if I can read anything between the lines about her, she'll be the *best* android; the fastest, the strongest. The best build. I know it's risky having the androids around, now we've seen what can happen. But what the *bloody hell* would we all do if Dr Neale, Bellatrix, showed up here and let rip on us without any androids on our side to help us?" He looked around at the drawn, worried faces of his crew mates. "She originally underestimated us, sending just her child to watch us while she stayed back and watched the settlement. We've been relatively lucky so far because of that. But if she's figured out that *we've* figured out her daughter is here, then she might come here too. That's when we'll be in real hot water. We need to press the last remaining vestiges of our advantage now, with all hands on deck, and get the android control device ASAP."

Ife nodded. "He's right, friends. It's risky, yes. But hell, that's what we get hazard pay for."

"Our bank accounts are all going to be so full when we get home," whispered Hernandez, and several people chuckled, including Ife.

"We can but hope. Now, moving on, what can we do about the cloaking device we think she has?"

"I believe I have a solution for that too, lieutenant commander," said Shaula. "But I will need help from a human engineer. I now possess memories of helping to make the cloaking device. I believe it can be interrupted by certain wavelengths. I need someone to help me find equipment aboard the *Sunda Tiger* that can produce those wavelengths."

Faolán grinned. Shaula was in her element, and he loved to see it. Also, it seemed everyone had come around after she told them the full story, and understood that she herself was no more dangerous than any other android at the moment. They were all dangerous until they had their hands on that device. Which they soon would.

"OK," said Ife. "Here's how we're going to do things. After we've eaten the meal that Faolán's making for us — that bread is starting to smell divine, by the way — I'm going to start talking to you one by one. We're going to put together a plan, and each person, particularly the androids, is only going to know the part they need to know. Understood? This is so that the plan can't be hacked out of an android brain. Any objections?"

"No."

"None."

"Sounds good."

"OK, then," said Ife. "We can do this, people. We've got a wide range of specialties here on this team. We'll be able to outsmart Dr Neale and her clone. I promise you."

CHAPTER 29

"**I** cannot believe that I have had the misfortune of being paired with you!"

"Believe me, the feeling is mutual."

"I am at least staying on target with the salvage, not sneaking away for romantic rendezvous like you are!"

He spluttered in response.

Listening to the argument between Lieutenant Chaudhary and Diphda was aggravating. If Shaula did not know better, she would think the pair were arguing for real. On second thought, they were likely taking the opportunity to let their genuine feelings out for the sake of the cause. At least it had a practical application.

Faolán tensed beside her as the raised voices approached. They were pretending to examine the scene of the explosion again, carefully combing over every square centimetre of the twisted, wrecked hover bed, even though they knew they would find no more clues.

"I wish I'd been paired with an engineer," said Sandeep loudly. "Maybe then you'd understand what I'm doing. The only reason you think I'm not pulling my weight is that you don't understand what I do."

"And you do not understand my job. Why do you think it is safe to sneak off on this wreck? Parts of the structure could yet give way."

The squabbling pair passed in front of the open doorway to the rest of the ship. They were carrying a crate between them on a small hoverbed, heading towards the next cargo bay, their new collection point, which was now permanently guarded by Vega and Ensign Latu.

Lieutenant Chaudhary stopped in the doorway and took his hands off the hover bed to prop them on his hips. "May I remind you I'm an engineer? It's my job to know if things are structurally sound."

Diphda also took her hands off the hover bed, and it floated to the ground. "You are not that kind of engineer. I am not that much of a fool."

"I still did my 100-levels in the other kinds of engineering, I'll have you know! And the Orion Navy requires all engineers to have knowledge in wider fields than their specialty."

Diphda threw up her hands and stalked off as if done with the conversation.

"Where do you think you're going?" Lieutenant Chaudhary pursued her. The sound of their argument continued, receding along the corridor.

Shaula kept her head down and pretended to continue her examination for a few more minutes. Then Faolán bumped her shoulder with his own, and she gave him a nod. They took off their gloves and went out into the corridor, lifted the hover bed, and took it to a small nearby office that Faolán had to tag open.

They righted a table inside the office and lifted the crate onto it. Shaula cracked it open. Inside was a boxy piece of equipment with a backpack portion, a cable, and a handheld wand. The box also held a physical instruction manual. There were small tags sticking out of the book.

"Don't see these very often," said Faolán as he leafed through the book.

"Why does this unit have an instruction book?"

"It's a field unit used on rugged terrain, far from the closest camp. No matter what technologies we invent, you still can't get better than a book when you're worried about power or information access."

"Fair." Shaula took the book from Faolán and looked at the tagged pages. Lieutenant Chaudhary had labelled the most pertinent instructions. In no time, Shaula had the geotechnical assay unit strapped on her back, powered on, and dialled to the exact frequency she needed. This unit was used to locate underground minerals and water in exploration missions. But Shaula was going to be using it for an alternative purpose.

Faolán stuck his head out into the corridor. "It sounds like the argument is heating up," he said. "Vega and Latu will be 'lured' away from their post soon — oop, there they go."

"Shall we wait a minute to give the clone time to get into place?"

"Negative," whispered Faolán as he took his pistol from his belt. "I just saw a door down the corridor open and close, but no one came through it that I could see. She's wasting no time."

"Then neither should we."

Faolán gave her a quick peck on the cheek, then he slipped out into the corridor in a defensive position. Shaula took Charm out of her hair and put it down on the table. "Stay back and observe," she whispered. She slipped her shoes off, more confident of her stealth without them, and followed Faolán. They both crept as quietly as they could. Shaula had never seen Faolán wielding his weapon before. It seemed so incongruous with his personality, and yet his hands on the weapon were sure and his posture precise. He was well trained in its use.

Faolán covered Shaula as she went around him and up to the doorway of the now unguarded cargo bay. She peeked around the doorframe. She could not see anything, but she detected a small sound like a scuff of a foot. Someone was in there.

The manoeuvre that Shaula had to perform would have been easier if the *Sunda Tiger* had been upright. If that were the case, she could have simply leaned around the corner and touched the device she carried to the floor. But she had to drop into the room, because the ceiling of the cargo bay had been higher than the corridor's. A few boxes had been positioned to act as makeshift steps down to the original ceiling. One box had been left 70 cm away from the wall, affording enough room for Shaula to drop behind. But the tricky part was that, since the clone was invisible, there was no way of telling where she was looking. Shaula would have to guess.

She listened closely. The small shuffles continued, seeming to mill around. There: it sounded like they were moving away. It was her best chance. Shaula stepped around the corner and dropped behind the box as quietly as she could. She barely made a sound, her body having some stealth coding in it somewhere.

Shaula listened for a moment to see if it sounded like the clone had heard her. But there was no taut tension of silence, only more light shuffles.

Shaula switched the machine on. Before the clone could have reacted if she had heard the click, she placed the point of the handheld wand on the floor/ceiling and pressed the trigger.

The pack on her back vibrated, as did the wand in her hand. That vibration travelled to the floor underfoot. Shaula gripped the floor with her toes, feeling like the vibration might upset her balance if she was not careful.

There was a higher hum originating from some-where in the room beyond. "What?" said an unfamiliar voice. Shaula felt a sense of grim satisfaction. She had been right. This unit had created a resonance with the cloaking tech and disrupted its operation. Now it was her task to make the disruption permanent. She dialled up the intensity of the signal. There was a popping sound. Or was there two?

Faolán stepped into the doorway above her, his weapon held at the ready. "Hey there, hands up. Whoa, whoa, easy. We're not going to hurt—fecking hell!"

Shaula looked up to see Faolán staring over in a different direction from where the girl's voice had come from. He gave Shaula a brief, wide-eyed look, then he turned and ran.

Shaula had a moment to wonder what the thunder-ing noise was before a large, heavily muscled and furred shape leaped over head and pursued Faolán into the hallway. Shaula jumped up on to the box. She glanced back to see a small, slim girl with wide, scared eyes standing in the middle of the cargo bay. Then she ran into the hall too. She fully, whole-heartedly threw duty to the wind and did what her heart bade her.

Ahead of her, the corridor was clear. She heard bangs and thumps coming from a side corridor. Shaula took off in pursuit. Once she rounded the corner, she parsed what was pursuing Faolán. It was a lion. A full-sized fe-male lion. It wasn't oddly coloured like the animal fa-miliars. This one was real, its tawny fur glinting red in the emergency lighting.

The corridor was long, running the length of the ship. Boxes and crates of supplies were stacked along the walls. As Faolán ran, he pushed boxes over behind him, forcing the lion to take a zig-zag path. It was a smart move. The lion was far faster than him.

Shaula put on a burst of speed, but it would still take her many long moments to catch up. How could a real lion be here? The terraformation process had not included any large mammalian species. At least not yet. It would be a few generations until the ecological web was ready for an addition like that. It stood to reason, then, that this too must be an animal android, despite its realistic pelt.

And had she not remembered a lion in her confusing deluge of memories? Its realistic pelt had not registered in her memories. This must be it. The young clone's familiar, her protector, who had also been cloaked.

Ahead of her, the lion was fast closing in on Faolán. If only Madigan were here; he would have protected Faolán. But he was not, so it was up to her. The lion must be running a protector routine, and since Faolán drew a weapon on the clone, things would not go well for him if the lion caught him. Shaula diverted as much power to her legs as she could, but now she too was being slowed down by the boxes in her path. She leapt and sprung off the wall to clear a pile. The move was cumbersome with the machine in her hand.

Yes. The machine.

If the lion was an android, it was susceptible too. If only she could get the right resonance frequency.

With another leap, she drew closer to the lion.

"Hey, you. Lion! I'll hurt your girl if you don't stop!" she yelled in desperation. If she could just get the lion to see her as the bigger threat. But still the lion ran. Shaula dialled the frequency of the machine to something lower, rougher. She dragged it along the wall as she ran, holding down the trigger. The wall rumbled. The wand jumped off the wall each time it hit a doorframe, but she pushed it back on, causing as much of a disturbance as she could.

"Hey, you! I will hurt your girl!"

The lion skidded to a halt and turned. Its golden eyes honed in on her and it bared its fangs. It stalked towards her. She stood her ground, her finger on the dial.

Beyond the lion, Faolán had stopped running. He looked at her, worry in her eyes. She shook her head at him. She did not need his help. She was far less vulnerable than him. He needed to get back to the cargo bay and restrain the clone, but she could not tell him to do so without drawing the lion's attention back to him.

The lion pounced at her, but she was ready. She brought the wand up. The lion hit her full-force on the shoulders, and she fell hard onto her back. But the wand was in its mouth. Unfortunately, so was the trigger.

"Shaula!" cried Faolán. She could not see him beyond the lion. All she saw was fur, and a snarling snout, and fierce orange eyes. Claws bit into the silicone of her shoulders, tearing large rents.

"Go!" she called to Faolán. Again, she did not want to say where she wanted him to go. But she hoped he would get the message.

Shaula lifted her knees and then pushed up with her feet, trying to lift the lion enough that she could pull the wand back and get her finger on the trigger. Above her toes, she could feel the workings of the lion. It was surely not flesh and blood.

She heaved. As heavy as the lion was, Shaula could lift it. The lion tried to spit out the wand, but Shaula shoved it back in, up to the roof of the lion's mouth, this time on an angle so the trigger stuck out.

Faolán appeared in her peripheral vision. She spared a glance for him. His face was pale, his eyes wide. He did not look like he wanted to leave her fighting the lion alone.

"Go!" she said once more and pulled the trigger.

The lion whined as vibrations shook its head, but it held on, its claws digging deeper. She started turning the dial, searching for the right frequency. She heard Faolán run away, but she kept her attention on what she was doing. *Not there... not there... a bit more...*

She started losing feeling in her arms as the vibration set into her. The closer she dialled the frequency to where she thought she might disrupt the lion's processes, the closer she came to disrupting her own. But it was her hands on the device, while the lion had it next to its CPU. She dialled further...

Her vision started to blur. She dialled further...

...Just a little more...

An alarm sounded within her, one she ignored.

Then the light of the lion's eyes went out and it became a dead weight above her. She released the trigger, and her own vision stabilised and her arms regained their feeling.

Shaula waited to see if the lion would move again. When it did not, she pushed it off to the side. She did not want to leave the lion there in the hallway in case it turned on again while no one was looking. So she squatted, got her shoulder under its belly, and stood. The lion's head and forepaws hung down her back, the paws brushing her calves, and its tail swished to the ground in front of her. But the weight of the large android familiar was within her carrying capacity.

Shaula walked back to the cargo bay, her bare feet thumping under the combined weight of herself and the lion. When she reached the cargo bay, she found most of the salvage crew clustered around the doorway looking in. Ensign Latu spotted her first, and her face paled.

"Fucking hell," someone muttered.

Shaula felt the ripple of fear in her colleagues. They still had not overcome their caution around her, and carrying a deactivated lion android was not helping.

"What are you carrying?" asked Naos.

"The clone's familiar," said Shaula.

"Are you all right?" asked Lieutenant Chaudhary, who now stood beside Diphda, no sign of their faux argument remaining.

"I will be fine."

Shaula stepped close enough to see into the cargo bay. She froze, feeling fear again. The girl stood in the middle of the cargo bay, a weapon drawn. Faolán stood ten paces in front of her, his empty hands up. "It's OK. We just want to talk," he was saying.

The girl's hand shook and wavered. But then she looked beyond Faolán and saw Shaula. Her face twisted with anguish.

"Sekhmet!" she screamed. "What have you done to her?" She tried to charge past Faolán, but he caught her around the waist, twisting the weapon out of her hand with a practised move, and tucking it into his own belt.

Shaula understood the girl's panic. No doubt this lion was her only friend. Shaula held her free hand up. "Please, may I run a diagnostic on Sekhmet? To see how she is?" As she said the name, she noticed how it paired with Bellatrix's familiar Bastet.

The girl's face contorted again, but she nodded in a jerking movement, as if she was shaking or unsteady.

"Could someone get a tablet and a cable?" Shaula asked.

"On it," said Lieutenant Chaudhary.

"Wait, I have one," called the girl.

Shaula nodded and stepped down onto the box step and then into the cargo bay. She then laid the lion familiar down with care.

Faolán led the girl over. She had a satchel hanging at her side over worn, patched clothes in blue and brown, and her dark bobbed curly hair was wild and untamed. The girl reached into her satchel and took out a hand-held device that Shaula had only recently remembered. It was the control device, the very one they needed. She passed it to Shaula. "You don't need a cable for this one," she said. "Sekhmet's control panel is in here."

Shaula tapped the device awake. It was like a much more sophisticated version of the device they used to program the familiars at the research centre. That one was only programmed to run the startup, calibration, and bonding protocols, and it only worked for the familiars. But this one had categories for both androids and familiars.

As tempted as she was to scroll through the android section, she went into the familiars instead and scrolled down until she found Sekhmet's name. It gave her the option of running a diagnostic.

Shaula ran the diagnostic while the clone stood nearby, shaking, and Faolán stood beside her, one hand on her shoulder.

Shaula held the screen out to the clone when the diagnostic was finished. "Your familiar is just in sleep mode," she said. "See here."

The girl gave a relieved sob and covered her eyes. "Can you turn her back on?" she mumbled.

"That's not a good idea," said Faolán.

"I concur," said Shaula. "Your familiar tried to kill Faolán."

"And you, too," he added. "Are you OK?"

Shaula poked at one of the slashes in her shoulders. She belatedly realised her grey shirt was in tatters. She must look an absolute mess.

"I am repairable," she said. "My clothes, not so much." She stood and stepped away from Sekhmet.

Kikelomo approached them from behind, Chaudhary on her heels. "We're going to make absolutely certain that lion is safe before we even consider turning it back on, OK?" said Kikelomo.

"OK," said the clone in a small voice. She sat down against the lion and stroked its pelt.

Faolán squatted down near her, but not too close. "Hey, my name's Faolán. What's yours?"

Considering what they suspected the girl may have done, his kind words surprised her. But then, the girl was so small and so scared, it was hard not to pity her.

"I'm Bex," said the girl. "Are you going to arrest me?"

Faolán tilted his head. "Do you think you should be arrested?"

"I don't know. Maybe? Some of the things Mum asked me to do, I think they weren't so good." Tears began leaking out of her eyes again, and she hid her face in her familiar's fur.

Faolán shared a look with Shaula, and she recognised the grim thoughts he was having.

This girl had committed some of the crimes against them. But it seemed likely she had been used, just a pawn in Dr Neale's plans.

Used by her own originator. Her mother.

CHAPTER 30

Faolán bumped open the door to the medical lab with his elbow and carried the plate of snacks inside. The med lab itself was empty, but he followed the voices to the rear cabin.

Shaula, Ife, and Sandeep stood around the edge of the small cabin, watching while Naos examined Bex.

The girl in question sat hunched on the sofa. She looked like she was about twelve, though she'd said she was fifteen. If so, she was underdeveloped in a way that showed her access to food hadn't always been the best. She was tanned, and her dark curly hair had an amateur cut. There was a racially ambiguous look to her, which made sense if she was Rebecca Neale's clone, as the doctor was from Mars. She wore adult-sized clothes that were patched, rolled-up, and tightened with a belt. One brown trouser leg had a blood-stained slash across it, and in the hole he could see a bandage on the girl's leg.

Naos finished a physical exam of the girl and stood up. "She seems healthy enough, considering the circumstances. I will check her blood results." She stepped through into the lab and went to a machine on the bench.

Faolán looked around at the others. Ife nodded at him. Food first it was, then.

"Hey," he said as he sat down on the floor near her and put the snacks on the coffee table. "You must be hungry. You want something?"

The girl glanced up at him, her grey eyes frightened. But then she grabbed a biscuit and shoved it into her mouth whole.

No matter what this girl had done, there was no way that Faolán couldn't feel compassion for her. Even if she was a murderer and a ship saboteur, how could a girl like this have done such things without being a victim herself?

The girl's shoulders stayed hunched. Since Faolán had been the one to restrain her and had held a weapon on her, she probably wouldn't find him an easy presence. He went to stand beside Shaula.

She'd changed her shirt since he'd last seen her, perhaps when she'd taken the inactive lion familiar into the engineering lab for storage. She was now wearing a white t-shirt that was large on her, which he belatedly realised was one of his own. That thought made the corner of his mouth twitch up. But then he noticed those rents in her skin.

"Can we help you with those?" he murmured.

"If I had ten minutes, I could at least patch them."

Ife had heard their interaction. "Go take that time now. We'll watch the girl. But come back after. I'll need a full debrief."

Faolán went with her to the engineering lab. The lion was draped over the main workbench, so they worked at

the side bench. Shaula took her top off and got two bottles and a cup out of a cupboard. She measured equal
amounts of liquid out of each bottle into the cup and
stirred vigorously. "Can you help me cover the holes?"
she asked him. "It does not need to look good, it just
needs to cover the slashes."

Together they got the mix slathered over the rents
using thin steel spatulas. It looked like her green skin
was drizzled with salad dressing. The mixture dried
quickly and went clear. She tentatively stretched the
area, then rotated her arms.

"This will do for now."

"Who will help you fix it up later?"

Shaula froze, and he felt like a fool. What a terrible
time to bring up her loss of Tiaki all over again, and the
betrayal of Bellatrix. But then she patted him on the
cheek. "Maybe I can teach you how to use the silicone
press. I think it would be similar to making pasta."

He grinned at the visual image.

Shaula brushed her thumb over his cheek, her golden
eyes shining bright. "I did not think I would get there in
time," she said. "I was afraid the lion would be your end."

Faolán remembered looking at Shaula wrestling with
the lion and knowing he had to leave her there, unaware
of whether she'd win the battle. Turning away had been
one of the hardest things he'd ever had to do. He'd only
been able to do it by reasoning that she could bear in-
juries far better than he could, and by recognising that
he was the fragile one there. Needing to protect him
would make things harder for Shaula. If not for that, he
wouldn't have been able to go.

As it was, he hadn't needed to go back to take Bex into
custody. Ensign Latu had been doing a good job of covering her when he'd got there.

The relief he'd felt when he saw Shaula had won the
battle... He stroked her cheek, gripped the back of her

neck, heedless of the scorpion in her hair. "I was worried about you too. I'm so glad you're OK. And thank you for saving my life. Because I wouldn't have survived that without you, I don't think."

She grabbed a handful of his shirt and pulled him in for a kiss. They could take a moment for themselves, surely?

Just a moment more.

OK, one more moment.

As he wrapped his arms around her and stroked his hands up her bare back, the door bumped open. They both startled and looked towards the doorway, only to see Latu standing there.

"Sir, LC Kikelomo would like you to..." Latu trailed off. Her eyes bugged out. "Oi, I don't wanna see that!" Any deference to rank she usually had went out the window as she threw up her hands, turned on her heel, and sauntered off, muttering to herself in her own language. Probably disparaging things about Faolán. Which was fair. He shouldn't have been making out with a topless woman while on the clock.

Shaula slipped out of his arms and pulled the white t-shirt back on. "I believe we were just summoned."

"Yes, and outed."

Shaula ran a hand down Faolán's arm. "We were deluding ourselves if we thought we could be discreet forever."

They walked back to the med lab. Though Latu hadn't finished delivering her message, it seemed like the logical place to go. Sure enough, Ife was still there. Naos nodded at them, but stayed at her workbench. In the cabin, Ife still stood against the wall, but Sandeep was now sitting on the sofa near Bex, far enough away so as not to crowd her.

"...so I sort of stay underground a lot," Bex was saying. "Mum says I have to stay out of sight. But she's been visiting less and less. She says she's busy, and I'm growing up, so it's OK. She makes sure I have food and training modules. But I get bored a lot. I've always figured that if I go the other way, away from the lake, and keep my cloak on, it will be OK." She had an unusual accent. He could detect a hint of Mars in her voice, but otherwise her accent was a jumble, and dramatically inflected, as if she had learned from holodramas.

Faolán leaned in towards Ife. "Where did she say she lives?"

"In an abandoned facility on the other side of the lake."

"The one Altair was talking about? We were going to go look for that after the salvage, weren't we?"

"Uh, huh. Guess we should have done that first."

Sandeep offered Bex another biscuit. "Why has she been getting you to hide from the androids?" he asked. "Couldn't some of them have been your friends?"

Bex looked down at her hands. "Mum says that if anyone knows about me, I'll disrupt the experiment. There aren't supposed to be any humans here. But now you're all here too. It's a real mess, and she's so worried."

"Why is she worried?" Sandeep asked in a gentle, almost nonchalant voice.

Bex wrapped her arms around herself. "I don't really know. She told me it'll be a happy surprise one day, when she gets it right. She'll tell me about it then."

It sounded like such a lonely existence. "So you've been without friends all this time?" asked Faolán.

"I have Sekhmet! She's my friend!"

"Oh, Honey," said Ife.

"Do you know what you are?" asked Shaula.

There was a tension in Bex's face when she looked up at Shaula. Was she afraid of androids? Or had it just been drilled into her for so long that she shouldn't talk to them? "What do you mean? I'm a girl. A human girl."

"Where did you come from? Do you know?"

"I was born here."

"How?"

"Um, I don't really know. I don't think I was born like normal human babies, because Mum's an android too. But she's so clever. She thought of something."

"Do you know you're a clone of your Mum?" asked Sandeep.

"Well, duh. There were no other humans here, so I couldn't have a dad. I had to be a clone." She spoke with full-strength teenage scathing.

Sandeep looked uncomfortable at the girl's words. If Faolán remembered rightly, he only had an older brother, so he was probably sailing into uncharted waters right now. But Faolán had three sisters, so this girl couldn't throw anything new at him.

"Oh, good," he said. "We don't need to tell you how babies are usually made. Because no one here wants to be having that conversation with you, I can assure you. But you knew your Mum used to be a human, right?"

"Yeah."

"But she took an android body at some point."

"Yeah. Obviously."

"But you don't know what her full aim here is? What she's actually doing, or why she doesn't want any humans around?"

Bex shook her head.

Faolán sat back down on the ground, leaning his elbow on the coffee table. "Look, I'm working on the assumption here that you're old enough that we can just talk things out. You don't need any coddling like a little kid, do you?"

"No!" said Bex indignantly and rolled her eyes.

"Good. So. Some weird stuff has been going on. Don't you agree?"

The girl hunched her shoulders again.

"Like exploding cargo bays."

Bex picked at the tear in the shin of her trousers.

"Sabotaged ships."

She gripped her hands together.

"And our head doctor and one of the android engineers turning up dead."

Bex hung her head nearly to her knees.

Faolán softened his voice as he said, "Where we come from, people get arrested for that sort of thing."

Bex's breath hitched.

"Unless they were clearly coerced and used. I'm probably way out of line to say this, but what you've said so far about how your Mum has raised you, it doesn't sound quite right. Like, you don't seem to have your freedom."

Bex looked up at him, her eyes blazing. "You *are* out of line. Mum does her best for me. It's not easy! And she didn't use to get me to do these things, but as soon as you all showed up, it *had* to be me! You all would have noticed if an android of the settlement was taking care of things!"

Faolán looked over his shoulder at Ife to see if she wanted to take over, now he was starting to get somewhere, but she just nodded to him to continue. "So, what did she get you to do?"

Bex seemed to realise her mistake. She clapped a hand over her mouth to keep her words in.

"I do hope you realise that the things she got you to do were horrible. She's made you responsible for destruction and death. Sabotaging the ship—"

"I didn't sabotage the ship! I just installed some spyware and left a monitoring station in the hangar bay!"

"Why did the ship crash, then?" asked Ife, her voice snapping.

"Mum said it was another SecSat..."

"I was in engineering. I can tell you it was a computer virus, combined with a bomb that exploded in the *hangar bay*."

By the way the girl's face turned white, she'd been, if not fully believing that she hadn't sabotaged the ship, at the very least deluding herself that it might be true.

Faolán spoke even more gently when he said, "And Tiaki and Dr McArthur? Did you also just 'install some spyware'?"

Bex turned her head, looking away from all of them.

Just then, the door opened, and a grey shape bounded inside. Faolán was enveloped in grey fur, licky tongue, and waggy tail.

"Madigan! You're back. Did you get the message there in time?"

Everyone forgot Bex for a moment, particularly Ife and Sandeep, Marcie's close friends.

"Yes," said Madigan. "Thanks to our warning, an assassination plot was foiled. A bomb was found in Altair's quarters and defused. They are safe. I can also report that Bellatrix had disappeared from the settlement before I arrived and reported her identity. Her location is unknown."

Faolán breathed a sigh of relief, as did several others.

"Oh, thank goodness," said Ife. She reached out and grabbed Shaula's shoulder. "Imagine what would have happened if you hadn't assigned this one to Faolán!"

He smiled to see Ife praising Shaula. Their professional relationship had so far been rocky at best, but this was a real improvement.

Faolán stood and walked over to have a quiet word with Ife. Shaula stood at his shoulder.

"This girl needs some comfort if she's going to trust us further," he said in a low voice.

"I agree, but I don't know what we can do," said Ife. "How could we possibly be comforting for her? She must be so scared of us."

He looked from Ife to Shaula. "I have an idea. A not good, very stupid idea. But it might work." When neither said anything, he elaborated. "What if we wake up her lion?"

"No," said Ife. "It nearly killed you."

"Sure. But it's her only friend, and Madigan is here now. Shaula, do you think Madigan could stop that lion?"

"Yes. When we were fighting the lion on the wreck, I wished that Madigan was around for that very reason. I... may have upgraded some of Madigan's protective protocols."

Ife raised eyebrows at Shaula in a way that demanded an explanation.

Shaula shrugged at her. "I have a vested interest in Faolán's safety."

Ife's eyebrows stayed up.

"I wish for him to remain fully functional, thank you."

"Stop explaining now, please." Ife pinched the bridge of her nose.

They all trooped over to the engineering lab. Bex let out a wordless cry when she saw her familiar and flopped across the lion's still form.

"Madigan, please ready yourself to restrain this lion if it poses any danger to anyone," said Shaula. She then attached a cable to the lion inside one of its joints and started flicking through menus on her tablet. A moment later, the light flicked on in the lion's eyes, and it twitched, then sat up on the table. The lion looked down at Bex and then around at everyone else. It growled and bared its teeth.

"Bex, do you require assistance?" growled the lion.

"No."

"Did these people hurt you?"

"No."

"Should I protect you now?"

Faolán tensed, his hand hovering over his weapon.

"No. I want a hug," said Bex.

They let the girl and the lion hug it out for fifteen minutes. The lion even licked Bex's hair as if she were a cub.

Eventually, when he thought she was calm enough, Faolán stepped forward. "Can you tell us now about what happened that led to Tiaki and Dr McArthur's deaths?"

Bex sniffed and looked up at him with red eyes. "The bugs had been recording your conversations."

"What bugs?"

"Familiars. I have a few bugs with me that have been listening in. That's how we know what's been going on with you."

Faolán breathed out a sigh of relief. If they were using familiars to spy on them, then Dr Neale didn't have an omniscient awareness of what every android was doing. He'd been afraid of that.

"Oh, I saw a grasshopper," said Shaula. "I thought nothing of it, but I saw a grasshopper at the murder site. It was a spy?"

Bex nodded.

Faolán looked at Shaula. "That's how they knew to wipe your memory when we found those prints." He looked at Bex again. "Right?"

Bex nodded again.

"We can sort all the details out later," said Ife. "I'll give you the benefit of the doubt that you didn't intend for anyone to die. But what are you even doing out at the wreck in the first place, why did you blow up our salvaged goods, and why did your mother want Camryn and Tiaki dead?"

Bex shrugged. "Like I said, it has to be me now, because otherwise someone would notice Mum was gone. She just told me to stall you and sabotage you so this takes as long as possible, so she has time to get contingencies in place. And she told me to blow up the goods to slow you down further. I made really, really sure to do it when no one was in the room, I promise! I didn't want to hurt anyone."

"But you did hurt people," said Faolán. "I can't sugarcoat this for you. You blew up medical equipment meant to help people who are suffering. What was it all for?"

Bex screwed her eyes shut. "Mum wanted to know things about the wreck. But then that yellow android said he knew where Mum was. She told me before I came here that if I ever heard someone say something like that, I had to run one of the programs on my tablet. The program's name was a code, so I didn't know what it was supposed to do. Then I deleted it from the device."

Over in the corner, Shaula had the device in question in her hand. She was scrolling through a menu.

"You won't find it," said Bex to her. "I'm not silly enough to leave it in the trash bin."

"Who?" asked Shaula.

Bex shrugged.

"We need to know so we can verify that the android in question is safe and will not run the program again. You are here with us now. You would not be safe either."

There was tension in the room from both Shaula and Naos. They were both listening with their complete attention.

"...Vega."

Faolán rounded up Latu and Diphda on his way to find Vega. Shaula tagged along.

They found Vega quickly. He was sitting on a rock with a placid look on his face, though he was rubbing his hands together in a nervous gesture. Simons was watching from nearby, a smirk on his face. Smug bastard. He was probably thinking that he was right about everything because an android was involved.

"It was me, correct?" asked Vega as they stopped before him.

Faolán sighed. "I'm sorry."

Vega looked at the wreck beyond the camp. "I volunteer to be shut down. I willingly comply. I do not remember doing anything, but my leg has been strange, and I have been too afraid to find out why. Shaula, may I ask you to investigate?"

Faolán sucked air in over his teeth. Now he thought about it, he had seen Vega being clumsy on his feet a few times lately. He'd barely noticed, because that happened to people sometimes. But Vega was an android. It shouldn't have happened.

Vega didn't wait to go back to the lab. He just stood up and took his trousers off, then sat back down. Faolán was reminded of a time when he'd been amused seeing Altair in a similar state.

But that day, Altair had been a calm and collected hero. Today, Vega was an unwilling villain.

Shaula took a tool out of her pocket, a small folding implement. She knelt before Vega and started peeling back the silicone skin on his thigh. Once she had a swathe pulled away, she peered in.

"Faolán, could you get gloves and a sample bag? I have found the murder weapon."

"Just a sec." He went to fetch them at a run. When he had given the items to Shaula, she eased a sharp metal tool out of Vega's leg, one he had seen in the engineering lab before: a hair rooting tool. It was covered in a dark red stain. Blood.

CHAPTER 31

Their next course of action took little time to deliberate. Vega was turned off and stored. Shaula checked that no lingering programs were running in his code, while Naos examined the murder weapon and verified that the blood belonged to Dr McArthur.

Then Shaula had a brief repair job to complete before she took Madigan and Charm with her to the engineering lab to charge. They would all need maximum battery capacity for the next few days. Because from what they had uncovered, although Bex and Vega had physically committed the criminal acts, they were not the ones responsible. They were merely the tools. The real criminal was Dr Neale, and their investigation would only be complete when they had her in custody. Bex's explanation of her home, plus what Altair had remembered, gave them a place to look.

By the time Shaula emerged with the familiars and a few full recharge packs, Faolán had all the other preparations complete: one of the ATVs packed with a tent and supplies, and with a few items requisitioned from Bex. Even though it was nearly evening, they departed immediately in the hope they could reach Dr Neale before she had moved on from the secret laboratory.

They left the salvage team behind, with Bex still in their care. The girl had no communications equipment she could use to warn her mother of their approach. Bex must have been telling the truth when she said that her mother had been keeping in contact with her using a bird familiar, just like they had been in contact with the settlement.

Shaula sat on the back of the ATV and put her arms around Faolán's waist as they drove along the channel the ship had scored in the ground when it crashed. Charm was in her hair, and Madigan loped along at their side. Faolán's broad back was warm before her, and the jacket he wore over his clothes rippled in the breeze of their passage. If they were not in pursuit of a murderer, the trip would be pleasant.

Pleasant. Since when had she come to see travel as pleasant?

They set up camp near the gorge that led through the hills to the river valley. While Faolán cooked and ate his camp meal and looked at the wreck of the *Sunda Tiger* in the distance, Shaula took out one of the devices they had taken from Bex: the android control unit. It was time to take a closer look at the list of androids.

Each listing included several functions: a list of their special attributes, including their enhancements; a menu in which their memories could be wiped; and a list of pre-programmed routines ready to be triggered. Currently, only Shaula, Charm, and Madigan had memories that could be wiped. The pre-programmed routines, also, could only be run in those present.

Shaula investigated, and as far as she could tell from the information on the device, it worked via an ancient proximity tagging and inventory system, which meant that the device needed to be near an android to trigger the routines. Also, although the code was visible in each item, each code was already uploaded and ready to be triggered in each android. The communications standard used would have taken a while to upload a whole new code, but could transmit a simple trigger in moments. This must be why nothing strange had happened to Madigan yet: it would have been too time-consuming to upload a new code from this simple device at the wreck.

All in all, the way the device worked was very awkward. Was this evidence that Dr Neale also had no access to satellite communications? Surely she would be using a more user-friendly system if she had access to one.

Shaula started looking through the list of pre-programmed routines under each android's name. Each was named with an alphanumeric string, just as Bex had described, and if she had little to no programming knowledge, the girl no doubt would not have been able to tell what she was activating. But Shaula could read through the code of each program, and each one she read made her more horrified.

She checked herself first, of course. Whatever program had been activated to make her try to kill Faolán was long gone. But three other programs sat there ready to go: one that would trigger her to take apart and incinerate an android, with a blank space in the code waiting for an android's designation to be entered; one that would cause her to destroy her own engineering lab; and one that would send her on a rampage, killing as many of the *Sunda Tiger* crew as she could. She deleted all three programs and emptied the trash. As she did so, she felt a 'lightening' within her processes. She was sure the programs were deleted, not just from the device, but also from herself.

Then she started checking other androids. There was a program that would cause Altair to murder Marcie when they were alone. Obviously, she deleted that one. She found a program that would make Diphda break into munitions storage in the *Sunda Tiger* and set detonators at key points to destroy the wreck. She deleted that one too.

She found an insidious program ready to run in Naos that would have the android administering all medicines at too strong a dose by an order of magnitude. That one could be hazardous to many people's health, so she deleted it. Later, she would have to take the device near each of these androids to make sure the changes were implemented.

Not all the programs were dangerous. Capella had no fewer than fifteen routines ready that would allow her to take care of a baby or child at various stages of development. Nursing routines. Nutrition routines. School routines. Each routine had a tag on it, allowing it to activate if Bellatrix was destroyed or rendered incapacitated. It was clear Dr Neale had made contingency plans in case Bex was left alone. If Shaula's memories were correct, Capella had even been the surrogate mother of Bex, so it made sense that she would have been picked for this role. Shaula left all of those routines intact for now.

Shaula spent most of the night lying beside Faolán in the tent while he snored gently beside her, deleting anything that would cause any android to become dangerous.

The following morning, they made their way back through the hills. They made faster time than the outward journey had taken, because they could move faster than the lab vehicles. By afternoon, they were a long way down the river. But Shaula and Charm's batteries ran low, and Madigan's was not much better. They stopped for a while to charge from the mobile packs. Shaula drifted in her charge cycle with little awareness of her surroundings. When she woke later, the sun had moved a significant portion across the sky, and evening was not far off.

Faolán stood at the river, skimming stones. Something about the way he flung the stones with more force than necessary made her aware of how much stress he must be feeling. Shaula unclipped herself from the mobile pack and picked her way across the stony riverbank to him.

He gave her a quick glance over his shoulder as she approached. "Hey, feeling better?" he asked.

"The mobile pack got me to 87% charged."

"There's no more?"

"No."

He skimmed another stone. It bounced twice. "What do I do if you run out of batteries?"

"Leave me behind and tell the androids in the settlement. Someone would take another mobile pack out to me and charge me enough that I could come home."

He selected another stone from near his feet and smoothed it in his fingers, tested its weight. "I don't like that idea. I don't like the thought of leaving you behind." He skimmed the new stone. This one did not bounce at all, but went straight into the river with a plop.

She stepped behind him and wrapped her arms around his torso. She rested her chin on his shoulder and smoothed his belly with her hand. "You are worried about our task."

"Of course. We don't know what we're walking into. We should have brought someone else with us. What were we thinking?"

"That the salvage needs to continue. People are relying on the salvaged goods."

"We already failed to a certain extent. We lost stuff in the explosion that can't be replaced."

"We will adapt."

He sighed. "Shaula. The unit that can make my ADHD meds was destroyed." He spoke with such a flat inflexion that it was as if he felt nothing about that loss. But she knew the opposite was true. He felt everything.

"I am sorry," she said.

"There's no need to apologise."

"I mean, I feel sorry." She squeezed him, and he put a hand on her forearm. "But also, I want to assure you: you are fine just the way you are."

He gave a huff of laughter. "That's not quite true. Sure, I'm still me, no matter what. But without my meds, I can't fully stay on top of all the things I need to do for my job."

"I have not seen you failing."

"But I've *felt* it. There's been so many times where I've nearly forgotten something really important until I've been reminded by you or someone else. It's only a matter of time until these small errors start piling up, and I won't be able to keep on top of things again."

"Then do not."

He turned his head to give her an incredulous look. "*Excuse me?* Shaula the workaholic is telling me to shirk my duties?"

"No. In our colony, a few times we have discovered that an android was assigned to the wrong role, and they were performing sub-optimally. The fix for this situation cannot be to change the android, because we only have so many resources and so much information available to us. The fix has always been to reassign the android to a role better suited to them. You have what is considered a disability for a human. But the disability is not only within you. It is caused by the interactions that you have with the community you live in, and the resources you have access to. If your role does not accommodate your needs when your access to resources changes, then perhaps you need a new role. You are fine just the way you are, because you are you. The problem is not with *you*."

He was quiet and still in her arms for a few minutes. Then he turned and gave her a chaste kiss. "Whoever said that your bedside manner was lacking just didn't understand you, I reckon. It always seems to me like you have the right words."

"Maybe I only have them for you."

He grinned, his eyes crinkling at the corners. "How about you? Have you had any more time to think about your enhancement, or about the memories you retrieved?"

She rested her chin on his shoulder again. "Emotions... I think you may be right about them. But as you mentioned, it is hard to verify, because how does one measure what they feel against what others feel? Are any differences because of the emotions being different, or how those emotions express through personality? Is there a difference in *how much* I feel or *how detailed* my feelings are? None of these concerns are measurable, none of them objective. I am not comfortable in this sort of thought experiment, where there is no clear answer. Is it easier to face such questions as a human?"

He snorted. "Not at all. Not even a little bit."

"But surely you must observe a difference in how I express my emotions and how humans do?"

"Hm." He tipped his head to one side. "You do seem uncomfortable expressing emotions. But I've known plenty of humans like that too. Don't get me wrong, Shaula, you're *exceptional*, but that's not one of your exceptions; not particularly."

"How about how I express my emotions with you? In our... intimacies. Surely I am different."

"Again, human nature is broad enough to cover any-thing different about you androids. Like, you seem to have a different relationship with your sexuality than I do. But then again, I dated this guy once? Back when I was young. And he was demisexual. You're actually quite similar in some ways to how he was with me."

"What is demisexual?"

"It's people whose sexuality is tied to love and famil-iarity. Like, they don't want to have sex just to get off, but only as a way of expressing affection. My ex was happy to partake of *bedroom activities* while in a relationship, but said he didn't miss it at all when he was single."

That was an apt description. "Yes. I think that is how I approach intimacies. Except for that first time, which was driven more by curiosity."

"Yeah, I figured." He patted her hand. "How about... the memories?"

"I think it will take me a long time to process the re-trieved memories. They change how I think about my place in this settlement, and in this universe."

"You've been wondering about that, huh? What do you think? Where is your place?"

Shaula smoothed her hands over his shoulders, flat-tening the creases in his jacket. "I do not yet know. De-spite everything, I feel like engineering is obviously still my place. My worries are about how it will all work with-out Tiaki. This salvage and investigation has taught me I am still bad at communicating with most people. But I do not know if I need to make adjustments."

"I think you put too much stock in 'not being person-able'. You *have* met Naos and Diphda, right? I think they're less personable than you." He reached up and squeezed one of her hands.

She frowned. "Surely not. I know they can be tricky—"

"—They're far more than tricky."

"—But I have always been known as the worst. Other androids make plans of how to approach me when they have large requests."

He bumped back against her. "Just because you have a reputation for being the trickiest, doesn't mean you earned it. Perhaps your stronger emotions discombobulate the other androids, and they don't see how there are other ways that some of them are even trickier to deal with? I don't know. You all have 30 years of history, during which you've all changed. And yet you all act as if you haven't changed much at all. It seems to be a situation that would lead to people getting unfair reputations."

Shaula hummed. "I had not thought of it that way."

"If you're still worried about it, you know who is considered pretty likeable, and is already winning her way back into most people's good graces after the wee blip her reputation took the other week?"

Shaula raised an eyebrow.

"Marcie. She's always been known as a pleasant sort within the crew. And people are getting over their shock about her relationship with Altair. Rely on her. She'll come through for you."

"Will you come through for me too?"

"Of course. Now, shall we get a bit more travel time in? There's still a few hours before sunset, and if we go further, we'll be able to make the hidden lab sometime late tomorrow morning."

"That sounds like a solid plan."

That night, while camped by the lake shore, instead of poring through the device, Shaula dedicated herself to Faolán. She used her fingers and her lips to tell him just how much she appreciated his presence at her side, and how much she valued who he was. He told her a similar message with caresses and kisses of his own. The night birds cried out and the wavelets of the lake lapped at the shore as their voices rose in passion. If things went poorly the following day, it might be their last time together.

For all that Faolán brought intense feeling after intense feeling out in her, Shaula experienced no more memories rising to the surface. It seemed she had already remembered what she needed to.

They resumed their journey early the next morning. Shaula knew her batteries would only last so long, and Faolán picked up on that tension. It was only midmorning when they arrived at an overgrown clearing by a stream that poured into a half-moon bay. Concrete foundation blocks, obscured by bushes, marked where the first settlement had stood. They left their ATV and Madigan behind and went on foot to peer through the tree line at the apparently abandoned area. It looked like no-one was there. But when Shaula pulled out the device and checked the listing labelled 'Bellatrix', she found the menus inside were active. If there was a preprogrammed routine within the listing, she could have uploaded it to Dr Neale's body. But of course, she had left nothing like that in her own listing.

"We are here," Shaula whispered to Faolán. "She is nearby."

He nodded. "Well then. Let's find Rebecca Neale's secret lab."

CHAPTER 32

Faolán held out his hand and looked down at the leaf litter through it. "This is so weird." He poked at the small, smooth piece of tech pinned to his chest, though it, too, was as invisible as he was himself.

"You are not really transparent," said Shaula. "Light is just being bent around you."

"It's still super weird."

Shaula had taken the cloaking devices from Bex and Sekhmet and repaired them. Since they only had two of them, they had reluctantly left Madigan behind with the ATV, though they had asked him to keep watch for movements to or from the hidden lab. Faolán would have preferred to have the wolf at his back, but Madigan was running low on batteries already, so perhaps it was for the best.

"How are we going to make sure we don't lose each other?" he said once his preparations were complete. "I can't see you, and you can't see me."

Shaula's fingers brushed past his crotch.

"Uh, *now*?"

"My apologies. I missed my target." Her hand found his, and she intertwined their fingers. "Shall we hold hands as much as possible?"

He never thought he'd hear her say *that*. He grinned, though she wouldn't see it. "Fantastic."

Together, they crept out of the tree line and into the remains of the settlement. It was easy to believe that the site had been (mostly) abandoned for three decades. All that remained were concrete foundations with a thick coating of soil, leaf litter, and even large plants and bushes on top of them. Trees poked up all over the place, their roots cracking the crumbling remains further.

"Over there," whispered Shaula in the general vicinity of his ear.

He couldn't see her pointing, of course, but she tugged him around to look over to the left. He soon saw what she had spotted. There was a wish path running out of the forest and around several bushes towards one of the foundations. As stealthy as Dr Neale had tried to be, she couldn't avoid putting her feet on the ground.

They circumnavigated the foundation the path led to. There were footprints across the top, leading to a bush near the middle.

"I want to check what data I can," whispered Shaula near his ear. She led him over to the tree line again, in a different direction from the well-trodden path. Once they were behind several rows of trees, Shaula let go of his hand and he heard a rustle and a small thump. She then turned off her cloak: she was lying on her belly at his feet. He kept his cloak on while she took out the android control device and started poking through the menu. She was green-skinned and grey-clad. She camouflaged in with the forest. He, in his human skin tone and white t-shirt, would be a lot more conspicuous if uncloaked.

"She is below somewhere. The signal keeps cutting in and out, though, as if she is far away."

"Maybe her underground lair is either sprawling or deep? So she's still where we think she is, but she's far away regardless?"

"Perhaps. I have an idea that I wish to run by you. There are no routines to trigger or time to code and upload one. But the listing for Bellatrix contains a menu to delete memories."

"Funny that," said Faolán.

"What is funny?"

"By giving herself an android body, she's opened herself to all the same vulnerabilities that the rest of you have. You want to delete some of her memories?"

Shaula put a hand over her mouth. "I do not want to. Not even after everything she has done. It is a terrible thing to have one's memories deleted. But I expect she knows Bex is in our care now and will be on guard. We are at an extreme disadvantage because we do not know what is down there. If we were to delete just enough memories that she is not aware we are coming..."

Faolán let out a gusty sigh and squatted down near her. The worry and discomfort showed on her face as clear as day. Now that she was aware of her enhanced emotions, she felt them and expressed them so keenly. She was now notably different from the other androids of the settlement.

"I appreciate how difficult this decision would be for you. Which would be easier for you? Me letting you make the decision, or me making it for you?"

"Tell me what to do, Faolán." Worry lines gathered between her brows as she looked up close to his face.

He chewed his lip. "This may sound harsh, but I think she forewent all right to receive the same consideration as all the other androids when she murdered an entire settlement, including the children. We've got words for people like that. Also, there's simply the fact that if she knows we're coming, we wouldn't have a snowball's chance in hell of getting into her lab. We really *have* to take her by surprise." He put his hand on her shoulder. "I say go for it, because it might make the difference between us bringing her to justice for what she's done, and failing to do so."

She looked down.

"Think of Tiaki," he added.

She nodded and then poked through the menu again. She brought up a code transcript and started scrolling through it. She highlighted an extended selection and deleted it. Then she ran her eyes back over the remaining transcript.

"I am new to this, but I believe that might let us take her by surprise. I have deleted the last several days to before she received her last message from Bex. I wiped back to the exact same time of day as now. If we are lucky and the timing works out, she may believe she has recently arrived here from the settlement. If we act fast, we may be lucky enough to catch her unawares."

"That's all we can do, I suppose."

Shaula put the device back in her pack and then cloaked herself. They waved their hands around until they could clasp them again, and then they went to examine the place the footprints led to. Bizarrely, they just... stopped. It was as if whoever walked here never went any further.

"Hold your hand out in front of you," whispered Shaula.

"Why?"

"So you do not hit your face or stub your toe."

"On wha—? Ow!" Faolán winced at the sound of his shod foot kicking... something. But the worst part was the burning embarrassment; considering what technology they themselves were using, it was obvious in retrospect that there was something here that was cloaked. just like they were.

He ran his fingers over the smooth surface in front of him. Nearby, he heard other fingers as Shaula did the same. He found the door handle first. It was locked, of course.

"Allow me," whispered Shaula as her hands brushed over his.

He switched places with her. "There is no panel to hack," she whispered to him.

"What do we do, then?"

"Shall we risk making a little noise taking the more destructive method?"

"It might blow our surprise arrival."

"I will be as quiet as I can possibly be."

He mulled it over. But without being able to see the door, they couldn't even pick the lock. "I don't know what else we could do. But this door is reinforced though, right?"

"No doubt, but so am I."

There sounded a thunk, a pop, and a brief screech of metal, quickly cut off. Then a line cut through the world before them.

The small building shielded before them was only shielded on the outside. The inside, once the door was open, showed like any normal building interior. The door itself, as Shaula swung it out, passed beyond the limits of the cloaking shield; it was a no-frills steel door with a small round glass window in it, now sporting a handprint-shaped dent in the metal near the handle. A handprint the precise size of Shaula's hand.

"Have I ever told you how handy you are to have around?"

"No. But you are right: I am."

Faolán looked into the short hallway for a camera, but couldn't see one. "I would have expected more security gear."

"Maybe she did not have any to deploy? We can only use what we had in stock, and we do not have spares in the settlement."

"Hm, I hope you're right."

They slipped through the door and eased it closed behind them. A sparse metal stairwell led underground, lit with a thin ceiling strip of cold white light. They descended. Faolán found it difficult to figure out where to put his feet when he could not see them — his sense of his body was already slipping.

At the bottom of the stairs was another steel door with a glass window in it. Beyond was a large rectangular space with several sofas and tables. It looked more like a waiting room in a fancy business than a living room. There were three doors off each side of the room, and double doors at the far end.

In front of him, the door clicked open — Shaula had opened it. She fumbled for his hand again, and together they tip-toed through and closed the door behind them. Somehow, he knew Dr Neale wasn't at this end of the facility. He couldn't hear a single sound that they were not responsible for. Still, they moved as quietly as they could. She would be somewhere at the other end, through the double doors, so not far away.

One by one, they examined the rooms off the main living space. Each was a windowless rectangular space, all the same size. On one side, they found a kitchen stocked with long-life foods, a bathroom, and a room with medical equipment including a treatment bed. On the other side were two bedrooms, one plain and lacking in personality, and the other clearly the bedroom of a girl, painted in moody purple and with clothes and personal items strewn about. There was a large fluffy pad on the ground along one side, like an over-sized dog bed. Cables ran into it. "Sekhmet's charging station," whispered Shaula.

"Speaking of which, do you think you could charge here? I'm worried about you."

There was silence for a moment. "I suppose," she said. "Though I would prefer to find a charge point that I would not need to curl up on the floor to use."

They went to check the last room. It was an office. It had the look of a scientist's office. There was a whiteboard on one wall with notes scribbled on it, and many filing cabinets. No matter how technology progressed, most scientists he had met still ended up printing out an inordinate amount of documentation and research for 'quick reference' — they couldn't help themselves. There was also a glass workstation with a leather-look office chair behind it. The chair creaked and the cushions settled as Shaula took a seat. A quiet beep followed a moment later.

"This chair is a recharge station," she whispered. "Convenient: I may charge while searching for information."

Faolán walked closer to the workstation. "You think she'll have, like, a manifesto?"

"It's unlikely she would spell out all her motivations. But we should check all the same." The workstation lit up and screens of data flicked by faster than Faolán could follow as Shaula started her investigation. "I have found something of note," said Shaula, pausing on one screen. "I have accessed an inventory of equipment. It appears there may be communications equipment in this outpost. The remaining battery power is low, but it seems to have enough charge for at least one more cycle. The range is not mentioned, but what if it could send a signal to the Weft relay your crew deployed?"

Faolán's stomach flipped. "You mean we could contact the Orion Navy?"

"I believe so, yes. Though I am not an expert in such equipment, and so we would need to inspect it to be sure. As we have not seen it yet, the equipment must be further in."

Even just getting word to his family that he was OK would be brilliant. His sisters would be worried. As would everyone else's families. Plus, there were a few unfortunate families that the captain would need to contact, to inform them of the loss of their loved ones. Not everyone had made it safely off the *Sunda Tiger*. If they could send a data packet updating those at Sol of how they were...

They'd have to look for that equipment. After they had Dr Neale in custody.

"Is there anything on there that would tell you where Dr Neale is now?"

"One moment," she said, tapping the workstation again. "I will just—"

A buzzing, crackling sound filled the room. Faolán's hair stood on end. He felt like he had the worst case of feet-on-carpet static he'd even had. He looked down as a shiver went through his body, and found he could see himself again. The cloaking device had failed. He looked up. "Shaula—"

She, too, was visible again. She thrashed in the chair, her head whipping back. Her eyes flickered with blue electricity. Charm scampered down her arm onto the workstation in a hurry.

"What do I do?" he asked Shaula, but she couldn't respond. Charm was tapping at her hand with its tail, but she didn't respond to it either.

He began looking around the room for something he could insulate his hands with. Was it too much to ask for a pair of rubber gloves to be lying about? He was so desperate, he barely registered the door clicking open behind him. There was a hiss, and then something hit his back. Something sharp. "Agh!" he choked out, unable to keep silent under the onslaught. Pain scored down his back. He reached back and brushed fur. He made another grab for whatever assaulted him, and stumbled into a filing cabinet, making a loud clang. A white blur landed on the filing cabinet beside him and then sprung towards his face. He instinctively closed his eyes and brought his forearm up, saving his face. Pain scratched down his arm. Finally, he could see what attacked him: a fluffy white cat, one with pink eyes.

A familiar. Of course she had a familiar. He'd even seen it around the settlement: the totally innocuous, dainty, and cute house cat familiar of Bellatrix.

He grabbed the cat by the scruff of the neck and flung it across the room towards some shelves. He'd normally never dream of flinging an animal like that, but it wasn't a flesh and blood cat and so was no doubt sturdier, and also he was in full 'get it off me!' panic mode. The cat crashed into the shelf, fell to the floor, and then sprung up again, its back arched and its tail fluffed. It hissed at him and bared its fangs. Its pink eyes glowed with malice.

Faolán glanced at Shaula to check on her. She was still locked in the chair, unable to move. Her eyes were wide and shocked, though they now were her own golden colour rather than the startling blue. But she was not looking at him. She was looking at the doorway.

He whipped around, just in time to duck the swing of a right hook punch. He gulped as he looked up at the tall white-clad purple form with the tumbling purple curls. "Dr Neale, I presume," he said with all the bravado he could muster.

Dr Neale looked at him with her emotionless purple face and gleaming eyes. "You would presume correctly."

CHAPTER 33

A pulsing signal writhed through her systems, aborting each process she tried to run. Her legs did not respond to her urging to stand. Her mouth did not respond to her desire to speak. Charm was trying to rouse her, but she could not let it know she appreciated its attempts. She could only watch as first the familiar Bastet attacked Faolán, and then Bellatrix, or rather Dr Neale herself, charged into the room and joined the fray.

Faolán ducked Dr Neale's punching once, twice. He pushed a filing cabinet in her path, and dove to the side as she kicked it back towards him. Fear was stark on his face. Although he was fast for a human, he would not last long against an android, and they all knew it.

Shaula tried again to break free of whatever process had been sent through the recharge chair to hamper her, but she was helpless in its grasp. She started an internal diagnostic, hoping for any clue about what to do.

Dr Neale took a moment to smirk at her. The unfamiliar look on the face of someone who Shaula had considered to be her colleague for many years made her feel a sharp stab of anger. This woman had fooled her and used her repeatedly. She had made her commit terrible atrocities. She had even made her disassemble her own lover. But now she had a new lover, and she would not lose this one to Dr Neale's machinations. She gritted her teeth and tried to force her way through.

"Did you think I wouldn't have weight sensors in the stairwell," said Dr Neale, "or the charge ports monitored? How foolish do you think I am?"

A heavy book hit Dr Neale in the head, then another bounced off her raised arm: Faolán was throwing things at her, trying to bring her attention back to him. The fool. Why would he do that? And why did the knowledge make her internals sing?

Dr Neale tilted her head as she perused Shaula. "You've tapped into your enhancement, haven't you? Not that it matters; yours gives you no advantage in battle. Having more emotions just made you easier to manipulate. It's an enhancement that's utterly lost on someone who never had a human self."

"Why did you make her that way, then?" demanded Faolán. "You're spouting lies. You don't strike me as the type to do unimportant things."

A small frown furrowed Dr Neale's brow for a moment, and Shaula felt sure that Faolán had struck close to the truth of something with his words, but she could not yet fathom what.

Dr Neale turned her attention once more to Faolán, pursuing him around the workstation.

Shaula, desperate to help, returned her attention to the diagnostic. For long moments, nothing seemed to come of it. But then she found it: whatever held her in its thrall was borne on a proximity carrier signal. Since she was not networked, the only carrier signal she could think of was the simple one used in the android control device they had removed from Bex. Or, perhaps, a twin device in Dr Neale's possession.

Dr Neale paused behind the workstation at Shaula's shoulder. "It's Sunday," she said. Then, louder: "It's *Sunday*. You wiped my memory! Bitch!" She seized Shaula and cracked her face against the glass workstation. Or, no: it was the workstation that cracked, all the writing on the screen blinking out as the panel broke.

"What have you done to my daughter?!" screamed Dr Neale in Shaula's ear as she yanked her up again. Out of the corner of her eye, Dr Neale's perfect android face contorted and tears rolled down her cheeks.

Faolán tried to pull Dr Neale off Shaula, but she swatted him away like a fly. "What have you done?" demanded the overwrought scientist once more, but Shaula still could not answer. She still could not move.

Unless...

If it were the control device, there was one thing she could do. But... how could she bring herself to do it? Sure, she'd done it before, to hide Madigan's allocation, but that was before she had remembered the full horror of what had been taken from her. The mere thought of all the memories Dr Neale had wiped from Shaula's mind made her feel a deep well of horror. The thought of losing even more... on purpose... by her *own hand*...

...but if she did not move soon, Faolán may be killed. He was still provoking their opponent.

"We haven't done anything to Bex," he said. "We're not like you. We don't hurt children!"

The fool. He was going to get himself killed.

Shaula reached into her own process logs. To remove any uploaded codes, she had to remove everything. All the processes that had run. All the memories she'd written. She concentrated on the last few minutes of her being, ever since the electricity overcame her. Then she chose to delete them.

...

She was looking for important data on the workstation when suddenly it powered down and a crack appeared across its surface. She saw no projectile, no blow that would have caused the damage. One moment, the workstation was whole, and the next moment it was destroyed. Charm had also moved. It had been perched on her head, but now stood on her wrist. It, and her arm, were now visible.

"You don't understand!" shouted a voice shockingly close to Shaula's ear. "It wasn't working! And it had to, it just had to!"

Shaula looked up in surprise at Bellatrix... no, Dr Neale, who stood next to her, wearing a strange white jumpsuit that Shaula had never seen her wearing. Dr Neale had her attention turned away from her towards Faolán, who was also visible again, and had a bruise on the side of his face and a small cut over his eyebrow. His t-shirt had a rip in the shoulder. When had all of this happened?

She had lost memories again. Had Dr Neale wiped her again? The thought filled her with horror...

...no, wait. Her process logs were open in her mind. It was her. She had done this. Why? She must have had a reason.

Faolán could tell her later. But only if she saved him now. Because Dr Neale made as if to rush Faolán.

She surged up out of the chair and grabbed Dr Neale from behind. The doctor grunted, a curiously human sound. Belatedly, Shaula noted that there had always been minor details about Bellatrix that pointed to her difference from the other androids: the way she spoke, some of her body language and gestures. The clues had always been there. How had none of them seen?

315

Dr Neale fought Shaula's hold. She tried to strike Shaula in the face with an elbow, but Shaula ducked her head to the side and avoided the blow. She held on as hard as she could. It was all she could do — Dr Neale seemed to have a stronger body than Shaula, and she had a height advantage too. She only got the upper hand because her attack was a surprise.

She peered around Dr Neale's shoulder. It was like the lion attack all over again. Faolán was watching, anguish in his eyes.

"Run," she told him. "Tell the settlement." She would hold Dr Neale here, no matter what.

"No!" he cried, his voice breaking.

It seemed he understood her intent. But Shaula had countless evil actions that her hands had performed to atone for, and this moment showed that it was now time for that reckoning.

"Go," she said. "Now."

He shook his head, but stepped out of the office nonetheless. His eyes did not leave her own until the doorway made it impossible to see her.

"He won't make it to the settlement," said Dr Neale. "You can only hold me until your batteries run out, and you're running low."

Shaula didn't dignify the doctor with a reply. But she was right. Shaula could only hold her for so long. Perhaps if she let go and then wiped the doctor's memory again with the control tablet?

But no: she would not have enough time. Would she be able to grab something sharp and incapacitate her with a stab to the back of the neck? But nothing sharp lay near.

The door clanged and feet sounded on the stairs to the surface, the echoes loud in the underground quarters. Good. Faolán was getting to safety.

"I'll get my retribution for whatever you've done to my daughter," growled the doctor, the threatening rumble of her voice vibrating Shaula's arms.

"We have done nothing to harm Bex. We questioned her and fed her. That is all."

"I don't believe you." The doctor lifted her legs, put her feet on the workstation, and pushed. Hard. Shaula toppled, and the doctor fell on her, scrambling away as soon as Shaula's grip slipped. Dr Neale darted for the door.

"No!" cried Shaula.

But before Dr Neale could get far, she fell to the ground. Or rather, was knocked. By a purple arm.

Shaula ran towards the doctor, intending to restrain her again, but the doctor rolled and leaped further into the outer room, away from her assailant. Shaula skidded to a halt in the doorway, taking in a most unlikely grouping of people. Vega, who was no longer inactivated, was the one who had stopped the doctor. Beyond him, closer to the door, was Faolán, who peered around Vega to lock eyes with her. Madigan stood at his side, hackles raised. Faolán held an arm out behind him, keeping someone shielded behind his body: Bex, who was riding astride her lion familiar. And over by the door to the stairwell was the most unlikely person of all: Simons. The disgraced engineer was surveying the proceedings as if wondering whether to get involved.

"Let my daughter go!" growled the doctor.

"It's not like that, Mum!" said Bex from behind Faolán. "Please. Stop this!"

Dr Neale's arms dropped and she gaped at her daughter. "What?"

"They're not holding me hostage."

"Why are you here, then?"

Bex gulped. "Did you lie to me?"

"What?"

"Was it a bomb you had me put on the ship? Was that program meant to sabotage their computers?" The girl's voice was a whisper. Shaula could not see her face from her vantage, but she could imagine.

"Honey, I—"

"Please tell me they're wrong!" the girl cried.

There was a long silence from Dr Neale.

"How could you?" whispered Bex. Underneath her, the lion growled. "Why would we need to make their ship crash? There were *bodies* in the wreck, Mum. I had to *bury* people."

"You weren't supposed to need to do that, Honey," Dr Neale said in a placating voice. "I never wanted you to suffer like that! How could I, when I love you? The ship was bigger than I guessed. The bomb was supposed to take care of it."

Bex reared back. "'Take care of it'? You mean, you tried to kill them all? You made me plant a bomb that was supposed to kill them *all*?" Bex started shaking, and tears rolled down her cheeks.

Faolán let out an aggrieved noise and covered his eyes. Shaula also felt horror at the revelation.

"The galaxy is a harsher place than you know, Honey," said Dr Neale. The doctor looked at her daughter for a long moment, shaking her head. "When you come to understand things as I do, let me know. I'll help you."

With that, the doctor turned and ran through the double doors at the end of the room, further into the facility.

"We must stop her," said Shaula, already running in pursuit, Madigan at her side. "There are resources here she must not access."

Vega followed close behind as she ran into a long corridor that looked more utilitarian than the living quarters behind. Evenly spaced doors along the corridor led into labs and storage rooms, glass panels in the doors showing their contents. She had seen these rooms before, in the memories she had retrieved. Shaula peered into each one down the left-hand side, while Vega took the right.

"Why are you here?" Shaula asked him.

"I cannot abide what she made me do."

"Who woke you?"

"Simons."

"Did he say why?"

"He said the girl had already gone alone, and a security guard was needed to pursue her."

"Why is he here?"

"He said he could offer engineering assistance."

Shaula did not believe for a moment that Simons was here for altruistic reasons. But there were more important things to deal with right at this moment.

She detected sounds from within a room at the end of the corridor. She opened the door and stepped inside. As she did so, her internal battery warning made itself known to her again. She was back under 5% batteries, and after her aborted charge earlier, she was not sure how accurate that measure was.

Dr Neale stood at a workstation tapping at the screen. Shaula charged forward, aiming low and hitting the larger woman around the thighs. They went down together in a heap.

Shaula could barely see under the white fabric of Dr Neale's suit, but she felt the woman flailing and punching and did her best to avoid the blows while holding her away from the workstation. Growls filled the air and additional weight settled on her as Madigan nipped at the doctor and held her down with his paws. Then the combined weight lifted off her, and she looked up at Vega holding Dr Neale in the air by the throat. He spun and pinned her to a wall.

"You made me kill," he said without inflexion but with finality. "You made me your weapon."

"You were always my weapon."

Vega drew his hand back, then slammed her onto the wall harder. Her hands scrabbled at his arms, but he was much bigger than her and had more reach.

Shaula crouched, holding the growling Madigan around his neck. She was no longer sure which android his defence algorithm would identify as the bigger threat.

"Mum!" screamed Bex from the doorway.

Faolán entered the room, holding his hands up. "Hey, Big Guy. I know you've got feelings you want to take out on her right now. But we need to keep her in one piece so she can be questioned."

Vega stayed motionless for a long moment, and then stepped away from the wall, changing his hold on Dr Neale to a restraining one.

Shaula stood and approached the workstation. The display showed a similar menu to the one on the android control device. She had pulled up menus for both Shaula and Vega and had been moments from executing code on both of them. Code that would have them kill Faolán and Simons, and then themselves.

Shaula looked up at Dr Neale, who startled at her expression. She wished she had a mirror so she could see how she looked at that moment.

Shaula deleted the codes and emptied the trash on the workstation too, to make sure those codes could not be revived. She felt a hand on her shoulder and found Faolán at her side. His eyes shimmered.

"Are you all right?" he asked.

"Yes. How about you? You must be injured." She pulled at his torn shirt, looking for wounds.

"Bruises only. Nothing to worry about."

That was not quite true, but maybe he was not aware. She touched the cut on his forehead, the scratches on his neck, and ran a finger over the bruise forming on his jaw. When she leaned forward and kissed him, she did it with the utmost gentleness so as not to hurt him further.

"Ew," said a voice behind them: the girl Bex.

Shaula looked around at the others in the room. She had not even thought to worry about observers before expressing her affection for him. Then she frowned. "Where is Simons?"

Faolán looked around in surprise. "Not again."

They all left the room, Vega still restraining Dr Neale. Shaula and Faolán both checked the rooms along the corridor. Shaula's low battery warning was strident now, at only 2%. She ignored it.

"What's in here?" asked Faolán, standing at one door peering through the glass. His shoulders were tense, and he was talking to Dr Neale.

The doctor started by smirking at him, as if she would not answer. But then she, too, frowned. "The communications equipment..." she said. "It's not strong enough to reach your Weft relay, though. And it's nearly out of batteries, hence why I've not been using it myself. The solar panel's cracked."

"That's why he was so keen to come here!" said Faolán. "All he wants is access to comms."

Faolán pushed through the door, Shaula close behind him. Simons was at a terminal hooked up to a large tower-like comms array that extended through the ceiling. It must have been cloaked from above, because the array seemed to extend into the open air.

"Stop!" said Shaula. She sped forward, but was too late. Simons completed the function and sent his message.

Shaula pushed the man out of the way and started checking what he had sent. He moved without resistance. He did not wear the smug expression she might have expected. Instead, he just looked relieved, and tears gathered at the corners of his eyes. He pinched the bridge of his nose and took deep breaths.

"Your message won't get to your relay," Dr Neale told him.

"He did not send his message to the relay," said Shaula. "He sent it in a different direction. He used an antique verification standard. I believe it was to an old relay network."

"What message?" asked Faolán.

She showed him the string of incomprehensible letters and numbers.

"Code," said Faolán. "Code sent to an old relay network, unknown to the Orion Navy." He glared at Simons. "I reckon he just contacted his space pirates."

"To say what?"

But Simons just turned away, refusing to answer.

"If what you've done ruins my work here, your life is forfeit," growled Dr Neale.

"You're not in a position to be giving ultimatums, lady," said Faolán. "Not with what you've done."

"Mum, what did you do?"

They all looked at the confusion and fear on Bex's face.

Dr Neale looked around at all of them. "I would do anything for my children," she said in a tight whisper. "*Anything.*"

Children? They all looked in surprise at Bex. She was not the only one? But Shaula only remembered one instance of cloning. Where was her other child, or children?

Or who?

Shaula's wondering had no chance to end as she received her final battery warning and...

0%...

CHAPTER 34

F aolán would have liked to go straight back to the settlement and hand over this investigation to someone else. He was over it. But the logistics of their return
were complicated, to say the least.

Shaula had collapsed in his arms, her battery depleted. If she had run out, Vega likely would soon too.
Unfortunately, Dr Neale was still active. Surprisingly, Simons had come through for them for once and showed
them how to turn her off. Whatever vitriol and snark
had powered the man before was oddly depleted, and
he was now solemn.

Once Dr Neale was inactive, they'd hooked all the
other androids up to charging points in the facility and
then made use of the kitchen to make a meal. There was
plenty of food stockpiled, and as it was Bex's own
kitchen, she knew her way around it. The meal was awkward, what with Simons being there and still not admit-
ting what was in his message. Also, that fecking white cat

jumped them half-way through the meal. Faolán had somehow forgotten about it in all the madness, despite having its claw marks on him.

But eventually, they'd got themselves mounted up on a combination of ATVs, wolf, and lion for the trek around the lake to the research centre.

They arrived late in the evening, far too late to do a full report. Faolán had reported the bare bones of what happened to the captain, saw that both Dr Neale and Simons were taken into custody, and then he'd crashed. He hadn't even gone back to his assigned tent. He just crashed on a sofa in the Mayoral office. His last memory that evening was of green hands draping a blanket over him.

He now stood in Mayor Sirius's office, an instant coffee in hand, blearily blinking sleep out of his eyes and doing his best to be present for this important meeting though his brain hadn't yet deigned to turn on.

Mayor Sirius and Captain Rodriguez were there, as were Canopus, Commander Mori, Vega, and Ife, who had arrived just that morning ahead of the rest of the salvage crew on the final ATV. Shaula was there too, standing shoulder to shoulder with him. While he was still in the rumpled, torn, and grass-stained clothes he'd been wearing the day before (and the day before that), she was clean and fresh in a white tank top and grey slacks.

Since Ife was the commanding officer of the salvage crew, she started the meeting by explaining everything that had happened at the *Sunda Tiger*. Faolán listened with one ear while focussing on his coffee. When Ife described how they had fought Sekhmet, Shaula bumped shoulders with him. He gave her a sidewards smile. She was thinking again that she was pleased he'd made it through that day, he could tell. He bumped her shoulder in return.

Then it was their turn to explain what happened at the hidden facility. Faolán explained most of it, with Shaula and Vega jumping in as needed.

When they had laid all the details out, the captain, who sat perched on the edge of Mayor Sirius's desk, took a long moment to mull it all over. She looked at Sirius, who had his elbows on his desk and his fingers steepled.

"It seems the last few weeks have brought a lot to light," she said. "I want to say how sorry I am that you went through such a traumatic experience. From what I understand, you all had to see the bodies of your colleagues. And you two found them, right?"

Faolán nodded when the captain looked at him.

"We lost one human crew member and one android in tragic circumstances, an event which touched the lives of everyone here. And I deeply regret that your small team had to deal with that whole situation in isolation. Both Dr McArthur and Tiaki will be sorely missed."

Shaula's eyes dropped, and Faolán took a hold of her hand, squeezing it. There had been something between Shaula and Tiaki long before he was in the picture. He knew she'd be mourning him for a while.

Both Sirius and Canopus seemed to stare at them and their intertwined hands intently, but Faolán didn't care what anyone thought anymore, and it seemed neither did Shaula, because she kept a hold of him.

"Our next major consideration," continued the captain, as if she had not too raised an eyebrow at Faolán and Shaula, "is that we finally have Dr Neale in custody, and that she's been amongst us this whole time, doing who knows what. We're going to have to investigate this situation closely. What can you add, Sirius?"

"As far as anyone has been aware, Bellatrix has been just another android of the settlement. It has come as a great shock to us that she was Dr Neale. We also do not understand at all how her mind could have been moved into an android body. We were not aware that was possible. Is that not the case, Shaula?"

"Indeed," said Shaula. "Even though I now have memories of observing the transfer, I do not know how it was achieved. But I believe that it may have been the crux of Dr Neale's research project; her true aim."

"You will investigate this matter," said Sirius.

"Of course I will," said Shaula. "That is a given."

Faolán squeezed her hand. She didn't like being told what to do, he knew, and it would rankle that she was being told to do what she was obviously going to do anyway. The tension went out of her arm.

"We're going to have to question Dr Neale closely," said Commander Mori. "There's so much we still don't understand, like her specific aim, why she's keen to keep this facility hidden. Why she cloned herself. Why you androids have special enhancements. Even though we've found her, there's still so much we don't know, and she won't be an easy person to get answers out of."

"Yes, and we need to decide how to get that information," said Captain Rodriguez. "We have a few options here, since she's an android. Do we wake her and question her? Or do we look through her memory records?"

Faolán pulled a face. Both options seemed terrible. One involved risking waking her up, and the other involved treating a person like a thing. His stomach soured at the thought. It seemed he wasn't the only one, as no one offered an answer.

"Let's think carefully about our approach before we do anything," said the captain. "And let's make that decision together." She nodded at Mayor Sirius.

The silence in the room continued. "How about the hidden facility?" asked Faolán to change the subject. "I think we barely scratched the surface over there."

Shaula bumped his shoulder again. "I cannot do everything, Faolán."

"I didn't mean you necessarily," he said in a low voice. "Delegate, woman!" But honestly, that she'd demurred was a vast improvement on how she'd been until recently. When he first met her, she wouldn't have trusted that investigation to anyone else.

Canopus stepped forward from where she had been standing by the wall, observing. "I shall lead that investigation myself, if no one opposes?"

"I concur," said Sirius.

"We'll send a team with you," said the captain.

"We have another matter of concern," said Commander Mori. "What about the girl? Bex?"

"She did run off when told to stay," said Ife. "And of course she did sabotage the ship."

There were sighs around the room. No one felt comfortable holding things against a child.

"It does all look damning," said Captain Rodriguez. "But she's so young."

"I really think she didn't understand it all," said Faolán. "She was so horrified when she realised she'd been used. Right?" He looked at Ife, who nodded. "Also," he continued, "what Dr Neale and Bex said to each other says that Bex has been kept in the dark about things."

"We have a duty of care to her," said Commander Mori. "She has no place other than where she's been, and she can't go back there. She's a child."

"Of course," said the captain. "It's not her fault that she's an unregistered clone, made out in the wilds of this planet. Think of how lonely she must have been all this time. We'll look after her, though I expect she won't always see our care as for her benefit."

"What teenager does? But we must look after her, no matter how angry some of the crew might feel towards her."

The captain nodded slowly.

"Speaking of Bex, there's something else that's been bothering me," said Faolán. He shuffled awkwardly when everyone looked at him with undivided attention. "Dr Neale said that she'd do anything for her children. *Children*, as in plural. So, where's the other one, or ones?"

Everyone looked around at one another's reactions. The captain and the commander both sighed. Canopus looked at Mayor Sirius as if he might have the answer, but he folded his arms and looked up as if in thought.

"I only remember one clone being born," said Shaula. "Which is not definitive, of course, because the memories I unlocked were merely those that had been wiped from me when Dr Neale used me as a tool. If other clones were born and I was not present, I would not know. But I wonder if by children she meant something else. Perhaps something to do with us androids. Did she mean all of us? Or is one or more androids not what they appear, just as Bellatrix was not?"

"You mean you think that hiding amongst the androids of the settlement is someone else who was once human, whose consciousness was transferred? Someone she'd think of as her child?" asked Commander Mori.

"Her son," said Faolán.

"What?"

He looked around at the puzzlement on the others' faces. His sister's fascination with the Hellas Basin incident was finally paying off, it seemed. "She had a son. He died years before the Hellas Basin massacre. There was a rumour that her heartbreak over losing him made her reckless with her work, and that's how things got out of hand."

"But that must have happened years before she started this research centre. It couldn't possibly be," said Ife.

Faolán sighed. "Right. It was just a thought."

"Whatever the case may be, we will need to investigate each android of the settlement again, to identify malicious code left by Dr Neale, if nothing else," said Sirius. "Shaula, your work in this area is likely to be extensive and ongoing."

"Is it not always so?" she said, and Faolán snorted at her wry humour. "But it will work well with my investigation into the lost memories. I will need to examine everyone for both reasons."

"Is that mystery not solved, though?" asked Canopus.

"What do you mean? I do not believe so. Or rather, not fully."

"Between how Altair retrieved his memories from before the Event Horizon and how you have retrieved memories erased by Dr Neale since, it is clear that all we need to do to retrieve each android's memories is interrupt their processes."

Shaula stiffened at his side, and her grip on his hand tightened. "I will have no part of such a method."

"It is your job."

"No."

"But—"

Shaula took half a step forward. "No. I will have no part of it. Because what you are proposing is *torture*."

"It is not—"

"I assure you it *is*. Dr Neale has already made me torture androids for her studies. Will you follow her down that path?"

Faolán looked around the room. He saw tension in the faces of the humans in the room, and stillness in the androids. Shaula was making everyone uncomfortable, and she was *damned right* to do so.

"While many memories may be retrieved by the method you suggest, there is another avenue of investigation that retrieves small scattered memories. As Altair did, I have found that leaning into one's enhancements

329

also helps retrieve isolated memories. The process is less sure and takes longer, but it is never torturous. That is the method I will pursue. Investigating everyone's enhancements, which I need to investigate anyway, and encouraging them to lean into those enhancements."

"But we need more than scattered memories—"

"No. Either you let me investigate using my chosen method, or I will not investigate at all." She stepped back to be level with Faolán again.

"You will achieve results," said Mayor Sirius in a way that made it clear it wasn't a question.

"I will," said Shaula.

"And if the memories retrieved are not sufficient—"

"Then we will learn to bear the unknowing," interrupted Shaula.

There was an awkward silence in the room, and Faolán scrambled to think of something to fill it. But it was Vega who filled the gap.

"I fear we would not all welcome a full return of our memories. Just enough to elucidate our missing history will surely suffice. I have... things I do not ever wish to remember. Though I understand if you need me to in order to complete your investigation."

Despite Vega's lack of expressive vocal tone, Faolán really felt for him. His distress lay in the empty places between what he could emote and what he was willing to say. Faolán slipped around Shaula so he could reach up and lay a hand on Vega's shoulder. "Hey, Big Guy. We all know you weren't responsible for what happened, even if it was done by your hand. We know what happened now; there's no need to make you remember just for evidence or whatever."

"While that may be," said Canopus, "Vega should still be examined carefully to make sure no malicious algorithms remain within him as a result of that reprogramming."

Faolán gave the Deputy Mayor a cool look. She was right, but she'd picked a poor moment to bring it up.

"I agree," said Sirius. "Unless either of you have anything further to add, Shaula, would you please take Vega to your lab and run every diagnostic you can think of? Just as Marcie Martin-Palmer did for you last night."

Faolán hadn't known that had happened while he'd been unconscious, but it made sense. Shaula had nearly been used as a murder weapon too, after all.

"Understood," both Shaula and Vega said. Faolán gave Shaula a quick look as she left the office to check if she was mad at being dismissed. But she seemed fine. Actually, she probably was looking forward to getting back to her quiet lab, now that she'd said her piece.

Faolán stayed and listened to the rest of the meeting, as everyone else discussed the practicalities of keeping both Dr Neale and Simons restrained while they investigated the full import of their actions, and also discussed plans to investigate the hidden facility. It all felt so distant for him. It shouldn't. He was part of the crew, part of the settlement. But ever since his talk with Shaula where she'd pointed out that if his needs had changed, then his place should too... This just wasn't where he wanted to be anymore. He made promises to speak to the rest of the security team about prisoner watching shifts, and he *would*, just...

The meeting ended and he trooped out of the office with everyone else. Commander Mori strode away and Faolán hurried to catch up with her in the hallway.

"Commander, a moment of your time? Just a moment; I know you'll want to get back to Damon."

The commander paused, though her face looked tight. The others trooped past, leaving just the two of them in the hallway. "Yes, lieutenant?"

"I've been thinking about my place in the crew. I know that I have had certain duties when aboard ship, but things are different now, and we have different needs. We have a lot of security officers, but there's something glaringly missing that I think I can provide. No, I know I can provide. If you give me just a moment of time to describe what I have in mind, I think you'll agree..."

CHAPTER 35

Shaula had been busy ever since she had returned to her lab. Nothing had been waiting on her; Marcie had kept up with the workload admirably. But simply investigating Vega while making a list of android enhancements she was aware of and annotating them with recommendations of how to unlock each android's memories kept her busy for a full night and most of a day.

She had sent her list with Charm to the Mayor's office early that morning. Now she was unclipping Vega from the terminal she had been analysing him with. He sat up and looked at her quietly, waiting for her verdict.

"I cannot see any lingering effects," she said. "You are no more dangerous than any of us."

He looked down at his clasped hands and wrung them together fretfully. Shaula had observed Altair displaying the same behaviour on occasion. Her own forays into embracing her emotions gave her an insight into his. He had suffered a trauma. His confidence was knocked, and he would be worried about her being mistaken, about having potentially overlooked something. But she had not. She was sure he was safe.

"I have asked him to come and talk to you."

Vega looked up. "Who?"

"Your brother."

Vega cocked his head to one side. "You mean Altair?"

"Yes."

"I do not want to worry him with my troubles."

Shaula hesitated a moment, then held Vega by both shoulders, looking him in the eye. "Do not see yourself as an imposition. He is your family. You may not remember what that was like, but he does. He will want to help you. So let him." She gave him the type of tap on the shoulder that she had seen Faolán give other people when they needed support. He had always managed to lift others' spirits with that gesture. Vega, instead, just looked up at her as if puzzled. She dropped her hands from his shoulders and stepped away. Improving her bedside manner would take further practice, it seemed.

"Anyway, I have asked Altair to accompany Marcie here to the lab when she arrives. You should speak with him then. I shall report to Mayor Sirius that I do not consider you to be an ongoing threat. Feel free to return to your duties when you may."

Shaula returned to her workstation to give Vega a moment to decide what he was going to do next without her looming over him. She needed Charm to return to her before she could send another message to Mayor Sirius, updating him about Vega. Perhaps that would change soon. Perhaps they would find communications equipment that they could implement safely. Perhaps they would find assurances that, with Dr Neale in custody, it would now be safe for them to re-network so they could communicate the way they had originally been intended to: directly from android to android. But for now, she had to wait for Charm, the slowest familiar in all the settlement.

Vega took his time putting his shirt back on and checking in with his familiar, who had been charging nearby. Shaula had examined the bird and found it also lacking in worrying programming. All seemed to be as it should be. But she still felt like she was missing something important. She had expected it to be something to do with Vega or his familiar, but now she had checked them... what else could it be?

Marcie and Altair entered the lab. Marcie grinned at Shaula and came to stand next to her. They both watched as Altair approached Vega and spoke to him in a low voice. After a moment, the two men sat on adjacent lab chairs. Altair listened as Vega spoke. They were so very similar in appearance; only their chosen skin colours and hairstyles differed.

"Thanks for your message," said Marcie. "He's been so worried about Vega after we heard about what happened." Then she wrapped an arm around Shaula's shoulders and squeezed her. "And thanks for your part in warning us about the plot against us."

"That was Faolán. He was the one who realised and sent the message. He saved you."

"Still. I've heard the two of you were working together out there. You usually like working alone. How was it working with a partner?"

She paused, considering her words. "Different from what I expected. Though the difference was due to him. I have a history of getting on people's wrong side, I suppose. But Faolán has consistently given me the benefit of the doubt."

Marcie gave her a long look. Perhaps she had let more slip than intended. It was hard for her to predict the intuition of a human.

"Did you receive my message about my intended avenue of investigating the missing memories?" she asked to change the subject.

"Yes. I think you're right. I was there when Altair retrieved memories through both methods, and although one way accessed scattered broken memories, I know that's the one I'd go with too. The other way... I'd never want anyone to go through what he went through under Simons' hand."

Shaula nodded. She was glad that Marcie concurred. "If they had tried to make me torture anyone, I would have left this settlement."

Marcie looked at her in surprise. "Where would you have gone?"

"To the wreck of the *Sunda Tiger*, I suppose. Some sections could be made habitable, even though the wreck is upside down."

"Well, thankfully you didn't have to do that. I know you prefer your solitude, but I reckon there's a few here who would have missed you if you'd walked out." Marcie gave her another squeeze. "I'm so sorry about Tiaki," she said in a voice barely above a whisper.

"Thank you. I am sorry about Dr McArthur too."

"Thank you. Though I wasn't as close to the doctor as you were to Tiaki, so it's not the same."

The door moved slightly and Charm entered the lab, scuttling over to Shaula and climbing to her shoulder. "Faolán requests your presence in the Town Hall," it said.

"The Town Hall?"

"Yes."

What could that be about? Marcie must have heard the message, because she had her eyebrows raised.

Shaula tapped Charm with one finger. "Understood. Please tell Mayor Sirius that I have cleared both Vega and his familiar for active duty. No malicious code remains."

"Understood." Charm scuttled down her body and away again on its new mission.

Shaula slipped away from Marcie's side. "Excuse me."

She received some odd looks as she walked through the settlement. It was not so common to see her out and about, after all. But she pushed on.

In the central square, she saw signs of change. When she had left for the wreck, it had still been the case that only androids loitered in the settlement proper, while the humans stuck to their tent settlement unless running specific errands. But now she saw humans sitting or standing and talking. She did not know most of them, but she did spy Hernandez sitting on the bench underneath the oak tree. He was sitting with Ensign Bailey, a member of the original human landing party. The two men were holding hands, their heads close so they could have a quiet, private conversation. Shaula left them to it and stepped into the Town Hall.

They had not used the hall much since the Event Horizon. They rarely had need of the space. Faolán was not in the main part of the hall, though she heard noises from further in the structure. She passed through the large hall, past tables and chairs that had formerly been stored in a back room but which were now set out scattered throughout the space.

Through a door and down a short hall, she found the kitchen. It was a large room with several benches and many implements, stocked with long-life foods. There were also many boxes in one corner and along one bench: goods salvaged from the *Sunda Tiger*. Foodstuffs.

Shaula stopped and stared when she saw Faolán. Just looking at him made her feel different. Lighter. She knew now what this feeling was. It was the fondness she felt for him. Why did she have enhanced emotions? What was the purpose? What was the purpose of any of this? But she trusted now they had Dr Neale in custody, they would figure it out in time. She also trusted that she would not have to figure it all out on her own. Everyone in the settlement wanted to know the mystery of 227C. If someone else pieced it all together, she did not mind. She did not need to do everything herself, because she was part of a team.

Faolán was wearing an apron and serving slices of a baked product onto plates. On the other side of the bench were five androids, one of which was Diphda. All the androids were ones that Shaula knew had working stomachs.

"It's not much," Faolán was saying to the androids before him, "but it's the best I can do until we unpack the salvaged goods. This is a pound cake, and it's not too bad, if I must say so myself. So, have a go."

The androids each took a plate and began cautiously nibbling the cake. Faolán looked up and grinned at her as she came around the kitchen island to stand at his side.

"Where is Madigan?" she asked. "I trust you were allowed to keep him."

Faolán grinned. "Yeah, I was. He has his own duties, though: he's guarding Simons."

Shaula felt satisfaction at that knowledge: Simons had seemed afraid of the wolf. Faolán's broadening grin and knowing look indicated he felt the same. She turned to look at the other androids and bumped Faolán's shoulder with her own. "Why do I feel like you are doing my job for me?" she asked.

"Well, I knew you were gonna anyway, so I thought I'd get a start on it. Canopus told me these were all the androids you'd found working stomachs in, and since I had to try out the kitchen anyway, thought I'd give it a go."

She looked at him. "Try out the kitchen?"

He turned to her and took hold of her forearm. "Your advice, remember? I had a think, and I know what I want to be here on 227C, at least while we wait for rescue. There are a lot of security personnel around, and all of them are probably doing better than me at managing the change in workload and schedule. But we don't have a cook, and we sorely need one."

Shaula looked into his twinkling green eyes. "You have requested a transfer of your role."

"Yup! I think I can do more good here. I have the training, and the chaos of a working kitchen can work well for me, particularly if I put some music on or whatever. I didn't think of it before, because I flunked out of culinary school because I couldn't keep up with the perfection and the time management. But people here don't need perfection, they don't need cuisine. They just need to be fed. And I can do that."

She smiled at him, the curl unfamiliar on her lips, but somehow so right. His own smile grew brighter in response, and his fingers caressed up and down her arm.

"Please, not while we are eating," said Diphda, then took another bite of her cake. As she chewed, she frowned. She swallowed, and then gasped. "I think I remember... a cake? A rainbow layered cake?" She looked up at Shaula with wide eyes.

"As I hoped," said Shaula. "Your experiences help to unlock your memories."

She stayed and watched the whole experiment. Most of the androids who were eating remembered, at the very least, eating something else in the distant past, and one even remembered the flood that Altair had mentioned. It was a resounding success.

After the other androids left, she helped Faolán wash the dishes. Or rather, she dried them while he washed.

"You are remarkable," she said.

He flushed red. "How so?"

"You made a decision to change your life, and did so. I find that remarkable."

He dried his hands and then leaned on the bench, one arm on either side of her, trapping her there. His eyes seemed a deeper colour, closer to a forest green. "While we're on the topic, I found it remarkable that you stood up to everyone at the meeting yesterday and told them what you would and wouldn't do because of your morals. So many people would just follow orders, but you stuck to your guns. It was inspiring. You're inspiring."

Shaula put the tea towel down on the bench behind her. "Is that so?"

"It is."

She reached up and ran her fingers over the stubble on his cheek. "What are we?"

He hummed and stepped closer to her. "I don't know. I'd never dream of making assumptions about what you'd be comfortable with. You're too strong willed for that. I'd be afraid to scare you off."

"I am not scared."

"Poor choice of words," he said with a crooked smile. "Make you back off?"

"Make me feel stubborn?"

"Something like."

"What if I feel like stubbornly pursuing this, despite what others think?"

He moved closer still. "I think that sounds like something I'd be interested in."

He moved forward as if to kiss her, but she held a finger up to his lips. "We do not know what will happen in the future. What if rescue comes tomorrow, and you leave again?"

"Then we'd better make the most of now, huh?"

Then she let him kiss her, and she returned the kiss. He took the opportunity of Charm's absence to run his fingers into her hair and tugged on it, tilting her head so he could pepper kisses down her neck. She moved her own hands around his hips, grasping at him.

"Oh!" sounded a voice behind Shaula.

They sprung apart and looked around guiltily. Marcie stood in the doorway, her eyes wide.

"I didn't mean to interrupt." She smirked at them. But the smirk fell away quickly, replaced by a worried expression. "Shaula, you're needed. Something's come up. Something serious."

Shaula stepped towards Marcie. "What has happened this time?"

"There's an entire fleet of SecSats in formation around the planet, and we think they're all active and armed. We think Dr Neale deployed them. Maybe round about the time you found her in her hidden facility."

Shaula looked at Faolán and saw he was thinking along the same lines as her.

"That gap in time between when we arrived and she ambushed us in her office," said Faolán. "I knew something felt off."

"Indeed. She took precautions once we were close to her communications equipment." She turned to Marcie. "Is there any hope of disarming them?"

"Not from here. We only just managed to detect them with the sensors in an escape pod. We're being sent to the hidden facility to look for a way to disarm them. But she's not stupid. She would have locked them down tight. Which means..."

Faolán sighed. "Which means the planet is effectively booby trapped against whoever comes to find us."

To be continued...

ACKNOWLEDGEMENTS

It's been a longer journey finishing this book than I expected. Shaula and Faolán's story got complicated, quickly. Thank you to all the readers who waited patiently for this one.

My thanks to those who helped me along the way, particularly Kim and Emma.

Also, I want to thank my husband for everything he has done over the last year. I wrote and revised this book while dealing with another new health condition (why?) and along the way I dropped a lot of balls. He's been graciously picking them up for me as I go.

AUTHOR'S NOTE

In this book, Faolán has struggled with issues relating to his ADHD.

If you don't have ADHD, you might be wondering why there was no 'resolution' to his main problem, or why there was no apparent 'end' to the plot line. Why his ADHD wasn't 'fixed'. The reason is because ADHD and other neurodivergences aren't problems to be fixed. They aren't something you 'grow out of'. They stay with a person for life, though often in different guises in different stages of life. Faolán will have ADHD forever, whether he's medicated or not. And that's OK. He's fine just the way he is.

If you have ADHD, you probably already understand the previous point. But you may have problems with how I characterised ADHD, or be thinking, "It's not like that!" If so, I want to assure you that I'm not trying to speak for your experience. Everyone experiences their own neurodivergence differently. We all have different takes. I'm only speaking to Faolán's experiences, not to anyone else's.

ABOUT THE AUTHOR

Calanthe is a writer from Aotearoa New Zealand. By day, she is a parent and freelance editor.

Calanthe writes scifi romance and fantasy romance that balances exciting adventure with the quieter moments of life. Think cinnamon rolls, golden retrievers, and black cats with hearts of gold.

Her stories usually have magic or science, almost always have cooking or gardening, and definitely always have green flag romances that, no matter the heat level, are comforting like a snuggly blanket and a mug of hot chocolate on a rainy day.

Calanthe is a pākehā (white settler) who lives and works on the ancestral lands of the Kāi Tahu iwi.

Find out more at www.CalantheColt.com